*Something about the man . . .*

"What do you say? Can we work together? I know Miami, so I can help you look for him here. Besides, two heads are better than one."

Darrell didn't respond, clearly contemplating the thought.

"No offense," Serena added, "but I'm really the one who ought to be wary. Considering you *are* Cecil's brother."

"I'm nothing like my brother," Darrell retorted. "Your comment makes me think your suggestion is a bad idea. Why would you want to spend any time with me?"

*God, what was she thinking? Hadn't she learned her lesson yet?* Cecil had been the first pretty boy to sweep her off her feet—and she'd fallen flat on her back. The last thing she wanted to do was make the same mistake again. Especially not with his identical twin brother. How different could they be? But she needed to find Cecil to get her money and stolen heirloom back.

"Look," she said, "this isn't the best situation for either of us. But I'm willing to work with you if you're willing to work with me. Deal?"

## Also by Kayla Perrin

IF YOU WANT ME

# Say You Need Me

# KAYLA PERRIN

HarperTorch
*An Imprint of HarperCollinsPublishers*

This is a work of fiction. Names, characters, places, and incidents are products of the author's imagination or are used fictitiously and are not to be construed as real. Any resemblance to actual events, locales, organizations, or persons, living or dead, is entirely coincidental.

HARPERTORCH
*An Imprint of* HarperCollins*Publishers*
10 East 53rd Street
New York, New York 10022-5299

Copyright © 2002 by Kayla Perrin
Excerpt from *Tell Me Something Good* © 2002 by Margaret Hubbard
ISBN: 0-380-81379-3

First HarperTorch paperback printing: February 2002

HarperCollins ®, HarperTorch™, and ❦™ are trademarks of Harper-Collins Publishers Inc.

Printed in the United States of America

Visit HarperTorch on the World Wide Web at www.harpercollins.com

10  9  8  7  6  5  4  3  2  1

*For Auntie Dell and Uncle Bov,*
*with love, always*

# Chapter 1

When she saw him, Serena Childs very nearly choked on her mouthful of succulent, medium-rare sirloin—the best darn steak she'd had in a long time. Her eyes first bulged with stunned disbelief, then narrowed with bitter realization, while the morsel of beef lodged in her throat. He'd seen her, no doubt about it, and as if he were some stranger casually flirting with her from the restaurant bar, the bastard had actually had the nerve to smile.

Somehow, Serena managed to swallow her food without gagging. "That shameless son of a *bitch!*"

Startled by Serena's outburst, Kiana, Serena's younger sister by a year, flinched and dropped her silverware. The knife and fork clinked as they landed on her plate. Her eyebrows bunched together as she regarded Serena with concern. "What is it?"

Serena and her sister were at a restaurant on Miami

Beach's Ocean Drive, seated at an outside table. Until now, Serena had been enjoying the lovely March evening. Just a hint of a breeze floated off the Atlantic Ocean, and the lively sounds of a salsa band made the atmosphere festive. Just the type of ambiance Serena had been looking forward to after a very stressful week.

Now, one look at the slime ball who had made her last few weeks a living hell, and the evening was ruined.

Kiana looked over her shoulder, following the direction of Serena's gaze to the restaurant's outdoor bar. She turned back to her sister and frowned. "What?"

"I don't believe it," Serena replied, her gaze never leaving the lying jerk's face. "It's *Cecil*."

Kiana's jaw dropped to the table. "*Cecil* Cecil? As in—"

"Cecil Montford."

"Oh, my God." Kiana whipped her head around, scanning the crowded outdoor patio and bar. "Where is he?"

"He's on the far side of the bar. Dressed in a white T-shirt and jeans."

After a moment, Kiana said, "Oh, yes. There he is."

Serena scowled at the back of her sister's head. Kiana's voice was dreamy, as if they were talking about Cecil the sweetheart, instead of Cecil the world-class prick. Having met Cecil once when they'd all gone out for dinner, Kiana had been very impressed with him. Afterward, Kiana had crooned on and on about how gorgeous and charming Cecil was, how he definitely knew how to treat a woman right. She'd been as smitten by him as Serena had.

Clearly, Kiana was still smitten.

Not that Serena could completely blame her. He *was* drop dead gorgeous fine, which was why Serena had been so flattered by his attention. Most of the time, Serena dressed in comfortable, roomy clothes when she went to work at the library—far from glamorous. She didn't own a mini-skirt, and the only time she wore tights was when she worked out—and even then she wore an oversized T-shirt to cover her hips and thighs. Usually, she opted for her glasses over her contact lenses, which helped contribute to her dull librarian image. So, at first, she hadn't been able to understand what such a gorgeous man would want with a woman like her. Men like him didn't give her a second look. But as she'd spoken with him time and time again when he'd come to the library, making it clear with his kind words that he was interested in her, she'd slowly let down her guard.

After witnessing her parents' wonderful love affair, Serena had held out her whole life for Mr. Right, and Cecil had finally seemed like he could be The One.

She gritted her teeth at the memory. She couldn't have been more wrong if she'd thought she was going to marry the Pope.

Kiana turned back to Serena, her short braids swaying as she moved. Instantly, her large brown eyes grew wide with alarm. "Serena! God, what are you trying to do? Strangle the wineglass?"

Startled by her sister's comment, Serena's gaze dropped to her hand. Her fingers were tightly wrapped around the wineglass's stem as though she planned to snap it in two.

Not a bad idea . . . if it was Cecil's neck.

Again, Serena looked at Cecil. How could he sit there so casually, eyeing her as if he hadn't done a damn thing wrong? Seeing her staring at him, Cecil raised his wineglass and smiled.

"Oh, no. He did *not* do what I think he just did. Did you see that?" Serena asked incredulously, flitting her eyes between Kiana and Cecil. "I can't believe he's . . . he's *flirting* with me!"

"Hmm." Again, Kiana's voice got dreamy. "Yeah, he's a charmer. Too bad he turned out to be such a jerk. Damn, he really is good looking."

What was wrong with Kiana? Serena had expected nothing less than outrage from her overprotective, worry-wart-by-nature sister. Instead, she seemed to be off in la-la land, still unable to escape Cecil's charm, despite what he'd done.

Casting another glance in his direction, Serena lifted her wineglass and took a liberal sip of her cabernet sauvignon, needing something to wet her throat. No doubt about it, Cecil was fine. Even now she couldn't help noticing his striking brown eyes, his I'm-gonna-make-you-love-me smile. And maybe it was the restaurant's lighting, but he actually seemed more attractive tonight than she'd remembered.

That had been her problem from the beginning. Falling for his pretty boy good looks and charm had gotten her into this mess.

Still, it was hard to reconcile the reality that the attractive man twenty feet away from her could have done something so heinous.

As if reading her thoughts, Kiana commented, "With that *mmm baby* look he's giving you, you'd never think he'd split town with all your money."

"I know." Serena frowned, wondering what his game was. Was he going to flirt with her all night from afar, or was he finally going to approach her and give her some lame excuse for what he'd done? Clearly, since he wasn't ignoring her, he must be planning to give her some line of bull. Otherwise he would have hightailed it out of the restaurant before she'd seen him.

Her thoughts were interrupted by the appearance of their overly chipper waiter. Smiling from ear to ear, he placed another glass of red wine on the table before her.

"I didn't order this," Serena told him.

"I know," he replied in a singsong voice. "This is compliments of the gentleman at the bar." The waiter nodded in Cecil's direction.

Startled, Serena whirled her head around to face Cecil. He flashed her another one of his sexy smiles, the type that had stolen her heart in the first place.

God, he really did have a lot of nerve.

Well, this time his charm wouldn't work.

Until now, Serena hadn't been sure how to handle the situation. Approach him? Wait until he approached her? But, as he continued to make goo-goo eyes at her, she knew exactly what she'd do.

He just wouldn't like it.

"Excuse me." Serena pushed back her chair.

"Serena," Kiana said, her tone wary. She threw a hand out to grab her sister's arm, but Serena was already out of her chair.

Serena picked up the glass of wine.

"Serena, I don't think—"

Serena took a step, then halted. Her sister was right. Why waste a good glass of wine? She put it back on the table. Then, she gave her sister a saccharine grin as Kiana stared at her from worried eyes. "This won't take long."

"Serena . . ."

Ignoring her sister, Serena casually approached the restaurant's outdoor bar. Cecil's smile widened as she neared him, revealing perfect pearly white teeth. Either he thought she was completely clueless, or he figured he could actually explain away the last few weeks. She'd love to see the jerk explain away the fact that his cell, business, and home numbers had been disconnected—right after he'd left her that cryptic note about having to leave town on some emergency.

"Hey, there," he said.

*Hey, there?* He'd taken off with her family heirloom, her check for ten thousand dollars that she'd given him as a down payment for her antique jewelry store, and he was greeting her with a *hey, there?*

"Hey, yourself," Serena replied flippantly.

Cecil's eyes crinkled as he grinned at her, and damn if Serena's heart didn't do a little jiggy in her chest. Yes, he looked especially handsome tonight, definitely more so than the last time she'd seen him. Why her heart should do a hyper pitter-pat now, given what he'd done to her, was beyond her.

*Nerves,* she told herself, squaring her shoulders.

"So," he said, chuckling softly.

Serena mimicked his chuckle, then abruptly gave him an evil glare. "*So?* You take off with ten grand of my money and all you have to say for yourself is *so?*"

Cecil's mouth dropped open. "What?"

"Oh, now you have no idea what I'm talking about. Let me guess," she continued, raising her voice and placing a hand on her hip, "you've never seen me before, right?" She guffawed. "Is that part of the scam once you've been caught? To make *me* look crazy?"

"Actually, you do look kinda—"

*Whack!* Serena swung her hand back, then slapped Cecil upside the head. Her palm stung from hitting him with such force, but she didn't dare show that she'd hurt herself. Besides, the pain was overshadowed by the feeling of intense satisfaction.

She'd wanted to do that—and more—for nearly three weeks.

Cecil's hand immediately went to his injured jaw.

"That's for stealing my money," she told him, not caring that everyone within earshot was listening. "And for taking the necklace my grandmother gave me— God, the sight of you makes me *sick*. I'd ask why you did it, *how* you could do it, but I know all I'll hear from you are lies. You . . ." She faltered, but went on. "You never cared about me. I can't believe I was so incredibly stupid to believe a word that ever came out of your lying mouth."

"Wait a second—"

"No, *you* wait." She shook a finger at him while doing a quick neck rotation, full of attitude. "I want my money back. And my great-great-great grandmother's necklace. You know that means everything to me."

"If you'll let me get a word in—"

"I don't want to hear a word out of your slimy mouth."

Cecil's eyebrows shot together. "*Slimy?*"

"If you have one decent bone left in your body, do the right thing." Serena blew out a ragged breath, her body suddenly trembling. "Look, I can live without the money . . . but the necklace." She hated that she had to beg this jerk for what was hers, but she'd do whatever it took to get back the heirloom that had been in her family for generations. "Even if you keep the money, at least return the necklace. You know where I work; you can bring it there." She looked him up and down with distaste. "God, I curse the day I ever let you into my life."

Cecil was speechless, and Serena's satisfaction grew. She had never caused such a public display before, yet she wasn't embarrassed by her behavior. Humiliating Cecil was entirely worth it. She only prayed that she got her point across and he would do right by her.

He opened his mouth as if he was going to speak, but before the lying bastard could say a word, she turned and stalked back to the table where she'd left her sister.

Her concerned expression replaced with a smirk, Kiana gave Serena two enthusiastic thumbs up. And then a smile erupted on Serena's face, the first genuine smile she'd had in nearly three weeks.

"Damn it," Darrell exclaimed, nursing his cheek as he watched the crazy woman who'd just publicly chewed him out stomp away. He felt the beginnings of a welt forming on his face.

Who would have thought the demure-looking woman could pack such a punch?

Groaning, Darrell glanced around the bar where he sat. While the place had been buzzing with chatter only minutes before, it was now significantly quieter. *Everyone*—wait staff, bar staff, managers and restaurant patrons—was looking at him, some scowling, all no doubt thinking that he was a first-rate asshole. Why would such a sweet-looking woman publicly humiliate him unless he deserved it?

It didn't matter that he'd never seen the woman in his life. Everyone here thought they were intimately involved, and that he'd screwed her over royally.

God, this was priceless.

He'd certainly picked the wrong woman to flirt with.

Making eye contact with the guy next to him, Darrell gave a sheepish smile, but the older man merely shook his head and glanced away.

So much for relaxing his first night in Miami.

The hell of it was, Darrell couldn't blame her for thinking she knew him. Two seconds into the woman's tirade, and he had known she'd mistaken him for his good-for-nothing scamming twin brother, Cecil. Clearly, she was another casualty left in Cecil's wake.

Surreptitiously, he stole a glimpse of her. But she saw him look, and she glowered. So did the woman sitting with her. Groaning, Darrell turned.

What had his brother done this time?

All his life, Darrell had been dealing with crap his brother had gotten into. Hell, that's why he was here in Miami now. But good grief, he was too old for this. How much longer would Cecil have him picking up the pieces of the messes he made? And once, just once, Darrell wanted someone to look at him with happiness and relief, not disgust and scorn. But that would probably never happen, considering he was Cecil's identical twin and Cecil had screwed over people all across the country.

Darrell snuck another peek at the crazy woman. Part of him wanted to head over to her and explain who he really was, if for no other reason than to mollify his bruised ego. But with the evil look she continued to give him, he knew she wouldn't buy a word he said.

Darrell glanced around and saw that everyone still stared at him like he was one of America's Most Wanted. No, forget explaining anything to the insane woman. It was time he hightailed it out of here before any other scorned women came out of the woodwork.

"Excuse me." Darrell stood and summoned the bartender. The attractive redhead already had his check in hand as she approached. Giving him a nasty scowl, she slammed it down on the bar in front of him.

"Thanks," Darrell said wryly.

The woman flashed him an I-know-jerks-like-you look, then turned and gave a customer a few seats over a huge grin.

Darrell dug a ten out of his wallet and tossed it on top of the bill. It was way too much for the beer, but he certainly wasn't about to stick around for his change. Pushing the bill and money toward the bartender, he doubted she would appreciate the tip.

The patio exit was directly behind the table where the crazy woman and her friend now sat. No way he'd go in that direction. He bent to retrieve his small suitcase, then headed toward the interior of the restaurant. It was the way he'd come in and the way he would leave.

As he stepped inside, he threw a glance over his shoulder. The crazy woman and her friend were rising from their seats. Shit. Why were they leaving now? Darrell certainly didn't want another confrontation, and he couldn't imagine things being uneventful if they both ended up on the sidewalk at the same time.

Yeah, Cecil had a way of bringing out the worst in women.

Darrell thought better of leaving at this moment and instead headed to the back of the restaurant and the restrooms. He'd hang out there for a few minutes to be sure they were gone.

Thankfully, no one else was in the small, dingy men's room. He certainly wasn't in the mood to defend himself for something he hadn't done. Besides, he wanted a moment of peace to check out how bad his face looked.

He stood over the sink and stared into the foggy mirror. The lighting in the bathroom was pretty crappy, but it was lit enough for him to see a welt on his left cheek. Yeah, she'd hit him good.

*God, Cecil. What have you gotten yourself into now?*

Again he had his brother to thank for another difficult situation. Cecil hadn't been in touch much over the past few years, and while he'd missed and worried about him, at least Darrell had had some moments of peace. He'd almost forgotten how it felt to be mistaken for his brother, blamed for his pitfalls, or just plain caught up in trying to get Cecil out of another jam.

And Darrell had actually made the mistake of hoping that the fact that he hadn't heard from his brother meant Cecil had finally smartened up. Clearly, he couldn't have been more wrong. Though he was thirty-one years old, Cecil hadn't grown up, and Darrell was starting to wonder if he ever would.

Darrell was startled out of his thoughts when the restroom door swung open. He checked his watch. A good five minutes had passed since he'd come in here. Surely it was safe for him to leave now.

He stared at the ground as he exited, not wanting to meet the other man face-to-face. But once back in the restaurant, he held his head high as he looked around. Then he started for the front door at a casual yet brisk pace, fully aware that all eyes were on him.

He breathed a sigh of relief as he reached the front

door. Another second and he'd be home free. After this, he'd stick to his original game plan, which was to find his brother and bail him out of whatever mess he'd gotten himself into. Cecil had called him in Orlando a couple days ago, saying that he needed his help. But when Darrell had pressed for more information, Cecil had hemmed and hawed, merely saying that he'd gotten into some deep shit. After a long pause and some frustrated breaths on his brother's part, Darrell had thought he was going to explain his current situation, but then the dial tone had blared in his ear. Darrell had waited for his brother to phone back, but he hadn't. He called his brother's condo and got no answer. A call to Cecil's other home, business, and cell numbers told him that they'd all been disconnected. Instantly, Darrell had been concerned, and when, a couple days later, he still hadn't heard from Cecil, his concern had grown to worry.

While he and Cecil were completely different, they *were* identical twins, and on some level they were connected; over the years, Darrell had often sensed when Cecil needed him. This was one of those times. A pressing feeling in his gut told Darrell that Cecil was in trouble. So when Cecil hadn't gotten back in touch with him, Darrell had dealt with the immediate business that needed taking care of at the small bed and breakfast he owned and managed, then gotten on a plane to Miami.

Darrell pushed the front door open with his shoulder, then stepped outside. He descended the few steps to the sidewalk. The night air was refreshing, but the lively sounds of Latin music did nothing to lift his spirit. His staff was always telling him he needed to take a break, and he'd decided to take their advice. He'd come here tonight for a relaxing evening South Beach style before starting on his quest to find his brother, but he now wished he'd gone straight to Cecil's condo instead of taking this ill-fated detour.

He'd known this trip would be grief when he'd left Orlando, but he hadn't expected it his first night here!

Silently cursing his brother, Darrell turned right. He walked a couple steps, then stopped. Was this the direction of the condo? No, it was the other way, he realized, turning and recognizing the large high rise in the distance.

"That's him, officers."

Darrell's blood ran cold as he saw the crazy woman and her friend standing between two Miami Beach Cops. Standing slightly behind the taller man, as if to shield herself with his body, the crazy woman pointed at him so there'd be no mistaking to whom she was referring. Both burly men, one Hispanic and the other white, marched toward him.

All Darrell could do was stand there in stupefied horror.

"Mr. Montford?" the Hispanic one asked.

Darrell swallowed. "Yes, but—"

The taller, white officer gestured to the side of the road. "Mr. Montford, if you'll step this way, please."

His initial fear gone, Darrell stared at the two cops. He was aware that he should cooperate—the kind of thing he'd done all his life—but he'd been embarrassed once for the night, which was enough for him. He wasn't about to be humiliated in front of the hundreds of strangers who populated Ocean Drive. So he asked, "Are you placing me under arrest?"

"We'd like to ask you a few questions," the white cop replied.

Darrell looked at the man's nametag. "Officer Springer, I'm sorry, but I'm not in the mood to answer any questions right now." His gaze wandering to the nutcase, he frowned. "My jaw's a little sore. So, if you don't mind . . ."

He moved to the right, stepping past Springer. The Hispanic cop, whose nametag read Perez, blocked his path.

"Actually," Officer Perez held up a hand to keep Darrell at bay, "we do mind. This lady says you've stolen her property and some money. That's a serious charge."

"And what about assaulting someone?" Darrell couldn't help raising his voice as he glared at the loony lady. To the woman's friend he said, "You saw her do it. You're a witness."

The friend arched a brow at him in a gimme-a-break expression.

"You deserved that," the woman quickly said. Then she whimpered and dabbed at her eyes. "I can't believe you're doing this to me."

"It's okay, ma'am." Officer Springer placed an arm around her shoulder and gave it a gentle squeeze.

*Great,* Darrell thought. The woman could cry on demand. Just what he needed.

"Why don't you stop with the games?" the friend asked. "Surely you can't expect to lie your way out of this one. I'm so sorry I didn't have you checked out before you started dating my sister."

"Sir." Officer Perez gestured to the side of the road.

"She's got the wrong person," Darrell said. He supposed it would be simple enough to tell them that the woman thought he was his brother, but he wasn't ready to sic them on Cecil without talking to him first.

Officer Perez said, "We'd just like to ask you a few questions. If this is a misunderstanding, I'm sure we can straighten it out. Show us your ID and if you're not the man we're looking for, you can go on your merry way."

Okay. That was simple enough. Strolling to the edge of the sidewalk, Darrell reached into his back pocket. Reached, but didn't find his wallet. Where the hell was it?

Damn, he must have left it at the bar. "Uh," he began, chuckling nervously as he patted down his pants and shirt pockets. "I think I left it inside the restaurant."

"So you have no ID?" Officer Springer asked him.

"Yes, I have ID," Darrell replied testily. "I just told you I left it inside. I have to go back in and get it."

The look both cops gave him said they thought he was full of shit.

"He's lying," the crazy woman said, her tone high-strung. "Just like he always does." Her bottom lip quivered. "Can't you just arrest him?"

"*Arrest* me?" Darrell leveled an angry gaze on her. "Woman, I don't even know you."

The woman looked crushed. "How can you say that?" she asked, her voice cracking. "We dated for two months."

"It's okay," the sister told her, placing an arm around her. "I should have had Geoff check him out, but we'll know better for next time. And at least he's going to jail, where he belongs."

At the sister's words, Darrell turned back to the cops. "You can't just throw me in jail for no good reason. This is America, where people are innocent until proven guilty."

"Innocent?" The sister gawked at him. "Oh, that's a good one."

"I'm wondering why you don't want to cooperate," Officer Springer said.

"Because you haven't arrested me for anything. I know my rights," Darrell added smugly. "Excuse me."

Darrell took a couple brisk steps, to the side and then forward, but he did so before seeing that someone was immediately in his path. To avoid a collision, he did a quick move to the right, but he moved too far, and his suitcase clipped Officer Perez on the leg.

The wacko and her sister gasped in unison, making the impact seem more serious.

"That's it." Officer Perez instantly reached for his cuffs. "You're under arrest."

"*What?*" Darrell looked at the cop like he was crazy.

"Assaulting an officer," Officer Perez explained angrily. "For a guy who knows his rights, you should know that that's a felony in this country."

"I'm sorry, officer." Gone was the indignant attitude, replaced with a contrite tone. "I didn't mean to—"

"You have the right to remain silent."

"Oh, come on."

Officer Perez moved behind Darrell and slapped the cuffs on his wrists while Officer Springer spoke into his radio.

"If you give up your right to remain silent, anything you say can and will be used against you in a court of law."

God, this couldn't be happening!

"You have the right to talk to an attorney and have him present with you while you are being questioned. If you cannot afford to hire a lawyer, one will be appointed to represent you before any questioning, if you wish."

"This is a crock!. This . . . this *psycho*—who slapped me, by the way—tells you I'm a thief and you take her word for it, no questions asked?" Darrell bellowed as Officer Perez finished reading him his rights. "Let me go back in the restaurant and find my wallet so I can prove who I am."

"You've just added disturbing the peace to the charges," Officer Springer said.

"Son of a—" Darrell managed to stop himself. He drew in a deep breath, but it did nothing to calm him. "Look, if she hadn't pointed me out to you two, none of this would be happening."

"Her accusations of larceny and fraud are another issue," Officer Perez explained. "Right now, you need to be concerned with the charges of assaulting an officer and disturbing the peace."

"I can't believe this," Darrell muttered.

"Yeah, okay. Ten-four," Officer Springer said into his radio. He turned to his partner. "Perez, I talked to dispatch and there's a warrant out for this guy's arrest."

God, his brother was in more trouble than Darrell thought. "No, there isn't," he protested. "If you'll give me a second to explain—"

"I've told you your rights. Do you understand each of these rights I have explained to you?"

Darrell groaned.

"Do you understand your rights?" Officer Perez repeated.

"Yes," Darrell mumbled.

"Having these rights in mind, do you wish to talk to us now?"

"Will you let me go back into the restaurant and get my ID?"

Officer Perez clearly took that answer as a negative, since he said, "Fine. Let your lawyer advise you."

As both cops continued to talk, Darrell tuned them out and closed his eyes. When he reopened them, he saw that a large crowd of gawkers had formed on the street and the sidewalk around him. All he needed to complete this humiliating experience was to see the crew of *Cops* filming this whole scenario.

Darrell glanced first at the sister, who continued to look at him like he was the world's biggest jerk, then met and held the crazy woman's gaze. She was no longer crying. Her arms folded over her chest, she wore a satisfied smirk.

"I'm *not* Cecil," he told her softly, hoping to finally get through to her.

"Oh, my goodness," the woman began in a sarcastic tone. "You're *not*? You mean this is all a big misunderstanding?" She paused. "And imagine, you just happen to be psychic, and know the name of the man who ripped me off. Oh, wait. I know." The woman snapped her fingers. "Cecil is your evil twin, right?" She flashed him a look of disbelief. "Save your pathetic lies for the judge, Cecil. You've scammed your last victim."

"All right, sir." Officer Perez gave him a shove. "Come with us."

The smirk disappeared off the crazy woman's face as Darrell stared at her, and her eyes filled with grief. "Yes, please. Get him out of my sight."

Darrell, who'd never been in trouble with the law in his life, was being carted off to jail in handcuffs. God, Cecil would pay for this when he found him.

Darrell stared hard at the dingbat as he passed her, but she wasn't looking at him. She was resting her head against her sister's shoulder, while her sister comforted her. When he looked at the sister, hoping against hope that he'd at least get through to her, she shook her head at him in dismay.

It was obvious Darrell wouldn't get through to either of them. Yet he said, "I'm telling you the truth. I'm not Cecil, but I do know—"

Officer Springer took his arm and jerked him forward. "We told you that you have the right to remain silent. We suggest you use it."

"But you're mistaken," Darrell protested. "I swear to you, I'm not guilty of anything."

"Yeah, that's what they all say," Officer Springer replied, and both cops chuckled.

Darrell groaned his frustration. He didn't find any of this remotely funny.

Yeah, he was going to kill his brother—if the cops or the women he'd scammed didn't get to him first.

# Chapter 2

Kiana's stomach was a ball of mangled nerves. Even though she was exhausted and hadn't slept a wink last night, there was no way she'd get any sleep this morning. First, she'd been wired after Cecil's arrest, both happy that the slime ball was where he belonged, and worried that he might never tell Serena where the necklace was. After dropping Serena off at her apartment last night, Kiana had rushed home to call her ex-boyfriend Geoff. Geoff was a cop in the city of Miami, and if anyone could help her and Serena where Cecil was concerned, or at least give them some advice, Geoff could.

While Kiana still cared deeply for Geoff and wanted a close friendship with him, she hadn't spoken to him in at least three weeks, mostly because whenever they spoke, he pressured her about getting back together. He hadn't stopped trying for a reconciliation in the four months since their breakup. However, Kiana didn't want that. For one thing, her constant worry that he'd get hurt at work had been a major issue in the downfall of their relationship. But aside from her concerns about his safety, there had been other problems. Like the fact that Geoff had hidden his emotions behind humor. All cops did, he'd told her, but Kiana couldn't relate to that. She'd seen her parents openly express how they felt about each other all the time. Kiana was the same way. If she was upset, she showed that. If she was happy, she expressed that, too. And if she was in love . . .

A wave of sadness passed over her, remembering. Whenever she had told Geoff that she loved him, he'd merely smiled and said something corny like, "I love me, too." At first it had been cute, but then it had started to bother her. Why hadn't he been able to express his feelings? And the times he did tell her he loved her—after she'd press him about how he felt—he never seemed quite serious.

However, Geoff had done a total one-eighty after she'd ended their eight-month relationship. According to him, he did love her, but just had a hard time expressing in words how he felt. But by then, Kiana hadn't wanted to go backward, mostly because despite the fact that he might love her, she'd realized there was no point in continuing a relationship that had no future. She simply couldn't deal with the reality of what it would mean to be a cop's wife.

Still, Kiana treasured his friendship and valued his opinion. Which was why she had called him the moment she'd stepped into her apartment last night. She'd gotten his answering machine and assumed he was at work. Then, as she'd prepared for bed, she'd caught a rebroadcast of Channel Seven's nightly news, and had been horrified to learn that a Miami police officer had been killed at a domestic call.

No name had been given, pending notification of next of kin, and as always happened when Kiana heard bad news like this, she had become sick with fear. She'd promised herself that she wouldn't worry, but that promise had been broken the moment she'd called Geoff again and found that he still wasn't home. She'd left him one message, then another, telling him it was urgent that he get back to her as soon as possible, but still he hadn't returned her call.

All night, Kiana had tossed and turned, waiting for him to get back to her. And now, as the sun began to rise, Kiana was doing everything in her power to keep it together. She'd picked up the phone to call Serena several times during the night, but had decided against it. Serena had enough on her plate. Besides, Serena would tell her that she was giving herself high blood pressure for no reason, that until she heard definite bad news, she shouldn't cause herself unnecessary grief.

She knew Geoff would tell her the same thing— provided he wasn't in a morgue somewhere!

It didn't matter how often Geoff told her that he could just as easily drown on his day off as get shot in the line of duty. He always expressed a casual attitude toward the dangers in his job, and after a while, Kiana found that it annoyed her. She'd loved him dearly, and had actually thought Geoff would be the one she'd marry. But she'd come to realize she couldn't handle being a cop's wife, wondering every night *if*, not when, her husband was coming home.

Kiana rolled over onto her stomach, hugging the pillow. Her eye caught the digital clock. Six fifty-eight A.M. Fear spread through her blood, making her shiver. If Geoff had been working last night when she'd called him, he should have phoned her back by now.

A small sigh escaped her, and Kiana sat up. The bad thing was, she *wasn't* his wife, and if anything happened to him, she'd hear about it secondhand—from a friend or on the news. After a quick glance at the phone, she couldn't stand the suspense a moment longer. She reached for the clock radio. It was always set to a news station, and Kiana turned it on, then adjusted the volume.

". . . *Weather and sports coming up in the next ten minutes. But first, our top story. Last night, a city of Miami police officer was shot and killed in Coconut Grove when he responded to a domestic call. The suspect, Fredrick Baker, who was under the influence of cocaine at the time of the killing, immediately fled the scene but was apprehended without incident a short time later. He has been charged with second-degree murder and is being held at the Dade County detention center until a bail hearing on Monday morning. The name of the officer has still not been released, pending notification of next of kin, who are believed to be out of town on vacation.*" Pause. "*Also this morning, all lanes of I-95 are still closed north of Hallandale Boulevard, after a truck carrying . . .*"

Her heart sinking to her knees, Kiana turned off the radio. Geoff worked in Coconut Grove. He hadn't called her back. Lord God almighty, it really could be Geoff who was killed!

Kiana let out a shaky breath, her eyes once again going to the phone. *Please ring,* she thought. *Oh, Geoff. Please be okay.*

*  *  *

Serena listened to the rhythmic *tick tock* of her wall clock, counting the seconds as they went by. She hoped that counting the seconds would be much like counting sheep, allowing her mind to drift away to nothingness so sleep could finally claim her. But after a full two minutes of miming along to the incessant *tick tocking*, Serena groaned, then dragged a pillow over her head to block out the sun, all the while knowing that wouldn't help her to get any sleep.

She hadn't slept more than a few hours last night. Her nerves were on end, both from excitement and from fear, knowing she was as close as she would come to getting her family heirloom back. Normally she cherished sleeping in on the weekends, but this Saturday morning, she didn't allow herself the luxury. She wanted to head out to the police station where Cecil was in custody, and the sooner, the better.

If Cecil was released on bail after appearing before a judge, she might never see him again—and she might never get her property back. That was a chance she wasn't willing to take. As much as she didn't like the thought of seeing him again, it was something she had to do. And she'd do whatever necessary to retrieve what was hers, even if she had to beg.

Serena showered, dressed, then made her way to her Mitsubishi Mirage. She was both nervous and excited as she started her car. Quite frankly, after she'd realized that Cecil had scammed her, she hadn't expected to see him again. For the past three weeks, she'd been angry with herself for trusting him, and depressed over losing both her family's heirloom and ten thousand dollars. The check had cleared, and she'd thought she'd seen the last of him. A bitter ending to something she'd mistakenly believed had held a lot of promise.

So, while seeing him again yesterday was far from a pleasant experience, it was actually a good thing. Because now that she'd had him arrested, she was one step closer to retrieving her family's heirloom and her money.

The reality that she might have a happy ending in this situation made her excited. But she was also nervous because she didn't know if Cecil's arrest meant she'd necessarily get her property back.

Sure, he might spend some time in jail for what he'd done, but maybe he'd remain tight-lipped about her property and sell it once he was released. She'd heard stories of that sort of thing, where thieves who robbed banks or jewelry stores went to prison, but when they came out, they still had what they'd stolen and went on to enjoy a life of luxury.

The necklace had been appraised at over a quarter of a million dollars, enough to make someone very comfortable. And fool that she was, Serena had told Cecil how much it was worth. She would never forgive herself for that colossal error in judgment.

But more disturbing than the thought of Cecil hawking the necklace once out of prison was the reality that she had no clue what he'd done with it now. What if he'd already sold it and had the money in an offshore bank account?

As Serena drove out of her apartment complex and toward the turnpike, she whispered a silent prayer that that was not the case.

The heirloom, an antique diamond and ruby necklace, had been passed down in her family from mothers to their first-born daughters for over a hundred years. Ultimately, the line went back to Serena's great-great-great grandmother. Tilly Hancock, who'd been born into slavery, had been given the necklace by a man from Morocco, whose family had been royalty. The necklace had been his present to her upon their wedding. In Serena's case, the necklace had been passed down to her by her paternal grandmother, because Grandma Louisa May had never had a daughter.

It was that very exquisite necklace, and its history as her grandmother had relayed it to her, that had spawned Serena's interest in antiques from the time she was a young child. Quilts that told stories of family histories, carvings, books, jewelry—if it was antique, Serena was interested in it.

She'd thought Cecil had shared her passion for antiques. The day she'd met him at the library, he'd commented on how much he liked the earrings she was wearing and had surprised her by asking if they were Victorian. Yes, she'd told him. When Cecil had asked to take a closer look at one earring, she'd slipped it off her ear and passed it to him. Again he'd surprised her with his knowledge that the rose-colored stones were garnets; and she was impressed that he knew the diamonds were diamonds, and not the less expensive marcasite, which was commonly used in jewelry of the early twentieth century. He also recognized the platinum ring she wore as Edwardian. Except at antique shows, Serena had never met anyone who knew one era of jewelry from another just by looking at the various precious metals, stones, and intricate designs.

The garnets in her earrings were set in silver with tiny rose-cut diamonds and had a one-and-a-half-inch drop.

Serena was particularly pleased with the set; she'd gotten them for a steal at a garage sale, and later learned they were worth nearly a thousand dollars. She had enthusiastically relayed that fact to Cecil when he'd asked her where she found them, and it warmed her heart that his eyes didn't roll into the back of his head—much the way others' eyes did when she got to talking about antiques—when she told him how much she enjoyed going to flea markets and garage sales to search for great finds. From there, she and Cecil had begun discussing all things old. Like her, Cecil loved antiques, but had an avid interest in antique jewelry.

His interest in what she was most passionate about had sparked her attraction to him. But she'd also found him very charming, humorous, and easy to talk to. She'd definitely liked him, and when he asked her out for dinner a couple weeks later, she'd accepted. One dinner had led to another, then another. The more time they spent together, the more Serena realized how much they had in common, and the more she liked him.

He had a way of making her feel like she was the only woman in the room when they were out, which was something she wasn't used to. Most of the men she dated had wandering eyes when beautiful women crossed their paths, and it was nice that Cecil wasn't like them—especially when she knew she wasn't the most attractive woman in the world. So, when Cecil had lowered his lips and kissed her after an evening of dinner and dancing on South Beach, Serena had been flattered. No one as attractive as Cecil had ever kissed her before. And the kiss had been . . . nice. Not too long, not too short. Enough to let her know he was definitely interested but wasn't going to be pushy about it. And just like that, their relationship had gone to another level.

All her life, Serena had been waiting to meet Mr. Right, and Cecil Montford had finally seemed like he could be The One. He'd never pressured her for sex like some of the other men she'd dated, which was a definite plus. He'd been patient, expressing a desire to get to know her first instead of getting down and dirty. Serena appreciated that about him, because she'd been saving her virginity for the man she would marry.

Serena still remembered fondly first learning about her parents' love affair one summer night when she and her mother had sat on their back porch. Her mother, Edith, had told her how she believed she and her father had been destined to meet. Both in their late teens, her parents had met at a train station in Buffalo. Her father, Maurice Junior, or M. J., as her mother called him, had been waiting for his uncle to arrive from Baltimore. Edith had arrived home from a trip to visit relatives in Chicago. Edith's ride had been late; a traffic accident had kept her father from getting to the train station on time. The train carrying M. J.'s uncle had been late. As a result, both Edith and M. J. had ended up at the train station together, waiting. When Edith had turned in M. J.'s direction, their gazes had met, and something wonderful had sparked in M. J.'s eyes—according to Serena's mother. Her father had been immediately smitten—at least, that's the way Edith told the story; but Serena suspected her mother had been just as smitten by her father.

Weeks later, they were madly in love, and months after that, they married. Her parents had been virgins when they married, something they'd been proud of, and their love remained deep and true until the day they'd both tragically died. To Serena, there was something uniquely special about the idea that they'd shared the intimate act of sex only with each other.

Since her early twenties, Serena had had two serious boyfriends, neither of whom had respected her desire to save herself for her husband. Now she was twenty-nine and she worried that she might never find a man who shared her values. People were so much looser these days, jumping into bed first and considering a relationship later. Serena didn't want any part of that. She didn't care so much if she was a virgin on her wedding night, but she at least wanted the man she shared the special act of love-making with to be the man she would marry.

Cecil had seemed to have all the qualities she wanted in a husband—compassion, devotion, understanding, and patience. After Serena had gotten to know him better—or so she'd thought—she'd had no reservations telling him about her family's heirloom. Then she'd showed him the necklace one of the few times he'd been at her place. He was blown away by its beauty, the same way she was every time she looked at it.

Serena was happy to find a man who not only shared her passion but supported her dream. Cecil said he understood her desire to open an antique store and he'd encouraged her to do so. Coincidentally, Cecil worked as a real estate agent, and he'd assured her he could help her find the perfect storefront.

When Serena's parents had died in a boating accident fourteen years before, there had been a bit of money from insurance, and over the years, that money had grown with wise investments. She'd used the bulk of her share as a down payment on a property in Coconut Grove that would house her antique shop. But Cecil, the agent who'd brokered the deal, had betrayed her, proving that he wasn't the man she'd thought him to be. She could only imagine what he'd done with the money she'd given him, because he sure hadn't used it for the store. Hell, he'd probably had a few rounds of cocktails on some exotic beach, toasting her stupidity after he'd cashed her check.

Thinking about everything that had happened was giving Serena a headache, so she concentrated on the beautiful view as she drove. She knew the way to Miami Beach like the back of her hand, and was surprised to find that she was already along the causeway. In the distance, she saw massive cruise ships lining the port. It was a sight that always amazed her, because the ships were so tall they looked like apartment buildings.

But now the sight was bittersweet. She'd always wanted to go on a cruise, but hadn't allowed herself that luxury. She'd been saving every penny to open her store.

Damn Cecil.

She couldn't get him out her mind as she continued to drive. She'd been naïve, for sure, but did she deserve to lose something so precious to her? To her family? Hopefully the courts would throw the book at him and lock him up forever. If he'd scammed her, she imagined there had to be others.

Once over the causeway, Serena maneuvered through the Miami Beach streets until she was at the police station on Washington. She parked in a lot nearby, then hopped out of her car. She was so close to getting her necklace back, she could taste it, and she hurried out of the parking lot, practically setting a new record in the hundred-meter dash as she sprinted toward the front of the station.

Inside the large entranceway, Serena halted, disappointed to see that there were a few people mingling in front of her, waiting to speak to the cop at the information counter. She paused a moment to catch her breath, then joined the line. Her nerves were raw from worrying so much, and even now, she prayed she wasn't too late.

The few minutes that passed seemed like hours, but finally she was at the front of the line. A middle-aged, friendly looking cop sat behind the counter. "Good morning, sir," she said, giving him a tight smile.

"Mornin', ma'am. How can I help you today?"

Serena leaned forward to speak through the hole in the fiberglass partition. "Last night," she began, "someone was arrested and brought here. I'm assuming he spent the night."

"Depending on when he was arrested, he might have already been transferred to the Dade County detention center. Do you know what time he came in?"

Serena's heart spasmed in her chest. God, Cecil had to be here. "He was brought in around midnight."

"Then there's a good chance he's still here," the cop said. "Last night was busy, and not everyone was processed."

Serena's shoulders drooped with relief. "Great." She gave the cop a small smile. "Um, I'm wondering if there's a chance I can speak with him." She paused, wondering if she should add that she was his victim.

The cop gave her a stern look. "Are you family?"

"No."

"His lawyer?"

"No."

"I'm sorry, then. Prisoners aren't allowed any visitors. This is just a holding cell until they're taken to the detention center. Once there, he'll be allowed visitors after seventy-two hours. But he'll have to put you on his visitor's list in order for you to see him."

"Oh," Serena replied, unable to hide her disappointment. As if there was any chance of that happening! What was she supposed to do now?

While she hesitated, the cop looked beyond her to the next person in line. He said, "Can I help you, sir?"

Hurriedly, Serena said, "Wait."

The cop looked at her once again. "Yes?"

"Can you check? If he's still here, I mean."

"Ma'am, I already told you—"

"Please," Serena said, interrupting the cop. Maybe if she told him what Cecil had done, he would understand her urgency in seeing him. "This man, I really need to see him." She lowered her voice, then continued. "He stole a necklace from me worth a small fortune. I'm wondering, now that he's arrested, am I guaranteed—"

"Do you know who brought him in?"

"The cop who arrested him, you mean? There were two—" Serena stopped short when she saw movement to her left on the far side of the foyer. Something made her turn. And then her heart slammed against her ribcage.

There was Cecil, walking toward the front door with a female police officer.

"Ma'am?" the cop behind the information desk prompted.

"Uh," Serena replied, never taking her eyes from Cecil. "Never mind."

Slowly, Serena started toward the cop and Cecil. Was he about to be taken to the detention center? If so, why wasn't he wearing handcuffs? And why were he and the cop smiling?

Good grief, had he charmed this woman, too?

Serena picked up her pace. Her stomach did a nosedive when she saw Cecil shake the cop's hand. She might know nothing about police procedures, but she certainly knew that cops didn't tend to shake hands with felons.

No, something didn't make sense. Worried, Serena hurried toward them. For the first time, she noticed that Cecil had a small suitcase with him—another bad sign.

Cecil and the cop separated as she closed in on them, and with a quick wave on both their parts, Cecil turned and headed to the exit while the cop retreated toward the back offices.

"Wait a second," Serena cried, unable to keep her voice low. Her eyes darted between the cop and Cecil. "Why are you letting this man go?" Something was terribly, terribly wrong. "How can you let him walk out of here, after everything he's done?"

A smug smile danced on Cecil's lips as he looked at her and replied, "I tried to tell you yesterday that I'm *not* Cecil. You were too hard-headed to listen."

Serena's eyes flew to the cop. "W-what?" she sputtered. She could barely think straight, much less make sense of this situation. "I-I don't believe this. You've fallen for his lies!" Facing Cecil, she gaped at him. "And what do you mean, hard-headed? I may have been a fool where you were concerned—"

"Ma'am." The female officer held up a hand as she approached Serena. "If you'll relax, I can explain everything."

"There *is* no explanation. This man is an expert con artist. Obviously, he's even good enough to fool you."

The cop's eyes said she was mildly offended, yet she went on, business as usual. "This man's name is Darrell Montford. When our guys brought him in last night, they thought he was Cecil Montford."

"Darrell Montford?" Serena continued to gape, unable to believe what she was hearing. "Okay," she quickly said. "So he's got an alias. Isn't that consistent with most criminals?"

"His ID checks out."

This was wrong, all wrong. Serena placed a hand on the cop's arm, giving it an urgent squeeze. "Please listen to me. I don't know what kind of game he's playing, but this is the guy who scammed me." She looked at him briefly, then back at the cop. "I'd know him anywhere."

"I'm his brother," Darrell interjected matter-of-factly. When Serena looked at him again, he added, "I believe you made some remark yesterday about an evil twin."

Oh, no. This couldn't be. Serena's head started to spin. "You're . . . are you saying . . . you're his *twin?*"

"Yep."

"I don't believe this."

"Ma'am, we ran his prints," the officer explained. "He has none on file. A couple beat cops also went back to the restaurant and retrieved his wallet. His story checks out."

"But . . ." Cecil's twin? God, how could this be? This made no sense at all. "If he isn't Cecil, then why didn't you release him last night?"

"There were other charges, but in light of the case of mistaken identity, those have been dropped."

"He was arrested for theft," Serena protested.

"Not at the time," the Cecil imposter countered. He met Serena's eyes with a hard stare. "They wanted to *question* me about your accusation, but I was brought in for assaulting a police officer and public disturbance. All because you wouldn't listen to reason."

"Sorry again, Mr. Montford," the cop said, giving him a contrite look.

"No problem. Have a good day." He glared at Serena. "I plan to."

Then he started off, and Serena could only stand and stare as Cecil's supposed twin headed for the door, her mouth hanging open.

This was all so unreal, she didn't know what to think. Cecil had never mentioned having a twin!

But if the cops were releasing him . . .

Placing a finger against her lips, Serena shook her head and looked at the floor. Her brain was working overtime and she could hardly form a coherent thought. But seconds later, her mind made sense of the situation. Cecil truly had a twin. There was nothing she could do but accept the disappointing reality.

Exhaling a frustrated sigh, Serena looked up. Instantly, her stomach dropped. She'd been so absorbed in her thoughts, she'd let Cecil's twin walk away.

Oh, God. She had to get to him. He was her next best chance of getting her family's heirloom back!

# Chapter 3

*Serena jolted into action, sprinting for the front* door. She threw it open and darted outside. A quick look around told her that Cecil's twin was already at the sidewalk, several feet away.

"Wait!" she called, running down the concrete steps outside the police station.

The Cecil look-alike ignored her and hurried to the edge of the road. His suitcase in one hand, he flung out the other one to hail a cab. "Taxi!"

The cab passed by.

"Please," Serena begged, hurrying toward him. "Wait."

Cecil's brother quickly headed south along the sidewalk, and Serena realized that he was planning to ignore her. Not that she could blame him, but he had to understand how she'd mistaken him for Cecil in the first place.

She charged toward the sidewalk and threw herself in his path. "Mr. Montford."

He turned and began walking in the other direction.

"I-I'm not going to hit you," she blurted, feeling stupid when the words left her mouth. And they didn't influence him one way or another, because he didn't stop. But Serena didn't give up. She scurried in front of him once more.

She said, "I'm sorry."

Giving an exasperated sigh, he stopped. "Lady, I do *not* have time for this."

"I'm sorry," Serena repeated emphatically, then looked at him long and hard. For the first time, she noticed things she should have picked up on last night. His eyes were brighter than Cecil's. And the fact that he wore a T-shirt and jeans should have been an immediate tip-off, because all the times Serena had seen Cecil, he'd never worn anything less than a snazzy outfit, even when he'd come to the library.

Her gaze went lower, checking him out completely. This man's nails weren't manicured nicely the way Cecil's always were. And his body was leaner, his stomach noticeably flatter, even in a T-shirt. Subtle differences, but differences nonetheless.

"All right," he said, clearly irritated. "You've apologized. Is that it?"

Serena shifted her weight from one foot to the other. "Your name again is?"

Darrell gaped at her, but she didn't even flinch. God, couldn't this woman take a hint? Apparently not. She was either completely clueless or completely nuts, because she continued to look up at him from wide eyes, expecting an answer from him.

"Darrell," he cautiously replied, hoping she'd soon be on her merry way. He glanced around for another cab. To his chagrin, he didn't see one. Damn. The last thing he wanted to do was stay here and chitchat with this crazy woman.

"My name is Serena."

Man, she was crazier than he thought. "This may surprise you," he began slowly, his tone sardonic, "but I really have no desire to get to know you." He paused for effect, hoping his words would register. "Now, if you'll excuse me, I have things to do." He turned and started walking away.

A few seconds passed, and Darrell thought he was home free. Then he heard, "Darrell. Wait."

The crazy woman's voice held a note of desperation, and damn if Darrell didn't immediately feel bad. He didn't like being rude to anyone. In fact, working in the hospitality industry, he was used to smiling even when people were uncivil with him. And even though this woman didn't deserve a moment of his time, with resignation, he stopped once again and faced her.

Her bottom lip quivered slightly as she looked at him. "Can you *please* just give me a minute to explain?"

Considering the fact she seemed determined to follow him until he listened to her, Darrell didn't figure he had a choice. He may as well hear her out. "Serena, you said?"

"Yes."

"All right, Serena." A frown played on his lips. "You've got one minute."

Serena blew out a frazzled breath before speaking. "I'm really not psychotic," she said, offering him a weak smile. "It's just that . . . you look exactly like your brother. Which makes sense, since you *are* his twin. But I didn't know. How could I have known? So when I saw you last night . . ." Her voice trailed off from her rambling. "I'm trying to say, to ask—can you forgive me for hitting you?"

"Hitting me?" Darrell asked, his tone incredulous as he remembered the embarrassing event. "That right hook could have leveled Mike Tyson."

"I-I know," Serena said remorsefully. "And I'm sorry."

"You had me arrested."

She bit down on her bottom lip. "Yeah. I'm sorry for that, too. Believe me. I'm not usually so . . . bent out of shape."

Darrell lowered his suitcase and folded his arms over his brawny chest. "Have you ever spent a night in jail, lady?" When she shook her head, he said, "Well, it's not pleasant. They strip-searched me, made me sleep on a concrete bed that God only knows how many lowlifes have slept on. The guy in the cell next to me smelled so bad, he obviously hadn't bathed in months. I slept with my hands over my face the whole night, but even now, the sick scent is burned into my nostrils. Hell, I didn't even sleep. I just lay there, waiting for the night to end." He paused. "I couldn't even use the toilet without someone watching. Do you know how humiliating that is?"

"God, if I had known . . ."

"I seem to remember trying to get a word in last night, to tell you I wasn't who you thought I was, but you were hell-bent on doing all the talking."

"I thought you were Cecil." Serena's shoulders drooped as she pouted. "Cecil never mentioned he had a brother, much less a twin. How was I to know?" Confused eyes studied his face, as if even now, she couldn't be sure he was telling the truth.

After a moment, she said, "Now that I look at you,

though, I can see some differences." She reached out to stroke his face, and he instantly threw his head back to avoid her touch.

Regret passed over Serena's face at Darrell's reaction, and something about it made him feel guilty. Hell, why should he feel guilty, considering the night he'd had on account of her?

"I know, I deserve that." Her tone was rueful. She stared him squarely in the eye, and he stared back, neither saying anything for several moments. "Gosh, I don't even know why I reached for you. It's just that . . . I'm hoping that mark on your face isn't because of me—"

"You mean the imprint of your hand?" Darrell couldn't hide his sarcasm.

Unease flashed in her eyes. Then, swallowing, she cautiously extended her hand again. This time, Darrell let her touch him. Her touch was surprisingly soft as it caressed the side of his face that she'd slapped.

"God, I never would have hit you . . . I never hit *any-body*. That was so out of character. But seeing you there, smugly sitting at the bar. *Flirting* with me. I feel so stupid."

"Yeah, so do I." Of all the women he could have picked to flirt with, it had to be one who'd had the misfortune of being involved with his brother. No wonder she'd slapped him upside the head.

The hell of it was, she wasn't his normal type. Her square-shaped glasses made her look a little dowdy, though behind them he could see she had beautiful brown eyes. She had a gorgeous smile; he'd seen it before she'd even noticed him. She wasn't stunning, but she was definitely attractive in a low-key sort of way. Perhaps that's exactly what he'd been drawn to, her silent beauty. He'd dealt with too many conceited women who flaunted their beauty in hopes of getting his attention.

Then ultimately getting into his wallet.

Not that he was loaded, but when most women learned that he ran a successful bed and breakfast, out came the hard-hats with glowing lights as they dug for gold . . .

"I really am sorry."

Her soft words brought his attention back to her eyes. She seemed genuinely contrite, and while he wished he could hate her for humiliating him last night, then getting him arrested, he knew that her actions had been directed toward his brother—a man who no doubt deserved her wrath. Cecil had left many pissed off women all across the continental United States.

Part of him didn't want to know, but the part that was used to bailing Cecil out of trouble did. "What did my brother do?"

Serena wrung her fingers as she spoke. "I thought he was nice. He was always polite when he came to the library. That's where I work. I'm a librarian. Anyway, one day we started talking—and soon after, casually dating. He was supposed to help me find a property for an antiques store. I know it seems stupid now, but I gave him a check for ten grand as a down payment. He said he was a real estate agent and even showed me his business cards."

"Yeah, my brother has his real estate license."

"I thought he was as interested in antiques as I was. He saw my earrings and asked me about them." Automatically, Serena's hand went to an ear, gently touching one of the dangling Victorian earrings.

"Those are antique?" Darrell asked.

"Yes. From the Victorian era. Garnets and diamonds set in silver."

Darrell shrugged. He couldn't tell costume jewelry from the real stuff, much less antiques from something made last year. But the earrings were definitely beautiful. "My brother always did have an eye for expensive things."

"If it was just the ten grand, I could walk away and not worry about it. Not to say that I'm rich . . . what I'm trying to say is that Cecil also stole my family's heirloom. I'd showed it to him once, then put it back in my apartment safe. I always keep it in the safe, because it's too valuable to leave lying around. Anyway, I didn't notice until a few days after he disappeared that the necklace was missing." Serena paused, then said, "Cecil was the only one who could have taken it. Other than my sister, he's the only one who's been in my apartment. I didn't give him the combination to the safe, but your brother's obviously a very talented man when it comes to stealing. Bottom line, the necklace is worth a small fortune and has great sentimental value and . . . and I need it back. So, can you please tell me where to find Cecil?"

His brother had stolen cash and a necklace from her. Good God almighty. Cecil was becoming a better criminal every day.

"My brother stole from you."

"Yes."

Darrell shook his head in disappointment. "I wish I could tell you where to find Cecil, but I can't. I have no idea where he is."

At Darrell's words, Serena's mouth quivered, and she

sank her teeth into her bottom lip. A simple action, something people did all the time, but Darrell suddenly noticed how full and sweet her mouth was.

"Surely you must be in contact with him. You're his twin."

Uncomfortable with how he'd just looked at this woman who was no doubt crazy—even if she did have her reasons—Darrell glanced away. "Being twins is about the only thing Cecil and I have in common. The closest we've been was when we shared space in our mother's belly." He met her eyes again. "I hate to tell you this, but my brother and I live two different lives, and we aren't always in touch. All I know is that he's gone AWOL. Which means you can kiss your property and your cash good-bye."

Serena whimpered, then her face crumbled. Turning away from him, she hugged her torso.

Watching her in pain, Darrell instantly regretted his words. Not because he didn't believe them to be true, but because he couldn't stand to see the woman suffer. Yes, she'd slapped him, publicly humiliated him, and because of her, his back ached from sleeping on that pitiful excuse for a bed in the cell. But she'd done so because Cecil had scammed her.

Darrell should have long ago washed his hands of his brother, but he'd been picking up the pieces of his brother's messes for years and didn't seem to know how to get out of the habit.

Like this time. Instead of staying in Orlando and dealing with his own business, he'd come to Miami as soon as possible to find his brother and take care of whatever was going on. He was particularly worried about Cecil. Not that Cecil hadn't been in his share of snafus over the years and gotten out of them one way or another, but the cryptic phone call from him still played in Darrell's mind. Whatever mess Cecil had gotten himself into now was major. Darrell felt that as surely as he felt the hot Miami sun shining on his face.

Slowly, Serena turned back to Darrell. "Well." She sniffled. "I guess there's nothing I can do to get my property back. This was my last hope, but now it's gone. I have only myself to blame for being so stupid . . ." Her voice trailed off. "I'm sorry about yesterday, and I'm sorry to have bothered you now."

Her eyes held sadness, even as she walked past him with her head high. Darrell listened to her footfalls on the concrete as she got farther and farther away. It was what he wanted, to be rid of her so that he could start the search for his brother. Yet the farther she walked away, the worse he felt.

Finally, he spun around. "Serena."

She stopped immediately and whirled around to face him. Her brown eyes were wide with anticipation. "Yes?"

He'd been planning to tell her that he would contact her if and when he found his brother and her property. But man, if that vulnerable look wasn't his undoing. He found himself wanting to wrap her in his arms and tell her he'd pay her back himself, if that's what it would take to erase her pain.

He made his way toward her, and she toward him. "I . . . I may be able to help you get your stuff back." God, what was he doing? He had no clue what was going to happen if and when he found Cecil. He had no right to give Serena false hope.

Yet the way her eyes lit up with optimism, he knew he'd give her the same line again.

"You can?"

"I got a call from my brother a few days ago. He's in some kind of trouble, but I don't know what. That's why I came to Miami. To find him. And when I find him, I may be able to get your property back."

"Oh, Darrell."

He held up a hand to quell her excitement. "Wait. I want to be clear on this—I'm not promising anything. From the bit I heard from my brother, I assume he's on the run and doesn't want to be found. So, this may not be easy. But I'll do what I can to help you." He paused. "I mean that."

"That's all I can ask."

Silence fell between them, heavy and awkward. Then Darrell said, "All right. Give me a number where I can reach you."

"Maybe I can help you find him," Serena blurted.

Darrell gave her an odd look. "I don't see how."

"The last I heard from Cecil, he left me a note at the library saying something urgent had come up and he had to leave town."

Darrell's heart slammed against his ribs. His brother had left her a note? "Did he say why, or where he was going?"

Serena folded her arms over her chest. "No. He just said he'd be in touch as soon as he could." Serena frowned. "I don't know. Maybe if I think back, something will come to me."

"It sounds like you know as much as I know. Which is nothing."

Serena's eyes narrowed, like she was thinking hard. "What exactly did Cecil tell you?"

"He said he'd gotten himself into some trouble he wasn't sure he could get out of. When I asked what, I heard the dial tone in my ear."

"If he's in trouble, why didn't he just go to you?" Serena asked.

"Lady, if I could understand the way my brother thinks, the FBI would hire me in a New York minute."

Serena's eyes bulged. "You don't mean that."

Yeah, Darrell meant it. His brother would keep any criminal profiler in business just trying to figure him out. But he saw fear in Serena's eyes at his implication that his brother was a career criminal, and he didn't want her to lose any more sleep than she already had. So he said, "My brother probably didn't come to me because I'm in Orlando. And I got the impression someone was after him and he needed to lay low for a while."

"So this is serious?"

"Seems that way to me. Which is why I'm here. I expected to hear back from Cecil, and when I didn't, I knew I had to come to Miami and look for him."

Serena nodded. She'd do the same if her sister were in trouble. Glancing at Darrell's small suitcase, she asked, "Where are you heading now?"

"To Cecil's condo."

Her eyes lit up. "You think he's there?"

"No," Darrell told her. "I'm certain he's not there."

The spark in her eyes fizzled. "So why are you going?"

"I need a place to stay. Plus I want to check it out for any possible clues as to where he might be now."

She paused. "And how do you plan on getting in?"

"I have a key."

"Oh," Serena said. "Why?"

"Why all the questions?"

Serena shrugged. "From what you say, it doesn't seem like you and Cecil are in touch all that often. You live in Orlando, he's in Miami. I'm just wondering why you'd have a key."

Most likely, she was wondering if he was lying to her about not knowing where his brother was. He answered, "Cecil has always given me keys to his places. One of those precautionary things, I guess—in case his antics land him in jail and he needs someone to water his plants."

Serena frowned, letting him know she didn't think he was being funny.

"My brother's always inviting me to spend time with him," Darrell continued in a serious tone. "Or at least come down here for a vacation. But since he's such a hard guy to get ahold of, and he's always on the go, he wanted me to have keys to his places so I wouldn't be stuck waiting outside his door if I came to town and he wasn't around."

"That makes sense," Serena said. "So you're going there now?"

"Yes."

"All right." Serena dug her keys out of her purse. "I can give you a ride."

"That's not necessary," Darrell quickly said. "I can catch a cab."

"Where's the condo?"

"On Ocean Drive."

"That's not far. I can take you." Darrell flashed her a wary look, and Serena added, "I owe you that much. Probably even dinner."

"A billboard announcing your error will be payback enough." He gave her a wry smile.

She grinned back at him. "What do you say? Will you let me take you to your brother's condo?"

"It's really not necessary."

"Okay," she said matter-of-factly. "I'll be straight with you. If you're going to look for Cecil, I want to help. And before you say anything," she continued, holding up a hand, "I'm not going to take no for an answer. Because I want to be there when you find your brother. And then I want to wring his neck until he gives me back what's mine."

Darrell should have known it was too good to be true. Five minutes of sanity, and the crazy woman had reverted right back to being insane.

"What did you say you do?" he asked in a sardonic tone, staring down at her. She couldn't be more than five foot five.

"I'm a librarian."

"Right." Darrell stretched the word out. "Maybe you went into the wrong profession. Ever consider wrestling?"

Serena made a face. "What, I don't have a right to be angry?"

This wasn't about her not having a right to be angry. It was about Darrell trying to reconcile the fact that the cute, seemingly demure woman who'd caught his eye at the restaurant yesterday wasn't actually demure. Then again, maybe she was normally sweet as pie, but his brother had brought out the worst in her. Lord knew Cecil had brought out the worst in so many people, including their father.

"Yeah, you have a right to be angry. You just . . . surprise me, that's all."

"I'm normally mild-mannered—until someone crosses me." Serena punctuated her words with a saccharine-sweet smile.

Darrell gave her a slow once-over. The woman was an enigma, and not just because her demure appearance clearly hid a strong, determined side. What the hell had Cecil seen in her? Not that she wasn't attractive, because she was, but she certainly wasn't the type Cecil normally got involved with. She dressed simply, not flashy, and Cecil always went for flashy. Darrell guessed her to be in her late twenties, a little young compared to the women Cecil usually conned. His brother tended to date older women, often married, but women who easily spoke of money and class and appreciated the attention of a smooth-talking playboy.

But Cecil was a man, and when he wasn't pulling a scam on a woman, he'd date a bombshell until he was bored, then move on to another one.

Which is exactly what bothered Darrell about his brother and Serena. Yes, she was attractive, but in a cute sort of way—not the sleazy way his brother appreciated.

So, how the hell had they ended up getting involved?

"Darrell?"

His eyes flew to hers. "Yeah?"

She gave him an odd look, clearly wondering what had been on his mind. After a moment, she shrugged. "So, what do you say? Can we work together? I know Miami. I can help you look for him here. Take you to all the places you might not easily find. Besides, two heads are better than one."

Darrell didn't respond, contemplating the thought.

"No offense, but I'm really the one who ought to be wary," Serena added. "Considering you *are* Cecil's brother."

"I'm nothing like my brother," Darrell retorted.

Darrell's quick answer made Serena think he'd been spouting that line his whole life, almost like a knee-jerk reaction. That, along with the way his jaw hardened and his body tensed, made Serena realize that she'd pushed one of his buttons. Which made her wonder what Darrell and Cecil's relationship had been like growing up and how different they truly were. Judging by Darrell's agitated demeanor, Serena guessed they were quite different, and that Darrell had often taken flack for his brother's actions.

"I didn't mean to offend you," she told him.

"Maybe not, but your comment makes me think your suggestion is a bad idea. Like you said, I'm related to the guy who ripped you off. Why would you want to spend any time with me?"

"Because I'm desperate."

"Oh, thanks," Darrell replied wryly.

"I don't mean . . ." She exhaled sharply. "Look, this isn't the best situation for either of us. We don't know each other. But we both want the same thing: to find Cecil. And I'm willing to work with you if you're willing to work with me."

"Is that so, Slugger?" Darrell raised an eyebrow, but grinned.

"I guess you'll never let me live that down."

"Hey, I like a woman who can protect me from the bad guys."

"Oh, stop." Serena felt embarrassed enough.

"I'm just playing with you."

Darrell smiled down at her, a genuine smile, and Serena's heart suddenly pounded so hard, it was like getting punched from the inside. She'd never had that reaction just from looking at a man, not even Cecil, and he was Darrell's twin. Did that make sense?

No doubt about it, Darrell Montford was drop-dead-gorgeous-fine. He had a lady killer smile that lit up his bright brown eyes, coupled with an athletic body that boasted well-sculpted muscles in all the right places.

A soft breath oozed from her body.

Serena's reaction to him surprised her. But it wasn't only his physical qualities that were attractive, she realized a moment later. There was something else about him, something she inherently trusted.

And she couldn't help wondering, *Why didn't I meet him instead of Cecil?*

God, what was she thinking? Hadn't she learned her lesson yet? Cecil had been the first pretty boy to sweep her off her feet—and she'd fallen flat on her back. The last thing she wanted to do was make the same mistake again.

Especially with his brother.

His identical *twin* brother. How different could they be?

Which was why, though she knew she should simply give him her number and tell him to call her when he found Cecil, she wasn't quite ready to say good-bye to Darrell. How could she trust him to keep his word and call her when he'd found him? Cecil could easily give him some cock and bull story that Darrell would want to believe—perhaps even pass her off as a jealous ex. If that happened, Darrell would no doubt choose to believe his brother over her.

No, she needed to work with Darrell for her own peace of mind. Serena extended a hand. "Are we in this together?"

Darrell didn't respond, merely looked at her, not sure what to do. What the hell was he in for if he agreed to work with her? But as Serena continued to extend her hand, Darrell finally reached out and took it in his. Her small hand almost got lost in his large one, and he couldn't help wondering how something so small could pack such a strong wallop.

She was feisty, yes, but he also sensed a vulnerable side to her, and that vulnerability brought out a protective side in him.

His eyes caught hers, and she gave him a peculiar look. He realized he'd been holding her hand too long. Quickly, he shook then released it.

"All right," he agreed. "I'll work with you."

He only hoped he didn't live to regret this decision.

# Chapter 4

*Shrugging into the collar of his Versace shirt,* Cecil hurried from his rented van toward the payphones outside the Publix grocery store. Throwing a quick glance over both shoulders gave him a modicum of relief. For a while, he'd thought the blue Neon had been following him, but now that he no longer saw it, he knew that wasn't the case.

Thank God. The town of Kendall was a good thirty minutes from Miami Beach, which was where he normally spent most of his time, and he hoped to have anonymity here.

Cecil paused to let a woman and two small children cross his path before stepping onto the concrete sidewalk. A couple long strides and he was at one of the payphones lining the building's wall. He lifted the receiver and brought it to his ear. Seconds later, he had an operator on the line.

"MCI operator. How may I help you?"

"I'd like to make a collect call," Cecil told the woman, then gave her the number to his brother's home in Orlando.

Cecil waited while the operator dialed Darrell's line. It rang and rang, then the answering machine picked up.

"Sorry, sir. I'm getting a machine."

"Try this number," Cecil quickly said. "Make this one a person-to-person call to Darrell Montford." He gave the operator the number to Sleep Well, the bed and breakfast his brother owned and operated.

A minute later, the operator told him, "I couldn't reach Darrell Montford."

*Damn.* "All right." Cecil moaned softly. "Thanks anyway."

The operator disconnected, and Cecil hung up the phone. What was he supposed to do now? And where the hell was his brother? He'd been trying to reach him for a couple days, but to no avail. If there was one thing he could count on, it was being able to reach Darrell when he needed him. Darrell was reliable that way. If he wasn't at work, then he was at home.

So where was he?

Cecil frowned at the phone. Darrell hadn't been around for a couple days. If this were any of his male friends, he'd figure they were off with some honey somewhere. But Darrell wasn't the type of guy to run off and leave his business for a rendezvous with a woman, at least not since his ex-fiancée Jessica.

But who knew? Life had a way of surprising you. Cecil certainly never expected to be in the predicament he was in now. So it wasn't impossible that Darrell had finally fallen for someone else.

Cecil could almost be happy for him—if his disappearance hadn't come at the most inopportune time. Given the fact that he couldn't reach Eddie, Darrell was the only one who could possibly help him now.

Gritting his teeth, Cecil dug some change out of his pocket. He'd try Eddie once again. He hoped to hell that he was home now, and that he had the answers he needed. Eddie might not like having to deal with this situation, but the way Cecil saw it, Eddie owed him. If it wasn't for him, Cecil wouldn't be in this whole mess.

"C'mon, Eddie. Pick up the damn phone." But one ring turned to two, then to three. Then to four. And it kept ringing. God, didn't he even have his machine on now?

Cecil disconnected, gathered his change, then dialed Eddie's cell phone number. If Eddie was on the road, he'd be sure to have his cell with him.

But after four rings, his voicemail came on. "I'm busy. Leave a message."

"Yo, Eddie," Cecil said, his tone urgent. "You know who this is. Look, I need to talk to you. You have to let me know if you got that jewelry back, man. My ass is on the line here. For real. If I don't get that jewelry back—and I mean yesterday—I'm gonna end up as gator food." The very thought made a chill run down his spine. "All right. I've gotta run, but I'll try you again in a few hours. Please be around."

Then Cecil slammed down the receiver, a sick feeling spreading in his gut. Eddie had been AWOL for a good thirty-six hours. Cecil knew he was head-over-heels for Sheila, the new woman he was seeing, and yeah, he could understand him spending all his time with her. But hell, Cecil had left a few messages for Eddie already, so he had to know he was urgently trying to reach him. If he hadn't spent the last thirty-six hours in a body-lock with Sheila—and he couldn't imagine that—then why wasn't he answering his cell?

Cecil could think of only two answers to that question. Either Eddie was dead, or he was avoiding him. Cecil doubted the former, but he could easily picture the latter. As the saying went, there was no honor among thieves. Either way, the fact that he hadn't heard from Eddie meant bad news.

"Shit," Cecil mumbled, then leaned against the wall. How on earth had he gotten caught up in this whole scam, anyway? He'd been at one of his favorite Miami Beach night spots, hoping to meet a new woman, when Eddie had sat next to him at the bar. After sitting in silence for some time, Eddie had turned to him and asked if he had a light. Cecil didn't, because he didn't smoke, but Eddie's question had broken the ice. They'd started talking, and had instantly hit it off.

Cecil wasn't sure why Eddie had sat next to him nor why they'd started talking, but he had entertained the thought that fate had played a role in it all. At first, it had seemed like an incredible stroke of luck that he should meet a guy like Eddie, because he'd needed a new way to make a buck, and Eddie had provided that. In hindsight, Cecil couldn't help wondering if Eddie had scoped him out because he recognized in Cecil a quality he had himself—the ability to con.

Shortly into their talk that evening, Eddie had flat out told Cecil that he only dated women who could give him things—material things. Cecil was pleasantly surprised to learn that he and Eddie had that in common. Eddie had said, "Some might call me a con artist, but hey, so be it. At least I'm driving a Porsche." They'd both laughed, then had shared stories about their "conquests" and all the goods they'd received from horny older women.

Cecil didn't particularly like the words "con artist." It wasn't that he had *planned* to use women for what they could give him, it had just happened that way. For whatever reason, older women found him attractive—older women who were usually looking for a boy toy. Connie, the first older woman he'd dated, had been married, like most of them after her. In the beginning, the fact that she'd been married had disturbed him, but Connie had lavished him with gifts every time he told her he thought they shouldn't continue their relationship. He'd meant it, but her gifts had kept him around. Who wouldn't stick around when someone bought you a sports car, or gave you a couple grand to go shopping?

At first, Cecil hadn't felt that great about himself, because every time he accepted a gift from Connie, he felt he was leading her on. But then he'd realized the truth: Connie wasn't in love with him any more than he was with her. She simply liked having him around, so much so that she'd bought him the condo on the beach so they could spend more time together outside of hotels. It was an expensive gift, yes, but why should he say no? She was using him for what he had to give, so why not accept what she could give him?

If a woman wanted to spend money on him and give him gifts, why shouldn't he let them? It wasn't his fault women wanted him so badly they'd do anything to keep him hanging around. Connie had opened him up to a whole new world in his early twenties, and it suited him fine. The best part was, after only six months of seeing her, Connie and her husband had moved to France. And he'd gotten to keep the condo. Not bad for six months of his time.

Some people might say he was shallow, but at least he wasn't the one breaking any vows. And he *did* have to worry about jealous husbands coming after him if his trysts with their wives were ever discovered. So there was a certain amount of risk to pleasing women like Connie. Why not get paid for his efforts?

And as for those who said he was shallow, yeah, he specifically sought out women who looked like they were made of money, and maybe he even gave them some hard luck stories to entice them to part with their husbands' well-earned bucks—but didn't women look for sugar-daddies all the time? No doubt his mother had. Surely what was good for the goose was good for the gander.

But accepting lavish gifts from women without any remorse had pretty much been the extent of Cecil's underhanded ways. Until he'd met Eddie. After hitting it off at the bar and learning that they were both smooth-talking playboys, Eddie had griped that he wasn't able to adequately maintain the lifestyle to which he'd become accustomed because women were tighter with their wallets these days—didn't Cecil agree? Hell yeah, Cecil agreed. That's when Eddie had told Cecil about his sure-fire plan to make mega dollars. In fact, Eddie had already been doing it for a while. Things had been going so well that he now needed a partner to help him keep up with the demand.

The plan, as Eddie had explained it to Cecil, was easy. Steal expensive jewelry from their well-to-do lovers and replace them with fakes. For several months, Eddie had been working with a guy who was an expert at making stunning fake jewelry based on the real pieces. Eddie had assured Cecil that he'd been doing it for a while without any problems and had made a fortune.

Well, Cecil was always open to new ideas, so he'd figured, why not give it a try? Again, he'd thought fate must have brought him and Eddie together. Why else meet Eddie at a time when he needed a new way to earn quick money?

He and Eddie had shook on it, agreeing to be partners.

Shortly after that, Cecil had met Tamara at the Delano on South Beach, a spot frequented by those with money to burn. The thirty-five-year-old bombshell had been immediately receptive to his charm. Cecil had struck up a conversation with her not only because she was stunning, but because she'd been wearing beautiful jewelry. Cecil had complimented her on it, and she'd proudly proclaimed that the diamonds and sapphires were real.

Tamara hadn't waited more than five minutes before telling him how unhappily married she was—so Cecil had bought her a drink to help her drown her sorrows. Then another. Soon, she was throwing herself at him like a wanton hussy. Again, Cecil had complimented her jewelry. Tamara then bragged that she had a safe full of expensive jewelry at home—compliments of her ancient, impotent husband.

Because she'd given him a sly grin, Cecil had laughed, and so had Tamara. "Well, he's not exactly impotent," Tamara had amended. "But viagara ain't exactly helping Lionel's problem, if you hear what I'm saying."

"I hear you," Cecil said, chuckling. "Okay, so he's not quite impotent. But he's really ancient?"

Tamara laughed long and loud like an idiot, clearly drunk. "Oh, yeah. He's ancient."

"How old *is* he?"

"Eighty-one."

"Wow." Cecil blew out a low whistle. "That's old."

"I know. I don't know what I was thinking." Tamara rested a hand on the stunning diamond and sapphire necklace gracing her long, slim neck. Then she flashed Cecil another sly grin—which told him she'd known exactly what she'd been thinking when she married Lionel.

"How long you been married?" Cecil asked.

"Seven years. Since I was twenty-eight."

"Holy."

Tamara speared the olive in her martini and brought it to her lips, letting her tongue play over it before she took it into her mouth.

Instantly, Cecil was hard. Not even a monk would have been unaffected by her charm.

But Cecil played dumb, once again discussing her marriage. "Well, you're still together. So many couples don't make it past the two-year itch." Cecil raised an eyebrow. "True love, I'm sure."

In response, Tamara tilted her head to the side and gave him a slow once-over, biting her bottom lip as she did.

True love his ass. But he was having fun playing this game. "So, Lionel . . . has he always had . . . a problem?"

Tamara raised her eyes to Cecil's, giving him a level stare. "If you're asking whether or not he's ever fucked me right, the answer is no."

Tamara's vulgarity shocked Cecil, but it also turned him on. "Sorry to hear that." He sipped his scotch, wetting his throat. "Must be hard."

"Honey, if it was hard, that would have been a start." Tamara erupted in giggles, then downed the dregs of her martini. As her laughter faded, she added sadly, "God, it's been a *nightmare*," as if she'd always been faithful to her sexually challenged husband.

"A beautiful woman like you . . ." Cecil *tsked*. "I can't imagine you living without sex." He ran a finger along her palm in a circular pattern. "*Very* good sex. You strike me as a very passionate person who has a lot to give."

"Baby, you don't know the kind of passion I've got pent up after all these years."

"I can imagine."

Boldly, Tamara trailed her fingers up his thigh. "Why imagine?"

Before Cecil could answer, Tamara had thrown her arms around his neck and kissed him silly.

Cecil couldn't have asked for an easier mark. And it was a bonus that she was gorgeous. Sleeping with her was easy—not to mention pretty damn incredible. She had an insatiable sexual appetite, as if she hadn't been laid right in several years.

There was no doubt she was smitten with him. And not only could Tamara not get enough of him, she liked living on the edge. She'd sneak him into her Star Island home when the husband was gone for a few hours; often, Cecil barely escaped in the nick of time. And when her husband was out of town, she had Cecil over the moment he was gone, as if his name was on the deed to the million-dollar property.

After a three-day lovemaking marathon one time when her husband was away, Cecil had finally gotten up the nerve to break into Tamara's safe and take a few of her more expensive jewelry items.

Eddie had been very pleased.

So had Cecil. The pieces had netted them over one hundred and forty thousand dollars. And after a good week, Cecil had thought he was home free—until Tamara had noticed that the jewelry was missing. Cecil had quickly admitted to taking the pieces, but had assured her he'd done so to have them cleaned. Why hadn't he told her? Tamara had asked. Why sneak into her safe? Well, because it was going to be a surprise, of course, Cecil had lied. Then he'd slipped his hand beneath her skirt and quickly gotten her excited. She wouldn't ask any more questions in bed.

His answer had seemed to pacify her, especially when he returned the jewelry a few days later. But only days after that, Tamara started acting suspicious. She wanted to know where he'd brought the jewelry, and had wondered aloud if it didn't look a little different. Cecil didn't have any answers for her, so he'd started avoiding her.

Her call to his home in Coconut Grove a week later confirmed that she knew the jewelry was fake; she'd sensed something was wrong and had brought the pieces in to have them appraised. At first, Cecil had panicked, not sure what to do. However, shortly afterward, he'd relaxed. The way he figured it, Tamara would have to keep her mouth shut about the theft, because if she told her old man about it, she'd have to admit that she'd not only had a lover, but she'd had him *in her husband's bed*. Surely, if she did that, her husband would kick her out in ten seconds flat, cut her off from the lifestyle to which she'd become accustomed—*and* cut her out of the will.

No, Tamara was too smart to let that happen.

But naturally, she was pissed. And while Cecil no longer worried about her snitching on him, he did miss the sex. And he got the impression that Tamara wasn't as upset about him stealing her jewelry as she was about the fact that he obviously didn't care about her the way she had hoped.

Sylvia, at least, had been an easy, less complicated target. She'd liked him, but she hadn't gotten possessive the way Tamara had. As far as he knew, she was fairly happily married to a man a few years older than her. But he'd been having affairs for the last ten years of their nearly thirty-year marriage, and Sylvia had decided it was payback time.

Who better than a man nineteen years her junior?

Sylvia hadn't missed the jewelry Cecil had taken from her. So after a month, he'd taken more. He'd scored big with Sylvia; her jewelry had been worth over two hundred and fifty thousand dollars. The only downside to the whole scam was that Eddie took fifty percent of everything Cecil brought him. That was his cut, he'd told Cecil, take it or leave it. It didn't quite seem fair, considering Cecil was the one putting himself at risk to get the jewelry, but Eddie was adamant.

There wasn't much Cecil could have done at that point besides accept Eddie's terms. Eddie was the one with the connections to sell the jewelry and have the fakes made, so Cecil needed him. Fifty percent of a big chunk of change was better than fifty percent of nothing.

But now he was in deep shit. A couple months after being with her, Jan, another woman he'd been involved with, had learned that her expensive jewelry had been replaced with fakes. With Jan, Cecil had tried a different approach, a plan he'd thought was foolproof. After complimenting Jan's jewelry and casually asking her how much it was worth, she'd told him she didn't know; her husband, who was currently in jail, had never told her.

Cecil had then given her a line of bull about having a friend who was a jeweler, and offered to have her jewelry appraised. Because Jan didn't know the value of the pieces, she'd agreed to Cecil's suggestion. And she hadn't questioned him when he'd returned the jewelry. Another successful hit.

Jan hadn't been like the others, though. She didn't want to continue seeing him once her husband, Rex, was out of jail. She'd wanted him only to keep her warm at night until her husband could once again. Which suited Cecil fine—given the fact that he'd gotten what he truly wanted from her.

So no one was more surprised to hear from Jan weeks after her husband had gotten out of the pen than Cecil. Jan had called him, quite worried and distraught. She asked what he'd done to her jewelry. Cecil had played dumb. Jan had gone on to explain that Rex had suspected something was wrong when he'd noticed the diamonds in her tennis bracelet were a little too shiny. So Jan had told him that she'd had a friend appraise it, but Rex had been immediately suspicious. He'd had all her jewelry checked out and learned that most of the pieces were fakes.

Rex wasn't buying the "friend" line, and ultimately, Jan had admitted to her husband that she'd gotten involved with another guy while he'd been in prison.

"You did *what*? Cecil had asked, horrified.

"I had to tell him, Cece. He knew anyway."

Cecil panicked. "Does he know who I am?"

"I told him everything. It was the only way he would forgive me. God, I've never seen him so upset. Except for that time he went after that guy who made a pass at me with a tire iron. Which is what landed him in jail . . ."

Cecil swallowed—hard. Great. This was just great.

"Listen, Cece, I'm sure he'll get over the affair—as long as you get the jewelry back. Can you go back to that jeweler friend of yours?"

"Uh . . ." Cecil had hedged. "Sure. I'll see if he knows what happened."

Jan had called him days later, asking if he'd had any success finding out what happened to her jewelry. Cecil had told her he was still working on it. Jan had reiterated that Rex could forgive her indiscretion—as long as she got the jewelry back. If Cecil couldn't retrieve her jewelry, and subsequently Rex didn't forgive her, he wouldn't forgive Cecil, either.

That was a bit of life and death pressure Cecil could have lived without.

When Cecil hung up with Jan, he had immediately called Eddie. Eddie confirmed what he already suspected: the jewelry had been sold months ago and he had no idea of how to get it back at this point. The best Eddie could do was look into it.

Cecil had figured he'd had some time—until Rex had called him and promised to break every one of his bones before throwing him into a canal if he didn't get the jewelry back ASAP. During this time, Cecil had gotten to know Serena, and he knew she had a necklace worth a quarter of a million. Serena was sweet, not like the other women he'd scammed. She was genuine, not flaky like the women who'd come into his life. She was the kind of woman he occasionally daydreamed about settling down with—*if* he was the type to settle down. But even if he was, deep in his heart, he knew he didn't deserve Serena. Still, he liked her, and he didn't like the idea of hurting her.

But he'd remembered what Eddie had told him about not letting your emotions get involved. So he'd planned to take Serena's necklace the moment he could, because it was worth a pretty penny—and that would certainly help him out of his bind with Rex.

However, after learning that the necklace had been in Serena's family for aeons and that the history of the necklace had spawned her dream of opening an antiques store, Cecil had decided against taking it.

But Rex grew more impatient with each passing day.

As a result, Cecil had given in to temptation and taken Serena's necklace, offering it to Rex as a replacement. But days after FedExing Rex a picture of the exquisite antique necklace, Rex had called with the shocking news that he didn't want a replacement. He wanted the jewelry Cecil had hawked because it had sentimental value. He'd given Cecil forty-eight hours to get it back before he taught him a very painful lesson.

By then, Cecil knew Rex meant business. The only other thing he could figure to do was get enough cash together to buy the jewelry back—provided he could find out who'd bought it in the first place. But forty-eight hours wasn't enough time to sell any of his swanky properties to get the necessary cash.

Eighteen hours into his forty-eight-hour deadline, Rex had laughed his head off at Cecil's offer of ten thousand dollars—the money he'd taken from Serena—as a measure of good faith that he'd get the jewelry back.

Right on time, Rex had started calling with death threats. Cecil had promptly disconnected all his numbers, except for the one at his condo, which was his main number—and the one only a few people knew. Jan didn't have that one—at least, that's what he'd thought, until Rex had left a message for him there. Cecil didn't return any of the calls, hoping Rex would figure he'd skipped town. But he knew it was only a matter of time before Rex caught up with him. In the meantime, he was hoping to get some money together. However, even if he could sell one of his places in time, he couldn't show his face at either of his homes without the risk of getting a bullet in his back.

That's why he'd tried to reach Darrell, to see if there was any way Darrell could come up with the money. But he'd had to hang up on his brother when he'd realized someone had been following him.

With that thought, Cecil took another look around. Men, women, and children filtered in and out of the grocery store. Thank God, he didn't see anyone suspicious. But he'd best get out of this public place now—just in case.

Heading back to his van, Cecil cringed. A Pontiac. God, could life get worse than this? He missed his Jaguar and his Viper, but there was no way he could drive them. Anyone who knew him would recognize both flashy cars.

Well, at least the Pontiac's windows were tinted. No one should spot him in this vehicle. Still, as he opened the door to the boring van, he couldn't help exhaling a frustrated breath.

Hopefully, he'd hear from Eddie soon and find out who'd bought the jewelry. And hopefully he'd get his hands on some cash so that he could buy the jewelry back.

Because this time, he'd crossed the wrong person. And if he didn't make this situation right—and soon—he was as good as dead.

## Chapter 5

*Thirty seconds into the short drive to his brother's* condo, Darrell couldn't help wondering if he'd made one of the bigger blunders of his life.

The woman beside him was clearly crazy. He should run, not walk, in the other direction. Five minutes in her presence last night had cost him his pride, and had given him a miserable night in Miami that he would never forget. Hell, maybe her insanity had rubbed off on him. Otherwise, why on earth would he have agreed to work with her? She'd given him a hellish twenty-four hours. What else could he honestly expect if he spent more time with her?

All right, maybe he wasn't being fair. She'd thought he was Cecil, so her wrath hadn't actually been directed toward him. Now that she knew who he really was, he shouldn't have to worry that she'd up and go berserk on him again.

He glanced at Serena. Feeling his gaze, she angled her head toward him and gave him a half-smile.

Darrell opened his mouth, but after a moment, he closed it. As much as he wanted to tell Serena to forget this arrangement, he couldn't. She *did* have a point; two heads were better than one. But she was a feisty little thing, and that attitude of hers might get them both into trouble.

Then again, maybe it would get them out of a snafu or two. Which he expected, given his brother's reputation.

Darrell's mind wandered to Cecil and what he possibly could have done wrong this time. Though the younger twin by a few minutes, Darrell had acted as Cecil's older brother his whole life. While Darrell had been responsible, Cecil had been irresponsible. Darrell had been studious and well behaved in school; Cecil had been a pain in almost every teacher's butt. Not to mention other students' butts. He fought so much as a young child that one might have guessed he was preparing for a career in the boxing ring.

Darrell had no doubt that Cecil's problems started when their mother abandoned them. He misbehaved as a way to get attention because negative attention was better than no attention at all. At first, he must have hoped their mother would hear of his antics and return. When she hadn't come back, he'd continued to act up, probably hoping to get a rise out of their father, who'd become despondent after their mother's disappearance and had turned to booze. But their father hadn't had the patience to deal with Cecil's antics, and in an attempt to control his son's bad behavior, he'd beaten him every time he'd done something wrong.

Darrell would comfort his brother at night after such beatings, having taken on the role of surrogate father almost from the moment their mother had run off with that filthy rich CEO she'd worked for. Time and again, Cecil promised Darrell he would do better, not their father. And as he held Darrell and cried and made all these promises, he sounded completely sincere. But no matter how much Cecil said he'd try harder to do the right thing, he never did.

At age thirteen, when Cecil got caught stealing a Walkman from a K-Mart store, their father had beat the living daylights out of him, then disowned him.

Since then, Darrell had officially taken over as father, and had tried to get Cecil out of each of his messes, all the while hoping Cecil would one day smarten up. He never had.

"Darrell?"

Serena's voice startled him. "Huh?"

"Which building?"

"Oh." Darrell looked outside the slow-moving car and pointed to the tall multi-colored condo at the end of the strip. "That one."

Serena gave a low whistle. "Wow."

"Yeah." Darrell paused. "Wait a minute. You've never been here?"

"No." Serena slowed the car to a crawl.

Why had she never been to Cecil's condo? Darrell wondered.

"Where should I park?" Serena asked, interrupting his thoughts.

"There's got to be..." Serena turned right, going

around another side of the building. "Ah, there's valet parking. Let's pull in there."

Serena did as instructed. A gentleman wearing black pants, a white shirt with black bow tie, and a red vest stepped in front of the car as she stopped.

The man was at her driver's side door before she put the car into park. He opened it for her. "Morning, ma'am." His eyes went past her to Darrell. "Ah, good morning, Mr. Montford," he said brightly. "Haven't seen you here for a little while."

Darrell had never seen this man in his life before, but he didn't know that. And right now, Darrell wasn't about to clue him in to the fact that he was Cecil's twin before he had a chance to go upstairs and look for clues.

"Uh," Darrell began, glancing beyond Serena at the man's nametag. "Hello, Miguel. I know, I haven't been around much. I've been busy."

"I see." Miguel raised a suggestive eyebrow and looked at Serena, as if to say he understood what had been keeping Cecil away. "Well, glad to have you back, sir." Then, he extended a hand to Serena, helping her out of the car.

Darrell gripped the handle and started to open his door.

"Please, Mr. Montford," Miguel said, rushing around to that side of the car before Darrell had the door completely open. "Allow me." Miguel took the door handle and opened it.

"Thank you," Darrell said, feeling somewhat awkward. He was used to opening his own doors, but could imagine his brother lapping up attention like this.

Miguel gave Darrell a brief once-over, his slightly wide eyes the only indication that he was surprised at Cecil's attire. Then he turned to Serena, who had strolled toward Darrell. "I'll take your keys, ma'am."

Serena was about to ask how much the valet service would cost, then thought better of it. Anyone who lived here or visited friends here wouldn't be concerned with such petty things as the cost of parking.

She passed him the keys.

"Great." Miguel smiled. But he didn't move. Instead, he looked from Serena to Darrell, an easy grin playing on his lips.

"Oh," Darrell quickly said. He dug into his back pocket and withdrew his wallet. He took out a ten and passed it to Miguel.

"Thank you, sir." His grin widened. "I'll make sure to take good care of this car. Hold a second for your ticket, ma'am."

Miguel returned with Serena's half of the valet ticket, then opened the front door of the condo for her and Darrell.

"Morning, Mr. Montford," the concierge greeted Darrell once they were inside.

Darrell gave the elderly man a nod. "Morning."

Serena felt weird in this opulent place, as if she expected the *Rich and Famous* police to come running from the back rooms screaming, "Imposter!" and kick her butt out of here before she could say Robin Leach. But she flashed the concierge a confident smile and held her head high, then walked with Darrell to the elevators. They stood behind an older woman who carried what at first seemed to be a gigantic fur ball. On closer examination, Serena saw that it was actually an enormously fluffy white poodle.

The giant fluff ball let out a low growl as it stared at Darrell and Serena.

"There, there," the woman cooed. "You'll be okay. They're not going to hurt you, Buttons."

A tongue appeared from the puff of white fur, lapping at the woman's mouth. The woman giggled as she kissed the dog back.

Serena rolled her eyes.

The elevator arrived moments later. Serena, Darrell, the woman, and her white fur ball got on.

"What floor?" Serena asked Darrell.

"Penthouse." Serena reached past the woman and pressed PH.

Though the woman was closer to the brass numbers than Serena or Darrell, she asked, "Honey, can you hit the tenth floor for me?"

Serena complied, mildly annoyed. What would the woman have done if she weren't here? Was Buttons too precious to stand on the elevator floor?

"Buttons is a champion show dog," the woman boasted, almost as if she'd read Serena's mind. "Aren't you, Buttons? Huh?" Buttons enthusiastically licked her lips again. "That's right, sweetie. Mommy loves you."

The woman continued to talk to Buttons as if it were a baby until they exited on the tenth floor.

Darrell and Serena shared a look, but continued to the penthouse level in silence. Serena wasn't quite sure what irked her so much about the woman, other than that she seemed to be the pretentious type who expected the world to wait on her and frou-frou hand and foot.

Yeah, that's what bothered her. The reality that women like her who lived in a place like this clearly had money; Cecil clearly had money. So why had he stolen from her?

It didn't make any sense.

And it made her angry.

There was a soft *ping* when the elevator arrived at the penthouse floor. Serena followed Darrell out of the elevator. He glanced down one end of the hallway, then started off in the opposite direction.

Moments later, Darrell stopped in front of PH2. Key already in hand, he inserted it in the lock.

The moment he and Serena stepped inside, Serena gasped. "Good God in heaven. This place is *huge*."

Stepping further into the condo, Serena looked around in wonder. Huge was an understatement. The place had to be five times the size of her apartment, which was a pretty good size. The window stretched across the entire length of the living room and solarium, which was shaped in a semicircle. With the blinds open, bright sunlight streamed into the condo.

To her right, there was a hallway with at least six doors. Good Lord, how many bedrooms were there? To her left, there was a lavish black marble bar, beside which was the kitchen. She guessed the dining room was somewhere through there. Serena slowly descended the three steps that led to the sunken living room. While the entranceway and hallway were adorned with gleaming hardwood floors, the living room boasted a cream-colored carpet. As Serena made her way across the room, she noted that the carpet was almost as thick as the mattress on her bed. Stunning paintings of vast landscapes hung on the walls. A black lacquer coffee table and end tables matched the black leather sofa and loveseat. The entertainment center was extensive and gave Serena the impression that Cecil loved to entertain. Absolutely everything in the room spoke of money and taste.

Serena didn't doubt Cecil had money, but she'd never dreamed he had *this* kind of money. This was the kind of place featured on *Lifestyles of the Rich and Famous*.

Serena continued on to the floor-to-ceiling window. Not very practical if a hurricane hit, but she was certain Cecil had hurricane shutters outside.

She took in the view of the Atlantic Ocean. She'd never seen it from this height before, except once when she was in the air, and the view was breathtaking. She thought the lake behind her property was beautiful, but there was simply no comparison. To wake up to this every day would be like not having a care in the world.

The thought burned her, and she whirled around, unable to take anymore. If Cecil was this loaded, why steal from her?

"I knew Cecil had fancy clothes and drove a fancy car, but I never dreamed he had this kind of money," Serena commented.

Her mention of money immediately rubbed Darrell the wrong way; he'd had too many experiences with women who'd been interested only in his pocketbook.

Not that she'd done or said anything to make him think she was a gold digger, but the feeling wouldn't subside. "You had no clue?" he asked doubtfully.

"None."

She wouldn't look at him. "You mentioned his car and clothes. You had to know . . ."

"Like I said, I was sure he had a good lifestyle, but this?" She gestured a hand around the room. "This is opulence beyond anything I ever expected."

Whether or not she had actually been interested in Cecil for his money, Darrell couldn't be sure. He let the matter drop. "Yeah, this place is pretty amazing."

Serena surveyed the room a moment longer, then looked Darrell squarely in the eye. "Does your family own a *Fortune* five hundred company or something?"

"Not even close," he assured her.

"Then I don't understand."

Approaching her, Darrell said, "My brother has lived off gullible women for years."

The words were like a knife in Serena's heart, because they were true. She *had* been gullible—all because Cecil had been charming.

Yet she'd had reason to trust him. He'd taken her to many different properties that could house her antiques shop. She'd had every reason to believe he was a legitimate real estate agent. How was she to know he'd rip her off?

"Hey," Darrell said softly.

Serena lifted her gaze to his, somewhat unnerved to find he was standing mere inches from her.

"What I said . . . I didn't mean it like that. I'm not saying you're gullible. You seem like a nice person, and my brother no doubt saw that. Believe me, I know how charming he can be. So don't take it personally." Darrell grimaced, then shook his head. "My brother . . . practically from the beginning, he's been determined to stay off the straight and narrow path. I tried my best to show him the right way, but he was never interested."

Serena nodded grimly.

"You're not the first woman he's taken advantage of, but hopefully you'll be his last."

"I just want my property back."

She was putting on a brave face, but Darrell could see that his comment had struck a nerve. He wanted to ask her outright how she'd gotten involved with Cecil, because she was so not his type, but he didn't really want to know the sordid details. "Like I said, I'll do what I can to help you get your property back."

"Mmm hmm."

"I'm gonna take a look around, see if I can find anything."

"Sure."

Darrell didn't like her sudden despondency, but he didn't know what to do or say to make her feel better. All he could do was try and find Cecil, the only hope to getting her necklace back. "Go ahead and make yourself comfortable," Darrell told her.

"Yeah."

Darrell watched Serena sink into the soft leather loveseat. Hunching forward, she rested her elbows on her knees and buried her face in her hands. He couldn't help thinking that she seemed so small and frail in this huge space. It was a sight that disturbed him, and he quickly turned and walked out of the living room.

He tried door after door and found lavish bedroom after lavish bedroom. The last and fourth one was the only one that looked lived in. Darrell stepped inside, checking out the large room as he did. He saw nothing out of the ordinary. Then again, Darrell had no clue what he was looking for.

He spotted an answering machine on the night table

beside the king-sized bed. Excitement tickled his stomach. The machine might hold some type of clue. He strolled toward it. A green light flashed, indicating there were messages. He hit the play button.

*Beep.* "Cecil, baby," the first message began. "It's Donna. Where are you? You've been avoiding me, baby, which is very, very bad." Giggle. "Call me."

*Beep.* "Hey, Cece." That was another woman. "I miss you, sweetheart. I guess you're still out of town, huh? I hope your mother's okay. Call me when you get back."

Christ, Darrell thought. Cecil, a thirty-one-year-old adult, was using their mother as an excuse for being out of town when she'd been dead for ten years. When was his brother going to grow up?

*Beep.* "Cecil," yet another woman's voice began, "I'm going *crazy* waiting to hear from you. Where are you, baby? Mmm . . . I need to see you. I am *so* horny. Call me as soon as you get this message."

Good grief, Darrell thought. Where did Cecil meet these women?

". . . But you can't hide. You crossed the wrong person this time and now you're going to pay."

Darrell was startled out of his reverie by the words of the subsequent message. His heart slammed against his ribcage. After a moment of shock, he quickly hit the rewind button. After a few seconds, he once again pressed play.

*Beep.* "You can run, Cecil, but you can't hide. You crossed the wrong person this time and now you're going to pay."

The person's voice was distorted, and he couldn't tell if

it was a man or a woman speaking. But there was no mistaking that this was a threat.

Darrell hit rewind and listened to the message again. A myriad of emotions swirled inside him, from anxiety to concern to confusion to downright dread.

Was this an idle threat, or a deadly serious one? And was the person behind this threat the person who'd sent Cecil into hiding?

That had to be the case. How likely was it that Cecil had more than one person out to do him harm?

Dumb question, Darrell realized. He could only imagine how many people his brother had crossed. In reality, there could be any number of women angry enough to hurt him.

Darrell tuned out the next couple messages, but perked up when he once again heard the distorted voice. "I knew you were full of shit, Cecil," the message began. "You can't avoid the inevitable. I *will* find you. And you *will* pay."

*Beep.* "Cecil, it's Donna. Where are you hiding, sweetness? Call me. I miss you."

*Beep.* "Darrell, if by any chance you came looking for me and are hearing this message—oh, shit!"

A chill swept down Darrell's back at the sound of his brother's voice. Anxious for a follow-up message, Darrell let the machine continue playing, but there was nothing more from Cecil—only more messages from hot and bothered women.

He rewound the tape until he heard his brother's message again, hoping he'd pick up on something he'd missed the first time. But of course, there was nothing more to the message than what he'd heard.

"Damn!" Darrell exclaimed.

"Darrell."

The feel of Serena's hand on his back startled him, and Darrell whirled around. He hadn't even heard her approach.

"Sorry," she said, pulling her hand back.

Darrell ran a hand over his hair. "It's okay." Though he suddenly wasn't sure if he was referring to the fact that she'd surprised him, or the fact that he hadn't minded her touching him. Unlike last night, her touch on his back was a gentle caress, a comforting one, one he actually liked.

How long had it been since he'd felt the comforting touch of a woman's caress? Too long. All this time, he'd told himself that he didn't need that special touch again, but now he knew how wrong he was.

As he stared down at her, he couldn't help wondering what it would feel like if she trailed her fingers along his jawbone, over his lips, into his mouth . . .

Darrell's gaze dropped to her hands. She had delicate hands and long, nicely manicured nails. Darrell liked nails, liked to feel them tease his skin.

The jolt of sensation to his groin startled him—and forced his brain to start working again. Whoa. He dropped a hand to cover his sudden hard-on. Thank God, Serena didn't seem to notice.

Why on earth had his thoughts wandered in *that* direction? Disappointed with himself, he shook his head.

Hell, maybe he *had* gone and lost his mind. Why else would he actually fantasize about Serena softly stroking his face? The first no-no was that she'd slugged him—he had to be nuts to have any sort of fantasy about a woman who'd done that to him. The second no-no—and perhaps the bigger one—was the fact that she'd been involved with his brother.

The same brother he was here in Miami to find. Darrell had best keep his priorities straight.

Besides, if Cecil and Serena had clicked in some way, then Darrell and Serena most certainly would not. He and Cecil were as different as night and day.

Once again, his brain wrestled with the reality that Serena and Cecil had been involved. Sure, Darrell could understand Cecil's interest in her—her expensive jewelry. But what had this seemingly sweet woman seen in his brother?

Maybe her prim and proper exterior hid a wild side. An image of Serena dressed in a racy black bra and panty set made Darrell's groin start throbbing again.

"Darrell, what's going on?"

*Oh, I'm just imagining what you'd look like without clothes on.*

Yeah, it was official. He had lost his mind.

"Darrell?"

The unmistakable look of concern in her eyes instantly killed the fantasy. Thank God. The last thing he ought to be doing was fantasizing . . . even if his body was telling him something completely different right now.

He cleared his throat. "How much did you hear?"

Serena crossed her arms over her chest. "Enough to be worried."

"I knew my brother's antics would get him into serious trouble one of these days, but this is worse than I thought."

"You think . . ." Serena's voice trailed off. "You think it's really serious?"

Darrell blew out a ragged breath as he contemplated Serena's question. He walked the few short steps to the window, glanced outside at the people on the beach below. Finding his brother would be like finding a needle in that sand, if what he feared was true. Cecil had pulled a disappearing act once before, when he'd tried to escape a woman who'd claimed he'd fathered her baby. He hadn't reappeared for months.

"Obviously, my brother crossed the wrong person this time." He faced Serena and added, "This time, I think someone wants to kill him."

# Chapter 6

Kiana grabbed the receiver on the first ring. "Hello?" she said anxiously.

"Hey, Kiana."

"Geoff!" Kiana exclaimed, relief flooding her. "God, Geoff. Where have you been?"

"What's up, sweetie?" Geoff asked. "I got your messages. They sounded pretty urgent."

"I called you a couple times. You didn't get back to me, and then when I heard that cop got killed . . . oh, Geoff. I'm so glad to hear your voice!"

"It's nice to know I'm missed."

Kiana inhaled a deep, satisfying breath, then released it slowly, the first relaxed breath she'd had in hours. "Where are you, Geoff? And why didn't you get back to me?"

"I'm out of town," he told her. "In the Keys with a couple guys from work."

"Oh." She paused. "You heard about the cop that was killed? He worked in the Grove."

"Yeah, we heard. I'd met him a couple times, but didn't know him. He was at a different station. Man, that's sad."

While Kiana felt awful for the fallen officer and his family, she suddenly felt stupid. Once again she had practically worried herself to death, only to find that Geoff was okay. She knew what he'd say if she told him about her sleepless night. He'd say what Serena would—that she'd almost sent herself to an early grave for no reason.

While dating, Geoff had always told her that she worried too much, but she couldn't help it. Though the fact that he was safe in the Keys right now proved exactly what he'd always told her—that she needed to relax and deal with crises only if and when they happened.

"So, what was so urgent?" Geoff asked.

Suddenly, nothing seemed as important as the reality that Geoff was okay. "I guess it's not that urgent after all," Kiana said. "Serena and I ran into Cecil last night on Miami Beach. Talk about a weirdo. He sat at the bar flirting with her, after everything he's done. We called the cops, and they arrested him. I'm still waiting to hear from Serena with any more news."

"Hey, that's great."

"Yeah. We're hoping he still has the necklace. I'm sure Serena will find out soon."

"Anything else?" Geoff asked.

Kiana's stomach did a nervous flip-flop. "Why? You have to go?"

"Yeah, actually. Me and the guys want to get in some diving today."

"I see." It didn't make sense, but Kiana felt a measure of jealousy. The last time Geoff had been in Key West, he was with her. Had he met someone else now that he was down there without her? Was that why he was in a hurry to get off the phone?

"I'll give you a call when I get back to town," Geoff told her. "Okay?"

"Yeah, sure," Kiana replied.

Then the dial tone sounded.

For a moment, Kiana held the receiver to her ear, not quite willing to believe that Geoff was no longer on the line. Normally, she was the one who said good-bye first. Often, she had to pull teeth to get Geoff off the line.

Clearly, that wasn't the case anymore. Did that mean he'd finally gotten over her?

Not that this should bother her. For months, she'd been telling Geoff to get on with his life—without her. So why did she feel a niggling of disappointment now?

Kiana replaced the receiver and hopped off the bed. She had a freelance article to write about dating in the new millennium. She'd be better off concentrating on that than thinking about Geoff.

Serena watched Darrell turn away from her and walk to the window, the large muscles in his back flexing as he moved. For a long while he stood still, simply staring outside. But she knew he wasn't taking in the stunning view.

She felt the strongest urge to touch him again, to make his pain go away. But with the way he'd whirled around so quickly at her previous touch, coupled with the strange look he'd given her afterward, she didn't dare.

Instead she clasped her hands together and asked, "Do you have any idea what Cecil did?"

Darrell didn't turn. "No doubt he conned someone else out of a small fortune, just like he did to you." He slammed a fist against the glass. "Damn him."

Serena flinched at this outburst. For the first time, she put herself in Darrell's shoes. He wasn't looking for Cecil the scam-artist, but Cecil the brother he loved. And he was afraid.

"Maybe it's not as bad as you think," Serena said.

Darrell did turn then. "Usually, Cecil is able to talk women out of their money as easily as he talks them out of their pants. They don't even realize he's using them, that's how smooth he is. What he did with you—outright stealing from you—is out of character for him. But then, maybe I've been deluding myself all this time."

"You love him," Serena said, stating the obvious.

"He's the only family I have left." Darrell spoke with a finality of tone, letting Serena know that's all he would say on the subject.

Still, questions tumbled in her mind. She wondered what had happened in their lives, and why Cecil was so different from Darrell. Maybe she was still naïve, but so far, Darrell seemed to be a man of principle, a man who would rather give the shirt off his back than steal one. And he obviously had a deep sense of family loyalty, since he'd come from Orlando to try and find his adult brother and help him out of whatever mess he'd gotten into. Serena got the impression Darrell had been doing that all his life.

"Let's go," Darrell announced.

"Go?" Serena asked, surprised. "I thought you wanted to check—" She stopped short when Darrell stalked past her. She followed him out of the bedroom and to the front door. "Darrell, maybe . . . maybe Cecil will call again."

"He's got another place," Darrell told her. "One in Coconut Grove. Maybe he's there."

Cecil had another place? Gosh, Serena hadn't known him at all. He'd told her he had an apartment in Kendall, close to where she worked. That's the number she'd had for him, plus his cell and business numbers—all of which had been disconnected shortly after he'd disappeared from her life.

"I take it you know how to get there," Darrell said, turning to her as he opened the door.

"Yeah. The Grove is on the way back to my place."

Serena stepped into the hallway, then Darrell closed and locked the door. He was silent, distant, and Serena didn't know what to say to bridge the gap. What could she? She didn't wish Cecil dead, but other than retrieving her family heirloom and her money, she didn't have a vested interest in whatever might happen to him. Darrell did.

Serena couldn't relate. Her sister, though a little melodramatic at times, had never been in trouble with the law. She'd always been a good sister to her. Her parents, God rest their souls, had been the best two parents anyone could ask for. They'd died in a boating accident on their wedding anniversary fourteen years ago. After that, her grandmother had raised her and her sister, and again, she'd been a wonderful parent. Serena couldn't have asked for a more close-knit family.

She and Darrell were silent on the elevator ride downstairs, quiet on the walk back to the valet. Serena dug the valet ticket out of her purse.

"You sure you have nothing better to do?" Darrell asked her.

Stopping, Serena faced him. "Not today."

Darrell shrugged. "All right."

"Here's the valet ticket." Serena passed it to Darrell.

"Wait here," Darrell said. "I'll head over to Miguel."

Before Serena could say a word, Darrell was off. And she felt helpless. Helpless to make this situation better. In fact, she had to be making it worse by adding pressure to find her missing property.

Darrell stepped up to the valet counter. As Miguel smiled at him, he handed him the ticket. "We're ready to head out of here."

"So soon?"

"Yep."

Miguel looked down at the ticket, then back up at Darrell. "Sir, would you prefer I bring up the Viper for you?"

"The Viper?"

"With it being such a beautiful day, I figured you might like to take it out."

"Uh, yes. Yes, I'll take the Viper for a ride."

"Hang on to this ticket," Miguel said, passing it back to Darrell. "Just give me a few minutes to get your car."

As Miguel headed in one direction, Darrell headed back to Serena where she stood at the building's front doors. She saw the ticket in his hand and asked, "Aren't you getting my car?"

"Nope. Miguel suggested I take the Viper out for a spin, so I agreed."

"Oh." Serena frowned. "What about my car?"

"We can leave it here. Or, if you feel like taking off, you can grab your car and we can head our separate ways."

"You're not getting rid of me that quickly," Serena said.

"As long as you're sure. I don't want to put you out."

"Your brother put me out when he stole my necklace," Serena retorted. Then, "Sorry. I guess I don't have to belabor that point, do I?"

"You're just telling the truth," Darrell replied. "It won't do me any good to stick my head in the sand."

Serena nodded absently. She'd have to try and be a little more sensitive. Yes, she wanted the necklace back, but Darrell didn't deserve her wrath.

Changing the subject, she said, "Well, I've never been in such a snazzy car before. I'll enjoy this."

"Of course." Why wouldn't she? Darrell had never known a woman who didn't enjoy anything that had money written all over it.

But then another thought hit him. "You've never been in this car before?"

"No."

Well, Cecil did have two cars that Darrell knew of, so maybe this wasn't so unusual. "How long will it take us to get to Cecil's house in Coconut Grove?" he asked.

"Depending where he lives in the Grove, anywhere from twenty minutes—"

"Wait a second," Darrell said, interrupting her. "What do you mean, 'depending where he lives'? Don't you know?"

"Nope," Serena replied matter-of-factly.

"You haven't been to Cecil's house?"

"I haven't."

Darrell narrowed his eyes on her, just as a shiny black Viper whipped in front of them at a fast rate of speed, pulling to a sudden stop a few feet ahead of them. The license plate read "2FINE."

"Too fine?" Serena shook her head.

"No one ever accused my brother of being modest."

Miguel put the Viper in reverse, parking in front of them. As he hopped out of the car, he gave Darrell a sheepish grin. "Sorry, sir. Guess I got a little carried away."

"No problem," Darrell said. He started for the open driver's side door. Miguel hurried past him to the passenger door, which he opened for Serena. He closed Serena's door and was back at the driver's side before Darrell had fully gotten inside.

Miguel took hold of the handle. "Enjoy your day," he told Darrell.

"Thank you." Darrell passed the man the last ten he had in his wallet.

"You're very welcome, sir."

"Later," Darrell said to Miguel. The moment Miguel closed the door, Darrell hit the gas and whizzed the Viper onto the street.

"Whoa." Serena gripped her seat at the edges. She'd never been in such a powerful car before.

"Which way?"

"Turn left onto Collins," Serena told him, pointing to the street just ahead.

"This is a beautiful car," Darrell commented. "God, the lifestyle my brother leads makes me feel like a pauper."

"What do you do?" Serena asked.

"I . . ." Darrell paused. He stopped before telling her that he owned and operated a small hotel in Orlando. Most women saw green when they learned what he did, and he wasn't ready to share that information with Serena. "I work at a hotel."

"Oh."

Darrell turned to her. "You sound disappointed."

"No. Just surprised."

"Like I told you, I'm nothing like my brother. And I certainly don't have his bank account."

Serena simply stared ahead and nodded. Darrell felt the familiar disappointment tickle his gut. Yeah, she was just like the rest of them. Hell, maybe she'd been attracted to Cecil's flash and pizzazz, hoping he had a pretty penny. He did, of course, but he wasn't the type to share. He was the type to take.

It wasn't like Darrell had a right to be upset with her—she hadn't pursued him for his cash. Yet he was. It's just that from the moment he'd laid eyes on her, he'd thought she was different from the other women he'd met. To learn that she wasn't was unsettling.

His mind went back to their unfinished conversation. "Not that it's any of my business," he began, "but I'm having a little trouble figuring out your relationship with my brother. You haven't been to his condo or to his place in Coconut Grove." Darrell paused to glance at her. "You *were* involved, weren't you?"

"You mean dating?"

"Yes."

"Yes, we were dating."

Darrell paused. "So, he always went to your place? Didn't he invite you to his? And if he didn't, didn't you find that a little strange? I mean, I'd think that would be the first clue that you should . . . be a little wary."

"I thought your brother had a small apartment in Kendall. That's all he told me about. And no, I never went there."

"And you didn't think that was weird?" Darrell asked again.

"He invited me once, but I told him no. I liked him, but we were taking things slowly," Serena replied. "Your brother respected that."

*Cecil*, take things slowly? If Serena hadn't slapped him silly, he would have bet money that she'd been involved with a different Cecil Montford.

"In light of everything that's happened, I'm glad we *did* take things slowly." Serena sighed. "I thought he was a nice guy, one who shared my interests. I—I thought he had potential. But obviously, I didn't know him at all. Oh," Serena suddenly said. "Turn right at this light. This will take us to the 395. Then we can head south to the Grove."

"Sure."

Darrell turned where instructed, then glanced at Serena. She gazed out the window.

She was upset. Darrell couldn't blame her. Who wouldn't be, after learning that someone they trusted had lied to them?

He felt a burst of anger. Of all the low, dirty things his brother had done, this was one of the lowest. Serena was a nice woman, a working woman. Had his brother lost even his basic sense of human decency? Clearly, he no longer had a conscience, not if he could rip Serena off without a second thought.

"I'm really sorry about my brother," Darrell said.

Serena's lips lifted in a faint smile. "It's okay." She paused, then asked, "Did you grow up in Florida?"

"New York."

"What brought you to Florida?"

"My dad wanted a change." And to escape the memory of his cheating wife. "We settled in Kissimmee, but that was always too boring for Cecil. He moved to Miami as soon as he hit eighteen."

Just before the causeway, Darrell pulled into the right lane and turned into the gas station.

Serena glanced at the gas gauge. "The tank's almost full."

"I don't need to fill up," Darrell explained as he pulled up to the station's door. "I need an ATM."

"Oh."

"I won't be long," Darrell told her.

As he walked around the front of the car to the door, Serena watched him. A soft sigh fell from her lips. There was something about him that made it impossible for her to take her eyes off him.

He was Cecil's twin, yes, but she found herself forgetting that fact. How could he look exactly like his brother, yet not resemble him in the least?

Character, Serena realized. He had some. Cecil didn't. And it made a world of difference physically, something she wouldn't have known firsthand if she hadn't met Darrell. She'd always believed that an ugly character made an attractive person ugly, and witnessing the clear difference between Darrell and Cecil proved that point. Yes, Cecil was attractive, but his eyes lacked the warmth that Darrell's held, and that warmth made Darrell infinitely more appealing.

Darrell exited the store and headed back to the Viper, flashing Serena a charming smile as he did. Her heart slammed against her ribcage.

"I don't know about you," Darrell began, settling in the car, "but what they gave me in jail didn't exactly qualify as a meal. I'm hungry. You?"

Serena nodded. "I guess I am."

"Then we may as well grab a bite to eat before we do anything else." Slipping into traffic, Darrell went straight. "There are a few places up here," he said.

He drove slowly, looking from left to right at the various buildings. "You ever been here?" he asked, slowing near a restaurant named Monty's on the right.

"Nope. Never."

"I'm sure they've got something edible."

Serena checked out the huge establishment that bordered the marina. "No doubt."

Darrell turned into the parking lot. It was crowded, and he wasn't sure which direction he should go.

As he crept along in the Viper, a lot attendant hurried toward the car. He lowered his head to the open window. "Hey, Cecil," the young man said. "Long time no see."

So his brother was a regular here. "Hi."

"There's space around the corner to the back."

"Thanks," Darrell said, then started in that direction.

Serena gave Darrell a sideways glance. "Seems your brother was quite the popular guy."

"Let's hope that makes him easier to find."

Darrell parked in the first spot he found. It took him a moment to figure out how to close the sunroof, but when he did, both he and Serena exited the car.

The loud sounds of calypso music filled the air as Serena and Darrell walked to the entrance of the restaurant. As they got closer to the door, happy sounds of laughter and chatter mixed with the music. Considering all the action for a Saturday afternoon, this place was clearly a hot spot.

Serena whipped her head around when she heard a

collective shriek of laughter. Four women walked behind her and Darrell. Four *gorgeous* women. All were wearing sexy outfits that flaunted their perfect bodies: short dresses, form-fitting skirts, and tops that showed off their midriffs. Serena instantly felt out of place. Compared to these women, she looked like ... like a librarian. She frowned. Why hadn't she put on something nicer, like one of her summer dresses, before heading out?

Because she hadn't been planning on going out for lunch or doing anything social when she'd left her apartment. Her only plan had been to go to the police station and see Cecil, for which she certainly didn't need to be dressed up.

The group of women continued to giggle as they hurried past Darrell and Serena. Self-conscious, she ran a hand down her oversized T-shirt, then said, "I'm not dressed for this."

"You look fine," Darrell replied succinctly.

*Fine?* Any other day, she'd be happy with fine. Why not today? "I wish I'd known we'd be going out."

"It's only a bite to eat, not a date."

"Yes, of course," Serena said, then quickened her pace, walking ahead of him up the ramp. But she couldn't walk fast enough to escape his stinging words.

But why should they sting? Darrell was right; this *wasn't* a date. They were simply getting a bite to eat before continuing their search for his brother.

Yet it would be nice to believe that Darrell found her attractive enough to *take* on a date. Cecil had led her to believe he'd felt that way about her, but he'd turned out to be the biggest liar she'd ever met. And with Cecil's betrayal came the bitter realization that she'd foolishly let herself give in to the dream that a hunky guy like him could actually be interested in a plain girl like her.

The top of the ramp connected to a walkway that led to the restaurant door. Besides the restaurant, there were other businesses along the path. But Monty's was by far the biggest establishment.

The row of payphones reminded Serena that she should call Kiana. Last night, she'd promised to call the moment she had some news. Her sister would no doubt wonder what was going on.

When Serena looked over her shoulder, she saw Darrell right behind her. His full lips curled in a small smile, one that said he hadn't noticed her sudden change in mood. What was wrong with her, anyway? Women in Miami routinely showed a lot of skin and dressed provocatively. She'd never felt inadequate before.

"Give me a second," Serena said. "I want to call my sister."

"Sure."

She walked the few steps to the payphones, surreptitiously glancing at Darrell as she did. She watched him stroll casually toward the restaurant's front doors. Two women sauntering along the path boldly ogled him up and down, then wiggled their fingers at him.

Serena felt an unexpected spurt of jealousy. The two women were dressed in short-shorts and bikini tops, barely covering the essentials, while she was dressed as if she was ready to clean someone's house.

Phoning her sister took a back seat to watching what would happen next. She expected the women to stop and flirt with Darrell, but if they'd wanted to, his actions discouraged them. He merely gave them a polite nod, then turned—and the two women continued on.

Again, Serena was mesmerized by his strong back muscles, his beautifully sculpted arms. Yes, the man was *F-I-N-E fine.*

Darrell stopped his turn when his eyes met hers. Serena felt a little jolt in her heart. Quickly, she lifted the receiver and held it to her ear, hoping he didn't realize she'd been checking him out. She fished in her purse for change and dropped it in the slot.

"Hey, Kiana," Serena said when her sister picked up on the second ring. "It's me."

"Serena!" Kiana exclaimed. "Where are you? I called you a couple times."

"I'm in Miami Beach."

"The beach? What—you went to the police station?"

"Yeah," Serena replied. "I wanted to talk to Cecil."

"They let you talk to him?" Kiana asked, surprised.

"No." Serena paused. "Kiana, you're not going to believe this. That wasn't Cecil we saw last night."

"*What?*"

"I know. I hardly believe it either. But it was Cecil's brother. His twin."

There was a pause, then, "No way!"

"Yes way. And let me tell you, no one is more surprised than I am. Cecil never said anything about having a brother, much less an identical *twin.* I feel like an idiot for slapping him last night, but how was I to know?"

"Exactly," Kiana crooned. "You had no clue. He shouldn't hold that against you."

"No, he doesn't." Serena's gaze found Darrell. He stood

with his back pressed against the building wall. "In fact, I'm with him now. His name is Darrell."

"Wait a second. Backtrack. Did you just say you're with him now?"

"Yes. He thinks Cecil's in some kind of trouble, so he's trying to find his brother . . . and I offered to help."

"What?" Kiana gasped.

"He says he'll help me get my stuff back, and the only way he can do that is to find his brother. Kiana, you know I have to get the necklace back."

"Yes, but not at any cost. If Cecil's in some kind of trouble . . . God, Serena, you don't even know this guy."

Again, Serena glanced Darrell's way. As if sensing her eyes on his back, he slowly turned and faced her. He smiled.

God, there was something about him. She could look at him all day and not get bored. With Cecil, Serena had been attracted to him, but she'd been drawn to what she thought he was. He'd sought her out and she'd simply gone along with the attraction. But something about Darrell compelled her to look at him, to want to spend time with him, even though her brain told her that if she was smart, she'd run in the opposite direction.

Maybe it was the sincerity she saw in Darrell's eyes when he'd looked at her and told her he'd do what he could to get her property back. Maybe it was the way his eyes seemed to come alive when they connected with hers.

Or maybe she was finding something where there was nothing out of the ordinary. Darrell was an extremely handsome man. What woman wouldn't be drawn to him?

"No," Serena said in response to her sister's concern. "I don't know him. But from what I've seen, he seems completely different from Cecil, and I think I can trust him."

"Serena—"

"There's so much I have to fill you in on, but I'll do that when I see you. Anyway, I might not be home for a while, so if I don't call until late, don't go worrying yourself to death."

"I wouldn't worry if you didn't give me reason," Kiana muttered.

"I heard that," Serena said.

"Please be careful. That's all I ask."

"You got it. I'll call you later, 'kay?"

"Okay."

Serena hung up, then made her way over to Darrell. "I'm ready."

His eyebrows raised in concern. "Everything all right?"

"Yeah, everything's fine. I figured I'd call my sister so she wouldn't worry about me."

"That was your sister you were with last night?" Darrell asked.

"Uh huh. Kiana. She's my only sister. Actually, my only sibling."

Nodding, Darrell opened the door. Serena stepped inside. A host greeted them instantly. "Table for two?" the young man asked.

"Yes," Darrell replied.

"Inside or outside?"

Darrell looked at Serena. "Do you mind eating outside?"

"It's a beautiful day. May as well."

"All righty, then," the host said cheerfully. "This way, please."

Serena and Darrell followed the young man. As they walked, Darrell placed his hand on her back, gently guiding her. But while the touch was gentle, it set off tiny sparks along her skin. When Cecil had casually touched her, her skin hadn't come alive with this wonderful tingling sensation. Darrell's touch felt good, better than it should have, considering she wasn't the least bit interested in him. Even more confusing, Serena felt the oddest urge to have Darrell wrap his arms around her and hold her like he meant it.

Hold her like he wanted her.

The thought shocked her. Why should she feel this way about Darrell?

They followed the young host to the exterior portion of the restaurant. There was a large pool immediately ahead of them, in which a team of men and women were playing pool volleyball.

"Here you go," the host said, placing menus on a two-seater to the far right of the pool.

Good grief, everyone here looked like they'd stepped off the covers of *GQ* and *Cosmopolitan*. What was Serena doing here?

This was bad. Very bad.

Sitting, Darrell gave Serena a confused look. "You gonna join me?"

Serena spun around and grabbed the host's arm as he started off. "Where's the bathroom?" she asked anxiously.

"Straight back there on your left," the host replied, pointing Serena in the right direction.

"Thank you," she told the young man. Glancing over her shoulder at Darrell, she said, "I'll be right back."

Then, clutching her purse under her arm, she hurried toward the restrooms as if her life depended on it.

 Chapter 7

Serena didn't break her stride until she was in the large handicapped stall. She locked the door behind her, then sagged against it, releasing a long, harried breath as she did.

"Okay," she said aloud, her mind scrambling, "what now?"

Looking to her right, she was relieved to find a private mirror and sink in the stall, as she'd hoped.

She heaved herself off the door and was at the sink in one second flat. Placing her purse on the sink's ledge, she stared at her reflection in the mirror.

And nearly had heart failure. *This* was how she looked? God, how horrible!

Her hair . . . *yuck*. When she'd gotten this short do, the stylist had told her that it would be easy to maintain and would look great with minimal fussing. Now, it was flat and dull.

She finger-combed it, trying to fluff it as much as possible. It helped a bit, but not much.

Her bigger concern was her face. She didn't have a drop of makeup on, and suddenly it mattered. She didn't want to look like a complete dolt, dressed like she was ready to pick weeds while she was at a place where everyone else looked ready to compete in a modeling competition.

Holy shine on her face! She dug inside her purse until she found her compact of pressed powder, then applied a liberal amount to dull the shine. She also applied lipstick and mascara.

Now, if only she had another outfit in her purse, she could actually go back out there and look presentable. Of course, she didn't. She hadn't dressed to impress this morning, but had dressed for comfort.

That was her style. Why was she suddenly trying to change it?

Serena exited the stall, but couldn't help stopping at the main sink and mirror to check herself out again. She frowned. Something wasn't right. Did she need more powder? Or maybe black eyeliner to highlight her eyes?

"This is ridiculous," she told her reflection.

"What's ridiculous, honey?"

Serena whipped around to see a woman standing behind her in the bathroom. She was tall, at least five foot eight, with dark brown skin. Her shoulder-length hair was thick, her body shaped like an hourglass.

All of which emphasized just how dowdy Serena looked.

Serena took off her glasses and stuffed them in her purse.

She would have put in her contacts this morning if she

hadn't been in a rush to get to the police station. "Uh, nothing really. Well, actually . . . tell me what you think. I'm trying to decide if my glasses make me look really . . ." She paused, searching for an appropriate word. "Bad."

"Trying to impress someone?"

"Kinda." Serena gave a wishy-washy nod. "Yeah, I guess."

"First date?"

"Well, it's not exactly a date. I just . . ."

"You want to look good."

"As good as possible." Glancing at her reflection, Serena frowned. "I didn't expect to be going out today."

The attractive black woman settled beside Serena, then did a slow perusal of Serena's body. "Well, there's nothing you can do about that outfit, unless you want to twist your T-shirt through the neck to create a halter effect."

"Uh, I don't think so."

"Okay, let's see you with the glasses on."

Serena fished them out of her purse and did as told.

A slight look of disapproval marred the woman's beautiful features. "Now take them off."

Serena slipped the glasses off.

"Keep the glasses off, honey," the woman told her emphatically. Then she faced the mirror and began fluffing her hair.

"Thanks." Serena leaned in close to the mirror and squinted. Yes, the woman was right. She looked better this way.

So what if she couldn't see?

Goodness, she was being a moron. She was who she was and if any man didn't respect her for that, that was his problem. But despite that thought, she didn't put her glasses back on. What was wrong with her? Maybe she was simply feeling out of sorts because of this whole mess with Cecil.

Oh, who was she kidding? She could lie to herself till the cows came home, but the truth was, she wanted Darrell to notice her the way men hadn't noticed her before. She wanted him to look at her like she had at least a measure of sex appeal. Why, she didn't know, but it suddenly mattered.

"Good luck," the woman said.

"Thanks."

Serena squared her shoulders. She'd done the best she could with what she had. Now, she would see if it made any impression on Darrell.

The moment the other woman disappeared into a stall, Serena started taking baby-steps out of the bathroom. No doubt about it, this was one of the dumbest things she'd done in her life. She could barely see a thing in front of her face. Before she made it to the bathroom door, she shoved her glasses back on, annoyed with herself.

But as she stepped outside and saw a gorgeous couple stroll by hand-in-hand, she removed her glasses once again and stuffed them into her purse.

She was back to taking baby-steps, knowing she must look crazy. And at the moment, she couldn't help wondering if she was.

She was farsighted, and could see Darrell in the distance fairly well. As he looked up from the menu, nerves suddenly tickled her stomach. Would he like the new look, or would he think she was as moronic as she felt? She hoped he liked it. Darrell brought out a need in her she hadn't experienced before, one she couldn't quite understand. She wanted his eyes to tell her she was beautiful, that she was just as irresistible as the other women in this place.

Maybe it was Darrell's comment about Cecil having lived off gullible women for years, but she wanted to believe that someone as attractive as Darrell didn't think she was the kind of woman who had to be grateful for the attentions of a gorgeous man. Because that's not what it had been about with Cecil. She'd liked him as a person, the person he'd let her believe he was, and she'd wanted to build a foundation from there.

She forced herself to stop thinking about Cecil as she continued walking. Thankfully, she made it to the table without making a fool of herself.

"Hi." Serena placed her purse on the tabletop, then sat down. But she missed half the chair, and it wobbled. Quickly, she threw both hands out and gripped the edges of the table, righting herself, but in the process, she knocked over her purse. It fell to the ground, the contents spilling out.

Darrell was immediately out of his chair, crouching beside the table to retrieve her purse.

"I can't believe I did that," Serena mumbled, embarrassed.

Darrell glanced up at her with an odd look. He was noticing the makeup. Suddenly, Serena felt foolish. Why had she been so hell-bent on her makeover anyway? So what if Darrell didn't find her attractive?

"How well do you see without your glasses?" Darrell asked.

"I can see."

"You're squinting."

"Am I?" Serena folded her arms onto the table—and knocked her fork and knife to the floor. "All right, maybe I need my glasses."

Darrell stared at Serena, trying not to grin. He watched as she dug her glasses out of her purse, then slipped out of his seat to pick up the silverware that had fallen. He passed them to a busboy who walked by.

Serena rested her face in her palm, directing her gaze toward the pool. There was that vulnerable side again, a side that was definitely growing on him. And to be completely honest with himself, it stroked his ego to think that she'd dolled herself up for his benefit.

He'd known her only a day, but he'd never met anyone else like her. She was strong, yet vulnerable; confident enough to be secure in who she was, yet real enough to feel insecurity. It was a combination Darrell liked.

Which made him wonder if his brother had truly appreciated her or if he'd simply taken advantage of her. Hell, what was wrong with Cecil, anyway? Would he ever learn to appreciate a good woman?

Serena held the menu in front of her face. "Do you know what you're having?"

"I like the glasses," Darrell announced.

Serena blinked, but didn't lower the menu. "Come again?"

"The glasses. I think they're cute. They suit you."

"Oh," she said, sounding surprised as she lowered the menu. She actually blushed, a genuine blush, something Darrell hadn't seen on a woman in a long time. "Thank you."

Yeah, there was something about her. Something he'd

sensed last night at the bar. While other women had dressed like vixens, hoping to get men's attention, she'd dressed in a classically elegant way. She'd caught his attention immediately.

Even now, in an oversized white T-shirt and black track pants, there was a quality about her that he found more intriguing than the scantily clad women here. Serena left something to the imagination, gave him something to wonder about.

His eyes ventured lower. He could see the faint outline of her lacy white bra. Lace beneath cotton. The combination was strangely erotic.

Their waitress arrived at that moment, saving Darrell's thoughts from continuing down their unexpected lustful path.

"Cecil!" The woman's pretty eyes bulged with shock and delight. "Where have you *been*?"

Darrell was momentarily startled to hear Cecil's name, but recovered without her noticing his surprise. "Hey." He glanced at her nametag. "Miranda."

"Come on, Cecil." She playfully swatted his shoulder. "You know I prefer being called Mimi." Her lips curled downward in a pout. "You're not mad at me because of the last time, are you?"

Darrell paused. "No. Of course not."

"Good. Because I warned you about Tamara, and seeing you with her . . . I guess I got a little stupid."

"I figured that." Damn, Darrell wished he knew what the hell they were talking about!

Mimi's gaze finally went to Serena. She looked back and forth between her and Darrell, as if trying to assess their relationship. "This your friend?"

"Yeah." Darrell picked up the menu. "We're getting a bite to eat."

Mimi's smile seemed relieved. "Hi."

Serena greeted the pretty, fair-skinned woman with a tight smile.

Mimi turned back to Darrell. "You said there was something you had to take care of last time you were here. How did that go?"

Darrell shrugged noncommittally. "I'm still working it out."

"Well, Tamara was here looking for you."

"She was?"

"Yeah. I warned you about her, but you wouldn't listen. The woman is nuts."

Darrell merely chuckled, then waited for the waitress to offer more information. She didn't.

Damn. How was he supposed to get information to help him find his brother if everyone thought he *was* his brother? Maybe he should tell this woman he was actually Cecil's twin and see if she knew anything that could be of help.

"Shall I start you off with your regular drink?"

"Sure, Mimi. Whatever."

Mimi faced Serena. "Oh. And you?"

"I'll take a lemonade."

"Sure, honey."

Mimi's gaze lingered a little too long on Darrell as she walked away, and Serena couldn't help feeling annoyed. What was it with women these days, anyway? Talk about downright rude.

"*Mimi?*" Serena made a face.

"Hey, I didn't date her."

"No, your other half did."

"My *brother*. Granted, he's my twin, but like I told you before, we're nothing alike."

Serena buried her nose in the menu. Anxiety and annoyance fought for control within her. And yes, a measure of jealousy. Though why should she be jealous? She had no dibs on Darrell.

If he found Mimi attractive, good for him.

But try as she might, Serena couldn't see a thing on the menu—not even with her glasses. It bothered her to realize how little she'd known about Cecil. And it bothered her to think that Darrell was probably as hot-blooded as his brother was. Which only served to make her feel even more inferior than she had when she'd stepped into this place. Who wouldn't find the Mimis of the world attractive? Large breasts—plastic surgeons sure made a killing in Miami—long, lean legs, small waist. Serena couldn't compete.

"Hey."

Darrell's voice interrupted her thoughts. It held a gentle, caring note, and lowering her menu, Serena met his eyes. "Yes?"

"I hope you're okay with . . . with all this."

"With what?"

Darrell flashed her an uneasy look, then spoke in a hushed voice. "It's clear my brother had a thing with Mimi. And from the messages on his machine . . . you two were dating, but it's obvious Cecil wasn't faithful."

"Ah. Well, I got over your brother the moment I learned he'd scammed me."

Silence fell between them, and both perused their menus. Mimi returned with a tall draft for Darrell and the

lemonade for Serena. After she took their order for na-
chos, she again referred to Darrell as Cecil, after which
Serena asked, "Why don't you just tell her you're Cecil's
twin?"

"I was thinking the same thing," Darrell replied. "But
I'm not sure it will help. From what she said, she hasn't
been in touch with Cecil for a while."

"She mentioned some Tamara woman. Do you think
she's the one who might be after your brother?"

Darrell didn't know what to think, and shrugged in
reply.

For the most part, they ate in silence, with Mimi showing up every few minutes to yak about unimportant stuff.
His brother sure knew how to pick winners.

Darrell was glad to finally be finished with the meal.
He hated beer and had only a few sips of the draft. He
summoned Mimi and asked for the check.

"You didn't drink your beer, hon."

"I know," Darrell said. "I'm not feeling that hot today."

"Oh, that's too bad." She raised a suggestive eyebrow,
topped off with a sly grin, making it clear to Serena that
she would have continued with a cheesy I-know-how-to-
make-you-feel-better line if Serena wasn't around.

"Give me a second. I'll grab the check."

"Sure."

Mimi disappeared inside, reappearing less than a
minute later. Darrell pushed his chair back and stood as
she approached the table. Serena followed his lead.

"There you go." Mimi handed him the check.

"Thanks again, Mimi." Darrell dug some money out of
his wallet and passed it to her.

"Change?" she asked, though the coy expression on her

face and the sexy tone of her voice said she expected him to say no.

The tip would work out to about four hundred percent, way more than necessary, but Darrell said, "No, that's okay. You keep it."

"Thanks, Cecil."

Mimi stuffed the money in her apron, sticking her chest out as she did. Serena was certain the move was deliberate, and her heart filled with joy when Darrell didn't seem to notice.

"I'll see you another time," Darrell told her. Stepping toward Serena, he placed a hand between her shoulder blades. Serena felt a moment of power. She might never be invited to the playboy mansion, but she had Darrell's attention, and that made her feel like a million bucks.

His hand still on her back, Darrell started toward the doors that led to the restaurant's interior.

"Uh, sweetie." Mimi quickly blocked their path.

Suddenly feeling proprietary, Serena gaped at Mimi, showing her displeasure. The woman was way too bold for her liking.

"What?" Darrell asked.

"I'd take the back way out if I were you." She gestured to a set of stairs beyond the pool.

Darrell flashed Mimi a puzzled look. "Why?"

Mimi replied, "Tamara, honey. Didn't you see her?"

"No."

"Well, lucky for you, I did. She's sitting at the inside bar, honey, shooting daggers at you with her eyes."

# Chapter 8

Darrell's gaze went in the direction Mimi pointed. A voluptuous brunette who looked to be of Hispanic heritage sat at the inside bar, one long leg crossed over the other, her fingers wrapped tightly around a tall glass.

If looks could kill . . .

Darrell gulped. The last thing he needed was another slap in the face. Or a bullet in the back.

"Thanks for the heads up, Mimi."

"No problem. Don't be a stranger, now."

When Mimi was out of earshot, Darrell said, "Let's get out of here."

"Maybe you should talk to her," Serena suggested.

If Tamara had gripped the glass any harder, it would probably have shattered. "I don't think so," Darrell replied.

"Isn't that what you want?" Serena protested as Darrell

guided her in the opposite direction. "To find people who know your brother and ask them questions?"

"What exactly do you think she'll be able to tell me?"

Glancing over her shoulder at the woman, Serena shrugged. "I don't know."

"Exactly. She's no doubt another one of my brother's casualties, and right now, I don't want a matching welt on my other cheek."

That shut Serena up. She let Darrell lead her past the pool to the set of stairs at the back of the restaurant. Darrell took a quick look around as they began to descend.

"Is she following us?" Serena asked.

"I don't see her," Darrell replied. "Thank God."

Mimi. Tamara. Where on earth did his brother find the time to date all these women, anyway? And how had he not gotten into more serious trouble before now?

Once again, Darrell thought of just how different he and his brother were. Darrell liked a beautiful woman just like any other guy, but he preferred one at a time. But mostly, he preferred what his own parents never had: true love. However, he'd met and dated enough women to know that that ideal was fictional.

And when he'd learned that Jessica, his last girlfriend, had actually loved his bank account more than him, he'd been turned off the idea of relationships altogether.

It was never a smart idea to play with people's emotions, to lead them on instead of being straight with them. These days, people were more prone to get violent than turn the other cheek. Which made Darrell wonder if trying to find his brother was a smart idea. Serena and Tamara were only two of the angry women Cecil had left behind. How many more would Darrell encounter—and how would he survive their wrath when he did? And trying to pass himself off as Cecil . . . He felt like an idiot. Cecil had always been good at playing games. Darrell hadn't.

Darrell and Serena walked through the back end of the parking lot and found the Viper. Seconds later, they were settled in the car.

"How do we get to the interstate?" Darrell asked.

"Turn left out of the parking lot."

Darrell did, merging into traffic. "All right. Left at this light?"

"Yep."

Serena's tone sounded clipped. Or maybe Darrell was simply paranoid. But he suddenly felt responsible for everything Cecil had done wrong. At least when they were younger, Darrell had been able to make things right for the most part. When Cecil had broken Mrs. Fletcher's window with a rock, Darrell had paid to replace it. When Cecil had shoplifted from the local variety store, Darrell had returned the items to the owner and had convinced him not to call the police. Back then, Darrell had known what Cecil had been up to, even if he didn't agree with it. Now, even if he'd wanted to right all Cecil's wrongs, Darrell wouldn't know where to start.

"Something wrong?" Darrell finally asked, when he glanced at Serena and saw a sour expression on her face.

"No."

"Tell me." He knew that look. It was a look he'd received from his father on more occasions than he cared to count, one that said, "Why can't you keep your no-good brother out of trouble?"

"I'm just thinking."

"Thinking what?"

Serena shrugged. "I guess I'm wondering how many times you and your brother have tricked women." She looked at him. "You know, you pretend to be Cecil, he pretends to be you."

"Oh, for crying out loud," Darrell exclaimed. "I told you once and I'm not going to tell you again. I am *not* Cecil."

"You got right into the role of playing him . . ."

"Because I'm trying to find him! Not that it worked, by the way. Hell, games are Cecil's forte, not mine." Darrell paused, then said, "We can forget this whole arrangement. Us working together. Yeah, I think that's the best thing."

"As if I'd trust you to contact me when you find Cecil," Serena retorted.

Darrell's eyes flew to hers. "Is that what this is about? You wanting to tag along with me?"

"I'm certainly not here for your charm! And keep your eyes on the road."

"Okay. Let me turn around and head back to the condo. You can get your car and be on your merry way."

"And kiss my property good-bye? I don't think so."

"I don't even know if my brother took anything from you. All I have is your word."

Serena gaped at Darrell, but he didn't look at her. "Now I'm a liar?"

"I didn't say that."

"But you meant it. Hell, you can't even look at me."

"I'm looking at the road," Darrell said sarcastically.

"Why would I slap you, thinking you were Cecil, if he didn't take a dime from me?"

"Because you're crazy."

Serena let out a startled gasp. "Why are you doing this?"

"How do I get back to the condo?"

"Once we're off the causeway, you can go south, then turn around."

"Good."

Silence fell between them, heavy and stifling. Why the hell were they fighting, Serena wondered. And if they were fighting, she couldn't help wondering if Darrell was right. They'd barely been with each other half a day and already they were getting on each other's nerves.

Yet she said, "I'm sorry."

Darrell didn't respond.

"I didn't mean that remark about not trusting you." For whatever reason, she knew in her heart that she could trust him. "I'm stressed, wondering if I'll get the necklace back or if Cecil has already hawked it to pay the mortgage at his luxurious condo."

"All my life, I've had to deal with people who thought I was Cecil, or expected me to be as bad as him because I'm his twin. It's like they judge me without taking the time to get to know me."

"I didn't mean to do that."

"Maybe that's why I always wanted to right all his wrongs. To prove to everyone that I *was* better than Cecil. But how long can I do this? This is nuts."

Serena was aware that Darrell had stopped talking to her and was talking to himself. She really didn't know what to say, so she said nothing.

"Darrell, watch out!" Serena suddenly shouted when a van veered into their lane.

Darrell hit the brakes. "Damn, I didn't even see him."

Serena glared at the driver as he passed them. "God, I hate the drivers down here. Are they this bad in Orlando?"

"I think they're bad everywhere."

"The problem here is that everyone is from somewhere else, so we get the whole country's bad drivers." Serena groaned. "Anyway, hug the left. You'll be taking I-95 south."

"This is the way to Coconut Grove, right?"

A faint smile touched her lips with the realization that Darrell still wanted her to go with him. "Yeah. Yeah, it is."

Darrell hit his turn signal and entered the left lane. But after a moment, he veered back to the right.

Serena's gaze flew to him. "What are you doing? You have to stay left."

"There's someone on my tail." Darrell stared in the rearview mirror. "What's this idiot doing? I just moved over, buddy."

"What?" Serena glanced over her shoulder.

"This guy's right on my tail."

Serena stared at the gold-colored Ford Explorer behind them. If the driver had wanted to pass them, surely he or she could have done that already. Instead, the driver continued to ride their tail.

The Explorer had tinted windows, making it impossible for them to view the driver. She looked ahead in time to see that they were about to miss the ramp to the I-95 south. "Darrell, our exit."

Darrell tried to swing left, but he couldn't do so without cutting off another car. "Why the hell is this guy on my bumper?"

"I'll try and get the plate."

"Hold on."

Darrell put the car into fifth gear and accelerated. The Viper picked up speed instantly. Deftly, Darrell zipped in and out of traffic, hoping to lose the guy.

Serena gripped the edges of the seat for dear life. After what seemed like hours, though it was less than a minute, Serena glanced over her shoulder again. "I don't see it."

"Did I cut that guy off or something?"

"I don't think so."

"Then what was his problem?"

"I'm telling you, the drivers down here are psycho."

Darrell blew out a ragged breath and continued to drive. "What should I do now?"

"Well, we can continue along this expressway and then go south to the Grove."

"All right. Tell me where and when."

Darrell continued to drive, more cautious now of other drivers. He kept looking in the rearview mirror for the Explorer, but didn't see it. After a few minutes, he relaxed.

"The store I was going to open," Serena began, "it was in the Grove. It was a great little store. Perfect location."

"I'm sorry."

Darrell sounded weary, and Serena turned to him. "I'm not telling you that for you to feel bad. I guess I was thinking out loud."

Darrell glanced in the rearview mirror and felt a moment of panic. Was that the same Ford Explorer gaining on them to their left?

No, it couldn't be.

"What?" Serena asked, sensing something was wrong.

His gaze flickered between the road ahead and the rearview mirror. "It kinda looks like that SUV."

Serena whipped around. "God, I think you may be right."

Darrell glanced backward to see that the Explorer was now only a car's length behind their vehicle. With each second, it got closer and closer.

Darrell hit his turn signal and moved to the far right lane.

The Explorer did a sudden jerky move to the right across three lanes of traffic.

"Oh, shit," Darrell mumbled.

"What?" Serena cried.

"This asshole's still on my tail."

Serena's body lunged forward, and she screamed. It took only a second to realize that their car had been hit.

"Son of a bitch!" The Viper veered to the right, and Darrell spun the steering wheel to the left before the car plowed into the guardrail.

"What is going on?" Serena asked.

"I don't—"

Serena's scream pierced the air as the Explorer rammed them from behind.

Again, Darrell sped up. Again, the Explorer gave chase. Darrell shoved the car into fifth gear and slipped to the left. When the Explorer did the same, Darrell cursed. "This car's got a lot of power . . . If there wasn't all this traffic . . ."

"Why not pull over?" Serena's voice was shaky.

"I would if—*hold on!*"

The Explorer pulled up to their right. Darrell saw it coming and stepped on the gas, but he wasn't quick enough to avoid the hit.

Serena gripped the edge of the door while shifting her body to the left. "Oh, God. Darrell . . ."

Darrell spun the steering wheel to avoid ramming the car to his left, but he spun it too far around to the right, and the Viper did a three hundred and sixty-degree turn to the right across two lanes of traffic. Darrell slammed on the brakes, and the car skidded onto the shoulder, then onto the grass. The wheels kicked up grass and dirt as the car did a final turn, then came to a stop just feet before plunging into the bordering canal.

Serena's scream reverberated in the small car. Darrell watched as the sports utility vehicle disappeared along the expressway.

"Oh my God, oh my God," Serena repeated, her chest heaving as she sucked in air.

Darrell turned to her. "Are you okay?"

Whimpering, she managed a nod.

Darrell reached for her face and palmed it, offering the only comfort he knew how. Then he glanced ahead at the water, the realization of how close they'd come to possible death hitting him like a kick in the gut. A long breath oozed out of him, and he dropped his head forward to the steering wheel. What the hell had just happened?

A second later, a car pulled up alongside them.

"Darrell . . ." Serena's voice held fear.

Once again, Darrell reached for Serena's face, cupping her chin. She met and held his gaze. "It's okay, Serena. I won't let anyone hurt you."

She managed a jerky nod, then turned to the left and hit the button to lower the window.

"You guys all right?" the older black man asked.

"A little shaken up," Darrell replied, "but we're okay."

The man said, "I tried to get that guy's plate, but he drove by so fast. I can call the police for you if you like. I have one of those cell phones."

"Yeah, please," Darrell told the man.

As the older man made the call, Darrell turned to Serena once again. She was trembling.

"Come here." He removed his seatbelt and leaned across the seat. Serena gave a soft cry and went into his arms.

For a long while, Darrell held her. Her soft body quivered against his, and he tightened his arms around her.

"You sure you're okay?" Darrell asked, pulling back. He ran his hands over her hair, then framed her face.

Serena nodded jerkily. Then, sucking in a sharp breath, she closed her eyes and threw her arms around Darrell's neck. "Oh God, Darrell. Just hold me."

He folded her into his arms again and held her tight. He didn't let her go even when the good Samaritan returned and announced that the police were on the way.

Darrell angled his head and thanked the man, then watched him head back to his car. All the while, he continued to hold Serena. He felt a measure of comfort when the pace of her breathing slowed from its erratic pattern. Even then, he didn't release her, enjoying the feel of her cheek pressed against his chest, the feel of her soft body in his arms.

God, it had been so long since he'd held a woman in such an embrace. And it felt good to be needed, to know that his touch gave her comfort.

Serena pulled her head back and slowly lifted her eyes to his. Darrell reached for her glasses and pulled them off, then placed them in the compartment between the seats.

Her lashes were long and thick, something he hadn't

noticed before. She really did have beautiful eyes. Wide and expressive, her dark brown eyes were compelling.

They glistened now, almost as if she was about to cry. *Was* she about to cry?

"Hey," Darrell said softly. He placed his right hand on her left cheek, skimming her smooth flesh with his fingertips.

"Darrell, I've never been so scared."

"Shh," he cooed. He trailed his fingers to her hairline. "It's okay now."

Serena's eyes fluttered shut as she exhaled a long breath.

"That's it," Darrell said. He slipped his fingers into her hair. "Breathe."

She inhaled and exhaled again.

"Better?" Darrell asked.

Serena slowly opened her eyes. "Yes."

"Good." And as if his lips had a mind of their own, he planted a gentle kiss on her forehead. A soft sound escaped Serena's lips, one that said she was startled.

Pulling back, Darrell lowered his gaze to hers. She raised hers to his. Gone was the fear he'd seen in Serena's eyes moments earlier. Instead, he saw a mixture of confusion and yearning in their dark brown depths, and the combination was strangely erotic.

Something told him he should pull away, release her, and step out of the car, but Serena tilted her head upward, parted her lips . . .

And suddenly, something was different between them. Her eyes darkened at the same moment he felt a little jolt in his groin.

And he was lost.

Darrell crushed his lips down on hers, swallowing Serena's surprised gasp. Her full lips were soft and sweet. Lord, she tasted good. Flicking his tongue over her supple flesh, he urged her closer. He couldn't get enough of her.

The feel of his tongue on her lips was thrilling, more thrilling than she could ever have imagined, and Serena moaned against his lips. Instantly, Darrell's tongue delved inside her mouth. His hot, wet tongue played anxiously over hers, while one hand slipped to her shoulder, then down her arm.

Darrell suckled her bottom lip softly, bringing his other hand from her hair to her jaw line, then lower, to the base of her neck. Serena's body erupted in flames. Never had a man's touch felt so good. But the foreign feeling was enough to knock Serena's senses back into place.

*This is dangerous,* she thought. Before Darrell's hand could move lower, she broke the kiss and pulled away.

Dark eyes met her own. Their ragged breaths filled the hot air in the small car.

After several seconds, Serena attempted to speak. "Um . . ." But her voice trailed off, unable to find any words.

"Whoa." Darrell ran both hands over his shortly cropped hair.

Serena watched him curiously, her heart beating so fast she feared it couldn't be good for her. Just as she opened her mouth to try speaking again, Darrell turned away.

Serena brought a hand to her face, gently touching her lips with the tips of her fingers. Good Lord, Darrell had just *kissed* her. And that had been no ordinary kiss. She'd been kissed before, but never had a kiss left her breathing ragged, her skin flushed, or her heart beating like she'd just finished running a marathon.

Finally, Serena found her voice. "W-what just happened?"

"I . . ." Darrell seemed at a loss for words. "We . . . I think we . . . got caught up in the moment."

"Yes." Serena's shoulders sagged as she said the word, a sense of relief washing over her.

Darrell met her eyes with a steady gaze. "We did, didn't we?"

"Yes, of course. That makes sense. Isn't it normal . . . in situations like this?"

"Yes," Darrell agreed, relieved to find an answer to his strange behavior. It wasn't like him to ambush a woman with a kiss, much less after a life-threatening experience.

But as Serena had suggested, it was their frightening experience that had led to the kiss. In the face of near tragedy, they had ended up in each other's arms, ended up *kissing*—comforting each other in the most primitive, instinctive way. What more life-affirming thing could they have done to prove they were thankful to still be breathing?

That the kiss was a spectacular one had emphasized even more the fact they were very much alive.

"Um." Serena's frail voice disrupted his thoughts. "Do you think . . ." Serena paused, swallowed. "Do you think that car running us off the road had something to do with your brother?"

Darrell's forehead wrinkled at Serena's suggestion. "I didn't think about that. But God, you might be right. That could be it."

"I thought I saw a gold Ford Explorer in the restaurant parking lot. What if it was Tamara?"

"Could be," Darrell agreed. "But then, Explorers are popular. It could have been anybody."

Serena looked around the interior of the Viper. "You think the car's okay?"

"Yeah. It'll have a few scrapes and dents that my brother won't be happy about, but I don't really care right now."

Serena looked at Darrell, but he wouldn't meet her eyes. The tension between them now was undeniable. One minute, she'd felt so comfortable in his arms, like she could have stayed there forever and been at peace. His arms had felt right around her. And that kiss . . . even now, she was still light-headed, and it had nothing to do with the accident.

It had everything to do with the electrical charge she felt between her and Darrell.

She didn't understand what had happened to her. The fact that she *hadn't* wanted to pull away was exactly the reason she had. She had liked being in his arms all too much, and if she hadn't ended the kiss, she wasn't sure if she would have been able to stop what might have happened next.

This car was too small for the two of them. Serena reached for the door handle. "Uh, I should . . . step outside. Stretch."

"Good idea."

"Where are my glasses?"

Darrell retrieved them for her.

"Thanks," Serena said, shoving them on. Then she opened the door and exited the car. Darrell did the same.

She paced a few feet, pivoted, and retraced her path, watching Darrell while he stretched.

"Well, nothing hurts," Darrell announced.

Serena bent over, stretching forward. "Ow."

"What?" Concern flashing across Darrell's face, he made his way around the Viper to Serena. But as he neared her, she walked in the other direction.

"My lower back," she said, walking away from him. "It kinda hurts."

Again, Darrell stepped toward her. "Let me—"

"No, I'm okay." She arched her body from side to side. "There. That feels better."

"Are you sure? Because I can give you a massage if you like."

Serena waved off his suggestion. "Don't be silly. I'm probably just imagining it anyway. I hear that happens a lot to people after accidents . . ."

"Right," Darrell said slowly. But disappointment tickled his stomach. Just minutes ago, Serena had leaned on him for support, yet now she acted like she couldn't stand to be near him.

It was the kiss, Darrell realized. The kiss had complicated things between them.

Maybe it was best that he resist the urge to comfort her. That comforting had landed them in this uneasy situation. What had started off simply enough had become complicated, and it was entirely his fault. He could say what he wanted about getting caught up in the moment, but Serena had no doubt sensed he wasn't telling the whole truth.

The truth was that while they'd been kissing, his thoughts had gotten X-rated. And damn if her little sighs hadn't started to turn him on. If they'd been anywhere else, he would have been tempted to slip his hands beneath that oversized T-shirt and caress her bare skin, her breasts. Even now, he wondered how she would respond to him. Would she arch her breast against his hand, guide his mouth to her nipple?

Whoa, whoa, whoa! Darrell shook his head, trying to toss the visual image of a topless Serena that had invaded his mind. Damn if this accident hadn't made him lose his brain. He was taking this life-affirming bit *way* too far.

Besides, how crazy was it to have sexual thoughts about a woman who'd slapped you upside the head as a way to say hello? Not only that, Serena had been involved with his brother, and Darrell *never* dated Cecil's exes. Maybe because so many twins played that game, Darrell found the idea particularly unappealing.

"Oh, look," Serena said, pointing behind him. "The police."

Darrell whirled around. Indeed, a Miami-Dade police cruiser had pulled onto the shoulder.

Thank God.

Anything to get his mind off thinking about Serena, even if that meant thinking about Cecil and the very real fact that someone clearly wanted his brother dead.

# Chapter 9

"No, no, don't worry," Serena said into the phone. "I'm all right."

"I don't like this, Serena," Kiana stated matter-of-factly. "I know you're not going to want to hear this, but maybe the search for Cecil isn't worth it."

That very thought had crossed Serena's mind as the Viper had spun out of control, that nothing—not even the family heirloom—was worth her life. But as soon as the frightening moment was over, she'd dismissed the thought. The necklace had been in her family for generations and since it was her fault that it was gone, it was up to her to get it back.

"I don't know," Serena said. "At first, I figured the accident was related to Cecil, but now I'm not so sure. It's not as if psycho drivers in Miami are any surprise."

"What, you think the accident was a coincidence?"

Serena paused a moment. "Yeah. That's the only thing

that makes sense." She was aware that she was trying to make herself feel better as much as she was her sister. "Besides, if it was someone out to hurt Cecil, what are the chances we'll run into them again?"

"Serena . . ."

Serena switched the payphone from one ear to the other. "I'll be okay."

"I understand why you're hell-bent on finding Cecil, but why not let Cecil's brother deal with this? Let him call you when he finds his brother. Didn't he say he would do that?"

Serena and Darrell were at a gas station near the airport, both using payphones. She glanced at him. All she could see were his shoulders and back as he stood in the phone booth next to her. His head was hanging forward and she couldn't hear what he was saying.

"I promised I'd help him," Serena replied. "And I'm going to keep my word. I have to work Monday, which leaves only tomorrow, so if we don't locate Cecil by then, I suppose Darrell will be on his own."

"And tonight?"

Darrell hung up and faced Serena. "Um," Serena said. "Uh, I don't know about tonight. Look, I'll call you later."

"Serena—"

Serena hung up. "Hey," she said to Darrell. "Anything?"

"I called home and checked messages," he told her, "but there was nothing from Cecil."

"I didn't hear from him either." Serena had called home and checked her answering machine before calling her sister. "Not that I expected to," she added. "So, what do you want to do now? I'm not sure I'm up for another round of Dick Tracy."

"What, you don't want to head to Coconut Grove?"

"I was thinking maybe we could head to my place." Realizing that might sound like a clandestine invitation, Serena added, "To regroup. Maybe get some rest."

"You mean *stay* at your place tonight?"

"Uh . . ." Serena hadn't thought past simply heading to her place to relax and change. "Why not?" she asked, her tone upbeat. "First thing in the morning, we can head to Cecil's house in the Grove."

"I don't think that's such a great idea."

*What, you can kiss me silly, but you can't come over to my place?* Serena felt rejected, and it hurt. "Why not?"

"It's probably better that I stay at a hotel."

"Oh."

"I'll drop you off, see where you live, then I can pick you up in the morning."

"Fine." Serena started for the Viper.

Darrell fell into stride beside her. "This isn't about you. It's about keeping things in perspective."

Serena stopped abruptly and faced him. "What? You think if you stay at my place tonight, I'll try to seduce you?"

Actually, he was thinking that he didn't want to see where she and Cecil had cozied up together. Not that it should bother him, but it did. "That's not what I'm saying."

"Then what's the problem?"

"Are you always this testy when you don't get your way?"

"*Testy?* You want testy—"

"I'm pretty sure you showed me testy last night—"

Throwing her hands in the air, Serena groaned and started walking.

"Let's face it," Darrell said, catching up with her. "We don't exactly get along."

Halting, Serena gaped at Darrell. "Do you make it a habit of kissing women you don't get along with?"

"That was . . ." Darrell ground out a frustrated breath. "We discussed that."

"Whatever," Serena quipped.

Darrell took hold of Serena's arm before she could walk off again. "What do you want me to say?" he asked. "It happened, it shouldn't have, and . . . and I don't want to complicate things."

That's all the kiss had been to him, a complication. Darrell's words stung, but Serena was determined not to let him see that. "Don't flatter yourself, Darrell. I was attracted to your brother. I'm not attracted to you. You don't have to worry about me throwing myself at you if you come to my place."

Darrell's fingers loosened on Serena's wrist. She'd spoken firmly yet calmly, leaving no room for doubt. Her words shouldn't have hurt him, but they did. They pierced him in a place that once again said, *You're not good enough. Cecil's better than you.*

It didn't matter that Darrell had been the "good" twin all his life, Cecil had always had more fun, more women, more everything.

But he said, "All the more reason for me to stay somewhere else tonight."

"Yeah, you're probably right."

"I am."

"Fine."

"Good."

They were silent on the way to the car, silent as they got inside.

Serena finally broke the silence. "This has been a very

long and frustrating twenty-four hours. For you. For me. I want us to be able to get along, to trust each other."

"So do I," Darrell agreed.

"I didn't mean to offend you with that crack about you thinking I'd try to seduce you. It's just that . . . it seemed like you didn't trust me. And after everything that's happened, I want you to know you can trust me."

Darrell met her eyes. "And I want you to know you can trust me. I don't want to think that every time you look at me, you figure you can't believe a word I say, just because I happen to look exactly like the guy who ripped you off."

"I don't think that," Serena assured him. "But yeah, I suppose that every time I look at you, I see Cecil. How can I not?" She paused. "But my frustration isn't with you, it's with me. Ever since he disappeared a few weeks ago, I've been asking myself how I could have gotten involved with him. I ask myself what's wrong with me that I trusted someone like him. As much as I'd like to delude myself, I don't think he ever had any interest in me other than to steal from me. I keep kicking myself. I was so naïve where your brother was concerned."

"For what it's worth, my brother is pretty good at what he does. Don't beat up on yourself." Darrell glanced at Serena, saw her staring at him peculiarly, like she was studying him. "What?"

She shook her head and looked away. After a sigh, she said, "It's amazing to me that you can look exactly like him, yet not be like him."

"Believe me, I'm used to everyone thinking the worst about me because I'm Cecil's twin."

"I guess that's a pretty hard thing to deal with."

"Oh, yeah." There was a pause, then Darrell asked, "You said my brother took off a few weeks ago?"

"That was the last I saw or heard from him."

"And what exactly did he tell you?"

"He didn't actually speak to me. He dropped off a note at the library where I work. I was at lunch, I think. Anyway, the note said that something urgent had come up and that he had to go out of town, but he'd be in touch as soon as he could."

"But you never heard from him?"

"No. After a week, I got worried, mostly because I'd been waiting to hear about the store I'd put a down payment on. So I called, but I didn't reach him at his home number—the one I thought was an apartment near the library."

"Uh huh."

"When I learned Cecil's home number was disconnected, I called his cell number, his business number—everything was disconnected. After that, I got a really bad feeling. I don't know why, but something told me to check the safe. I did . . . and the necklace was gone."

Darrell shook his head. "That's it?"

"Yeah."

"Hmm."

"What are you thinking?"

"I'm thinking that I'd like to go to Cecil's house tonight. With you," Darrell quickly added. "If you want. I know it's been a long day, but I figure I can get a head start at searching the place to see if anything turns up. Or if Cecil's there. Then, later, I can bring you back to your place."

"Sure," Serena agreed. They'd come this far today, they

might as well continue looking. Besides, the Grove was on the way to Kendall, where she lived.

Darrell started the car. "Which way to Coconut Grove?"

"Turn left. Then we can continue south down this street until we get to US 1."

Darrell did as instructed. The rest of the drive was in relative silence, with Serena giving Darrell directions to Cecil's house in Coconut Grove based on the address he'd provided her.

When they pulled up to the large house partially hidden by a variety of mature palms, a lump formed in Serena's throat. *This* was Cecil's house? Having seen his condo, she should have been prepared for this, yet she'd hoped to see something less swanky.

She might as well have the word "sucker" tattooed on her forehead. Because this house was absolutely stunning—and even more proof of Cecil's deception.

Darrell got out of the Viper, and Serena followed him, though her legs felt like lead as she walked to the front door. Part of her didn't want to go inside, didn't want to see the tangible evidence of her naiveté. But denying reality wouldn't change what had happened.

The house was larger than the condo, with a stunning entertainment center in the backyard, as well as a large pool, and a jacuzzi. As Serena stared out the window at the lavish backyard display, a sick feeling washed over her. She didn't even want to know how many bedrooms this place had.

She closed her eyes and exhaled slowly. *It doesn't matter that Cecil lied to me,* she told herself. *It only matters that I get the necklace back.*

The feel of Darrell's hands on her shoulders startled her, and she flinched. But a second later, she relaxed against his touch, unable to deny herself the comfort she knew it would bring. She didn't want to. Instead, she fought the urge to turn in his arms and place her face against his strong chest. This was all much harder to deal with than she had anticipated.

"You okay?" Darrell asked.

Serena shrugged. "I don't know. I'm still trying to understand it all."

"I don't think anyone has ever figured Cecil out. Not my father, and certainly not me, though Lord knows I tried."

"I suppose there's no point in crying over the past." Serena stepped away from Darrell and hugged her torso.

"I wish you wouldn't do that," Darrell said softly.

"What?"

"Walk away from me when you think about Cecil."

Serena gave Darrell an odd look.

"Like I said before," he continued, "it's like everyone sees Cecil when they see me . . . and it'd be nice not to have to go through that for a change."

Serena nodded. "I'll try."

"I'm gonna take a look around," Darrell said. "See if I can't find the necklace."

Serena's face instantly lit up. "Oh," she said excitedly. "I didn't think of that. Gosh, do you think the necklace could be *here*?"

The way she looked at him, with complete trust and hope in her eyes, filled Darrell's heart with warmth. He wanted nothing more than to say that yes, he believed the necklace was here, as long as it meant she'd never look forlorn again. What was it about her that had him wanting to do anything in his power to make her smile?

"I have no clue," he admitted, knowing he couldn't give her false hope based on no evidence. "But who knows? My brother spent a lot of time here, obviously. Anything's possible."

Serena held her hands to her lips in a prayerful gesture. "God, I hope so."

Walking toward her, Darrell closed the distance between them. Reaching for her face, he ran a gentle finger along her cheek. "If the necklace is here, I'll find it."

Serena held his gaze, her eyes saying implicitly that she believed him.

And good God almighty, he wanted to kiss her again. How inappropriate would *that* be? What the hell was wrong with him, anyway?

He dropped his hand from her face and crossed his arms over his chest. He had to put some space between them before he complicated matters further.

"Why don't you sit on the sofa and relax? I'll take a look around."

"I can help," Serena told him.

"No," Darrell quickly replied, softening his anxious tone with a smile. "That's okay. You just . . . relax. I'll be back in a little while. Hopefully, with some answers."

# Chapter 10

*Serena awoke suddenly, her eyes popping open.*
She felt a moment of panic when she saw her strange sur-
roundings, realizing she had no clue where she was.

And then she remembered. She was at Cecil's house.

Well, one of his houses.

Serena stirred, turning onto her side. That's when she
noticed the down-filled comforter covering her body.

*Wait a second,* she thought, bolting upright. She was on
the sofa, that much she could tell. Narrowing her eyes, she
glanced around—and realized she couldn't see. A hand
went to her face to confirm what she already knew. She
wasn't wearing her glasses.

Where were they? Squinting, she checked out the near-
est object, the coffee table, but didn't see any shape that
resembled her glasses. She glanced in the other direction,
to the side of the sofa where her head had been, and saw
the shape of a lamp. The lamp had to be on some type of

table. Sliding her butt along the sofa, she reached for the base of the lamp. Her fingers closed around her glasses.

Serena put them on. All right, she was still in the living room, still on the sofa. Last she remembered, Darrell had left her here while he'd gone to search the house for the necklace.

But if she had a blanket covering her, then Darrell must have placed it on her because she'd drifted to sleep. How long had she been out?

And why was the house so quiet? The sun seemed brighter than when she'd arrived, almost as if it was morning.

Good Lord, it *was* morning. But how could that be? If it was morning, that meant she'd slept through the night. Had she been that tired that she'd completely zonked out for several hours?

And where was Darrell?

Serena yawned, then rose from the sofa. After giving her body a good stretch, she headed out of the living room.

Sunlight spilled into the hallway through open bedroom doors. Serena peeked her head into the first room, but didn't see Darrell.

She continued down the hallway. "Darrell," she called. "Darrell?"

A door several feet ahead of her opened, and Serena's head whipped in that direction. Darrell stepped into the hallway. Clad only in shorts, sunlight bathed his body, emphasizing all his beautiful features. He looked, quite literally, like a god.

Strong muscles defined the entire length of his golden-brown arms. His abdomen was washboard flat, a marked contrast to his bulging pecs. His upper body was virtually hairless, with just a sprinkling of dark hair around his belly-button. Serena's gaze dropped lower, to his waist, then lower, to his legs. Her lips parted at the sight of his powerfully built thighs.

Oh yes, this man was a pure Adonis.

"I trust you slept well," Darrell said.

His voice startled her out of her gawking. "Uh, yes." Serena planted both hands on her hips. "At least I think so. What time is it?"

"A little after seven."

"As in A.M.?"

"Yeah."

"My God. I didn't realize I was that tired."

"A lot happened yesterday."

"That it did," Serena agreed. The accident, the kiss . . .

Darrell was suddenly walking toward her, and Serena's heart went berserk. He stopped about a foot in front of her, and the smell of soap, probably Irish Spring, filled her nose. But there was something else, a distinct scent that was all male and totally enthralling. Try as she might, it was impossible to ignore his masculine appeal.

She suddenly wondered if she could be this close to him without salivating. Abruptly turning, Serena started back toward the living room. "I can't believe I slept that long," she commented as she walked. "Why didn't you wake me?"

"You were tired. I let you sleep."

In the living room, Serena went back to the sofa where she'd slept. She sat down. Knowing she must look awful, she ran a hand over her hair, smoothing it as best she could.

"Did you . . ." She halted when Darrell moved toward

her. Pushing aside the comforter, he joined her on the sofa. "Uh." For a moment, she couldn't remember what she was going to say, that's how flustered she was with him so close to her. Why was he sitting next to her like this, anyway? As if they'd spent many a morning together?

Her brain started working again. "Did you find anything?" she asked.

"I searched this place top to bottom, and no, I didn't find your necklace. I did, however, find something interesting."

"What?" Serena brought a leg onto the sofa and angled her body to face his.

"Cecil has a computer in one of the rooms. In the printer tray, there was a printout from some online auction site, detailing the rules and regulations regarding selling items online."

"Oh, my God. Do you think Cecil was going to sell the necklace online?"

"You say it's an antique diamond necklace."

"I just had it appraised. It's worth . . ." Serena hesitated, remembering that it had been her big mouth that had gotten her into this situation in the first place.

"I assume it's worth a small fortune."

"Two hundred and sixty-five thousand dollars."

"*What did you say?*"

Serena repeated the figure.

"And you told Cecil this?"

"Yeah. We talked a lot about antiques—"

"My God, Serena. You can't dangle a gold carrot in front of someone and expect him not to take it."

Serena jumped to her feet. "I know. I was stupid. Don't

you think I realize that? I trusted your brother. He approached me, told me how much he loved antiques. I didn't tell him about the necklace right away, not until I'd gotten to know him. It was nice . . . nice to find someone else passionate about antiques the way I was. So I told him about the piece, but I didn't show it to him until after he began helping me look for a store. How was I to know he was a fraud?"

Darrell stood. "A quarter of a million?"

Serena nodded, a glum expression on her face.

"Well, now I understand why you're so hell-bent on getting it back."

"It's not the dollar figure. That necklace has been in my family for generations."

Placing his hands on his hips, Darrell paced the hardwood floor. "God, until now, I'd figured that if we didn't find my brother, I would cut you a check. But I can't afford that kind of money."

Serena frowned at Darrell. "I don't expect you to cut me a check."

"My brother stole from you, Serena."

"Yes, your brother. Not *you*. Darrell, you're not responsible for Cecil's crimes."

In his heart, he knew that, yet what Serena had just told him made Darrell feel a ton of guilt. Where had he gone wrong when trying to show his brother the right path? Why hadn't he been able to stop Cecil from choosing a criminal lifestyle?

He contemplated the situation a moment longer. "There's no way I can afford anywhere near that kind of cash."

"Did you hear what I said?" Serena was now standing in front of him. "The only person who owes me anything is Cecil, not you."

Darrell didn't think when he reached for her face, didn't think when he stroked his fingers across her skin. "God, I'm sorry."

Serena covered his hand with hers. "Darrell, it's not your fault."

"Maybe it is."

"No, it isn't."

His heart filling with pain, he looked down at her. She met his eyes with an intense, sincere gaze. She meant her words. She didn't hold him responsible for what Cecil had done.

And while that realization gave him a measure of joy, it also gave him a measure of pain. Because he knew without a doubt that he wanted to make things right for Serena where his brother was concerned, but if his brother had already hawked her necklace, he had no clue how he'd do that.

It was a heavy burden to bear, and Darrell stepped away from her. He faced the floor-to-ceiling windows bordering the impressive backyard. His brother had all this, yet he'd stolen from Serena. Where had Darrell gone wrong?

"You don't understand," Darrell said softly. "No one understands."

"I think I do."

Darrell turned and stared at her, but didn't say anything.

"I've never met anyone like you," she told him. "Except perhaps my father. You have a deep-rooted sense of right and wrong, of good and bad. Anyone who spends any time with you has to see that."

"Then where did I go wrong?"

"You can't be held accountable for what Cecil does, Darrell."

"I was all he had. I tried to show him the right way."

"Because he didn't follow it doesn't mean it's your fault."

"I feel like it is. He depended on me."

"It's not, Darrell."

Darrell sighed. "My brain says you're right, but I can't undo years of feeling like that overnight."

"You sound like his father, not his brother."

"Like I said, you don't understand. I pretty much *was* Cecil's father. He didn't have anyone else, certainly not our dad."

"What about your mother?"

Darrell huffed. What mother? She'd left them when he and Cecil were only seven. To this day, Darrell figured that was the root of Cecil's problems. Their mother had wanted the finer things in life, all the things money could buy, the things her husband—who'd earned a modest living as a garbage collector—couldn't provide her. Perhaps because she was beautiful, she'd thought she deserved more out of life. Ultimately, she'd found a man who couldn't resist her charms, the CEO of a bank in New York. After working for him for a few short months, she'd left her husband and her children and had never looked back.

Was it a coincidence that Cecil scammed rich, beautiful women? Darrell doubted it.

"Darrell?" Serena prompted.

"My mother died ten years ago."

The confused look on her face said he hadn't answered her question, but this was a subject Darrell wasn't in the mood to chat about. So he returned the discussion to the issue at hand. "I didn't think of online venues before, but considering the value of that necklace, it's obviously something Cecil couldn't just bring to a pawn shop. He must have sold it over the internet."

One minute, Darrell had been discussing his guilt over his brother's lifestyle, but the moment she'd mentioned his mother, he'd shut down. Serena didn't have to ask to know that there was pain associated with the subject of his mother. But was the pain regarding her death and the fact that he missed her, or something else altogether?

"Yeah, that's a very real possibility."

Serena's mind finally registered what Darrell had just said. "Wait a minute. You think he *sold* it?"

"Or tried to sell it."

"Over the internet?" She couldn't prevent the note of hysteria from entering her voice.

Darrell held both palms up in a frustrated gesture. "I don't know. I checked his saved e-mails but didn't find anything that would give me answers one way or another."

Serena's breath snagged in her chest. Were she and Darrell on a wild-goose chase? Was her family heirloom already gone forever?

God, no.

Her eyes flew to Darrell's. In a voice barely above a whisper, she said, "I have to get it back."

"I know." Darrell dragged a hand over his face. "I know." He blew out a harried breath. "All right. Let me think. When Cecil called me, he was still in Miami—at least, based on the area code. I tried calling the number back, but it was a payphone. I don't know why, but my gut says that if he was still in Miami a few days ago, he's probably still in Miami now."

"Why?"

"Let's assume someone was after him a few weeks ago when he left you that note at the library. He disconnected his numbers, obviously because he didn't want to be reached. But why not head out of town? If he's still around—which he was when he called me—then there must be a reason for that. Something's keeping him here, but he's laying low. The question is why, and where." Darrell paused. "Do you have *any* idea where he might be?"

"I have no clue." Frustrated, Serena threw her hands in the air, then dropped them against her thighs. "Obviously, I didn't really know Cecil at all."

"Nowhere the two of you used to hang out? No one he mentioned in particular?"

"Again, this might sound weird, but we didn't discuss Cecil's friends. I never met them. We went for lots of dinners, chatted about antiques. And he met my sister. But I have no clue who his friends are. I didn't even know he had a twin."

"Somebody's gotta know something." Darrell walked to the backyard window and peered outside. After a moment, he turned to Serena. "We should head out and meet the neighbors this morning. See if any of them know Cecil, and know where he might be."

"All right."

"You want to shower or something? Cecil's got a ton of T-shirts and shorts around if you want to change into something fresh."

"I'd rather start going door-to-door."

"It's too early for that."

"Oh," Serena said, remembering the time. "Well, I guess I do need to freshen up. Where's the bathroom?"

"End of the hall on the right."

Serena started off.

"Uh," Darrell said, and she halted. "You should probably pick out some clothes to wear before you head in the bathroom."

"Of course. Which bedroom?"

Darrell walked toward her, then led her to one of the bedrooms. The closet was full of silk shirts and dress pants, but the drawers had T-shirts and sweats. Serena wouldn't have known that Cecil owned anything so casual if she hadn't seen this with her very eyes.

She decided on a black T-shirt and black sweat shorts. She drew the line at choosing any of Cecil's bikini briefs.

"I saw some toothbrushes in the top left drawer in the bathroom," Darrell pointed out. "In brand new packages."

"Great," Serena said. She wondered how many women Cecil had entertained here that he'd have a supply of toothbrushes.

*It doesn't matter,* she told herself. And it didn't.

The bathroom was something out of a fairytale. Cream-colored marble floors and walls, huge jacuzzi tub, separate shower stall, his and hers sinks with gold-colored faucets. It was the kind of bathroom where one went to relax and stay awhile.

How nice it would be to lie back in the oversized tub and do just that, but there would be no joy in it for Serena. All she felt was bitterness.

*My brother has lived off gullible women for years.*

She was simply one of those gullible women who'd enabled Cecil to continue living his luxurious lifestyle.

Pushing that thought out of her mind, Serena went into the shower. She let the warm water knead her flesh, massaging away the knots formed in her shoulders because of all the stress she was experiencing.

The shower did her a world of good. Feeling fresh, she exited the stall and dried herself, then slipped into Cecil's T-shirt and shorts. How odd to dress in a man's clothes when she hadn't been intimate with him. She remembered how her mother used to dress in her father's shirts and such, and she'd dreamt of the day when she could share that simple intimacy with someone.

There was nothing special about the experience now.

*Forget it,* she told herself. *Don't dwell on what you can't change.*

The sooner she got over Cecil's betrayal, the better.

Darrell was lifting a Teflon skillet from a cupboard below the sink when he heard, "Where's the dryer?"

He whirled around.

"I need to dry my undies."

The skillet slipped from his fingers, falling to the ceramic-tiled floor with a loud crash. He bent with lightning-fast speed and retrieved it.

*Great,* Darrell thought. She wasn't wearing any underwear. He gave her body a quick once-over. Though she was wearing thick fleece shorts, she may as well have come into the kitchen topless, that's how X-rated his thoughts became.

He turned and faced the stove. "You want to dry your . . ." Darrell's voice trailed off, his mind conjuring images of just what kind of underwear Serena wore. Practical cotton undies that matched the way she dressed, or did her oversized clothes hide naughty, racy underwear beneath? White lace, black? Bikini or thong?

"I'm not going to wear Cecil's."

"Um . . . I . . ." Darrell turned on one of the stove's burners. "Aren't we heading out?"

"Yeah, but it's still early, so I figured while we eat breakfast, I can dry my underwear."

"I don't know if there's a dryer. If there is, I didn't see one." He did a sidestep to the fridge and removed the carton of eggs, all without looking at Serena. "This place has everything. I'm sure there's one around somewhere."

"Are you all right?" Serena asked.

"Sure." Darrell tried to make his tone casual. "Why wouldn't I be?"

"I don't know. You're not looking at me."

"Just trying to make some breakfast. There's eggs. How do you want them? Naked?"

"What?"

"Scrambled. That's what I meant." *Damn, calm down, Darrell.* He was acting as if he'd never seen a naked woman before, much less fantasized about one.

"Sure." Serena's tone was puzzled. "I'm easy."

*Easy.* Like he needed to hear another sexual innuendo.

"I'll go look for the dryer."

Darrell waited a full two seconds before turning. And got a full view of Serena's butt. It was round and firm beneath his brother's shorts.

He gulped.

Her round butt led to long, shapely legs. She had the kind of thighs a guy wanted wrapped around his body.

Darrell's groin tightened, leaving him with a painful erection. Never, ever had he looked at any of his brother's other girlfriends in any way other than platonically—and they'd all been stunning. Yet Serena, sweet, pantyless Serena, had him all hot and bothered without even trying.

"Breakfast, Darrell," he told himself. "Make breakfast." Trying to forget the image of Serena's beautiful buns, Darrell busied himself with finding a bowl for the eggs, butter for the skillet, and the other items he needed to make breakfast.

But the knowledge that Serena was somewhere in another room, walking around with no underwear, was what made his mouth water—not the aroma of the food he was cooking.

## Chapter 11

*When Kiana walked into the kitchen and saw the* answering machine flashing, she immediately dropped her grocery bags on the counter beside the phone. Of course, the phone hadn't rung once this morning, but the moment she'd stepped out to get groceries, someone had called.

She hoped it was Serena. Try as she might to remain calm, the worry was setting in. Serena didn't know Cecil's brother from Adam, and despite what she said about feeling she could trust him, Kiana couldn't be sure.

Kiana hit the machine's play button.

"Hey, Kiana. It's Geoff. I'm back in town, so give me a call."

Geoff. Kiana's breath snagged. So, he was back.

She hesitated a full half-second before she reached for the receiver. She dialed Geoff's number.

"Geoff, it's Kiana," she said when he picked up.

"Hey, sweetie." Kiana could hear the smile in his voice. "You called."

It was times like this, when Geoff sounded like she'd made his entire day, that Kiana missed their relationship. At least she still had his friendship. "How was your trip?" she asked.

"It was great. Nice to get away. You know how stressful my job can be."

"Yes, I know." Geoff had always enjoyed taking impromptu trips when he and Kiana were together. He still did. But since their breakup, Kiana hadn't done much other than hang out with Serena from time to time.

"You know how much I love the Keys," Geoff said.

"Yes," Kiana replied softly, knowing he was referring to the fabulous week they'd spent there together.

As silence filled the line, Kiana was sure Geoff was going to bring up that week. He often reminded her of the happy times they'd had together in an attempt to persuade her to give their romantic relationship another chance. But he didn't. Instead, he asked, "So what's happening with Cecil?"

"Gosh, there's so much to tell you," Kiana said, her thoughts shifting from her relationship with Geoff to the situation with Serena. "It turns out Cecil has an identical twin brother. That's who we saw Friday night. That's who Serena had arrested."

"No way."

"He's out of jail now, given the misunderstanding."

"And where's Cecil?"

"That's the problem. His brother doesn't know. I'm not sure I told you about that note Cecil left for my sister at the library."

"Yeah, you told me."

"It looks like something really crazy is going on," Kiana said. "Darrell—that's Cecil's twin—came to town to find Cecil because he thinks he's in trouble. And he must be, because someone tried to run him and Serena off the road yesterday!" A sick feeling swept over Kiana. "God, Geoff, they could have been *killed*!"

"Sweetie," Geoff said firmly yet gently.

"Yeah?" Kiana's voice wavered.

"Serena's all right, right?"

"Yeah, but—"

"But she's okay. Nothing happened to her. That's the most important thing."

Geoff's words made Kiana remember the positive, not dwell on the negative. He was right. The fact that Serena was okay was the important thing. She had to hold on to that.

Kiana blew out a steady breath. "I'm worried about my sister. She's got *no* clue what she's doing. She's so hell-bent on finding that good-for-nothing ex of hers . . . who knows what kind of trouble she'll get into?"

"That's a legitimate concern," Geoff said.

Kiana paused, surprised at Geoff's statement. "You really think so?"

"Of course."

Relieved that Geoff understood her point, Kiana continued. "Serena's already told me that she still plans to look for Cecil—with his twin—a guy she met for the first time when she slapped him in the face Friday night."

"She slapped him?"

"Yeah. Well, she thought he was Cecil."

Geoff chuckled softly. "Ouch."

"I know." Kiana grinned, thinking of the irony of it all. She'd bet anything Darrell regretted flirting with Serena that night.

"One thing about your sister, she's a sweetheart—but don't cross her."

"Ain't that the truth!" Kiana giggled.

"She'll be just fine," Geoff said with confidence.

"I hope so."

"All right, sweetie," Geoff said. "What do you want me to do? Run a criminal background check on this Darrell Montford guy?"

A smile touched Kiana's lips. Geoff knew her so well. And he had a special way of making her feel better. Minutes ago, she'd been so worried about her sister. Now, she was still concerned, but she didn't feel as anxious. "Yes, Geoff. I'd love that."

"No problem."

"And maybe . . . I was thinking you could do a search and find out all Cecil Montford's known addresses. Maybe even acquaintances and stuff. Anything that might help Serena find him as soon as possible."

"I don't know . . ." Geoff said playfully. "That's a lot to ask."

"C'mon, Geoff. You know I'd be forever grateful for any help you can give me."

"Really?" Geoff bantered. "What's in it for me?"

"I will honor you with my friendship for life."

"Oh, my wounded heart."

"Funny, Geoff, I don't remember you having one."

"That was cold." But there was a lightness in his voice. And at least Kiana was laughing. "You're so silly, Geoff. So, can you hook me up with the four-one-one or what?"

"I'll see what I can do," Geoff replied.

When she and Geoff had been an item, they'd rarely laughed—probably because she'd been so worried about him at work, and no matter how he tried to make her feel better with light-hearted comments, she hadn't appreciated his humorous approach to comforting her. Now that they were strictly friends, she could laugh at his humor because she didn't have as much invested in him. Yes, she cared about him and always would, but the pressure of worrying if her future husband would come home in a body bag was gone. As a result, they got along a hundred times better.

Clearly, she couldn't deal with her fears. Granted, that was her flaw, but if she couldn't deal with her fears, why continue a relationship?

Still, Kiana often thought of the time they'd spent together. She still remembered how they'd met while walking in Coconut Grove two years ago. He'd been working. She'd been surprised when he'd stopped in her path to say hello. The spark had been instant, and when he'd jokingly told her that he would have to arrest her for possessing an illegal weapon—her smile could knock any man flat on his butt—she'd wanted to get to know him better. By the end of their chat, they'd exchanged phone numbers. Geoff had called her that night, and soon afterward, they'd started going out.

But things had gone awry when a couple months into their relationship, Geoff had started canceling dates for off-duty gigs, concerned with paying off the enormous debt he'd incurred as a student. And the more she cared about him, the more she worried about the dangers associated with his job as a police officer. Geoff had always downplayed her concerns.

The memory of the negative issues brought Kiana down. "Okay, Geoff. I'll talk to you later."

"Or maybe I can take you out for dinner."

Kiana paused, nerves tickling her stomach. "I don't know, Geoff. Maybe that's not a good idea."

"And that would be because . . . a law was passed against friends going out for dinner while I was away?"

"No, but . . ." Kiana exhaled sharply. "I'm pretty busy today. I've got a deadline I'm trying to meet."

"I see," Geoff said, but his tone said that he didn't.

"I'll call and let you know if I've got time."

"You do that."

"Thanks for agreeing to look into all that stuff for me."

"Just remember you'll owe me," Geoff warned, his tone playful once again. "And I *will* collect."

Kiana chortled. "Good-*bye*, Geoff."

"Remember what I said."

"Bye." Then Kiana hung up, a smile still playing on her lips. The man never gave up.

"Okay, how do you figure this will work?" Serena asked, strolling into the living room. "You want us to separate or work together?"

Darrell shot to his feet as she neared him and took a couple steps backward.

Halting, Serena cocked her head to the side and asked, "Everything okay?"

"Yeah, of course." He swallowed. "Are your . . . did you finish with the, um, dryer?"

"The dryer?"

"Your underwear. You're finished? Dressed? Ready to go?"

"Oh." Serena gave him a confused look. "Yeah."

"Great, great," Darrell said, feeling like an idiot. But he had to know if she was still pantyless. He didn't need any more visions of what she *didn't* have on beneath his brother's shorts dancing around in his head.

But the knowledge that she was now wearing underwear didn't help any. Because Darrell's thoughts had already turned sexual, and he couldn't stop his eyes from roaming Serena's body with interest. He couldn't help noting the way his brother's shorts hung loosely over her full hips. What would it feel like to skim his fingers along her skin, beneath those shorts, around to her full behind? Darrell's gaze ventured lower, to her flawless mocha-colored legs and her pretty, bare feet.

Man, they were the prettiest feet he'd ever seen.

A long breath oozed out of him.

Serena's skin grew warm as Darrell looked her over from head to toe. Even if she hadn't been wearing her glasses, she would have easily seen the raw, sensual heat blazing in his eyes. His lustful gaze seemed to burn right through her shorts, with a look that said he wanted to eat her up with some melted butter. And though she was fully clothed, Serena suddenly felt naked.

She crossed her arms over her chest, then dropped her hands and linked her fingers across her abdomen. Darrell's gaze didn't waver.

Serena cleared her throat—loudly. Darrell's eyes flew to hers.

"Why are you looking at me like that?" she asked.

Darrell's Adam's apple rose and fell as he swallowed. "Like what?"

Serena hesitated a good two seconds, then replied matter-of-factly, "Like you're stripping me naked with your eyes."

Darrell's mouth hit the floor, his surprise at Serena's forthrightness obvious. Hell, even *she* was surprised. What demon had possessed her body and made her say something so . . . so *provocative*?

As her heart rate accelerated, a little voice whispered, *You know exactly what possessed you.* There was a side to herself she was rapidly discovering, a side that enjoyed this feeling of being sexually alive. It was a new feeling, one that was thrilling, and it led to a need she didn't know she possessed—the need to see if she could exert any sexual power. With subtle gestures on her part, could she make Darrell want her, make him find her irresistible? Or would her feminine appeal be completely lost on him?

She moved instinctively toward him, calling on a sexual assuredness that was a surprise to her. "Hmm?" she asked, her voice soft and seductive. "Is that what you're doing? Stripping me naked with your eyes?"

Darrell didn't move as she stepped toward him, almost as though he was paralyzed. When she stopped a couple feet in front of him, he said, "Damn. You are . . . you are something else."

She cocked her head to the side. "In a good way or bad way?"

"Definitely a *good* way. I'm kinda wondering what was wrong with my brother."

"I don't want to talk about Cecil."

Darrell raised an eyebrow. "You don't?"

"Uh uh."

Darrell reached for her, softly running his fingers down her arm before taking her delicate wrist in his hand. "Neither do I."

His voice was deep and smooth and utterly sexy, causing Serena's heart to flutter. Why was she teasing him like this? She'd never been so bold before.

But then, no one's gaze alone had ever set her body on fire.

He linked one hand with hers, then the other. He urged her toward him, stopping her just before their bodies touched. Serena's core thrummed, a passion burning within her that she'd never experienced before.

"What are we doing?" Serena's voice was barely above a whisper.

"What do you want me to do?"

Ooh, he was teasing her right back, giving her a dose of her own medicine. Serena had stepped into dangerous territory, thinking she could play this game. But she suddenly felt ill matched, like an amateur.

She must have looked like a deer caught in the headlights, because Darrell grinned and said, "It's okay. I won't bite you."

Serena's legs turned to jelly. God, what a turn on the very idea of him biting her was! "What . . . what if I . . . want you to?"

"Baaaby." A growl rumbled deep in Darrell's chest. "Prim and proper on the outside, wild on the inside. God, that's an irresistible combination . . ."

Irresistible. He found her irresistible.

Oh, God . . .

Darrell lowered his head and brushed his velvet lips

against her jaw line ever so lightly, yet the mere touch set the skin beneath his lips ablaze.

"Darrell . . ." Serena hardly recognized her voice. Okay, she'd tested him. She'd proven that she could turn a man on. But she had long crossed safe territory and ventured into the unknown. She had to stop this . . .

"God, Serena." Slowly, agonizingly, he trailed kisses along her sensitized flesh, from her jaw line to her earlobe, down to the base of her neck, then up to her mouth.

And Serena stopped thinking altogether.

An electric bolt coursed through her veins, awakening her body to feelings she had never known existed. Feelings oh so delicious. She could easily get lost in a sea of desire, relishing Darrell's intoxicating touch.

Darrell brought his lips down on hers. Serena moaned softly and melted against him. Taking her face in his hands, Darrell slipped his tongue into her mouth, flicking it over the tip of her tongue, over her teeth.

Serena's fingers crept around his neck as Darrell wrapped his arms around her body. His mouth was hot, his breath heavy. The kiss wasn't a gentle kiss, but one that told Serena in no uncertain terms that Darrell wanted her.

He moved his mouth to her ear. "Serena, you're driving me *wild*."

Wild . . . oh, God. Serena's head was spinning. She was caught up in an inferno of passion and had no idea how to escape.

Darrell gripped her buttocks and pulled her close, and Serena felt something hard.

Her eyes flew open at the realization that Darrell's erection was pressed against her abdomen.

Good Lord!

From somewhere in her mind, the voice of sanity emerged, screaming, *You can't do this!*

She mewled as Darrell slipped a hand beneath her shorts, skimming the edge of her behind. *But it feels so good,* she protested.

*You cant!* the voice of sanity replied. *Stop this—now!*

Oh, man. The voice of sanity was right. She *couldn't* do this. She was saving herself for her husband, not the first man who got her hot and bothered. She couldn't let her emotions take over, or she was bound to make a mistake she would regret.

No matter how tantalizingly wonderful those emotions felt right now.

Groaning softly, Serena broke the kiss.

Startled, Darrell stared at her. A mix of emotions warring inside her, Serena stared back at him. For several long seconds, neither said a word, their faces so close their heavy breathing mingled.

Then suddenly, they both jumped apart.

"I think—"

"We need to—"

They spoke at the same time, then stopped. Quiet, they again stared at each other. The confusion on Serena's face matched how Darrell felt.

"Cecil," said Serena softly.

"Yes, Cecil." Darrell took another step backward, putting much needed space between him and Serena. Yet he couldn't stop looking at her. The rise and fall of her breasts with each ragged breath mesmerized him.

Serena promptly crossed her arms over her chest.

And Darrell promptly looked away. Good Lord, what had happened to him? His hormones were raging out of control as if he were a horny teenager. He wasn't acting like a man who'd traveled a few hundred miles to find his brother, but rather like one who'd come here hoping to score a piece of ass.

And what an ass . . .

"We should go," Serena said.

Serena's voice was like a splash of cold water in the face. *What is wrong with me?* He gave himself a mental kick in the butt to smarten the hell up.

"Yeah, we should," Darrell agreed. "Yes, it's time to find my brother." He clapped his hands together and inhaled deeply. Then he turned and started for the door. He needed to get outside, and the sooner the better.

In the foyer, Serena bent forward as she slipped into her sandals, once again giving Darrell a delicious view of her butt. Man, was she doing this on purpose, or was she completely clueless to the fact that she was torturing him?

He reached for the door.

"You want to separate or go door-to-door together?" Serena asked as she stood tall.

"I think it's best if we do it together. I mean, *go door-to-door* together."

"I know what you mean," Serena said.

Darrell met her eyes as he reached for the door. The mix of desire and confusion mirrored exactly what must have shown on his face.

"Yeah, I'm sure you do," he said after a moment.

"I do," Serena assured him.

Darrell opened the door. A cool breeze swept over him, for which he was grateful. "All right," he said softly. "Let's do this."

"Yes, let's."

* * *

"Cecil, sweetie," Virginia called from the bedroom. "Come on back to bed."

"In a minute, baby doll," Cecil replied.

"Don't keep me waiting," Virginia crooned, ending her words with a loud, lustful moan.

Cecil rolled his eyes. God, the woman was insatiable. All those studies that said older women were much more comfortable with their sexuality than their younger counterparts were definitely true.

Not that he minded, but right now, he had more pressing concerns than sex. He paced the living room floor, waiting for Eddie to return his call. Eddie still wasn't answering his home phone, nor his cell, but he usually responded to his beeper.

He damn well better respond, Cecil thought, gritting his teeth. It was going on ten minutes since he'd beeped Eddie, and still Virginia's phone hadn't rung.

Sighing, Cecil made his way to the living room window. As was his habit these past couple weeks, he pulled the blinds back ever so slightly and peered outside.

Nothing out of the ordinary. Thank goodness. Not that he expected any problems here, but one could never be sure.

He'd been hiding out at Virginia's house in Aventura for the last week, ever since Melanie had kicked him out of her Fisher Island home because her husband had returned from his overseas business trip. Melanie had proved to be a nice distraction, but she was a tightwad, and he didn't mind the fact that he'd had to find somewhere else to go.

Hopefully, he could chill here for a while, because Virginia didn't have a husband who would walk through the door at any minute. And Virginia was much more prone to parting with her deceased husband's well-earned dollars.

But he didn't want to come right out and ask. That wasn't his style. So he'd dropped hint after hint that he needed money. Virginia could easily write him a check for a hundred thousand, but this time, she was playing deaf. Probably because after the last time she'd helped him out of a bind, he hadn't kept in touch with her as he'd promised.

Women were all the same. After a while, they wanted to get serious, no matter how much they said they didn't. Even the older broads, like Virginia. He'd started off as her boy toy, someone to satisfy her because her much older husband couldn't, but now that her husband was dead, Cecil knew she wanted him around on a more permanent basis.

Hell, he'd just have to deal with that reality. At least she'd taken him in, no questions asked. It hadn't been hard. A few compliments, a few strokes in the right places, and she had been begging for him to stay with her.

Though she was happy to have him around full-time, she hadn't given him a dime.

Maybe he was slipping. He used to know how to play women right to get from them just what he needed, but in the last little while, he'd made some mistakes. Those mistakes had gotten him into the predicament he was in now.

If only Darrell were around. He still couldn't reach his brother and couldn't help wondering what was going on with him. *Was* he off on some romantic getaway?

The phone finally rang, and Cecil dove for it, answering it after the first ring. "Where the hell have you been?" he barked.

"Sorry, man," Eddie replied.

"Sorry? Eddie, you know I've been trying to reach you for days. What the hell is going on?"

"I've been busy," Eddie replied, as if that explained everything.

Cecil ground out a frustrated breath. "All right, give me the dirt. Did you find the buyer?"

Eddie spoke so softly, Cecil couldn't hear. "What'd you say? Speak up, man."

"Sheila's sleeping."

"I don't give a damn about Sheila," Cecil retorted. "Did you find the person who bought that jewelry or not?"

"Not."

"You *didn't?*"

"Yet," Eddie qualified.

"Damn it, Eddie. Don't you realize this is life or death for me? You *have* to get that jewelry back, you understand?"

"The guy didn't want that other piece you offered him?"

"No, he didn't want that necklace," Cecil replied testily. "I already told you that."

"Right."

Cecil pulled the receiver from his ear, stared at it, and frowned. Sometimes he thought he was dealing with the world's biggest idiot.

Putting the receiver back to his ear, he said, "Who can I call?" It was high time he took control of this situation.

"Man, I already told you I can't give out my contacts."

"Fuck your contacts," Cecil said. "This is my life."

"Relax, man."

"*Relax?*"

"Yeah, relax. You're gonna give yourself heart failure before Rex ever gets ahold of you."

"Thanks," Cecil replied wryly.

"I'm gonna call my sources again, okay? Then I'll call you back. Will you be at this number for a while?"

"Yeah, but don't call me till I beep you again. Okay?"

"All right. Give me a few hours. Well, it's Sunday morning, and people are probably still hung over—so give me until this evening."

"Whatever."

"Hang tight, man," Eddie said.

Easier said than done, Cecil thought, as he hung up the phone.

As Darrell and Serena walked down the long, winding driveway outside Cecil's house, Serena said, "You mentioned before that you weren't sure if you should pass yourself off as Cecil today. I'm kinda thinking you shouldn't."

"I decided I won't. I think it's better that I admit I'm Cecil's brother. That'll probably be my best chance to get info about him."

When they reached the sidewalk, Darrell paused. "Which way?" he asked.

"This way." Serena pointed to the right.

"Okay."

Pivoting on his heel, Darrell headed the way Serena had suggested. The first house to the right had a long curved driveway, much like Cecil's. While Cecil's house was a pale peach, this one was a pale yellow. Both houses were large with stunning landscaping, and Serena couldn't help wondering why this house didn't have a gate.

Still, as she and Darrell headed up the driveway, she was wary. People who owned houses like this were routinely paranoid about trespassers; she hoped they didn't react badly to seeing two strangers on their doorstep.

At least no dog barked crazily when Serena and Darrell reached the door. Darrell rang the bell.

Several seconds later, a woman who looked to be in her early sixties answered the door. Quelling Serena's fears, the woman smiled brightly when she saw them. "Hey, there," she practically sang. "What brings you by today?"

Darrell smiled back. "Hello. Um, you probably think I'm my brother. He lives next door." When the woman gave him a confused look, Darrell added, "I'm his twin."

"Oh." She chuckled. "Well, how nice to meet you."

"Likewise," Darrell said. "Look, I don't mean to bother you, but I'm wondering if you can tell me when you last saw my brother."

The woman pursed her lips, deep in thought. "Hmm. Not for a couple weeks, at least. Why? Is something wrong?"

"No," Darrell responded without hesitation. "I thought I'd surprise him with a visit, but now that I'm here, he isn't. It'd be just my luck to show up here and he's gone out of town, touring the world or something. He's got a lot more free time than I do." Darrell chortled. "Does he by any chance get you to watch the house when he's gone?"

The woman shook her head. "I'm afraid I can't help you."

"Well, thanks anyway."

Darrell and Serena got the same response at the next two houses, and at two houses across the street. Yes, the neighbors had seen Cecil around, but no, they didn't know where he might be. And no, they didn't water his plants when he was away.

"I don't know, Darrell," Serena said. "This isn't getting us anywhere. With Cecil having a condo on the beach, maybe he didn't spend much time here."

"Let's try a couple more houses on the other side of the street, then call it a day."

Again, Darrell led the way, and Serena followed. At the front door of the next house they got to, Darrell rang the bell. They waited.

As he was reaching for the bell again, the door swung open. A gorgeous petite black woman, dressed in a white silk robe, appeared.

Her eyes registered first shock, then anger, as they narrowed on Darrell.

"Hello," Darrell said.

"Hello?" the young woman replied, then guffawed. Her eyes darted to Serena, then back to Darrell. "How *dare* you?"

*Oh, no.*

"Let me—"

But before Darrell had a chance to say a word, the woman drew her hand back and slapped him across the face.

# Chapter 12

*Son of a bitch!* Darrell thought, his hand flying to his face. *Not again!*

"I can't believe you'd have the *nerve* to show your face here," the woman hissed. "And with . . ." She looked Serena up and down with distaste. "With some *tramp*!"

Serena's hands flew to her hips. "Tramp?" she replied, taking a step forward. This from a woman who answered the door in her lingerie? "Lady, you don't even—"

"Wait a second," Darrell interjected. He gripped Serena by her upper arm and pulled her back. Serena's eyes flashed fire at him, but he gave her an expression that told her to let him handle this. Then he looked at the woman again. "Please, just give me a minute to explain."

"Explain? Oh, that's beautiful. There is no explanation for what you did to me. I will never, and I mean *never*, believe another word that comes out of your mouth." She paused briefly, pain filling her eyes. "How could you treat me the way you did? After everything we meant to each other . . ."

"You really ought to listen to what he has to say," Serena stated in a straightforward tone, making a marked effort to curtail her anger. After all, the woman's wrath wasn't really directed to her or Darrell, but to Cecil.

"You shut up," the woman snapped, wagging a finger at Serena. "You have nothing to do with this."

Serena gaped at the woman, then at Darrell, before once again turning her stunned face back to the woman. The anger returned full force, and Serena squirmed, trying to break free of Darrell's grip. But he held her tighter, pulling her backward as he took a few steps away from the door.

"Down, Slugger," Darrell said.

"Did you hear how she talked to me?" Serena protested. "That is rude to the nth degree—"

"What, you want a piece of me?" the woman taunted.

Serena was so livid, her nostrils actually flared.

"Let's go," Darrell said.

"She slaps you in the face, insults me, and you don't even want to tell her the truth?" Serena asked, appalled.

"You think she's going to listen to reason?" Darrell retorted.

"That's right, Cecil," the woman said. "Take your tramp and get off my property. Before I call the police."

"You don't even know me," Serena yelled over her shoulder as Darrell dragged her away.

"Forget it, Serena," Darrell told her.

But Serena didn't want to forget it. She'd never met

anyone so rude in her entire life! Tramp? No one had ever called her a tramp before, and she sure as hell didn't appreciate it now.

"Don't come back," the woman continued. "Oh, and you should be happy to know that I lost the baby."

At those words, Darrell halted. If Serena wanted to break free of his grip, she easily could have now. But she no longer cared about telling the woman a thing or two about her attitude. She was too absorbed in watching the grief-stricken expression on Darrell's face.

"What did you say?" Darrell asked.

"I lost the baby. You can call my doctor if you still don't believe I was pregnant." She squared her jaw. "So now, there's nothing more tying me to you." The woman's voice trembled as she spoke the last words, and whirling around, she hurried into the house. A moment later, the door slammed shut.

"Oh, my God," Darrell muttered. A sick feeling swam in his gut. His brother had gotten this woman pregnant? For Christ's sake, hadn't he learned a damn thing during his thirty-one years? Cecil knew firsthand what life had been like with an absentee father, so why the hell would he want to pass on that legacy?

Darrell had no doubt that with the lifestyle Cecil led, his brother wouldn't be a part of any child's life he might have. Hell, a kid needed a father. Cecil was a big boy and he knew better. If he was going to get involved with different women, how could he do so and not take better precautions?

"Darrell?"

Serena's voice was soft and pain-filled, and Darrell's gaze fell to her.

"I don't know about you," she began, "but I've had enough of this. At least for now."

"Me too."

Darrell took one last look at the woman's house before turning and heading to the sidewalk. Serena fell into step beside him. But seconds later, when he rounded the corner to Cecil's driveway, Serena veered away from him, hustling to the Viper.

It didn't take a rocket scientist to figure out what she was feeling. Even he couldn't believe how much of an SOB his brother apparently was. The reality was clearly too much for Serena to cope with.

Serena yanked on the passenger side door, but when it didn't open, she slammed a palm against the Viper's hood. Then she dropped her head on the roof.

A lump formed in Darrell's chest the size of Key West. Slowly, he approached her. "I'm sorry," was all he could say.

"Open the car door," she said.

"Serena."

Determined eyes met his. "Open it."

"Serena, I know this is hard. My brother's turning out to be a bigger slime ball than I ever imagined. God, all I can do is apologize."

"Pregnant?"

Darrell could only shake his head with disbelief and chagrin. "As unfortunate as it seems, it's probably best that she lost the baby."

Serena's eyebrows shot up as disbelief crossed her face. "How can you say that? A child is precious—"

"And deserves to be raised by two loving parents. A kid needs a father, Serena. Cecil is a prime example of what can happen without one."

Serena didn't say anything, just slumped against the car. She wanted to tell Darrell to take her back to the condo so she could retrieve her car. When she'd agreed to join him in his search for Cecil, she had no idea she'd learn he was a first rate pig. Maybe the search for Cecil and her family's heirloom simply wasn't worth her pride.

She drew in a few calming breaths, and as she accepted the extent of Cecil's deception, she rethought her position. She'd learned the worst about Cecil the day she'd discovered the necklace gone. Anything else—like him being involved with a thousand other women—wouldn't be worse than that. She could only thank the Lord that she hadn't given him her heart and body as well as her material possessions.

Her pride wasn't an issue. She'd do whatever it took to get her family heirloom back. How could she not? God willing, they'd find Cecil by the end of the day—and she could have the satisfaction of wringing his neck before she headed back to work tomorrow morning.

Serena looked at Darrell. He wore an expression filled with disappointment and sadness. More pain filled her heart—for Darrell. Yes, this was hard for her because she'd been lied to, scammed, and robbed, but how hard must this be for Darrell? She tried to imagine what it would be like if she learned that her sister was a criminal. The thought was incomprehensible.

Serena pushed away from the Viper and started for the front door of the house. Quietly, Darrell followed her.

As he unlocked the door, he said, "I'd be happy to take you home, if you want. I give you my word that I'll contact you the moment I find Cecil."

It was a tempting offer, yet Serena said, "No. I said I'd help, and that's what I intend to do."

"God, Serena. I feel bad, and I'm not in your shoes. If what we've learned so far is any indication of what we're going to find out, this search is going to be full of disappointments for you in terms of how much of an asshole my brother was to you."

"I'm over it."

"Are you? I saw your reaction to that woman's news that she was pregnant."

"I was surprised, that's all."

"You don't have to play tough, Serena. I know this isn't easy."

"What do you want me to do? Tell you how much of a jerk I think your brother is?" She gave him a pointed look. "I'm sure you'd appreciate that."

Darrell shrugged. "If that's what you need to do."

"Come on. I know you have a sense of right and wrong, but Cecil is your brother. I wouldn't want anyone badmouthing my sister to me, no matter what she did."

"I'm sure your sister wouldn't do what Cecil did."

"Never."

"Exactly. You obviously had a Cosby family life. Mine was the exact opposite of that. Yeah, Cecil's my brother, but given everything he's done, I have no right to get upset with anyone who badmouths him."

"Cecil's already done what he's done. Going home and moping about it won't help me get my necklace back."

"No, but—"

"No buts," Serena said. "What do you want to do next?"

Darrell wasn't sure why, but he was happy that Serena

refused to leave. He wasn't quite ready to say good-bye to her.

"How about we take a break?" he suggested. "Get some food."

"That's a good idea. Coconut Grove is a really neat place. Have you been here before?"

"No."

"Then let's get a bite to eat at Coco Walk. I can also show you my store. Well . . . the store I'd thought was going to be mine. Maybe it's still available."

"Are you sure that's a good idea?" Darrell asked. "I mean, what if it isn't available any longer? Why torture yourself?"

"There'll be another storefront, Darrell." Serena spoke with confidence. "Seeing it again will make me more determined to succeed. I *will* open an antiques store one day."

Darrell liked Serena's spirit. She carried on in the face of adversity, refused to fail when others in a similar situation would have thrown in the towel. "All right."

"Let's drive closer to the downtown area, park, then do the tour of Coco Walk and area. It's very scenic."

Darrell agreed, and after a quick stop in the house to grab his wallet and Serena's purse, they were on their way.

"Wow," Darrell said as he cruised along Grand Avenue. "You're right. This is beautiful."

"This is the heart of Coconut Grove," Serena explained. "If you hug the right, that will take you to a marina. You should see the boats down there."

"You want me to go that way?"

"No. Stay straight. See that on the left?"

Darrell checked out the three-story structure with

walkways and escalators that led to various shops and eateries. "Yeah?"

"That's Coco Walk. It's like a city block within a block. It's filled with shops and restaurants from casual to up-scale. There's even a platform in the center, where there's nightly entertainment. Salsa dancers, Latin bands. That sort of thing."

"Sounds fun." Not that Darrell knew the meaning of the word. This trip to Miami to search for his brother was as close as he'd come to taking a vacation in years. "Where should I park?"

"Whoa," Serena said, pointing to the left. "That guy's leaving."

Indeed, a man in a Mercedes was pulling out of a spot by a meter. When the man drove off, Darrell spun the Viper around and easily slipped into the spot.

He parked and got out. By the time he rounded the car to the sidewalk, Serena was putting money in the meter.

"That should do it," she said.

"Thanks," Darrell told her.

"No problem." She secured her purse strap over her shoulder. She and Darrell started toward Coco Walk.

"You want to eat first," Serena began, "or do you want to see the store I was telling you about?"

"Let's check out the store."

"It's off the main road, but still in a high traffic area." They strolled past Coco Walk. At the light, Serena started across the street and Darrell followed her. A crowd of peo-ple walked between them, and once they hustled by, Dar-rell reached for Serena's hand.

"Lot of people out here," Darrell commented.

"Uh huh. I'm telling you, this is a great location for a store. For any business."

Serena stopped walking when she reached the sidewalk. Three roads diverged at this intersection—the one that housed Coco Walk, the one that led to the marina, and another smaller road that led to fewer attractions.

Darrell looked in the direction of marina. "Which way?"

Their hands still joined, Serena twisted her body toward the smaller street. "This way."

She headed down the less populated road. Mature palm trees added to the beauty and serenity of the street and its upscale boutiques and outdoor restaurant patios.

"Quick," Serena said, pulling Darrell across the street when no cars approached. As their feet hit the sidewalk, Serena abruptly stopped. Her hand tightened around Darrell's.

"This is it."

Though she could have released his hand as she scurried up the walkway to the store, she didn't. And Darrell found he didn't want her to.

"It's small," Serena said, "but it was all I needed." Her eyes were wide with excitement as she looked up at him. "On the left, that's where I planned to have my pottery display. I got some wonderful California pottery at an estate sale. It's not quite antique—something has to be a hundred years old to be officially antique—but it's highly collectible, and since the Great Depression, the value of the pottery has gone up substantially.

"And on the right," Serena pointed in that direction, "I figured I would have a display of antique dolls."

"Dolls?"

Serena glanced at Darrell. "Oh, yeah. You wouldn't believe how many different kinds of dolls are out there. And let me tell you, there are some serious doll collectors. Fanatical, almost." Serena chuckled.

"I never would have guessed."

"Oh, yeah. Porcelain dolls, rag dolls." She paused. "You see that little ledge right there?" She pointed to a spot near the base of the window. "I've got this set of turn-of-the-century Victorian quilt pillows. Just gorgeous, and in immaculate shape. They would be perfect right there, along with this fabulous American quilt I found at a flea market."

"Where do you have all this stuff?" Darrell asked in wonder.

Serena spun around. Her face literally shone as she gazed up at him. "I have a small storage unit with most of the items," she explained. "Other pieces are in my apartment."

"How long have you been collecting antiques?"

"Oh, at least a few years. Well, that's when I started seriously, with the intent of opening a store."

Darrell found himself smiling. Serena's excitement was contagious.

"Gosh, I'm probably boring you with all this." She stepped away from the store and started down the walkway toward the main sidewalk. Darrell grabbed her hand, stopping her.

Perplexed eyes met his.

"Tell me more," he said.

Serena's nose wrinkled as she gave him a tentative look. "You sure I'm not boring you?"

"I love to hear you talk about this. Your whole face lights up."

"Really?"

"Yeah." Pause. "Is the ring antique?"

"This?" Serena extended her hand, offering the platinum ring for Darrell's inspection.

"Uh huh." Darrell took her hand in his and ran a thumb over the ring that graced her middle finger.

"Yes, this is from the Edwardian era."

"Hmm."

"What?" To her surprise, she sounded breathless.

"You have beautiful eyes, Serena."

Suddenly self-conscious, Serena pulled her hand back and brought it to her face. "You think so?"

"Definitely."

As her gaze held Darrell's a moment longer, Serena's lips curled in a slight smile. Then she turned back to the store. "Oh, Darrell. This place would be so perfect." She placed both hands on the glass. "Even the floor—" Stopping short, Serena suddenly whimpered.

"What?" Darrell asked.

"Oh, darn. The store's been leased."

Disappointment tickled his stomach. "How do you know?"

"Right there." A frown cast a shadow over Serena's face as she glanced over her shoulder at Darrell. Taking a step backward, she pointed downward. "I can't believe we didn't see this."

Darrell followed her gaze. A cardboard sign at the bottom of the glass door read: BETTY'S BOOKS COMING SOON.

"Damn," he muttered. Again, he felt bad for her. And guilty for what Cecil had done.

Serena's petite shoulders rose and fell. "This was such a great location," she said wistfully. "The necklace, my family heirloom, I wasn't planning to sell it. But because it's worth so much, I was able to use it as collateral. That was Cecil's idea, and it was a good one. That's why I had it appraised . . ." Her voice trailed off. "Oh well. There'll be another store."

Darrell placed a hand on the back of her neck and gently squeezed it. "Yes, there will be."

At his touch, Serena sagged against him, resting her back against his chest. Darrell trailed both hands down her arms.

"I'll make this right for you, Serena."

She didn't say anything, merely turned her face into his chest and sighed.

Something tugged at Darrell's heart. Had his brother heard her talk so passionately about her dream? And if so, how could he have taken it from her?

Well, there was one thing Darrell knew: he'd do whatever was necessary to get Serena's necklace back, even if that meant traveling halfway across the world. Serena didn't deserve what Cecil had done; he *would* make this situation right for her.

Serena pulled her head back and grinned at him. "Ready to eat?"

"If you are," he said.

"I am."

"Mmm." Darrell's eyes went heavenward as he took a bite of the huge, juicy burger.

"I swear, this place makes the *best* burgers," Serena stated.

"I haven't had a burger in ages. Probably because for a while, I was eating so many of them."

"Why, no home cooked meals?"

"Who has time?" Darrell asked. "I spend so much time at work."

Serena finished chewing her mouthful of food, washed it down with some soda, then said, "Speaking of home and work . . . did you leave someone behind in Orlando?"

Darrell swallowed. "You mean a wife?"

"Well, I'd be surprised if you were seriously involved with anyone," Serena said, giving him a sheepish smile.

"No," Darrell replied succinctly. "I'm not seeing any-one."

"Oh," Serena said, her tone cheerful. She couldn't deny that she was happy to learn there was no one special in Darrell's life.

Darrell suddenly reached for her face, and Serena's heartbeat sped up. With the pad of his thumb, he wiped something from her chin.

"What?" Serena asked.

"A bit of mustard. That's all."

"Oh." Serena dabbed at her mouth with her napkin.

Darrell stared at her a moment longer, enamored with her bashful look. This morning, she'd shown him a com-pletely different side, one that was sexually confident, but here she was, actually blushing because he'd wiped a bit of mustard from her face.

It was that whole demure quality coupled with the wild side. And damn if it wasn't a turn-on.

Darrell took another bite of his burger. Serena picked at her fries, surreptitiously watching him watch her. Just what game were they playing?

Her mind drifted to this morning, to how hot and bothered the two of them had gotten. How far would things have gone if she hadn't put a stop to it? For the first time in her life, she'd been tempted, *really* tempted, to throw caution to the wind and let her emotions control her. That was so completely out of character for her, and she couldn't help thinking, *Why Darrell?*

Perhaps she was looking for a complex answer where a simple one made the most sense. Maybe the passion that had exploded between her and Darrell was the normal, biological result of a man and woman spending time alone together. Since she'd met him at the police station, they'd practically been joined at the hip. She'd never spent this much time alone with a man before, so she hadn't known what to expect. But it was now crystal clear to her that the question shouldn't have been *if* sparks would fly between her and Darrell, but *when*.

It was simply a matter of physics.

And knowing that was the first step in making sure she controlled her emotions, and not the other way around.

Deliberately making herself think of something else, Serena asked, "So, you like your job?"

"I'd better. I spend enough time there."

"You said you're a manager at a hotel?"

"Actually"—Darrell wiped a napkin across his mouth—"I also own it." Having spent time with her, he now trusted Serena with the truth. She wasn't a gold digger. "It's a small hotel, a bed and breakfast, actually, and I oversee everything. It's like a wife. Demanding and not always rewarding."

"Ouch. Were you married?"

"No, but I've had friends who were. My parents were . . . until my mother got bored."

"What do you mean?"

"Nothing."

"Your parents divorced?"

"Don't fifty percent of all couples? Hell, it's more than that nowadays, isn't it?"

"Not everyone gets divorced," Serena pointed out.

Darrell reached for his soda. "All I know is that everyone I've ever known who's gotten married has ended up miserable—whether or not they stayed together. So why bother?"

"That's pretty narrow-minded."

"It's the truth."

Serena frowned. "How can you say that when you haven't even been married?"

"I almost did get married," Darrell replied. "Thank God I saw the light."

A painful knot formed in Serena's stomach. Memories of how close she'd come to giving herself to Darrell now taunted her. God, what a mistake she would have made. Not only would she have let her emotions control her, she would have given herself to a man who didn't even believe in marriage!

She continued, "So your relationship failed and now the institution of marriage is bad?"

"You're a woman. You won't understand."

"Excuse me?"

Darrell shrugged. "Women always have this ideal about marriage, which in theory, is great. In reality, it's a fairytale."

Serena felt annoyance with each of Darrell's answers. She didn't know why they bothered her, but they did.

"Well, my parents happened to have had a wonderful marriage," Serena replied, a tad defensively.

"Had," Darrell responded. "That's the key word."

"They died."

Darrell's eyes first widened, then contrition passed over his face. "I'm sorry. God, I'm an idiot. I shouldn't have—"

"They were always happy," Serena continued. "Right till the end." Remembering the loss of her parents always made her throat grow thick with emotion. "The only consolation is that they were together at the end. I think that's how they would have wanted it."

"I'm sorry."

Serena crumpled her napkin into a tight ball. "So am I. But because of them, I know that true love exists. It's not a fantasy. And I don't want to settle for anything less."

It was amazing to Darrell that Serena had ended up dating his brother, a man who balked at commitment with the best of the players. Maybe she'd been susceptible to believing she might have a future with him because she'd been blinded by her own ideal of the perfect relationship.

All Darrell knew was that for him, the reality of marriage wasn't a pleasant one.

He'd been willing, once. In fact, he'd wanted to get married, settle down, and have a family. But thank God he'd come to his senses. When he'd learned that Jessica had been siphoning money from the bed and breakfast's restaurant till shortly before their wedding, he'd learned that she was more interested in his wallet than in him. When Darrell had confronted her about the theft, having caught her on camera after he suspected something weird was going on, she'd had the nerve to call him cheap and had said that if he'd loved her, she never would have had to resort to stealing *their* money. He had no idea where she got the idea that his money was hers, considering they weren't married yet, but more than that, Darrell had been appalled with her gall. Hell, everything she'd asked for, he'd given her—within reason. Her major complaint had been that he'd gotten her a two-carat rock instead of the five-carat one she'd fancied.

In hindsight, he wondered if she had ever planned to marry him, or if her plan all along had been to steal from him, then leave him before he caught on. Being a sucker, he didn't have her arrested. And when she refused to give the rock back that he'd bought for her, he hadn't pressed the issue. He'd simply been happy to get her out of his life, realizing it was costing him less in the long run.

In a way, he could empathize with Serena falling for Cecil. Jessica had been outgoing, seemingly generous, and caring—while they'd gotten to know each other. She'd cared about everything he did, or so she'd said. After working long hours as a legal assistant, she found time to come to his workplace and put in hours there—all because she'd said she couldn't get enough of him.

Darrell had been flattered. And gullible.

Of course, he'd no doubt easily fallen for Jessica because she was beautiful, but it was that very beauty that had given her the false impression that he should have worshipped the ground she walked on.

After ending their engagement, Darrell had sworn off love and marriage. Jessica had turned out to be just like his mother—out simply for what a man could give her financially. Those were the kind of women he'd met over the years, probably because he mostly met women at work, and his position at the bed-and-breakfast wasn't secret. Once women found out what he did, they wanted to get into his wallet.

So much for love.

Maybe for some, it existed, but he hadn't found it. And he certainly wasn't about to hold his breath.

"That's strange," Darrell said, frowning when he slipped the key into the lock at Cecil's house. "I locked the door, didn't I?"

Instantly alarmed, Serena's eyes flew to his. "Of course you locked the door."

Darrell extended a hand in front of Serena, guiding her behind him. "Stay back."

"Darrell—"

"Stay back."

Darrell opened the door slowly, then peered inside. A quick glance at Serena, and he stepped into the house.

She held her breath as she watched him disappear. She didn't like this, not one bit. If someone was inside the house . . .

God help them, who could it be? Cecil, perhaps? Or had someone broken in? And if someone *had* broken in . . .

Though seconds ticked by, it seemed like hours had passed without a peep from Darrell. God, was he okay? Serena could no longer stand the waiting. Silently praying that Darrell was all right, she hurried into the house.

# Chapter 13

"Oh, my God!" Serena exclaimed. She froze when she saw that the house they'd left intact over an hour ago was now in complete disarray.

Darrell whipped around when he heard her. "I told you to stay back!"

Serena flinched at Darrell's angry outburst, and she felt a sinking feeling in her stomach. "You didn't come out . . . I-I was worried."

"Do you realize the kind of danger you could have put yourself in if the intruder had still been in here? Damn it, Serena, I came in here to make sure this place was safe."

"I . . ." She promptly shut her mouth.

"Serena, I'm sorry," Darrell said, his tone softer. He started toward her from where he stood in the middle of the living room. "I didn't mean to yell. It's just that I'm so frustrated. I have no clue what's going on." He stopped a couple feet in front of her. "Damn, if someone had still been in here, and you'd been hurt . . . I'd never forgive myself."

"I chose to walk through that door. If anything happened to me, it would be my fault."

"You're with me, Serena. It's my job to keep you safe."

Serena was bewildered by the conviction she saw on Darrell's face. My God, he truly *did* feel responsible for her. Was it merely a sense of obligation, or was there something more to his concern?

The very thought that he might care about her well-being for a deeper reason made her stomach quiver.

But perhaps she was reading more into his motives. He'd traveled from Orlando to Miami on what was turning out to be a wild goose chase to find his brother, and from everything he'd said, Serena got the impression that he felt responsible for everything Cecil did wrong.

Why? She couldn't help wondering if that sense of responsibility had been drummed into him from the time he was a child.

And Serena's heart suddenly ached for him. Darrell needn't carry such a burden.

Darrell glanced around the immediate area. "Well, I don't think whoever broke in is still here."

"We should call the police," Serena said.

"I want to check the place out first."

Serena wondered what that would possibly tell him other than the obvious. Someone had clearly come in here and gone berserk. The place was an absolute mess, with the sofas ripped, coffee tables upturned, and paintings pulled off the walls. Serena hadn't seen damage this bad since Hurricane Andrew had hit South Florida.

"Stay with me," Darrell said. "I don't want you alone for a second."

Darrell's words once again made Serena's stomach quiver. There was something about his tone and his expression that made her feel he would do anything to protect her.

Slowly Serena moved to Darrell's side. She took hold of his upper arm and instantly felt safer. His arm was strong, beautifully sculpted, and as he cautiously headed down the hallway, Serena remembered exactly how thrilling it had felt to have those arms wrapped around her, a thought that was totally inappropriate under the circumstances.

It was hard to believe that just hours earlier, Serena had been so ensnared in a web of desire that she might not have been able to stop Darrell if he'd wanted to take her on the living room floor. Now, that living room floor was in complete disarray.

The memory of her lust was disrupted by a moment of panic. What if the intruder had entered the house while she and Darrell had been in each other's arms? What if he'd had a weapon?

Serena tightened her fingers around Darrell's brawny arm. Sensing her fear, he paused, then placed his hand over hers. He gave her a reassuring look, and Serena said, "I'm okay."

Every room in the house looked the same way the living room did. Beds were overturned, drawers were pulled out and their contents dumped.

"How could this have happened since we left here?" Serena asked. "I mean, was it a coincidence that someone came here and trashed the place today? Or does this mean someone is watching us?"

Darrell moved down the hallway to another room. "You didn't notice anyone following us?"

"After that SUV, no."

Another bedroom door squeaked in protest as Darrell slowly opened it. "This room's been trashed, too."

Serena peered around Darrell's body into the room. She shook her head at the site of the once nicely kept room in a state of utter chaos. "You don't think it was . . . that psycho neighbor your brother was involved with?"

Darrell didn't know what to think. "I can't see someone as small as her tearing apart a place like this."

"She was pretty angry. You never know."

When they moved to the next room, Darrell uttered, "Aw, shit."

Serena's heart dropped to her stomach. "What?"

"The computer," Darrell said, his eyes scanning the overturned desk. "It's gone."

"Gone?"

Darrell stepped away from Serena and into the room. Heading toward the desk, he carefully made his way over the strewn items that littered the floor. In the middle of the room, he dropped onto his haunches and began sifting through the loose papers.

Serena sank to the floor beside him. "What are you looking for?"

"That paper. The one that had the auction information. It was the only real lead we had to finding your necklace."

Moaning softly, Serena lifted a sheet of paper, then tossed it aside. Then another, and another. Darrell did the same.

"It's not here," Serena said, anxiety lacing her voice. "It's not here."

Frustrated, she attempted to throw the piece of paper she held, and when it merely fluttered, she batted it to the ground.

"Serena—"

She fell from her knees to her butt, covering her face with both hands.

Darrell took her in his arms and pulled her body to his. But she shrugged him off, moving out of his embrace. She crawled a foot away, then sat and wrapped her arms around her knees, pulling her knees to her chest. A knot formed in Darrell's stomach as he watched her. God, he felt helpless. He didn't like her pushing him away, but he understood her frustration. What good were condolences and empty promises? He could tell her he empathized with her, he could apologize until he turned green, but there was only one thing Darrell could do for Serena that would make this situation better: find his brother. And soon.

Serena took off her glasses and rubbed the heels of her hands over both eyes, then put the glasses back on. "You don't remember the name of the auction company?"

"I only saw the word 'auction.' Serena, I'm probably the only person alive who's pretty much clueless when it comes to computers." He paused. "I'd figured we'd take a look at it when we came back, maybe even see if we could access Cecil's e-mail account for new messages."

"And now the computer's gone."

Slowly, Darrell stood. Placing his hands on his hips, he did a full turn around the room. "This is bad. Damn it, Cecil. What have you gotten yourself into this time?"

Serena stared at Darrell, but he looked past her to the room's window. Until now, she hadn't truly considered the big picture. Yes, she'd realized that there was some kind of danger, and that she and Darrell had gotten caught up in it. But until this moment, her eyes had always been on the prize—retrieving her family heirloom.

She hadn't considered the very real threat to Cecil, perhaps his life. Did someone actually want to *kill* him?

She'd been somewhat selfish, she suddenly realized, wanting to help Darrell find his brother only so that she could get her necklace back. She hadn't shown any sensitivity to Darrell's plight over his brother's well-being.

She'd wanted to dismiss the SUV that had run them off the road as an irate driver, because it had been easier to deny that there was a real threat to her and Darrell's safety. But now, given the condition of the house, she couldn't help wondering how serious this situation might be.

"You think someone wants to . . . *really* hurt Cecil?"

"Hell, yes," Darrell replied, spinning around to face her. "You think someone came in here and slashed and trashed everything, then took the computer, just because they were irritated with him? Sure, they were looking for something, but the way they went at this place—there's no doubt they also wanted to leave Cecil a message."

Serena lifted the phone's receiver. "There's no dial tone. I forgot—his line was disconnected. We'll have to use the car phone to call the police."

Darrell righted the desk chair, then slowly lowered himself onto it. "I need to think."

Serena didn't question him. After a moment, she said, "Give me a second."

Darrell looked at her with alarm. "Where are you going?"

"The bathroom."

Serena headed out of the bedroom and down the hallway. Inside the bathroom, her eyes immediately went to the mirror.

"Darrell." Her mouth formed his name as she scanned the mirror, but no sound came out. Then, flinging open the door, she fled from the bathroom. "Darrell!"

Darrell charged out of the bedroom at full speed and nearly collided with Serena as she ran to the door. He halted to avoid slamming into her, but immediately reached for her, gripping her by the shoulders. "What?"

"The bathroom," she managed between deep breaths. "There's a message for Cecil."

Darrell hesitated for only a second before bolting to the bathroom. Serena was fast on his heels. As soon as he crossed the threshold to the lavish lavatory, he saw what Serena was talking about. On the large mirror, in bright red lipstick were the words:

*Cecil, you can run but you can't hide.*
*I gave you a chance, but you didn't take it,*
*and now you're gonna pay the hard way.*
*ASSHOLE!*

Darrell took a step toward the mirror. "Gee, the person forgot to sign this note," he said sardonically. Then he turned to Serena. "Yeah, this is bad."

"Darrell, we have to call the police." When Darrell didn't respond, Serena continued, "You said yourself, this is worse than we expected."

"I'm not sure that's going to help."

"Why not?"

"Well, for one, we have no clue who's doing this. Two, the

police will probably be more interested in taking Cecil's butt to jail than in investigating who might have broken in here." Darrell balled a fist against his forehead. "And now I'm wondering if Cecil is still in Miami. I thought for sure he was, but if he's in serious trouble, he may have left the country."

"Left the country?" Serena repeated. "Where would he go?"

"He's got a villa in Montego Bay."

"*Montego Bay?* As in Jamaica?"

"Yes."

"Good grief," Serena muttered, leaning her back against one of the bathroom walls. "A condo on South Beach. A house in Coconut Grove. A villa in Montego Bay. Does it ever end?"

"Those are the three homes he has, as far as I know. The villa isn't that big, at least the way he describes it, but hell . . ."

Serena dropped her head and closed her eyes, tuning Darrell out. She didn't want to hear another word about Cecil's third property. All she wanted to do right now was hide from the world. How had she ever thought Cecil was a nice guy?

Perhaps Darrell was right; she shouldn't blame herself. Con artists were good at what they did or they'd never succeed at scamming anyone. Serena had never met anyone like him before and hadn't been prepared for that level of deception.

Still, knowing that she couldn't logically blame herself didn't make her feel better. God, she'd give anything to turn back the clock and erase the day she'd ever met Cecil.

Yet if she'd never met Cecil, she would never have met Darrell.

That thought troubled her, and she stole a glimpse at Darrell. Her heart fluttered. No, she didn't regret meeting him in the least.

Even if he was a constant reminder that she'd been a very big fool where Cecil Montford was concerned.

It seemed that every step of the way on her search for Cecil, she was bound to uncover something that would further humiliate her and throw her total bad judgment in her face. And if Darrell was right, if someone was threatening Cecil's life, what was the likelihood that they'd ever find him—at least, before he wanted to be found? And by then, she highly doubted he'd still have the necklace.

Once again, she wondered if this search for Cecil was worth her pride.

"What are you thinking?" Darrell asked.

"Just wondering if someone is following us. First that car running us off the road, now this house is trashed. I doubt it's a coincidence."

"That's exactly why I'm more convinced than ever that you shouldn't be a part of this search. I don't want you hurt."

"And what about you?" Serena challenged.

"Cecil's my brother."

"Your *twin*. How smart is it for you to be playing detective when you look exactly like him? If anyone's asking to get hurt, it's you. At least no one knows who I am. *I'm* the one who should play detective, not you."

"Out of the question."

"Why not?" Serena challenged. "I'm the better person to ask around about your brother."

"Absolutely not."

"It makes sense."

"No."

Serena and Darrell stared each other down in a silent challenge, neither wanting to back down from his position.

After a moment, Darrell headed out of the bathroom, as if the conversation was over.

Serena followed him, saying, "I'm not the one they're looking for."

Darrell stopped. "But you've been seen with me, right? So yeah, if what's happened isn't a coincidence, they know what you look like."

"I'm still the best bet—"

"You heard what I said." Darrell started down the hallway again.

Serena threw her hands in the air as she followed him. "What, you make a decision that affects both of us and that's just it?" She waited for Darrell to respond, but he ignored her, walking to the living room. "Great, now you won't talk to me?"

Darrell turned suddenly. "I am not going to let you put yourself at risk."

Serena's heart was zapped with a bolt of electricity as she looked at the firm set of Darrell's jaw. She almost wanted to ask *Why*, just to see if he'd tell her he didn't want her at risk because he cared.

She'd been able to say what was on her mind this morning. How hard would it be to do that now? All she had to do was open her mouth, say the word . . .

She opened her mouth, the question on the tip of her tongue. "I don't want you at risk, either." No, that's not what she'd wanted to say. Where had the guts she'd had this morning gone? "Obviously, if you're gonna spend time at Cecil's homes, whoever is out to hurt him can get to you." Gosh, her mouth had a mind of its own and didn't want to cooperate at all! "So, I'm thinking . . . we should go to my place. They don't know where I live." *And I can see if there are any more sparks between us . . .*

Darrell gave her an intense look, and Serena wondered if he could read her thoughts in her eyes.

After a long moment, he said, "I think that's a good idea. Are you ready?"

"No time like the present."

## Chapter 14

"Make yourself at home," Serena told Darrell, once they entered her first-floor apartment. "I'm gonna call my sister. She'll be beside herself with worry if she doesn't hear from me soon."

"Sure."

Serena kicked off her shoes and trudged into the apartment, bending to pick up a couple of magazines as she made her way to the living room. On the sofa, she found one of her bras and quickly scooped it up. Had she known she'd have company, she would have cleaned the place before she'd left.

Serena did a final sweep of the area, satisfied that there wasn't anything in the living room that shouldn't be there; at least, not anything that would embarrass her. She started off, then paused. "You want a drink or something?"

Darrell lowered himself onto the sofa. "I'm cool. Go ahead and call your sister."

"Okay." Serena hustled out of the living room and went to her bedroom, where she closed the door behind her. She threw the magazines and her bra onto the foot of the bed, then sat on the bed's edge. She reached for the phone on her night table and punched in her sister's number.

"Thank God!" Kiana exclaimed when she answered the phone. "Where have you been?"

Serena chortled. Clearly, her sister had checked her caller ID box before answering the phone. "Hey, sis."

"I thought you were going to call me ages ago."

"I was." Serena sighed. "It's been a long and interesting day, that's for sure." Serena explained what Darrell had found at the house about the online auction, how the house had been ransacked once they'd left, and that they were now at her apartment.

"Oh, my God. Serena, tell me you now realize this is serious business."

"I guess I can't deny that any longer."

"What did the police say?"

Serena hesitated. "Well . . . nothing, really."

"What do you mean 'nothing really'? You called them, didn't you?"

"Darrell didn't want to call the police," Serena replied matter-of-factly.

"What?" Kiana moaned her displeasure. "Serena, don't you think that's a *little* fishy?"

"Actually, I think he has a good point. The police are only interested in arresting Cecil, at which point, who knows if I'll get the necklace back. I mean, what if he's sold it to someone and he's the only one who can get it back? If he's locked up, that's not going to do me any good."

"I don't like this, Serena. Not one bit."

"I don't like it either," Serena conceded, "but what am I supposed to do? Kiana, I have to get the necklace back."

"You need to let the police handle it."

"If I thought they were going to make the necklace a priority, I would. Don't get me wrong. I'm not against calling the police. But I agree with Darrell that we need a few more answers first."

"And if the necklace is gone for good?"

"I can't allow myself to think about that."

"The necklace isn't worth all this."

Every time Serena considered that exact thought, she dismissed it. The necklace symbolized her hopes and dreams, and if she gave up trying to find it, she might as well give up her plans for the future.

"I'll be fine. I'm with Darrell—"

"And that bothers me, too. The man isn't only Cecil's brother, he's his twin. Who's he really looking out for— you, or Cecil?"

Kiana's words gave Serena pause. Blood was thicker than water, as the saying went. Darrell's loyalties un- doubtedly lay with his brother. Yet Serena didn't doubt for one minute that Darrell wanted her to retrieve the necklace as much as she did.

After a long moment, she said, "He has nothing to gain from me."

"Who knows? If he's anything like his brother, maybe he'll want the necklace, too."

"No," Serena said confidently. "That's definitely not the case."

"If I were you, I wouldn't trust a member of that fam- ily as far as I could throw him."

"Like I told you before, he's different," Serena replied, meaning every word. "I can't put my finger on it, except to say that with Darrell, I absolutely *know* he's a man of his word. I think where Cecil was concerned, I just wanted to believe that." Serena paused. "You've heard of that whole good-twin/bad-twin thing. With Darrell and Cecil, it's obviously true."

"Okay, fine. You can trust him. But anyone looking for Cecil will think Darrell's him. Someone already ran you guys off the road. They broke into Cecil's house. That is too close for comfort, Serena. And if you continue hanging out together . . . ? Am I the only one who sees this?"

Serena blew out a long, weary breath. As much as she wanted to dismiss her sister as a worrywart who was making a mountain out of a molehill, she had a very good argument. But Serena was nothing if not stubborn. "I hear what you're saying, Kiana. And the good thing is, anyone looking for Cecil won't know where I live. Darrell made sure to circle the area several times as we headed to my apartment. No one was following us."

"All right," Kiana gave in. "I see I won't be able to talk you out of this. I hope you know what you're doing."

"I do." Serena spoke firmly. Any sign of doubt and Kiana would stress herself that much more. Yet Serena couldn't help wondering if she wasn't trying to convince herself that she would be all right as much as she was her sister. Serena had no clue what she was doing; she only knew that she was determined to get the necklace back one way or another.

"I asked Geoff to run a background check on Darrell."

Of course. Even now, Kiana blamed herself for not having had Geoff run a check on Cecil. Kiana had suggested it, but Serena had insisted that her sister not do that, because it hadn't seemed right. Of course, hindsight being twenty-twenty, checking Cecil out would have been the best thing.

Kiana hadn't always been so overprotective, but after they'd lost their parents at an early age, she'd changed. The reality that one tragic event could change your entire life had hit home in a very strong way.

Serena asked, "And what did Geoff find out?"

"I haven't heard back from him yet. I'll let you know as soon as I do."

"Okay." Serena appreciated the gesture. While she trusted Darrell in a way she never should have trusted Cecil, she didn't want any surprises. "Let me know what he says."

"What are you gonna do now?"

"I don't know. I suppose take a break and try to figure out what to do next."

"Darrell's gonna stay there?"

"Yeah," Serena replied, as if that was the most natural thing in the world. "That makes the most sense." Besides, they'd already spent one night together. What could another one hurt?

"All right, hon," Kiana said, surprisingly giving no argument. "Please be careful."

"I will. Oh, and about what I told you regarding Cecil's house being broken into—don't mention anything to Geoff. I don't want him feeling obligated to look into it, or tell anyone else in the Grove to look into it. Like I told you, Darrell doesn't want to report it—"

"*Please* be careful," Kiana reiterated. "You really don't know Darrell."

"I think he's just watching out for his brother. Like the night at the beach, he could easily have told the cops that he was Cecil's twin and saved himself a lot of aggravation. But he didn't." Serena paused. "And I can't say I blame him. I'd do the same thing for you."

"I hope that's all it is."

"I'm sure it is." If the police went through the house, they might find something incriminating against Cecil, and Darrell wouldn't want that. At least not without finding Cecil first and helping him out of the mess he'd gotten into. "Anyway, Darrell's in the living room, so I've gotta get off the phone."

"Call me later."

"I will," Serena promised.

Serena replaced the receiver, then stood. She gave herself a quick once-over in her dresser mirror, frowning at her image. *Oh, what the hell. Darrell's already seen me looking my worst. Fixing my hair's not about to make a difference now.*

That thought in mind, she headed back to the living room. She found Darrell standing at the patio doors, looking out.

Serena lived in the Hammocks, a quiet and beautiful residential area in Kendall. What she'd loved about this place when she'd moved here was the fact that the apartment backed onto a lake. Ducks frequently waddled through her backyard or swam on the lake. On days when she felt confused or stressed, she needed only to head into her backyard to find some peace.

She approached Darrell and glanced past his body to the outside. Several ducks swam on the nearby lake.

"It's beautiful here," Darrell commented.

"Yeah, it is."

"I can't imagine Cecil liking it here. This is so . . . tame."

Serena shrugged. "What's not to like? There's such an interesting variety of wildlife. Palm parrots, iguanas, cranes, ducks. It's like living on a nature reserve or something."

"I guess."

"What about where you live?" Serena asked.

"It's a nice place. Very scenic. It's got a golf course and a lake nearby. A pool. Tennis courts. Not that I ever get to enjoy it."

"You have to make time."

Darrell chuckled mirthlessly. "This trip to Miami I've taken—this is my vacation for the year."

"This is hardly a vacation."

"Disney is in my backyard, yet I haven't been there in years. I'm too busy."

"Oh, Darrell."

He shrugged. "What's a guy to do?"

"What it is with some men? All work and no play. My sister's ex was like that. In the beginning, he liked to do things . . . go for dinners, go away for the weekend. Then suddenly, he got so concerned about paying the bills that he stopped having fun. So many men let life pass them by, then they drop dead of a heart attack the moment they retire."

"It's a good thing I don't have a wife. Or a family."

"Maybe that's exactly what you need."

Darrell tipped his head back, chortling sarcastically. "Oh yeah. That's exactly what I need."

Like when she'd mentioned family before, Serena felt her stomach drop at Darrell's instant dismissal at the idea of having one. "Kids keep you young. Make you remember what's important in life."

"Not for this guy, thanks."

"Never?" Serena asked, shocked.

"Never."

Though it shouldn't matter to her, Darrell's disinterest in having a family bothered her. He obviously cared a lot about his brother, and he had a lot of love to give. Why didn't he see that?

"Maybe I had too much responsibility with Cecil. I was practically his father, and look how he turned out. I'm not good at the daddy thing."

"You're being way too hard on yourself."

"Hey, some things you just know."

Serena didn't know what to say to counter Darrell's conviction, so she said nothing. After a long moment of silence, she opened the patio and screen doors, slipped into her flip-flops, then took Darrell's hand. "Come here."

"What are you doing?"

"Just come here." She led him onto the concrete, then said, "Wait." Hurrying back inside, she went to the fridge and got a loaf of bread. Then she went back outside.

"Watch this," Serena said, walking toward the lake.

"What?"

"Just watch."

By the time Serena took a few steps toward the lake, the ducks that lazed around on the grass started toward her. She opened the bag of bread and took out a slice. As she tore it into pieces, ducks rushed to her feet.

She giggled as she dropped a piece of bread and two ducks fought over it. More ducks seemed to come from nowhere, flying from across the lake, waddling from all directions.

"Here." She passed Darrell a couple slices of bread.

Darrell was about to break up the slice when a duck flew up and grabbed the bread from his hand. "Whoa, wait a second. There's plenty to go around."

The ducks went at the slice of bread as if it were their last supper.

"I need more bread," Darrell announced.

Serena handed him several slices, then continued dropping pieces to the ground for the ducks. White ibis appeared behind the ducks, at a safe distance, though still hoping for food. Serena shot several pieces farther away and watched the birds run to them.

"Whenever I'm in a bad mood," Serena began, "all I have to do is come out here to the lake with a bag of bread and feed the ducks. Or, sometimes I just come out here and go for a walk. See the walking path?" She pointed to the asphalt path after she dropped more bread. "It goes for ten miles around this lake, behind several of the properties in the Hammocks. You can walk, jog, cycle. I love it."

"These ducks are tame. They're taking the bread right from my hands."

"Yeah, they're kinda like family. In a couple months, there will be a whole bunch of little ducklings. Last year, I had a mommy and her babies practically living in my backyard. It was so cute. I got to watch them grow up."

Darrell tossed a piece of bread and watched the ducks rush for it. One duck, however, stayed put at his feet, staring up at him. He dropped a chunk of bread and the duck caught it.

"Hey, there's Buford."

Darrell's eyebrows shot up as he stared at Serena. "You name the ducks? And how on earth do you know which one is which?"

"Buford is easy to spot. He walks with a limp."

"Buford?"

She smiled. "Yeah. I don't know how I came up with that, but I think it suits him. Here, Buford."

Darrell's gaze followed the direction of where Serena tossed a morsel of bread. The duck hurried toward it as quickly as possible, but the animal limped badly.

"Oh, I see him," Darrell said.

Another duck nabbed the piece of bread Serena had thrown before Buford could.

"Hey, that was mean," Darrell said to the other duck. Then he asked Serena, "What happened to Buford, anyway?"

"I don't know." She frowned. "Maybe a kid on a bike ran over one of its legs or something. Or maybe a dog got to it."

Darrell threw bread toward Buford, but again, another duck got it before Buford could. He started toward it, but when Buford saw him coming, he swiftly hobbled away.

"You have to go slowly," Serena said. "Gain his trust."

Darrell stopped to turn and face her. "You take your duck feeding seriously."

"Uh huh." She laughed loudly when two ducks fought over some bread she'd just dropped.

Darrell enjoyed watching her. Her laughter warmed his heart and made him smile.

He faced the injured duck, which now eyed him warily. He lowered himself onto his haunches. "Here, Buford," he called softly. God, he felt ridiculous. Here he was, trying to gain a duck's trust so that he could feed it a piece of bread.

The injured duck cocked its head to the side, but slowly took a step toward him. A few other ducks now moved toward Darrell, hoping to get bread from him. He tossed a piece in the other direction, and they ran toward it. Then, he quickly threw a piece toward Buford. Buford just as quickly gobbled it up.

"Hey, he got a piece," Darrell announced proudly. He threw Buford one more fragment of bread, but another duck was faster. "That wasn't for you," Darrell told that duck.

"You have to create a diversion when you feed Buford. The other ducks are stronger and quicker."

"Okay. Throw some bread a different way."

Serena shredded a slice of bread and threw the fragments to the far left. While the other ducks fought for those pieces, Darrell quickly shot another morsel toward Buford. Buford grabbed it. "There you go," Darrell said. Then he laughed. "God, I can't believe I'm talking to a duck."

"But you're not thinking about your problems now, are you?"

"No."

Serena gave him a victorious smile. Yeah, she had a point. Hanging out here feeding the ducks was mutually beneficial. Who would have thought he'd feel such a sense of happiness doing this?

He remembered feeding ducks once or twice when he'd been a kid in New York. It was one of the few happy memories he had of his mother before she'd split.

"These sure are funny looking ducks," Darrell commented. They were a mix of black and white, with red fleshy skin around their bills. They weren't like the ducks from the north.

"I call them turkey ducks."

Darrell stood. "I need more bread."

"I'm out."

Darrell frowned. "Buford didn't have enough to eat."

"He'll be okay," Serena assured him. "Other residents will come out and feed them."

Darrell headed toward Serena, glancing back at Buford. It stared at him, as if hoping there was more bread coming. "You sure? Maybe we should go buy more bread."

"Buford will be okay. Everyone looks out for him." When the ducks gathered around her feet, Serena spread her arms wide to show them that she wasn't hiding any bread. "Sorry, guys. That's all."

Serena headed toward her backyard, and Darrell followed her. So did the ducks, he realized when he turned. "They're still hungry."

Serena opened the patio door. "Quick. Get in."

"Why? They'll follow you inside?"

"Yes. They're very tame. And when you feed them— they love you. I told you, they're like family."

"You weren't kidding."

"I wasn't." She flashed him a grin as she closed the patio door. "I love it here. I really do. If you want, we can take a walk around the lake later. Hopefully we'll get a glimpse of the water bird."

"Water bird?"

"Yeah. It swims under water, searching for food. It stays

under for quite some time, coming up for air every minute or so. It's really cool."

"Wow."

"And there are turtles out there, too, though you don't see them as often."

"This is a nice place."

"How can you not take advantage of all this when it's literally in your backyard?"

Serena's question brought Darrell back to reality. "Because the real world has to come first."

"This is the real world. Part of it, anyway. Like I said, you have to make time to enjoy it. Life's too short to let the good things pass you by."

Darrell conceded that Serena was probably right. Still, he couldn't think about the good things in life until he'd found Cecil.

"Speaking of short lives . . ." Darrell's voice trailed off as he contemplated the seriousness of the situation. For the first time in his life, he was truly afraid for Cecil. Yes, his brother had done some unthinkable things, but he certainly didn't deserve to pay for them with his life.

Serena said, "Darrell, for what it's worth, I'm sorry. I know you might think I don't care what happens to Cecil, but I do. Yes, we have different reasons for wanting to find him, but I don't want to see him hurt any more than you do."

"Thank you," Darrell said softly. "That means a lot."

Serena headed further into the apartment, but Darrell stayed by the patio door, still staring outside. If only his biggest worry in life could be whether or not he'd fed the ducks enough bread.

"You okay?" Serena asked.

"Yeah," Darrell replied, not turning to face her. Though he wasn't, really. He wouldn't be, not until this was over and Cecil was safe.

Even if that meant safe in a jail cell.

For the zillionth time, Darrell wondered how he and Cecil could come from the same embryo yet be so entirely different. And he wondered if he wasn't crazy for having left his life in Orlando to come down here and search for Cecil. Didn't animals let their young fend for themselves once they were old enough? Perhaps because Cecil always knew Darrell would be there for him when he got into trouble, he'd never made the effort to smarten up once and for all.

Darrell had done what he could to help raise Cecil into a decent human being, but he'd failed. What else could he possibly do for his brother now?

The more Darrell thought about it, the more he realized how crazy it was for him to be here in Miami. What could he realistically do for his brother besides convince him to turn himself in? If he indeed was in serious trouble, that might be the only thing that would save his life.

Darrell was imposing on Serena, and quite possibly getting her involved in something that was beyond his control. His brother had already scammed her, and Darrell would never forgive himself if something bad happened to her.

"I'm gonna take a bath," Serena announced.

"What?" Darrell asked. Instantly, an image of what Serena would look like naked danced in his head.

"A bath. I won't be long. Then I'll make you some dinner."

From zero to hard-on in ten seconds flat. Darrell shifted uncomfortably on the sofa. "Uh . . . you don't have to. Make me dinner, that is."

"I want to." Planting her hands on her hips, Serena gave Darrell a sweet smile. "It's been a long day, and we have another long day ahead of us tomorrow."

*And a long friggin' night tonight,* Darrell thought. Why did she have to smile at him like that? And was she deliberately sticking out her chest, trying to get a rise out of him? Hell, she'd already done that.

"Okay. See you in a bit." With that, Serena twirled around and headed down the hallway. Darrell couldn't tear his eyes from her perfectly round behind.

Darrell dropped his head back against the sofa. A frustrated breath oozed out of his body. It had been *way* too long since he'd been with a woman. All work and no play and the first time he was spending some real time with a member of the opposite sex he couldn't keep focused on what was important.

Man, what was wrong with him?

And how the hell was he supposed to spend the night here with Serena if he couldn't stop thinking of her in a sexual way?

When he heard the bath water start running, Darrell sat forward and rested his elbows on his knees. His decision to leave was solidified by the fact that he obviously couldn't focus while staying here.

First thing in the morning, he was heading back to Orlando.

# Chapter 15

"My parents were such lovebirds," Serena commented, as she opened a cupboard and withdrew some spices. "They always took time to enjoy life, enjoy each other. Every evening after dinner, they would sit on the front porch of our house—we had a porch swing—and they'd talk and laugh. I remember that vividly."

"Uh huh."

"They had a wonderful relationship," Serena continued. "You could see the love in their eyes as they looked at each other . . ."

For the next several minutes, Darrell was mesmerized watching Serena prepare dinner and listening to her talk about her parents' love affair. Maybe it was the way her whole body seemed to come alive as she spoke, but Darrell was enthralled with the story of how in love her parents had been. It was nice to know that real love existed outside of books and movies, even if he hadn't experienced it himself.

". . . Smitten right from the moment they met. At least, that's what my mother said. I believed her, because my father always looked at her like she was the only woman in the world . . ."

Darrell suddenly found himself thinking about an old dream he'd given up on years ago. What would it be like to have a wife and children to come home to every night after a hard day's work? What would it be like if he had a family to give his life purpose outside of his career?

Serena almost made him believe his old dream could possibly come true. For a while he'd believed it—until Jessica had shattered all those hopes once and for all. But Serena . . . she was definitely wife material. She went about preparing food for him as if he was a longtime friend . . . or even a lover. No doubt about it, she was completely different than Jessica or any other women he'd known. She had a caring, giving nature, and that nature could grow on him.

His brother had had a good woman in her, but he'd been too dumb to see that.

*His loss,* Darrell thought.

Darrell lifted his glass of cold lemonade to his mouth at the same moment Serena ran the back of her hand over her forehead. Such a simple gesture, but it caused her close-fitting cotton shirt to hug her beautiful breasts, and just like that, Darrell's mind drifted from a vague fantasy of family life to imagining that *Serena* was his wife, that it was *her* warm smile that would greet him every evening, her soft body he'd hold against his every night.

"Oh, damn," Serena suddenly said. She met his eyes, and Darrell had to wonder if she'd read his thoughts. She continued, "I have no more jerk sauce. I hope you didn't get your hopes up for jerk chicken."

Her honest concern for what he would like and not like gave his heart a little lift. "I'm sure I'll enjoy whatever you make."

Serena went back to work, and Darrell actually stretched his feet out beneath the kitchen table and relaxed. And damn if it didn't feel good to do that. In Orlando, he ran around all day, much like a chicken with its head cut off, so much so that he'd almost forgotten what the word *relax* meant.

Feeding ducks, having a woman to come home to . . . he could get used to this.

The moment of pleasure instantly soured, and he frowned. Who was he kidding? Yeah, it was a nice fantasy, but that's all it was—a fantasy. Hadn't his own mother proven that to him? That when you no longer got what you wanted or needed, you moved on without looking back? Darrell had seen what his mother's blasé attitude had done to his father, and it was the last thing he wanted for his own life.

He'd almost made the same mistake with Jessica that his father had made with his mother.

"You want it a little spicy? Because I have some hot sauce, but it's not the same as jerk."

"However you like it," Darrell replied.

"You're easy to please," Serena said, then giggled. Then she went back to work.

Darrell continued to watch her. There was a quality to

Serena, something he didn't remember ever seeing in his mother or in Jessica, that made him think she'd be different.

Darrell's stomach twisted into a painful knot. Even if Serena was different, and even if he wanted to delude himself into thinking she could be the one woman to make him happy, he couldn't pretend that he could make *her* happy. From the way she talked, she wanted a husband and kids—the whole nine yards. Darrell had given up that dream ages ago. Hell, he was no good at being a father, that much he knew for sure. What did he have to offer her?

The whole direction of his thoughts made him anxious, and Darrell realized that sitting around doing nothing wasn't helping him one bit. He needed something to occupy his mind and keep his thoughts from venturing to territory it shouldn't go.

Standing, he strolled the short distance to where Serena was now bent over an open bottom cupboard. For a moment, he simply stared at her, at her round butt in the floral skirt she'd changed into, at the glimpse of her back between the skirt and shirt the view allowed. Why couldn't he take his eyes off her?

Serena straightened, then saw him. Gasping, she threw a hand to her chest. "Goodness, you scared me."

"Sorry."

She got a peculiar look in her eye as she stared at him. "Did you want something?"

"Um . . . yeah." Hell, yeah. He wanted to lift that skirt over her hips, run his hands along her smooth skin, slip his hands beneath her panties. . . .

"Darrell?"

"Uh, sorry. I . . ." He cleared his throat. "I was wondering where I'm going to sleep tonight."

"Oh. I have a guest bedroom. You'll have to share it with some antique dolls, though."

Dolls. *Why not with you?*

"Darrell?"

"Sorry," he mumbled. God, what was wrong with him? "I figured I'd lie down for a minute." He forced a yawn. "Until dinner's ready."

"You do seem a little tired. The bedroom's the second door on the left."

Darrell acknowledged her with a quick nod, then quickly left the kitchen.

He hurried to the spare bedroom, hoping that a quick nap would restore him with the lick of sense the good Lord had given him.


The next morning, Darrell's mind was made up. He was heading back to Orlando, and the sooner the better. Not only had he come to the conclusion that he couldn't help Cecil, he felt a measure of anxiety hanging around with Serena twenty-four/seven.

She was good and sweet and made him think of things he shouldn't want.

A quick sweep of the bedroom told Darrell that there was nothing in here to write on. Between him, the dolls, the various trinkets, and what he believed was an antique fountain pen, there wasn't a modern piece of paper on which he could jot a note. Not that he should leave a note for Serena—it was the coward's way out—but he wasn't sure he could stomach her disappointment when he told her he was leaving.

He exited the small bedroom and strolled to the living room, hoping to find a piece of paper and pen to write a note. He stopped short when he saw Serena sitting on the sofa with a thick photo album on her lap.

Hearing him, she looked up. "Hey," she said softly, smiling.

So much for an easy getaway. "Hey, yourself. What're you doing?"

"Looking through my family's photo album." She patted the spot next to her. "Come here. I want to show you this."

Darrell moved across the room to the sofa, then sat beside her. She wore a terry-cloth robe that reached her mid-thigh, as well as a pair of fluffy white slippers. One leg was crossed over the other, allowing him a glimpse of chocolatey-smooth skin. Man, this was getting harder by the minute. Last night, she'd prepared him dinner as casually as if she'd done it a million times, and now, here she was dressed only in her robe, as if they'd woken up every morning together for the past several years.

"Darrell."

His eyes flew to hers. "Huh?"

"I asked if you want any coffee. I can put on a pot."

"Naw, I'm fine." He was too wired to sleep. He glanced down at the open album. "That's a huge photo album."

"It's got a lot of pictures. Many of them have been passed down from generations ago. I guess it's kinda like a photographic family tree."

"You can see without your glasses?" Darrell asked.

"I'm wearing my contacts," Serena explained, then opened the album. "I wear them sometimes, though I prefer my glasses."

The first picture was a grainy black and white photo of a well-dressed man who appeared to be in his early twenties. "Who's that?"

"This is my great-grandfather, Devon Jackson."

"Great grandfather. Wow. You actually have a picture of him?"

"It was taken in 1898, when he was seventeen years old. His father owned a few bakeries in upstate New York, so they were fairly well off." Serena turned the page. "This is Ann-Marie Bennett, the woman Devon married. She's my great-grandmother. And here they are on their wedding day."

"I'm impressed."

"The necklace dates back to my great-great-great-grandmother." Serena flipped to the back of the photo album. "This is the only picture we have of her."

Darrell looked down at the charcoal sketch. "This is amazing."

Serena smiled. "Yeah. It's really neat to be able to look back and see where you came from."

"You kinda look like her. Your cheekbones. Your eyes."

"Mmm hmm. Tilly Hancock. She was born a slave, but shortly after her birth, slavery was abolished. Her mother, Emily, tried to find her husband once she was free—he'd been sold before Tilly was born—but she never did find him."

Darrell fingered the picture. "Tilly?"

"Yeah."

"She's fairly light-skinned. At least that's the way it looks in the sketch."

"There was some mixing along the lines. I think Tilly's

grandmother was mulatto—the product of a slave master and his slave. You know how that goes." Serena shook her head with chagrin. "Anyway, a little while after Emily and Tilly were free, they moved from the south to the north, somewhere in Ohio, from what I understand, where Emily got work as a maid. Apparently, her employer was very generous and Emily was able to save enough money to send Tilly to the university. During her first year at the New York Medical School for Women, Tilly met Armande Giroux, a man from Morocco. I'm not sure where they met, but as the story goes, the moment Armande saw her, he fell head-over-heels in love."

A smile touched Darrell's lips. "Like your parents."

"Yeah, like my parents," Serena agreed, a hint of nostalgia lacing her tone. "Unlike my mother, however, Tilly wasn't interested in Armande. While Armande was olive-skinned and didn't have the same attitude toward blacks that the average American did at the time, she was very proud of her heritage and planned to marry a black man. But as much as she rejected him, Armande eventually won her over with his charm. And get this, after he proposed, he told her that he was from a royal family. His wedding gift to her was a diamond-and-ruby necklace."

"I can't believe you know all this."

"This is the story as it's been told to me, and these are the pictures that go along with the history. I have the album because I'm the oldest, I guess. One day, I'll pass the album and the necklace to my oldest daughter. It's a tradition that my great-great-great-grandmother Tilly started, and I plan to keep it going."

Serena turned the page. There was a yellowed black and

white wedding photo. "This is my great-great-grandmother, Amanda. I suppose she was named Amanda after her father, Armande. That's kind of a sad story. Just a couple years into Armande's and Tilly's marriage, Armande got ill and died. Amanda was their only daughter, and Tilly never remarried. This is Amanda upon her marriage to Richard Jackson. They were Devon's parents, the first picture you saw." Serena turned the page. "I really should go through this and put the pictures in their proper order."

She pointed to the color photo of an older woman. "This is my grandmother, Louisa May. And this is my grandfather, Maurice Childs, with my grandmother shortly before he died. He died a couple years before my parents did. Cancer. After my parents died, Grandma Louisa May raised us. She had three sons, no daughters. My father was her firstborn, and I was his firstborn daughter. Hence the necklace went to me."

"What an impressive story."

Serena closed the album and held it to her chest. Pride shone in her eyes. "Yes, it is. That's why . . ." Her voice trailed off, ending on a sigh. "That's why it's so important for me to get the necklace back. It's not just a necklace, Darrell. It represents my family's history."

She sighed softly, and for a moment, Darrell wondered if she would cry. But she didn't. She remained strong, though this whole situation must be tearing her apart. Now, Darrell understood how much.

For her, losing the necklace was like losing a very real piece of her.

"Here are my parents," Serena said. Once again, she had the album open, this time to the photo of an attractive couple on their wedding day. "They died in a boating accident, and in so many ways I feel I never got to know them. Maybe that's why this album is so important to me."

When Serena closed the album again and looked up at him, her eyes were filled with tears. "I miss my grandmother so much. She died last year of a stroke. She was only seventy-three. I'm glad I had her for so many years. And the necklace . . . it's the one special connection I had to my grandmother and our history."

"My brother," Darrell said suddenly. "You told him what you told me? You showed him this album?"

Brushing a stray tear, Serena nodded.

"Hey." Darrell didn't think, he acted. He stretched an arm around Serena and pulled her close.

"I didn't mean to get emotional," Serena said. "It's just that . . . looking through this album, seeing all the pictures . . ."

"I know," Darrell said. He pressed his cheek against her hair, and the perfumed scent of the shampoo she'd used wafted into his nose. It was distinctly feminine, and he suddenly wanted to run his fingers through her hair, hold her close, and tell her that everything would be all right.

While Darrell had planned to tell her that he was leaving this morning, he no longer had the heart to do that to her. He couldn't leave. He owed it to Serena to get the necklace back. Deep in his heart, he knew he wasn't truly responsible, but Cecil was his blood, and if his blood had robbed her of so much, then he couldn't rest until he'd made everything right again.

"I'm going to make sure you get your necklace back," Darrell vowed.

"I want to believe that." Her voice was soft and low as she spoke against his chest.

"Believe it," he told her. "Because it's true." It didn't matter that he didn't know how or when he'd keep his word, but he *would* keep his word—even if it meant hunting down the buyer if Cecil had already sold the necklace.

Sniffling, Serena pulled away from Darrell. She wiped at her eyes. "Gosh, I didn't mean to get all sentimental."

"It's okay."

No, it wasn't okay. She hadn't meant to get all emotional in Darrell's arms, but there was something about him that made her feel safe showing her emotions. Still, she was now embarrassed. Scooping up the album, Serena brought it to the coffee table, where she placed it in one of the coffee table's compartments. Not glancing back at him, she started for the kitchen.

"Serena."

Hearing her name, Serena stopped. Yet she didn't turn. And though she didn't hear Darrell approaching her, she sensed it. Her whole body tensed as she waited for him to touch her.

For she knew he would.

A little sigh escaped her as Darrell's hands made contact with her body. Starting at her shoulders, he ran his hands down the length of her arms, then back up. Serena's eyes fluttered shut as a wave of emotions washed over her. She liked Darrell's touch, liked it way too much.

"Serena." His voice was gentle, yet it seemed to vibrate through her entire body. "Turn around."

She did.

Placing a finger under her chin, Darrell lifted her face, forcing her to meet his eyes. "I know you think I'm giving you an empty promise when I tell you that I'll get the necklace back for you, but I'm not."

Serena didn't say a thing. Darrell's gaze had her mesmerized.

"Unlike my brother, I'm a man of my word."

Serena flinched when Darrell's fingers grazed her face, then she relaxed. He smoothed a tendril of her hair against her forehead.

"I'm going to make this right for you, Serena. I owe you that much."

"You don't—"

"Yes—" He brought his fingers to her mouth. "—I do."

The air between them was charged, so much so that Serena found it hard to breathe. Her eyes roamed over Darrell's attractive face, settling on his full lips. God, she wanted to kiss him again.

"You're very lucky," he said softly. "You have a wonderful family. It's something I never had, and I envy that."

As Darrell said the words, Serena heard pain in his voice, saw it in his eyes. What had his life been like growing up? Why had Cecil chosen a criminal path while Darrell had chosen a straight and narrow one? And why did Darrell seem to believe that he was responsible for all the wrong Cecil had done?

Everything he'd said to her in the time that she'd known him indicated that he'd had a not-so-wonderful family life, and Serena couldn't help wondering just how bad it had been.

"Tell me about your family," Serena said.

Darrell's fingers stilled on her cheek, then, dropping his hand, he stepped back. She watched as a mix of emotions—pain, sadness, and anger—passed over his features.

"There's nothing to tell," Darrell said, his voice void of emotion.

"Tell me anyway."

"Actually, I . . . need to take a shower. Where do you keep your towels?"

Serena frowned, but Darrell was no longer looking at her. The moment of intimacy between them was gone. Clearly, the subject of his family was off-limits, which bothered her, because it made her feel like he didn't trust her.

"I'll get you some towels," Serena told him.

But as she headed to her hallway closet, she found herself ever more curious about the complex Darrell Montford.

"I'm serious, Serena," Darrell said. "Go to work."

Holding the receiver in one hand, Serena stared at Darrell from across the living room. She'd been planning to take the day off to help him search for his brother, but he was insisting that she not miss work because of him. "I don't mind," she assured him.

"There's no need," Darrell told her. "I'm gonna head back to the house in Coconut Grove and go over it with a fine-toothed comb. After that, if I don't find anything, I'll call the police. I thought about it all last night and whatever trouble my brother is in, he may be better off if the police are actively involved."

"Darrell, I want to help you."

"And I appreciate that, but there's not much you can help me do that I can't do for myself today. If I don't find anything, we'll regroup tonight and figure out what the next step is."

Serena got the impression that Darrell was avoiding her—especially since he hadn't met her eyes as he spoke—

and she didn't know why. Maybe he just needed space to deal with this whole situation, to deal with how he was feeling. A lot had happened in the past few days and neither of them had really had any breathing space separate from each other. Serena and Darrell had spent every moment together since she'd met him at the police station. It wasn't too much to ask that he have some time to himself.

"All right," Serena conceded. "But if you learn anything at all, please call me at work." Hanging up the phone, she reached for a notepad and pen. She jotted down the number to the library, then passed it to him. "You remember how to get back to Cecil's house?"

"I'll figure it out."

"Let me give you directions."

Serena spent the next few minutes giving Darrell detailed directions to Cecil's home. "Be careful, Darrell. If you see any sign of trouble, make sure you leave and call the cops."

"I will." Darrell paused, then asked, "You need a ride to work?"

"No. The library is only about a ten-minute walk."

Darrell stuffed the information she'd given him in his jeans' pocket. "All right." His eyes lingered on hers. "I'll see you later."

"I'll be off at six."

Serena's face flushed. Was she mistaken, or did Darrell want to kiss her? Or perhaps that was wishful thinking on her part. Because she did want to lock lips with him, just as her parents had always shared a kiss before parting.

Her heart pounded. Why was she feeling like this about Darrell?

"Serena?"

"Huh?" she replied, startled.

"I'm going to head out."

"Yes, yes. Of course." Serena swallowed her disappointment that Darrell *didn't* lean close and cover her mouth with his.

"See you then."

When Darrell was gone, Serena laid her head against the wall and released a long sigh.

# Chapter 16

Darrell's heart leapt to his throat when he pulled up in front of his brother's Coconut Grove home and saw two Miami police cruisers in the driveway. The car had barely stopped moving before he jumped out and ran up the rest of the driveway to the door.

Lord help him, was he too late? Had his brother returned home and met with foul play?

A police officer stood at the door, and when he saw Darrell, instantly stepped forward.

"What happened here?" Darrell asked, glancing over the cop's shoulder to see inside the house.

"You the owner?"

"No. My brother is." Darrell paused. "Is everything okay?"

The cop looked him up and down curiously. "You have some ID?"

"ID?"

"Yeah," the officer replied succinctly.

Whether the cop had seen a picture of Cecil inside the house or had seen his mug shot on a wanted poster, Darrell wasn't sure. But he knew the cop suspected he was Cecil, and Darrell wasn't about to play that game again.

He dug into his back pocket and withdrew his wallet. He opened it to his driver's license and passed it to the cop.

"Wow," the officer said. "You two are twins?"

"Yes."

The cop closed the wallet and handed it back to Darrell. "A lot of people are looking for your brother."

Darrell asked, "What happened?"

"The place has been robbed and ransacked," the officer explained.

When Darrell started to move, the cop held up a hand to his chest, keeping him at bay. "I can't let you in there."

"It's my brother's house."

"Your brother's, not yours. Besides, we're in the middle of an investigation, sir."

"Fine," Darrell said. "It's just that I've come in from out of town and . . . was hoping to find him."

"You always show up without calling first?"

"Is that a crime?"

The cop shrugged. "Nope, I guess not."

"I know, it wasn't smart, but I figured he'd be around. You have to understand why I'd be worried, coming here and seeing the police outside his door."

"Of course."

"You say the place has been robbed. If my brother's not around, who reported it?"

The officer hesitated for a second, as if deciding

whether or not he should give Darrell any information. Then he spoke. "The housekeeper called us a couple hours ago. She showed up this morning to do her weekly cleaning and found the place like this."

"Housekeeper?" Excitement tickled Darrell's stomach.

"Uh huh. Lucky for her, the perps weren't here when she got here."

"No doubt."

The officer gave Darrell another skeptical look, then added, "According to her, your brother's been out of town for a couple weeks."

"Oh." Pause. "Is she still here?"

"She left about twenty minutes ago, after giving her statement."

Damn. Maybe she could give him a few clues as to where his brother might be. "Was anything taken?" Darrell asked, as if he didn't already know.

"I can't discuss that with you, sir, since you're not the homeowner. But if you're in touch with your brother anytime soon, please tell him to give us a call."

The way the officer's eyes narrowed at his last words gave Darrell pause. Yeah, he knew there was a warrant out for Cecil's arrest.

Darrell wanted to stay and ask more questions, or at least find out the housekeeper's name and number, but he had the feeling he ought to hightail it out of there before they detained him for something. What sucked about being the identical twin brother of a wanted man was that *he* was now constantly looking over his shoulder, when he hadn't done a damn thing wrong.

Darrell turned to leave, then doubled back. "Sorry to bother you again," he told the cop. "I'm sure you can't give out the housekeeper's information, but if I leave you mine, can you tell her that I'd like to talk to her? I'm trying to find my brother."

"Sure," the cop replied.

He gave Darrell a pen and paper, and Darrell scrawled down the number to his home in Orlando. "Thanks."

"No problem. Again, if you talk to your brother, please tell him to give us a call. We have a few things to speak with him about regarding the break-in."

"Of course," Darrell replied, then started off again.

*Yeah, right,* he added silently.

Kiana was heading through the front door when the phone rang. Pivoting, she ran into her nearby kitchen and grabbed the phone from the wall.

"Hello?"

"Hey, cupcake."

Leaning her back against the wall, Kiana smiled. "Geoff."

"Have you kicked the other man out of your bed yet?" he asked playfully.

Kiana rolled her eyes. For as long as she'd known Geoff, it didn't matter what time of day it was—he never lost his sense of humor. Strange, considering the man had worked so much and hadn't made much time to play.

"Ha ha. Very funny. I assume you're calling because you have some info for me."

"Well, that too."

"What did you find out?" Kiana asked.

"How long you gonna be around?"

"I was stepping out to Office Depot," Kiana replied. As a freelance writer, she worked from home. Normally, she didn't get out of her pajamas in the morning, but she'd run out of ink for her printer and therefore had to.

"When will you be back?"

"Thirty minutes, max."

"Great," Geoff said. "I'll see you then."

"Geoff," Kiana began, protesting. But he'd already hung up.

Later, when the bell rang, Kiana opened the front door to find Geoff on her doorstep. Seeing him always evoked the same response in her—her heart fluttered and she felt light-headed. From the first time she'd met him, she'd had that reaction. At six foot four, Geoff had a commanding presence, especially in uniform.

He wasn't in uniform today, however. Yet Kiana still couldn't tear her eyes from his beautiful form.

"Hey, babe," Geoff said, his lips curling in a charming smile.

"Hi." Kiana spoke as casually as she could. Fleetingly she wondered when she'd stop seeing Geoff in a sexual way.

"It's so good to see you." He leaned forward and kissed her on the cheek.

Geoff's lips made her skin tingle; uncomfortable, Kiana pulled back. Turning, she walked into her living room. Geoff followed her. She sat on the armchair, leaving Geoff no choice but to sit on the opposite sofa.

"Okay," Kiana began, crossing one leg over the other. "Hit me with the news."

"All right." Geoff opened the folder he held and glanced down at the contents. "Let's start with the easy stuff. Darrell Montford, Cecil's brother, he's clean. I couldn't find anything on him, not even an unpaid parking ticket. He lives in Orlando currently, owns a small hotel."

"Okay," Kiana said, relieved that Serena's instincts about him were correct.

"Cecil, however, is a different story altogether. He's been in and out of trouble practically since the day he was born. He spent a little time in a juvey detention center for theft, but that was it. Seems he stayed out of trouble as he got older, but there are numerous complaints about him from angry women—ex–lovers. Claimed they gave him expensive gifts like boats and cars, but that he used them." Geoff shrugged. "Well, the cops couldn't do anything. The women gave him this stuff of their own free will. One woman even left him a villa in Jamaica in her will."

Kiana shook her head, amazed. "How do guys like him get so many women to give them stuff?"

"Wish I knew," Geoff replied, holding her gaze. But clearly he wasn't talking about Cecil or men like him and what they could get from women. He was talking about what he wanted from Kiana.

Her heart throbbing, Kiana looked away.

Geoff continued. "Anyway, on to the good stuff. Aside from all the gifts he got, a couple women recently reported that he stole jewelry from them."

"Women other than Serena?"

"Mmm hmm. One woman, Jan McDonald, says he stole almost a hundred and eighty thousand dollars' worth of jewels from her. Another, Tamara Alvarez, says he took close to a hundred and fifty thousand dollars' worth of jewelry from her. A couple of Miami Beach cops were investigating the allegations and found enough evidence to build a case against Cecil. According to what I learned, they tried to find him at his various residences, but he was nowhere to be found. That's why there was a warrant out for his arrest when you and your sister met up with his twin that night."

"God, I can't believe it."

"Looks like your sister picked a real winner."

"I knew I should have had you check out Cecil right from the beginning. I told Serena, but she refused."

"I can't entirely blame her. There's a lot to be said for trust in a relationship."

Kiana rolled her eyes. "Trust? Does anyone know the meaning of the word anymore? There are so few people you can trust these days, you may as well use the resources available to you to check them out before you get involved."

"If you have to, I guess."

"I'm glad you agree. Because I'll be sure to have you check out any man I meet in the future."

Geoff's eyebrows shot together. "Really?"

"Makes sense, doesn't it? I'm sure you wouldn't want me—"

Kiana broke off when Geoff rose from the loveseat and marched to the armchair. He stopped in front of her, his large, muscular body impossible to ignore.

"Here's a newsflash," Geoff stated. "Any guy you have me check out will get a thumbs-down from me."

"I'm sure I'll find someone nice—"

"And safe, who works nine-to-five and gets two weeks off a year. You're doing this on purpose, aren't you?"

"Doing what?" Kiana asked, feigning ignorance, but she knew exactly what he was talking about.

He lowered himself before her. "Testing me. To see how I'll react to your talk of dating other men."

Kiana's breathing grew shallow. "I . . ."

"That's what I thought," Geoff said. He casually rested his hands on both her knees. "Did I ever make you feel insecure when you were with me?"

"I wasn't always sure you cared," Kiana admitted.

"I know that, and that's why for the past four months I've repeatedly told you how I feel. There's no need to test me, Kiana. You know how I feel."

Geoff trailed his fingers from her knees to her thighs, and though she should have, Kiana didn't stop him. God, it felt so good to have him touch her again.

Geoff's fingers stopped at her mid-thigh. "We should be together. Deep in your heart, you know that."

Kiana's heart beat erratically at the way Geoff was touching her, at the familiar pleasant feelings his touch brought to her skin. Yet she said, "We tried that before, remember? It didn't work."

"It didn't work because I didn't listen. But I'll listen now."

Kiana attempted a chuckle, but it sounded like a throaty moan. "It's not about changing, or listening, or telling me how you feel. Geoff, it's you and me. We're not compatible."

"That's bullshit and you know it."

To prove his point, he leaned forward and covered her lips with his, too fast for her to move or even protest. And damn her, she instantly melted in his arms. The kiss was deep and passionate, and proved exactly what Geoff had said.

"What were you saying about compatibility?" Geoff's eyes sparkled with victory.

"Fine, so we were great sexually," Kiana conceded. She stood, but Geoff blocked her path. "Sex isn't everything."

"It's a damn good start." Geoff winked as he reached for her arm.

Kiana smacked his hand and stepped to the side. "That was always part of the problem," Kiana pointed out. "You making jokes when we're having a serious conversation." She paused. "You and me . . . we're so different. I know both you and Serena tell me I'm too serious sometimes, but I can't change how I am. And I can't change the reality that you're a cop."

She'd worried about him every single time he'd gone to work. If she heard there was a robbery or a high-speed chase or an officer down, she immediately feared that Geoff had been involved.

Now that they were just friends, she still worried about him, but not in the same way. Having a relationship required so much more than just caring about someone. How could she build a partnership with him when she didn't know if he'd come home at night?

Geoff folded his arms over his solid chest. His demeanor told her he was annoyed.

"I've said it once and I'll say it again," Geoff said. "Nobody knows what's going to happen to them when they leave their house. I could get hit by a bus before I ever get shot."

The very mention of him getting shot had Kiana's stomach in knots. "Geoff . . ."

He blew out a harried breath. "All right, Kiana. You go back to worrying. I'm gonna head out and see if I can't enjoy the rest of this beautiful day. I'd hoped you'd want to do something with me, as this is my last day off, but I guess I was wrong."

Kiana swallowed painfully. Why was he making this

so hard for her? "I have to get this piece done for the magazine."

"Right." Geoff's nod said he didn't believe her. "Call me if you need anything else."

"Geoff . . ."

He ignored her as he stalked past her to the door. A second later, he was gone.

A soft moan escaping her, Kiana dropped herself onto the sofa. A feeling of emptiness spread through her entire body.

Dejected, she threw her head back on the sofa and closed her eyes.

Every time the phone rang in the library's back office, Serena's heart went into overdrive. And every time it was someone calling about library business, she was disappointed.

She had hoped to hear from Darrell by now, even if he only told her that nothing was going on.

For the zillionth time, Serena glanced at the wall clock. It was just after one P.M. She had another five hours to go. God, was time moving forward in slow motion or something?

Serena groaned. She should have told Darrell to check in with her whether or not he found out anything about Cecil. And after not hearing from Darrell for most of the day, she had to concede that she was perhaps more like her sister than she wanted to admit. She was worried about Darrell, unable to stop herself from wondering if the fact that he hadn't called her meant he wasn't okay.

But she wasn't only worried. She missed him.

A lot.

Which was one helluva surprise to her.

But it was true, she realized. Without a doubt, she missed Darrell. Having practically been joined to him at the hip these past few days, she'd grown accustomed to his presence. In fact, she could hardly remember what her life had been like before he'd come into it.

Ever since meeting Darrell, her life had been a whirlwind of excitement. The threat of real danger aside, the excitement was, to a degree, stimulating. Exhilarating. At least, that's what she'd realized today as she sat at her desk in the library office, which is where she'd *always* sat, Monday to Friday, for the past six years. She didn't want to be here, not today. She wanted to be with Darrell, searching for her family's heirloom like she should be.

The fact that doing so made her feel like she was living out a story she would otherwise only read about in a book was simply a bonus.

No one—certainly not her co-workers at the library— would have expected anything other than predictability from her. And car chases and house break-ins were certainly not predictable.

If she was trying to throw caution to the wind, she was doing it in grand style. And she'd no doubt knock ten years off Kiana's life before this search for the necklace was through. Yet for the first time in all her years, she felt truly alive . . . though she had a sneaking suspicion that whether or not there was any danger involved with this search for Cecil, she'd still feel amazingly alive—and that had everything to do with the tall, dark, and too-fine Darrell Montford.

Hell, she felt wonderfully alive every time he touched her, every time he *looked* at her. Was that normal?

A soft sigh fell from her lips as Serena thought of him, thought of his magnificent body clad only in shorts. There was something about him that made every nerve in her body scream with sexual awareness, and that was something she was not used to.

But it was most definitely something she found she liked.

Perhaps too much.

Serena wanted to get to know Darrell better, and only hoped she had the opportunity to do so. Because there was so much about him that intrigued her. He was mysterious. A deep thinker with a sense of responsibility that astonished her. But he had a lighter side, a side that often made her smile.

Yeah, she missed him.

The phone rang, startling her. With lightning fast speed, Serena's hand shot out to grab it. "West Kendall Public Library."

"Hello," a man said. "I'm wondering if you can tell me whether or not you have a book."

"Oh." Disappointed, Serena slumped forward on her desk. "Sure. What's the title?"

Serena spent the next couple of minutes on the phone with the library patron. The moment she hung up, she dropped her head onto her desk.

Then, inhaling deeply, she sat up and pulled herself together. Determined to put Darrell out of her mind, she went back to cataloguing new library items on the computer.

A short while later, Phyllis, another of the library's workers, interrupted her. "Your sister's here," Phyllis announced. "You want her to come on back, or will you go out to meet her?"

"Send her back here," Serena replied, pleasantly surprised by the diversion. Finishing up an entry, she pushed her chair back from the computer and stood as Kiana sauntered through the door.

"Hi, sis," Serena said, walking toward her.

"Hey, Serena." Kiana stopped short when she saw her. "Whoa. You look nice."

"Oh." Serena smoothed her hands over the ruby-red sundress she wore. "Thanks."

"You're not wearing your glasses."

"Contacts."

"And your hair. What'd you do? Go to the salon this morning?"

"What? Can't a girl do something a little different now and then without getting the third degree?"

Kiana half-nodded, half-shrugged. "I guess. You do look nice."

Serena spread her arms and was about to give Kiana a proper greeting when a small frown marred Kiana's pretty face.

Serena dropped her arms to her sides, her eyebrows bunching together with concern. "What's the matter, Kiana?"

"Nothing, really." She shrugged. "I can't seem to get any work done at home today, so I figured I'd use the computer here."

Serena gave her sister a skeptical look. "You sure that's all?"

Kiana waved a hand, dismissing Serena's concern. "Uh huh. And I figured I'd come by to see if there's any more news on the Cecil front. Any word yet?"

"No. Darrell's gone back to Cecil's house in the Grove

today, though, to see if he can find anything we might have missed." Serena's eyes ventured to the phone. "He's supposed to call me if there's any news, but I haven't heard from him."

Kiana slumped into the chair Serena had vacated minutes earlier. "Well, I have a bit of news."

"Uh oh." If her sister's body language was any indication, the news wasn't good. "What?"

"Nothing bad," Kiana quickly said. "The background check on Darrell came back clean."

"I thought it would," Serena commented. But still, a smile spread on her face. It was good to know her instincts had been right where Darrell was concerned.

"Cecil, however, has apparently been in trouble all his life. He's gotten a ton of *gifts* from women, which seemed to be quite a lucrative deal for him."

Serena sat on the edge of the desk. "Tell me about it. You should see his condo on the beach, Kiana. Not to mention his house in the Grove. Darrell said he's also got a villa in Montego Bay."

"That one I heard about," Kiana said. "Geoff said some woman left him the villa in her will."

"How old was she?" Serena asked, mildly surprised.

"I have no idea." Kiana tsked. "I don't understand why that wasn't enough."

"Neither do I," Serena said.

"Geoff did tell me that you're not the only one he's stolen jewelry from. A couple other women have filed complaints."

Serena balled a fist against her lips, thinking. Then she said, "Either he's gotten into something and needs money badly, or his lavish lifestyle is too expensive to keep up."

"I left the printout with all the info at home, but the

two other women who filed complaints are Tamara something-or-other—"

"Tamara!" Serena exclaimed. "That's the woman from the bar! My God, I wonder if she's the one who ran us off the road."

"Given the fact that Cecil stole a small fortune from her, I wouldn't doubt it."

Serena stood tall. "We need to try and reach these other women. Talk to them, see what their mind-set is. Maybe one of them is out to get Cecil."

"You've got to be kidding."

"No." And the adrenaline rush was back. "If we can talk to them, question them, then it's quite likely we can figure out who's threatening Cecil's life."

Kiana gave Serena an incredulous look. "Did you change your name to Shaft?"

"I think it's a good idea."

"What are you going to say if you talk to them?" Kiana asked.

"I don't know. Fish for information. Tell them I'm also one of Cecil's victims," she added proudly, as if the idea was a stroke of pure genius.

"As if anyone's gonna admit to trying to hurt him." Kiana reached for Serena's hand and gave it a firm squeeze. "Let the police handle this."

Serena simply shrugged.

"Serena . . ."

"Have you ever known me to do anything stupid? Besides getting involved with Cecil," she added, flashing her sister a wry grin.

"I'm concerned about you," Kiana said in reply. "And rightly so."

Serena didn't respond as she drifted off in thought.

"Serena?"

"I was just thinking," she began, already moving toward a different computer, one with internet access. Her sister quickly followed her. "I told you that Darrell found something pertaining to an online auction site at the house, right?"

"Yeah."

"Gosh, why didn't I think of this before?"

"What?"

"Checking the internet for a listing of online auction companies. I know about E-Bay, but that's it. There's got to be more, however." Her eyes lit up as she glanced at her sister. "If Cecil has the necklace up for auction, I can try to find it. And if I find it, I can find out who he sold it to, if he already sold it." She paused, thinking as she accessed the internet via the computer. "If he hasn't, then I can let the auction company know that the necklace has been stolen, and maybe they can stop the auction."

"What a good idea."

Serena sat before the computer. "I don't know if it will work, but at least it's something to try. I'm sure reputable auction companies don't want to sell stolen goods."

"I can talk to Geoff about what's done in situations like these."

Serena glanced up at her sister. "You and Geoff are still pretty tight."

"Of course. We're still friends."

"Uh huh."

"What's that supposed to mean?"

"You turn to him for advice for *everything*."

"Like I said, we're friends."

"Whatever."

"Don't give me that, Serena. You know why our relationship didn't work."

"I know what you told me, but I also see how you are every time you mention his name."

"What are you talking about?"

"Your eyes light up. You talk highly of him all the time, thinking he can solve every problem. Almost like . . ." Serena paused for dramatic effect. "Almost like you're still in love with him."

Kiana rolled her eyes. "Oh, please."

Serena's eyes narrowed on her sister. "*Try* and tell me I'm wrong."

"Aren't you supposed to be looking something up online?"

"That's what I thought," Serena replied, knowing she'd proven her point.

Through her peripheral vision, Serena saw her sister glance at her watch. "I'm gonna leave you down here and head upstairs. I've got to get this article done. But if you hear anything about Cecil, come get me, okay?"

"Sure."

Kiana hurried off, and Serena chuckled to herself. *That's it, sis. Run away.*

A blind man could see Kiana was still madly in love with Geoff Winters.

Serena went back to work, much more content to think of Kiana's love life than the inexplicable feelings she was having for Darrell.

# Chapter 17

Later that evening back at home, Serena ran to answer the door when she heard the knock. Peering through the peephole, she breathed a sigh of relief.

She opened the door. "Darrell!"

"Hey."

He stepped into her apartment and slipped out of his sandals. "Man oh man."

Serena closed, then locked, the door. "What? Did something happen? Didn't I tell you to call me at work if something happened?"

"I figured I'd see you soon enough."

Serena felt a niggling sense of disappointment. She'd practically gone crazy not hearing from him all day, yet he'd barely given her a second thought.

Darrell strolled to the living room. Feeling like an idiot, Serena followed him. He'd breezed past her as if she was wearing a burlap sack, not the beautiful red sundress everyone had complimented. For the first time since hanging with him, she actually looked attractive—and Darrell hadn't even noticed.

Serena sat on the sofa's armrest. "So, what happened?"

"Well." Darrell sat near Serena on the sofa. "I didn't get to search the house for anything because the cops were there when I showed up."

"What?" Serena asked, instantly worried.

"Apparently, the housekeeper went there this morning, found the place ransacked, and called the cops. They wouldn't let me in. Besides, I couldn't very well go in there and search for clues with them around."

"Who's the housekeeper?"

"I don't know. She wasn't there when I got there, and they didn't give me her name."

Darrell stood and walked to the patio doors. Serena watched his back muscles expand and contract. Then her gaze dropped. For the first time, she checked out his butt—really *really* checked it out. It was firm and shapely. Strong.

She sighed. Lord, what a beautiful behind.

Darrell peered outside, then turned to face her. His hard stare knocked some common sense back into Serena.

After a moment, Darrell said, "I was thinking—"

"Well, I did some—"

They spoke at the same time.

"You did some what?" Darrell asked.

Serena moved her butt from the armrest to the sofa's cushy area. "I did some investigating at work. I checked out the biggest online auction companies, but I didn't find any listing for the necklace. I don't know if that means it was already sold and I couldn't get info on it, or if Cecil never listed it. In any case, I couldn't find anything, so without Cecil's computer, that's a dead-end."

"Hmmm."

"Now, what were you going to say?"

Darrell strolled to the sofa and sat beside her. "I think I did a half-assed job searching the condo. I mean, I didn't even look for a little black book, and you know Cecil's got to have one. Maybe he has it on him, maybe he doesn't, but I've at least got to head back there and check it out."

"I think you're right. We've been spinning our wheels, hoping we'll happen to find Cecil. But if we can figure out who his friends are, we can probably find out who he's staying with."

"Not only beautiful, but smart, too."

Darrell's comment caught Serena off guard. "Excuse me?"

"Nothing," he said, with a wave of the hand.

Serena stared at him curiously. Did his comment mean her dolled-up appearance hadn't been lost on him? She rarely wore her contact lenses to work, much less a nice dress versus comfort clothes. Yet as she'd glanced at her image in the mirror before leaving for work, she'd liked the look. It was more . . . feminine. Why didn't she dress that way more often?

Darrell's eyes lazily roamed over her, as if he was noticing her for the first time. "You look really nice."

"Thanks."

"That's a nice dress."

Serena couldn't believe it—she actually blushed! She glanced at the floor, hoping Darrell couldn't tell. "Thanks."

"I miss the glasses, though."

Serena's head whipped up.

"Not that you don't look good without them," he quickly amended. "I don't know. They add character or something."

A small smile lifted Serena's lips. Truth be told, she preferred the glasses as well. And in her heart, it mattered that Darrell did, too.

For a moment, Serena thought Darrell would say something else, but he didn't. As she looked at him and he back at her, neither said anything, and Serena suddenly felt awkward.

Because she wanted to kiss him, but she didn't know if he wanted to kiss her, and she sure as heck didn't want to make the first move.

But she'd long ago thrown caution to the wind, so why not go after what she wanted?

Darrell abruptly stood, leaving Serena cold with the gush of air resulting from the sudden action.

"Anyway." Darrell began pacing the floor in front of the sofa. "Like I said, I didn't get to search the house because of the police, but I called home and work to see if Cecil left any messages for me."

"And?"

Darrell shoved his hands into his pockets. "And nothing."

"Maybe he wants to talk to you in person if he's in trouble."

"Maybe. I also called his villa in Jamaica, just in case. There was no answer. That doesn't mean he's not there, but I don't think he is."

"Why not? That might be the best place for him to have taken off to."

"Yeah, but I just have a feeling he didn't leave Miami."

Serena gave him a quizzical look. "Is that one of those psychic connections or something?"

Darrell nodded slowly. "Kind of. I guess we've always had it, in a vague sort of way. I always sensed when Cecil was in trouble . . . but maybe that's because he was pretty much always in trouble." Darrell smiled, but it didn't reach his eyes.

Serena leaned forward, linking her fingers. "All right. So you want to head back to the condo and look for a little black book?"

"Yeah. But first, let me call home again and check messages."

Darrell walked to the loveseat and sat, then lifted the receiver from the adjacent end table that held the phone.

While he made his call, Serena's mind drifted. Darrell seemed completely comfortable in her space, but more so, she liked having him around. Having him here felt natural. Right.

She wasn't exactly sure why. But she did know that the thought of Darrell calling home, a place that was far from here, bothered her. It reminded her that he had a life he'd return to once they found Cecil.

"Pen," Darrell suddenly said. He snapped his fingers to indicate the urgency.

Serena glanced anxiously around her living room. After a moment, she saw a pen and pad of paper on the coffee table. She picked them up and hurried to give them to Darrell.

He scribbled down a number, then hung up.

Serena looked at him expectantly.

"Cecil's housekeeper. She left me a message."

"What did she say?"

"She said to call her," Darrell replied, already punching in the digits to the number he'd written down.

"Nothing else?"

Darrell held up a finger to Serena, silently telling her to wait. After a few seconds, he frowned. "Hello, I'm trying to reach Mariana. This is Darrell Montford, Cecil's brother. Please give me a call at—" His eyes went to Serena. She scribbled her number on the pad and he repeated it into the phone.

Darrell repeated Serena's number, just to be safe, then added, "I'll be here this evening, so if you can call me tonight, that'd be great. Thanks."

He hung up and stood to meet Serena. "Okay. Guess that means I have to wait for her call and head back to Cecil's condo later."

"That could be a while," Serena said.

His eyes suddenly fell to hers, darkening to sparkling obsidian. "Guess we'll have to find some way to pass the time."

Serena reached for his T-shirt and picked at an imaginary piece of fluff. "Did you . . . have anything in mind?"

Darrell placed a hand over hers, flattening her own over his chest. "This is a pretty damn good start."

Serena inhaled a quick, jerky breath. "This?" she asked, bringing her other palm to his chest and running it over his pectoral area.

"Mmmm. That feels good, but I bet it would feel even better if you slipped your hands under my shirt."

Serena swallowed. God, she wanted to touch his bare skin. But she was no temptress. She was a librarian who'd been saving herself for Mr. Right. What if she failed to turn him on?

But what if she did? What then?

Instead of slipping her hands beneath his shirt, Serena

brought a hand to his face. As he looked down at her, she studied him. Her eyes roamed over the firm set of his jaw and his full lips. As her gaze ventured along his cheek, she noticed something she hadn't seen before. A faint scar that ran along the curve of his jaw to his ear.

Impulsively, she reached out and touched it.

Darrell's hand shot up with lightning speed, grabbing her hand. Just like that, the mood was dead.

Serena met his eyes with a steady gaze, ever more curious about him. "That scar looks painful," she said softly. "Like you got it painfully, I mean."

Darrell dropped her hand and stepped away from her.

"What happened?" Serena persisted.

Darrell headed to the patio window. "Feel like getting some dinner?"

Darrell's whole body language had changed. His shoulders drooped, and he had his arms folded over his chest in a closed demeanor. Serena's heart ached for what he must have gone through. "Darrell—"

"What?"

He sounded annoyed, and while his tone hurt her, Serena didn't back down. She'd been raised to believe that talking about things helped you feel better, and she wanted Darrell to feel better. "I'm willing to listen—"

"It doesn't matter."

"Obviously, it does."

Turning, Darrell gave her a pointed look. "Drop it, okay?"

A lump of emotion formed in Serena's chest. She wasn't quite sure if it was because Darrell didn't want to share with her what had happened, or because she knew whatever had happened was horrible.

After a moment, Darrell blew out an annoyed breath. "Like I told you, I didn't have a Cosby-type family life."

"Did your father hit you?"

Darrell didn't respond, but a flash of pain crossed his eyes. The room was still and quiet as Serena waited for Darrell to say something, *do* something, almost as if they were the only two creatures in the world.

"He was drunk," Darrell said after a moment, his voice barely above a whisper. "Hell, when wasn't he? I don't even remember what happened."

Serena began walking toward Darrell.

"My dad pretty much blamed me for everything Cecil did wrong. One of the times the cops showed up at our door with Cecil, my dad got pissed as hell. He asked me why I'd left Cecil alone after school, said that if I hadn't, he wouldn't have gotten into trouble."

"Oh, Darrell."

"My dad didn't even wait long enough to hear that Cecil had skipped school that day, as usual. He was drunk, or he wouldn't have done it, but he grabbed a record from the record player and threw it at me. The edge caught me along the jaw."

Serena stopped in front of Darrell, and this time when she reached for his face, Darrell didn't flinch. Her touch felt good, like a tender, loving caress; it was a touch he'd never truly experienced.

And suddenly Darrell couldn't shut up. But damn, it felt good to get all this off his chest. Until Serena, no one had really cared.

"Cecil had been out with some thug friends of his, doing stupid shit. I don't even remember what. But not enough that the police wanted to bother charging him.

After my dad beat the crap out of Cecil, I also suffered the brunt of his wrath."

Serena traced the outline of his scar with the tip of her finger. "That's why you feel so responsible for him, isn't it? Even now."

"He's my brother."

"No one is going to hold you responsible for Cecil now, least of all me." Boldly, Serena trailed her finger to his chin. "Darrell, look at me."

After several seconds, he met her eyes.

"Honestly, if it means me giving up my search for the necklace right now, I will—to prove a point."

All the moisture in Darrell's mouth dried. Warily, he stared down at her, the tempo of his heart as wild as the salsa dance. "I know how much that necklace means to you."

"Exactly." Her gaze never wavered. "But I get the feeling that if we don't find Cecil, or don't find him in time to retrieve the necklace, you're going to feel extreme guilt over that. And I don't want that, Darrell. You . . . you've been through enough on Cecil's account."

Darrell could hardly think, much less breathe. Was she for real? As Serena continued to stare into his eyes, her fingers still gently caressing his face, a faint smile lifting her lips, a bolt of electricity zapped his heart.

Good Lord, she was serious. She *would* give up her search for the necklace if it meant easing his burden of guilt.

*Why?* Darrell asked himself. *Why, why, why?*

That question was followed by the thought that Darrell didn't want to think anymore. Taking Serena's face in his hands, he brought his lips down on hers fiercely. He sucked the startled breath from her mouth, swallowed it, then opened his mouth wide for more of her.

He kissed her ardently, as if he could suck every bit of goodness from her body and renew his wounded soul. He kissed her as if her lips alone could erase the pent up frustration that had grown within him over the years.

God, he couldn't get enough of her.

He drew Serena's bottom lip between his teeth, biting it gently. When Serena mewled and threw her arms around his neck, Darrell's blood started to boil.

Slipping his tongue into her mouth, he wrapped his arms tightly around her, molding her body to his. He tore his lips from hers, trailing hot kisses along her jaw, down the side of her neck.

"Oh, God, Darrell. I've never felt like this—"

His hands moved over her body with a desperation he didn't know he possessed. Lord help him, he actually *needed* her. He groped her buttocks like a hot and bothered teenager, then brought a hand around to her breast. But, surprising himself, he covered her breast gently. He wanted her with a frenzy he'd never experienced, but he also wanted to savor her. And he wanted her to enjoy this.

"How do I get this off?" Darrell asked urgently.

"The zipper," Serena replied breathlessly. "At the back . . ."

Darrell's hands went to the back of the dress, fumbling for the zipper.

The phone rang.

"Ignore it," Serena said. She kissed the length of Darrell's jaw urgently, pressing her fingers into his back as she did.

Pulling away, Darrell groaned. He looked down at Serena's slumberous eyes. God, he didn't want to end this, but . . .

"Mariana," he said, when the phone rang again. Turning, he hurried to the phone and grabbed the receiver. "Hello?"

"Hello," came a tentative female reply from a woman with a Spanish accent. "I'm looking for Mr. Darrell Montford."

Darrell sank onto the sofa. "This is he."

"Hello, Mr. Montford. This is Mariana Ortiz, your brother's housekeeper."

*Yes!* "Hello, Mariana." Excitedly, he waved Serena over. "Mariana, I'm so glad you called."

"I'm not sure if I can help you," she said. "Like I told the police, I only clean your brother's house once a week. I don't know when it was broken into."

"That's okay," Darrell told her. "Actually, I'm wondering if you can help me locate my brother. I recently came in from out of town, hoping to find him. But he's not around."

"Oh," Mariana crooned. "I don't know where your brother is. Mr. Montford said he was going away for a while."

"When was that?"

"Um . . . I think a little over two weeks ago."

"He didn't say where he was going?" Darrell asked.

"No, sir."

Darrell frowned. When Serena looked at him with questioning eyes, he shrugged. "To tell the truth, Mariana, I'm a little concerned about my brother. The last time I talked to him, I got the impression he was in some kind of trouble. Did he say anything at all to you about that?"

"Oh." Mariana sounded worried. "No. He didn't say anything to me."

"What about acquaintances? Anyone that he was seeing, maybe?"

"I'm sorry, sir. I don't know much about your brother's life. I only clean his house."

Damn. Mariana didn't seem to be much help. After a moment, Darrell said, "I guess that's it. Thanks for getting back to me."

"Wait," Mariana quickly said. "I forgot. Yes, your brother was seeing someone. A woman named Tamara. They broke up not too long ago. Yeah, he had a real bad fight with her on the phone about a month ago. I . . . I didn't really hear what he was saying."

Darrell sensed the woman's hesitation, as if she had indeed heard more of the conversation but was embarrassed to admit that. So he said, "Nothing at all?"

"Well . . . I did hear Mr. Montford say something about paying her back soon. That's all. He kept promising to pay her back as soon as he could. That's all I heard."

"How can I reach her?"

"I don't know."

"Do you know Tamara's last name?"

"No, sir. I'm sorry."

"All right." Darrell frowned. "Thanks, anyway."

"What'd she say?" Serena asked as Darrell replaced the receiver.

Darrell looked up at her. "She doesn't know anything."

"Great."

"She did mention Tamara, however. Said that she and Cecil had a really big fight about a month ago."

"God, I don't think I told you this. My sister had her

ex–boyfriend do some digging—he's a cop—and she learned that Cecil stole jewelry from Tamara, too."

"So that's why she's pissed with him."

"That, and the fact that your brother no doubt led her on." Serena started for the sofa, then hesitated when Darrell gave her an odd look. She suddenly felt awkward. Had she said the wrong thing? Did Darrell think that comment was meant for him?

Whatever the cause, Serena's stomach bubbled with tension.

Hell, she wasn't used to this. She'd never gotten hot and heavy with a guy, only to be distracted, then wonder what on earth was happening between them anyway.

Serena slowly lowered herself onto the sofa, wondering exactly that. What *was* happening between her and Darrell? The tension thickened. Was she too close to Darrell, too far? What was one supposed to do after a moment like the one they'd shared—talk about it, or pretend it had never happened? And if one didn't talk about it, what did that mean?

Lord, she was so confused. Maybe if Darrell would look at her again the way he had before the phone rang, she'd have some idea of how to gauge his feelings. Minutes ago, they'd been ensnared in a web of passion, yet now it was back to business. Serena didn't want to delude herself, but she felt that something was growing between her and Darrell, something powerful. But did he feel the same way, or had she simply been a momentary distraction for him?

"Yeah, Tamara seemed like the jealous type," Darrell commented, interrupting her thoughts. "I can only imagine the line of bull my brother gave her."

"You think she was the one in the Explorer?" Serena asked.

"Maybe." Darrell dug the heels of his palms into his eye sockets. "God, this is all one big headache."

"If Tamara's as crazy as Mimi intimated, I'm surprised she didn't make a scene at the restaurant."

Darrell's eyes shot to hers, a smirk forming on that sexy mouth of his. "The way you did the night I met you?"

Serena's face flushed, remembering her own outrageous behavior. She wanted to say something to refute Darrell's words, but there was nothing she could say. But amazingly, slapping Darrell seemed like a lifetime ago.

"Tamara probably wanted to play it cool at the restaurant," Darrell said, "especially if she had payback in mind."

"You mean running us off the road."

"Yep. If she'd caused some big scene, everyone would remember her. This way, she got to run us off the road with no one giving her a second thought."

"I'm sure my sister's boyfriend—her ex—can get more info on Tamara. At least her number."

"And find out what kind of vehicle she drives. If it's a gold Ford Explorer . . ."

"Then we know for sure she ran us off the road," Serena completed.

Darrell nodded. "And then we pay her a visit."

*Chapter 18*

*Even if Serena relied on an alarm clock to get up* each day, she wouldn't have needed it this morning. She'd tossed and turned all night, and at the first sign of daylight, she'd been up for good.

She'd been way too wired to sleep. Every time she closed her eyes, she remembered Darrell's hands on her butt, on her breast, and how close he'd come to taking off her dress. How much she'd *wanted* him to. And damn if she didn't want to finish what they'd started!

Sitting up, Serena stared at her reflection in the mirror opposite the bed. *Who are you?*

That was the million-dollar question. And she had no lifelines to help her with this one.

All night, she had alternated between hoping Darrell would come into her room, and wondering if she should go into his. And if she'd gone into his, what would have happened? That thought alone had scared her, because it was so *unlike* her. Never had she wanted anyone to touch her body, make her hot with need, as much as she had wanted Darrell to. What had happened to the cautious woman who wouldn't dare think of tempting a guy because temptation could lead to . . .

Well, lead to sex.

She'd been saving herself for Mr. Right for twenty-nine years. So why was the thought of compromising everything she'd believed in crossing her mind, even in fantasy?

Because there was a part of her, something in her heart that went a little crazy every time Darrell looked at her. It was the kind of feeling she'd read about in books, had seen in movies. She'd heard her mother talk about it several times in reference to her father. So, God help her, Darrell *felt* like Mr. Right.

But was he?

The biggest mystery was when she'd even started to feel this way. One minute she'd been slapping him across the face, the next it seemed she was falling for him.

Lord, she *was* falling for him.

Serena let out a soft cry. She *was* falling for him. Oh, God. Was it simply that they were spending so much time together and she couldn't resist his potent male sexuality?

*It's more than that.* Darrell was a very special kind of man, and other than her father, she'd never met anyone quite like him. He had an integrity she admired, a devotion to his brother she respected, and damn if he wasn't the most irresistible man on the planet.

But he was a Montford, and how in her right mind could she ever get involved with the lying, scamming Cecil's brother?

The question disturbed her, and Serena dropped her

head back against the pillow. She had to stop thinking about Darrell! Glancing at the phone, she willed it to ring. Kiana should call any minute with some news about Tamara. Serena had called Kiana last night and updated her on the situation, and Kiana had promised to call Geoff right away.

So why hadn't Kiana called back yet?

Darrell . . . Again, Serena's mind drifted to the fine brother who was in the bedroom next to hers. It was still early, and she wondered if he was awake, unable to sleep, as she had been.

If Serena lay here all day, she wouldn't stop thinking about him. She was better off getting up and doing something, *anything*, to keep her mind off Darrell. Serena sat up and swung her feet off the bed and reached for her glasses. The apartment was quiet. Darrell was probably still asleep. She'd go shower before he got up.

Serena rose, stretched, slipped into her robe which lay across the rocking chair at the foot of her bed, then strolled to the bedroom door. After a brief pause to listen for sound, she opened the door and stepped into the hallway. But at the same moment, Darrell stepped into the hallway from the bathroom.

Serena couldn't help it—her mouth dropped open. Darrell was naked—except for a white towel wrapped around his waist. Man, she'd known he was sexy as hell after seeing his torso a couple days ago, but with beads of water glistening on his magnificent body, and the towel split at his thigh, he was like an oasis in a desert.

And man, was Serena ever ready to quench her thirst.

"Morning," Darrell said slowly. "Um, I took a shower."

*No doubt,* Serena thought, glad she somehow kept herself from speaking out loud. "Yes, I see." She met his eyes only briefly before perusing the rest of his body once more. He had long, lean legs and strong thighs. Her gaze traveled the length of the slit in the towel, from just above his knee to where it stopped below his hip.

Lord help her, it was getting hot in here. Had the air conditioning died?

"Serena?"

Her eyes shot to his. "Hmm?"

"Did you . . ." Darrell paused. "Want something?"

Oh, yes, she wanted something all right—the incredible man before her. "Oh, I was going to . . . take a shower."

"I'm done. The bathroom's all yours."

*Stop it, Serena,* she scolded herself. *Stop staring at him like you want to serve him up as the main course.* But God, that's exactly what she wanted to do.

Inhaling a deep breath, Serena dropped her gaze to the floor. That was the only way she could stop looking at him. Her head lowered, she hurried toward the bathroom door.

As Serena reached him, then took a step past him, Darrell should have let her continue on. Instead, he darted out a hand and took hold of her upper arm.

Startled, Serena looked first at her arm, then raised her gaze to Darrell's face. She had long, thick eyelashes, and damn if it didn't seem as if she was giving him a coy look. One minute, she'd been looking him up and down with an I-want-you-in-my-bed gaze from behind her glasses, yet now she giving him a shy glance. Darrell had always been a sucker for the sweet-and-demure-with-a-wild-and-sexy-side type.

He was used to women staring at his body with both subtle and obvious appreciation, but somehow, Serena's stare was different. He wanted to be perfect for her, to believe that she found him completely irresistible in a way she hadn't found any other man.

He tightened his grip.

Serena's mouth opened, as if she was about to say something, but no words escaped those beautiful, full lips. With her lips parted and slightly moist, Darrell's hormones went wild. His groin tightened at the thought of smothering her mouth with his, of crushing her soft body against his hard one.

His other hand went to her face, gently stroking her smooth skin. Then, his fingers tangled in her short hair as he angled her face upward and lowered his.

A soft sigh escaped her lips as his face neared hers, and Darrell watched her eyelids flutter shut. God, he wanted her so badly, more than he'd wanted anything in his life.

He turned her in his arms, pulling her body to his. He brushed his nose against hers. Serena moaned and wrapped her arms around his neck.

Darrell pressed his body against hers. He felt his erection rise just as his towel start to slip away.

Quickly, he grabbed the towel before it fell. Serena jumped back.

And just like that, the moment was gone.

"I'm gonna shower . . ." Serena scurried into the bathroom and closed the door. Darrell heard the lock turn.

Darrell threw his head back and groaned. Then, holding the towel securely around his waist, he stomped into his bedroom and closed the door. Once inside, he pressed his forehead against the wood and closed his eyes.

Man, what was he *doing?* Darrell wanted her, no doubt about it, but hell, crossing the line with Serena would be the biggest mistake of his life. He'd come to that realization when he'd thought about her all night long, and had repeated that fact beneath the cold stream of the shower a short while ago.

Yes, he was attracted to her—he couldn't deny that—but Darrell could not get involved with her. Serena wasn't the kind of woman a guy simply slept with, then walked away from.

He had no doubt that sex with her would be fabulous, which was half the problem. Serena probably didn't realize it, but every time she looked at him and fluttered those sexy lashes of hers, Darrell practically got hard. That whole combination of good-girl-with-a-wild-side was literally making him crazy.

Wasn't it exactly that combination that all men wanted in a woman? The quality that made them fabulous-in-bed wife material?

There he went again, thinking the "wife" word. He didn't want a wife. He'd known that before Jessica, but had conveniently forgotten that when he'd been involved with her, only to have her drive the point home for good with her deception.

So, yes, he wanted Serena in his bed, but the problem was that for Serena, it wouldn't only be sex. From everything she'd told him, he knew she was a woman with a deep commitment to family. She'd definitely want her own, and that was something he couldn't give her.

Darrell finally moved from the door and went to the bed, where he lay down. He had to remember what he was doing here in Miami. He was here to find his brother. He didn't need any distractions.

And he sure as hell didn't need any complications.

* * *

Later, Serena was sitting at the kitchen table when Darrell strolled into the room. At the sight of him, her heart thumped hard in her chest.

She was still reeling from the fact that he'd almost lost his towel—and from the startling revelation that she'd *wanted* him to. When the moment had been broken, she'd run scared not because she was afraid of what could happen, but because she knew without a doubt what she wanted to happen.

She had never, ever felt such a strong attraction to any man before. Why Darrell?

In the shower, she'd thought and thought and thought about him. He was so obviously not marriage material, at least, not for her. He'd flat out told her that he didn't want a family, and she most definitely did. So how could she even be attracted to him?

It had to be lust. The kind of lust that made you lose all reason—something she wasn't accustomed to. But, thank the Lord, they'd both regained their senses before she got caught up in something she couldn't control. Because it would be a mistake. She didn't want casual sex, and she knew that's all Darrell would offer. Call her an old-fashioned prude, but she wanted more.

Then why did it bother her that Darrell's eyes no longer held the spark they had in the hallway?

"Hey," he said, pulling out a chair and sitting across from her.

No, the electrically charged moment they'd shared in the hallway was definitely gone. The realization disappointed Serena.

"Did I hear the phone ring a while ago?" Darrell asked.

Serena tried to swallow her disappointment, but it got stuck around her heart, which was firmly planted in her throat. "Yeah. My sister called. She told me she still hadn't heard from Geoff yet—her ex-boyfriend who's the cop."

"So no way to reach Tamara."

"Not unless we find Cecil's black book at the condo. You still want to do that?"

"Yeah, I'll go check it out. If that fails, I can try and find Mimi. She might know."

"You want some breakfast before we head out?"

Darrell's eyes narrowed. "We?"

"Yeah." Butterflies danced crazily in Serena's stomach. "I figured I'd go with you."

"Don't you have to work?"

"I already called in and told them I can't make it."

"Serena—"

"I want to go back to the condo with you." Even now, despite what she'd told herself about there being no hope for a relationship between her and Darrell, she still wanted to spend more time with him.

"I don't like the idea of you missing work over this."

"I have to get my car anyway," Serena pointed out, but once again she felt disappointment. Couldn't she take a hint? Darrell clearly didn't want to spend more time with her. Why couldn't she let go?

"I forgot about that," Darrell said after a moment.

Silence fell between them, and when the phone rang, both Serena and Darrell jumped, startled.

"One second," Serena said when she recovered, then hustled to the living room to answer the phone. "Hello?"

"Serena."

That voice. A chill swept over her, then nervous excitement.

"Serena, it's Cecil. Please, don't hang up."

"Where are you?"

"That's not important. Are you okay?"

"Yes, I'm okay. What's going on?"

From her peripheral vision, Serena saw Darrell rise. He made his way toward her.

"I don't have time to talk right now. I just want you to know . . . I'll be in touch soon. And I have your necklace."

Serena heard a voice in the background.

Cecil hurriedly said, "I have to go."

"Cecil, wait—"

Darrell grabbed the receiver from her and held it to his ear. "Cecil? Cecil?" He slammed down the phone. "Damn." Facing Serena, he asked, "What did he say?"

Stunned from the call, Serena paused. Then she said, "Not much, really. He asked if I was okay, then said he had my necklace."

"And then he hung up?"

"Yeah." Serena checked the phone's caller ID box. "His number didn't show up."

"Why did he hang up?"

"I don't know. I heard noise in the background, a voice, then he said he had to go. I didn't even get to tell him you were here."

Darrell headed to the window and looked outside.

"What are you thinking?"

"I'm wondering why he called, only to hang up." Darrell faced her. "Does that mean someone's after him right now? God, I feel so helpless."

"I wish I knew."

"At least he said he has your necklace. That means he plans to give it back."

Serena gave Darrell a skeptical look.

"If he was going to hawk it, he wouldn't have called to tell you he has it."

"If he didn't want to hawk it, he wouldn't have taken it in the first place."

Darrell paused, then said, "Whatever. If we're going to go, then let's go."

Clearly, Darrell was miffed, but what did he expect Serena to think? That Cecil had suddenly become a trustworthy guy? She might think Darrell was decent, but that didn't change the fact that his brother was slime.

"You ready?" Darrell asked.

"Sure," Serena replied testily. "Just let me grab my purse."

Cecil replaced the receiver, but he wasn't fast enough. Virginia had seen him.

She strolled toward him. "Who was that?"

"No one," Cecil lied. "I was checking messages."

"Really?" Virginia raised a dubious eyebrow.

Cecil shot to his feet when she neared him and reached for her. She swatted his hand.

"Cecil, what's going on?"

"Nothing."

Virginia planted her hands on her hips and stared at him.

"What?"

"I love spending time with you, Cecil, but you have to admit this is a little much for you."

"C'mon, baby doll." Cecil stroked her face. "You know I love being with you."

"Oh, Cecil. Save your lies."

Cecil frowned. "Why would I—"

"Cecil, you normally stay here for a night or two, max."

"Yeah, well . . . I've missed you."

Virginia said, "You think I don't know the real reason you've been hanging out here? I'm sure it's not because you like my new implants."

"Of course I like them," Cecil replied. He reached for a breast beneath her silk robe, but she knocked his hand away.

"I know you're in some kind of trouble," she continued. "And you obviously had no one else to turn to, or you wouldn't be here."

"That's not true."

"You're not in any trouble?" she challenged.

Cecil gave her a sheepish look. "You were the first person I thought of to turn to."

"You mean the only one who would take you in. Let's face it, if any of the young women you play with would have you, you'd be there, not here."

Cecil was about to respond that he liked mature women, but it would be a lie. At fifty, Virginia wasn't exactly his first choice, even if she was still attractive and in excellent shape. She gave him a knowing smile. "I played this game once too, remember? So, tell me. How much do you need?"

"Two hundred thou."

"Two hundred thousand?" Virginia repeated, mortified.

"I swear, baby doll, I will pay you back every cent just as soon as I can."

"I doubt that."

"Honestly."

"Whatever. It doesn't matter. I can't help you."

"*Please*, baby doll," Cecil begged. "I wouldn't ask if my life didn't depend on it."

"I can't." Virginia shrugged helplessly. "Walter's kids are contesting his will, so all the money's frozen."

"Shit!"

"You can stay here for as long as you want—or until I get bored with you." She softened the words with a grin. "But that's all I can offer you. Sorry, sweetie."

Kiana was on her second cup of coffee when she heard a banging at her front door. Expecting a package from her editor, she quickly hurried to answer it.

"Geoff," she said breathlessly as she opened the door.

"Hey."

She stood back to let him in. "I thought you were going to call me."

"I was on my way to work, so I figured I'd stop by."

"You have some information for me?"

"Yeah."

Geoff was different today. He wasn't his normal, bubbly self.

"What's wrong?" Kiana asked.

"I don't have much time," he said, digging into his back pocket. "So, here's what you wanted. Numbers for the people who accused Cecil of theft. Of course, you didn't get these from me."

He passed her a sheet of paper, but Kiana didn't look at it as she accepted it. "Geoff, what's the matter?"

"Nothing. You wanted information, I brought it to you."

"And that's . . . it?"

"What? You want something else?" His eyes held hers in challenge, and when Kiana didn't respond, Geoff added, "That's what I thought."

"What's with the attitude, Geoff?"

"You should be happy. Aren't you the one who always says you don't want me coming on to you?"

"So if you're not coming on to me, you can't be nice?"

"I'm gonna go." Geoff turned to leave.

"Wait a minute," Kiana said, scrambling after him. She placed a hand on his arm, and he stopped. "I don't like this."

Geoff first looked at her hand, then met her eyes. "You want to know something? I don't like it either. You say you appreciate me and care about me, yet you only call me when you need me."

"Is that what you think?"

"Tell me it's not so."

"Come here." Kiana opened her arms and wrapped them around Geoff, hugging him tightly. "You know that's not the case."

Geoff didn't hug her back, and after a few moments, abruptly stepped away from her. "Why do you do that?"

"What?"

"Hug me like that. You know I'm still attracted to you. Hell, I'm still in *love* with you. It almost seems like you're deliberately teasing me."

"No," Kiana quickly replied, frowning. "Of course not."

"I'm not sure you know what you want. When you look at me, touch me, I see your attraction. But when you open your mouth, something entirely different comes out."

"I want us to be friends," Kiana replied succinctly.

"Friends." The muscle in Geoff's jaw flinched. "Friends stay in touch, Kiana."

"I'm sorry. I've been busy."

"Yeah, that's what you always tell me when I call you. But the moment your sister needs info to track down her ex, you're suddenly in touch with me, and I'm hearing from you a few times a day? You've got to realize how that looks to me. Maybe it wouldn't bother me if I didn't care about you, but I do. You told me before that I didn't let you know how I feel enough, that that's one of the reasons you ended things, but now that I tell you—"

"What do you want me to say?"

"I want you to admit that you still have feelings for me." He gave her a frank look. "Because I know you do."

"I still . . . care."

"You know, if I didn't see that you still loved me every time I looked in your eyes, I wouldn't bother you about us."

"Why we broke up . . . it was about more than you not telling me how you feel. It's what you do, it's who you are."

"My being a cop."

"After the honeymoon phase was over, you worked way too much, canceled our dates. I worried about you all the time."

"But being a cop is fine when you need something, right?"

"Do you not want me to call and ask you for anything anymore?" Kiana asked, exasperated. "Is that it?"

Geoff gave her a disappointed look. "Yeah," he said softly, "maybe it is. If you can't be honest with yourself and with me, maybe we shouldn't talk at all."

"Fine," Kiana said, though her heart began to ache.

"All right. I hope what I've given you helps your sister out."

Kiana knew she should say something to Geoff as he made his way to the door, tell him that she didn't want him to walk out of her life, but she didn't say a damn thing.

And when he left, she felt as if they'd broken up all over again.

# Chapter 19

Darrell wasn't in the mood to be friendly when they arrived at Cecil's condo, and clearly the condo staff recognized that. When Miguel took the car he was cordial, but not chatty, which suited Darrell fine.

Serena had been silent for practically the entire trip there, except to give him directions. He didn't like the tension between them, but he didn't know what to say to change it.

In a way, he was mad at himself. He hadn't come down to Miami for a holiday, and he felt like he'd been wasting time. His brother was in trouble, and he should be spending every waking moment trying to find him.

He had no time for duck feeding and talking about his past and thinking about getting naked with Serena. That he'd been so easily distracted in the face of his brother's dilemma bothered him.

Darrell opened the door to the condo. "Okay," he said,

getting right down to business. "I'll go to my brother's bedroom and search there. You start in the kitchen."

"All right," Serena agreed in a wooden voice.

"Look for anything you can find that seems relevant. Business cards. Scrawled numbers. His black book, of course."

"Yeah."

Darrell headed down the hallway, and Serena went to the kitchen. Pushing aside the bitter feeling in her stomach at the distance Darrell had put between them, she set herself to the task at hand. She rummaged through each drawer and cupboard, but found nothing other than everyday kitchen items. The place was pristine to the point where it pretty much didn't look lived in.

Which, Serena realized, it probably wasn't.

The place was lavish and way too large for one person. And given how much Cecil liked to socialize, he no doubt ate out most of the time.

Next, she went to the living room, but one complete glance told her there wasn't anything in here that could help her. There wasn't even so much as a scrap of paper on an end table.

Somewhat frustrated, she headed to the master bedroom, where she found Darrell sitting on the bed. Beside him, the night table drawer was open and he was carefully sifting through its contents.

"Did you find anything?" Serena asked.

"My brother is certainly neater than I remember him being."

"There was nothing in the kitchen, not even a fork out of place."

"I get the feeling he spent more time at his house in the

Grove. He had a computer there. Here, he has clothes, linens for the bed, but not much else."

Serena wandered to the other night table. "Have you looked through here yet?"

"No. Go ahead."

Serena sat and pulled open the drawer. Her face flamed as she saw the immediate contents. A pack of condoms, a bottle of lubricant. She cringed.

"What?" Darrell asked.

"Uh . . . maybe you should go through this drawer."

"Why?"

"Well." Serena rubbed the back of her neck. "It's a little . . . *personal*."

Darrell's eyebrow peaked with curiosity. "Personal?"

"Yes," Serena said emphatically. Her eyes caught something shiny. Handcuffs, she realized a moment later.

Darrell scooted around to her side of the bed and glanced down into the drawer. He chuckled for the first time today. "Oh. I see."

Great, he thought this was funny, while she was so embarrassed she didn't even want to touch anything.

He lifted a small aerosol can. "Stay hard spray. Hmm. Maybe Cecil wasn't quite the don he thought he was."

"Oh, my God!" Serena exclaimed, jumping up. "*Stay hard* spray?"

Darrell lifted something from the drawer that looked like a stiff condom. "Ah. A French tickler."

Serena held up a hand and looked away. "I don't even want to know."

"And a whip."

Serena groaned her disgust.

"I take it you've never used any of this stuff before?"

"God, no!"

Darrell shouldn't tease her, but he couldn't help it. This was the first laugh he'd had for the day. Serena's initial reaction made it obvious she'd never used any of this kinky stuff, and he couldn't help chuckling at her innocence. It pleased him to know that she was, at her core, still sweet.

"Have *you* used any of this stuff?" she asked.

"No," Darrell replied.

Glancing at the drawer, she grimaced. "Then how do you know what all this stuff is?"

Darrell shrugged. "I'm a guy. You hear things from other guys growing up."

She gave him a doubtful look.

He placed a hand over his heart. "Honestly. When I make love, I don't need or want any of these toys."

Staring at him, her expression softened. No, she thought, her heartbeat accelerating, she couldn't imagine Darrell needing anything to help him in that department. The thought made her as hot as she'd been only hours ago.

"I don't know how anyone can call that stuff toys," she said after a moment.

"Neither do I. But, to each his own, I guess."

Serena headed toward the bedroom's closet. "Have you gone through here?"

"No, but I went through all his other drawers. Go ahead."

Serena opened the closet door and cautiously peered inside. She didn't want any more surprises. The interior was the size of her apartment kitchen. She stepped inside and looked around, but again, it looked to be in the same pristine shape as the living room and kitchen.

"Here we go!" Darrell exclaimed.

Spinning around, Serena darted out of the closet. Her eyes met Darrell's across the room.

He slapped something against the palm of his hand, then lifted it to show her. "Cecil's little black book. I found it."

Cecil was glad when Virginia finally left the house. She said she was heading to Miami Beach to do some shopping, which meant she'd be gone for hours. He could use a little peace and quiet.

He supposed he should be thankful that she wasn't kicking him out, even though she was onto him. What the hell, like she'd said, she'd been a player herself. She understood him. And most of all, she enjoyed his company. At least he hadn't completely lost his touch.

He was waiting on Eddie to call him back before making a move, but the lying son of a bitch wasn't keeping in touch. He beeped him; Eddie didn't call. With each passing day, Cecil saw the reality of getting Jan's jewelry back dying.

Yeah, Jan was pissed. But if it was just her he had to contend with, he was sure he could smooth things over. But her husband Rex was out for blood.

No doubt he was as good as dead if they ever found him. His only option was to offer Rex cold hard cash and hope that appeased him. He'd been counting on Virginia, but now that had fallen through. He couldn't turn to Tamara. She was mad as hell with him as well. And there was no point going to Sylvia, a woman whose jewelry he'd already stolen and replaced. There was no way she'd give him the kind of cash he needed, not after he'd disappeared from her life without an explanation.

The only person he could logically turn to was Darrell.

He didn't know if his brother had that much cash on hand, but if he explained the situation to him, that this was a matter of life and death, surely Darrell would do what he could to come up with the money. He could always count on Darrell in a bind.

After this, he was going straight. No more conning, no more crime.

Which would no doubt be easier than he hoped. Because if Jan's husband didn't kill him, he'd most likely end up in cell block D in the state pen.

It was pretty damn hard to remain a criminal from behind a jail cell.

"Cecil's black book?" Serena asked, excited. She rushed to Darrell and plopped down beside him on the bed.

Darrell flipped through the book. "Oh yeah. This is it. Wow. There are a ton of numbers in here."

Serena glanced over his shoulder. From what she could see, all the names were of women. But surprisingly, she felt no more disappointment or disillusionment over Cecil's deceit.

She'd had to accept that Cecil was a liar, a cheat, and a thief. Now that she had, it was much easier to realize he was a master con artist. She'd stopped beating herself up for getting involved with him and was able now simply to concentrate on what was important—getting the necklace back.

"I should start calling some of these people," Darrell announced. His nose still in the black book, he strolled around to the other side of the bed where the phone rested on that night table. He lifted the receiver. Then he frowned as he replaced it. "There's no dial tone. Cecil must have disconnected this phone, too."

"Let's head back to my place," Serena said. "We can make the calls from there."

"Okay."

"Did you want to look around anymore?"

"I don't see the point. Like you said, except for the sex toys, it doesn't seem like my brother even lives here."

Serena's face warmed at the mention of the sex toys, and the realization that she had sat on a bed where Cecil had used them with God only knew how many women.

No, she had no desire to stay here any longer.

Darrell walked to the bedroom door. "You ready?"

Serena took one last look at the bed and the drawer that held the sex toys, and shuddered. "Yeah. I definitely am."

"Yo," Cecil said into the receiver. "How you doing, sweet thang?"

"Cecil?"

"Yeah, Mimi. It's me." It was a long shot, but Cecil thought he remembered Mimi telling him that her father was some business tycoon with tons of money. Maybe she could help him out.

Mimi yawned loudly. "Do you know what time it is?"

"Time I saw your lovely face again," Cecil answered. "You miss me, baby?"

Mimi chuckled. "Your ego amazes me."

"It's just a question, sweet thang. Since I haven't been around for a while."

"Mmm hmm. You get rid of that goody-two-shoes girl you were hanging out with a few days ago? And spare me the details about her being a friend. I saw the way she was looking at you."

Cecil's forehead scrunched. "Come again?"

"That girl you were with on Saturday. The one who looked like she escaped from the convent."

"I wasn't at Monty's on Saturday."

"Why are you even gonna lie?"

"I wasn't," Cecil insisted.

"What kind of drugs are you on? I served you, you idiot. You don't remember Tamara staring you down like she wanted to kill you right there in the bar?"

"Sweet thang, I was *not* there this past Saturday."

"Then you must have a twin."

There was a pause as the truth hit Cecil.

"Come on," Mimi said. "I talked to you like you were you. Even if it was your dead ringer, he wouldn't have pretended he was you."

"Oh, shit."

"What?"

"Mimi, I *do* have a twin. Shit, he must have come to town." Darrell must have gotten worried about him after their last phone call and headed to Miami.

And he'd *happened* to show up at Monty's? What was going on?

"You have a twin?" Mimi asked, doubt lacing her tone.

"Yeah. That would explain why he played along like he was me."

"You're shitting me."

"He was there with a woman?"

"Yeah," Mimi began, still skeptical. "Like I said, she looked like she'd come straight from a convent."

*Serena.* How the hell had Darrell hooked up with her?

"I have to go," Cecil announced.

"Wait, Cecil. What's going on?"

"Hell if I know, sweet thang. Hell if I know."

As Darrell had done the previous day when they returned to her place, Serena circled the block of her apartment complex a few times. Behind her, Darrell followed in the Viper. When she was sure the coast was clear, she turned into her apartment's parking lot. She parked, and Darrell parked beside her. Minutes later, they were inside her apartment.

Kicking off her sandals, Serena asked, "How do you want to work this? Split up the list and we both make calls? I only have one phone line, but your brother's got a car phone. You can use that."

"Sounds good to me."

"Wait." Frowning, Serena paced left and right. "Maybe that's not such a good idea. If you call these women, they'll think you're Cecil—and considering he's screwed at least some of them over, they won't be happy to hear from you." Serena shook her head. "No, I'd better make the calls."

Darrell nodded. "That makes sense."

"Well, there's no time like the present. I'll start now."

"What are you going to say?" Darrell asked.

Serena stopped. She hadn't thought about that. "I'm not sure. I suppose I'll play a jilted girlfriend, someone who's as pissed with Cecil as the rest of them probably are."

"All right."

"You have another idea?"

Darrell shook his head. "Here you go." Darrell passed her the black book. "I'll go to the Viper and call home for messages."

Serena took the book into her bedroom. Sitting on her

bed, she flipped it open. She could hardly believe there were so many names and numbers in there. From the amount of time Cecil had spent with her in the time she'd known him, she would never guess he had such an extensive list of . . . *friends.*

Oh, well. None of that mattered anymore.

Serena decided not to search for specific names and just started from the beginning of the book. She dialed the first number, which belonged to an Annie Collins.

The phone rang four times, then a machine picked up. Serena hung up. She certainly didn't want to leave a message.

There was no answer at the first several numbers— obviously, given the time of day, people were at work.

Serena flipped the page. The next number belonged to Virginia LeBeau. After two rings, a woman answered. "Hello?"

Nerves tickled Serena's stomach. "Hello."

"Who is this?"

"Uh . . ." Her mind scrambled to come up with something. "My name is Carol. I'll just come right out and be honest with you. I found your number in my boyfriend's little black book. We had a bad fight, and I know he's mad at me, and he moved out. I'm trying to locate him through his friends." God, she hoped that sounded plausible. "His name is Cecil—"

"Cecil?"

"Yes. Have you been in touch with him?"

"Cecil's a big boy. If he wants to talk to you, he'll call you."

Serena sighed. Maybe this wasn't going to work. "Look, I don't care if he's moved on, but he has some things of mine I'd like to collect."

"I haven't heard from him. Sorry."

Serena heard a click, then moments later, the dial tone sounded in her ear.

Well, that hadn't worked. And she didn't know what to think. If Cecil had screwed Virginia over, wouldn't she have been inclined to badmouth him?

Serena reached for a pen, then put a little check beside Virginia's name, indicating that she'd reached her. She moved on to the next number.

Jan McDonald. Wasn't that one of the women who had reported Cecil to the police? Yes, Serena was sure that's what her sister had told her. She dialed the number.

After several rings, it was apparent that no one was going to answer, so Serena hung up.

The next number belonged to Frances Ottey. After one ring, a man answered.

"Uh, hello," Serena said. "I'm looking for Frances."

"One sec."

Moments later, Frances came to the phone. "Hello?"

"Hello, Frances. This will probably sound weird, but I'm trying to locate my boyfriend, and I found your number in his black book. We've broken up, so I don't care if he's moved on, but he's got some property of mine—"

"Who's your boyfriend?"

"Cecil Montford."

Frances guffawed. "Honey, kiss your things good-bye. That man has a way of milking a woman dry."

"What did he do to you?"

"If you still have a roof over your head, be glad, and cut your losses. Cecil's slime."

While Serena tried to think of something else to say, Frances hung up.

She spent the next twenty minutes going through the remaining numbers in the book. Tamara's number was there, but like Jan, she wasn't home. Serena didn't leave a message.

She reached a few more women, none of whom seemed particularly thrilled to hear Cecil's name, but if they knew where he was, they certainly weren't talking.

Serena went back to the living room and was startled when she didn't see Darrell. She did a three-sixty around the room and saw him through the patio doors. She headed that way. As she neared the window, she saw ducks surrounding Darrell's feet.

A smile touched her lips. He was feeding the ducks.

She slid the patio door open. Darrell turned when he heard her.

And smiled.

He had a sweet smile, one that lit up his whole face. Especially his eyes.

She walked onto the concrete and slid her feet into her flip-flops. "Feeding the ducks?"

Darrell tossed some bread. "I came out to see if Buford was okay."

"And is he?"

"He is." Darrell threw the last pieces of bread to the ducks, then strolled toward Serena. "What'd you find?"

"Nothing much. Most of the women weren't home, so I didn't leave messages. Of the ones who were home, I got mostly condolences on having been involved with Cecil or congrats that our relationship was over."

"Great."

"I'll try the numbers again in a little while." Serena's

gaze went to the ducks. They'd followed Darrell. "I didn't have much bread, did I?"

"No."

"Wanna go buy some? We can feed the ducks, then I can make some more calls."

"Sure."


Cecil's head whipped up when he heard a sound. Virginia stood with her arms crossed over her chest, leaning against the doorjamb. He'd been sleeping and didn't know she had returned.

"When did you get back?" he asked, sitting up.

"Who's Carol?"

"Carol?"

Virginia strolled casually into the room. "I don't mind putting you up, but please—tell your other girlfriends not to call here for you."

"What are you talking about?"

"I just got off the phone with Carol. Says you two broke up, but you have some of her things."

"I don't know any Carol."

Virginia flashed Cecil a plastic smile. "If you're going to stay here, I at least expect some respect. Don't treat me like a fool."

"I'm telling you the truth!" Cecil bolted up from the bed. "Shit." He began to pace. "I told you already, I'm in a bit of trouble. Someone's obviously looking for me." His eyes flew to hers. "What did you tell her?"

"That I didn't know where you are."

"Okay, good. Damn, how would anyone find me here?"

"Look, I don't want any trouble here," Virginia said in a

matter-of-fact tone. "This place still isn't quite mine. Not until after this whole business with court."

"No, no," Cecil replied quickly. "Everything's cool."

"Are you sure?"

"Yeah. Even if someone has your number, they won't know where you live." Cecil frowned. "But something's up."

"Is it?"

The tone of her voice changed, and Cecil met Virginia's eyes. One perfectly sculpted eyebrow was arched and her dark eyes flashed heat.

"You've been ignoring me all day, Cecil."

"You haven't been here."

"True enough." She smiled. "I'm here now." Virginia began unbuttoning her blouse.

"But I'm trying . . ." Cecil's voice faltered as she did a sexy strut toward him. "I need to think . . ."

She dropped her silk blouse to the floor and unfastened her bra. "There'll be plenty of time to think—later. Right now, I need a reminder of why I'm keeping you around."

She dropped the bra to the floor.

One look at those double D's and Cecil was lost.

Virginia was wrong. Cecil loved her new breasts as much as she loved showing them off. And damn if she didn't have it going on as much as a woman fifteen years her junior.

What the hell. He'd wanted to call Serena again and see if she was around, especially since it made sense that Darrell was with her. But that could wait.

After all, he had to keep Virginia happy.

Before she kicked him out on the street.

\*   \*   \*

Time certainly flew when you were having fun. After a trip to the grocery store for a couple loaves of bread and spending some time feeding the ducks, the day had practically flown by.

It was early evening when Darrell and Serena stepped back into her apartment.

"I'm gonna make those calls now," she announced. There was no reason she couldn't make them with Darrell around, so she added, "Just let me grab Cecil's black book from my bedroom."

Serena scurried to the bedroom. So far, she felt she was doing a lousy job at playing detective, but she didn't know what else to do. She was still kicking herself for not blurting out to Cecil that his brother was with her, but she'd been so stunned by his call. And she certainly hadn't expected him to hang up seconds later.

In the bedroom, she reached for the black book on top of her bed—and noticed that the answering machine on her phone was flashing a red zero-one.

She depressed the play button.

"Serena, this is Cecil calling back. Damn, I was hoping to find you home. I spoke to a friend earlier today, and it sounds like my brother's in town. I don't know what you all are doing, but please tell Darrell to lay low. I'm in trouble, and if anyone thinks he's me . . . It could be bad. That's why I haven't been able to return your necklace, but I should be able to as soon as this is all worked out. In the meantime, watch out for a man and woman traveling together. If you see them, don't stop. Better yet, tell Darrell to stop looking for me—I know he is. Oh, and whatever happens, do not call the police. All right, I have to go, but I'll try and be in touch later."

Serena could only stare in wide-eyed disbelief at the machine once the message was over.

She hurried back to the living room to get Darrell. "Darrell, you have to come and listen to this message. It's from Cecil."

Hearing Serena's words, Darrell's eyes lit up. "My brother called?"

Serena nodded, then pivoted back in the direction she'd come from. Darrell was fast on her heels.

After listening to the message, Darrell faced her. "Okay, so he knows I'm here. He'll probably call back."

"Hopefully."

A soft grin formed on Darrell's lips. "I don't know when whatever mess he's in will be resolved, but at least he still has your necklace and plans to do right by you."

Serena wasn't quite ready to share Darrell's enthusiasm. "We'll see."

Annoyance flashed in Darrell's dark eyes. "I could understand your skepticism when he called this morning, but if he was full of it, why call twice?"

"To keep me from going to the police. You heard what he said."

"I know my brother," Darrell replied a little testily. "He's going to do the right thing. Maybe it took this situation to finally set him on the right track."

"You admitted Cecil has been a criminal almost since day one. This call is probably about doing whatever he can to save his own butt," Serena added, unable to hide her irritation.

"I say we give him the benefit of the doubt."

"Like I did before?" Serena asked, then scoffed.

"You'll get your necklace back," Darrell said. He'd

raised his voice and was clearly angry. "I already promised you that."

Before Serena could say anything else, Darrell stormed out of the room. She was going to go after him, but instead she emitted a loud groan and dropped herself onto her bed. God, she just wanted this whole situation over and done with.

Yet the thought of Darrell leaving made her stomach take a nosedive into a pool of disappointment. She especially didn't want him to leave angry with her. She appreciated everything he was doing to help her.

Serena waited several minutes, giving Darrell time to cool off, then went out to the living room. She felt a moment of panic when she saw that Darrell wasn't there. She hurried to the apartment door to see if the Viper was still outside, but stopped short of opening it when she realized he might be in the bedroom. Going back down the hallway, she gently rapped on that door.

"Yes," came Darrell's soft reply.

Relief washed over her. "Um, I was wondering if you're hungry."

After a moment, he replied, "I guess."

"I'm going to order a pizza. Anything you want on it?"

"Whatever you get is fine."

Serena frowned her displeasure. He was mad at her, and she didn't know what to do or say to make things right.

Darrell had said she should give Cecil the benefit of the doubt, but it was something she simply couldn't do. Where Cecil was concerned, she'd have to see it to believe it.

# Chapter 20

*Darrell was as uncomfortable as hell.*

Though he and Serena were sitting at her kitchen table eating dinner, and though she'd been nothing but cordial to him as she'd gotten him a plate and a drink, the tension between them was thick enough to make mud balls with and sling at each other.

They'd barely spoken two words, and Darrell had just finished his last slice. He was lousy at small talk and didn't know how to diffuse a situation that was an emotional time bomb. Give him something real to solve—like bailing his brother out of jail—and he could deal with that. But figuring out a way to get a woman to stop sulking—he was clueless on that front.

Which drove home the point that he was lousy at relationships. With his last girlfriend, he'd shut down when it came to arguments. Only after a bout of fussing and pouting and ultimately crying on her part did he finally break down and apologize, then try to comfort her. It was something he hadn't seen his own father do when he and his mom had gotten into their crazy spats, so Darrell had figured it couldn't hurt. But when he found himself always apologizing to Jessica, only to realize that she *never* apologized, he'd figured out how big a fool he was. Of course, he'd figured that out once and for all after he'd caught her stealing from him. He'd vowed never to be that kind of fool again.

He knew Serena had a right to be pissed with Cecil, and he understood her hesitation in trusting him, but why would he call twice and promise to return her necklace if he had no plans to honor his word? It would be a new kind of low to so obviously screw her twice—once, by taking the necklace, and twice, by pretending he was going to return it. Cecil wasn't the most honorable guy around, but he wasn't that bad. Besides, that didn't make any sense.

Darrell glanced at Serena. She was carefully cutting her slice of pizza into bite-size pieces. Hell, she had to know he was staring at her, but she refused to look at him.

That, Darrell realized, was the bigger issue. She was angry with Cecil, but she might as well be angry with him—that's how bad he felt over the whole situation.

Serena had told him he wasn't responsible for Cecil's actions, but Darrell had taken responsibility for Cecil's wrongs his whole life. He'd done his best to get Cecil to do right, but he'd failed majorly. So yeah, Serena's criticism of his brother also seemed like a criticism of him.

Darrell pushed back his chair.

"I'm sorry we argued earlier," Serena said, before Darrell could stand. She met his eyes briefly, then looked away. "It's just that I'm so mad at your brother for all he's done, and I'm stressed, and I'm worried. I don't know what to think."

Just like that, Serena broke the ice, and Darrell was glad. He hated the strain between them. But his heart did a little dance in his chest at the knowledge that he *was* right about Serena. She *was* different. He'd never known a woman to offer an apology first after a squabble.

"I'm sorry, too. I'll admit, I'm a bit testy where my brother is concerned. All those old protective instincts kicking in."

Serena nodded, speared a piece of pizza with her fork, then rested the fork on her plate. "It still amazes me how different you and Cecil are."

"Believe me, it's a question that haunts me."

"From what you've told me, it seems you took the role of father to Cecil from early on. Were you ever simply brothers?"

"You mean did we hang out and stuff?" Darrell shook his head. "Not really. When we were really young, yeah, but not after Cecil hit puberty. He ran with a rough crowd, the in crowd, and I didn't care about that. As a result, we did totally different things. I played soccer, football. Cecil learned how to break into cars."

"Yet you still feel close to him."

" 'Obligated' is a better word. My brother and I have nothing in common. Well, that's not entirely true. My father was hardly there for as long as I remember, so Cecil and I had to fend for ourselves." A small frown played on Darrell's lips. "I suppose it's our shared past that makes us close."

"As opposed to familial ties?"

"Cecil and I both got a bum rap growing up. In a way, I know why he choose the path he did, even if I didn't chose it for myself. I know some people use rough childhoods as an excuse for every evil thing they do, but in this case, I *saw* it all unfold. If my father had been there for Cecil, I'm sure he would have turned out differently."

"What about you? You needed your father just as much as Cecil did, and you didn't turn out the way he did."

"Cecil was needier, I guess." Darrell shrugged. "I don't know. Somewhere along the line, we adopted different roles than just brothers. Cecil was needier; I was there for him.

"My father ignored us so much that Cecil needing me started to feel nice at one point—like my life actually had a positive purpose."

Serena gave him a sad look. "God, that sounds awful."

"Hell, maybe I didn't do enough to discourage the path he took, just so I *could* always be there to bail him out."

Surprised at Darrell's comment, Serena met his eyes. But Darrell didn't hold her gaze. "I don't believe that," Serena told him. "I know you did the best you could."

"It wasn't good enough."

Once again, Darrell's body language changed as he spoke about Cecil. His shoulders drooped as if they carried the weight of the world on them. It was absolutely beyond Serena's comprehension that someone could so deeply feel responsible for another's faults. Her grandmother was a firm believer that parents held only so much responsibility for their children, then they were on their own.

And here, Darrell hadn't even been the parent.

Which made her wonder about his mother. It was obvious by the fact that he never mentioned her that she'd never been there for them, either.

"You never mention your mother in reference to Cecil. Where was she?"

"My mother split when Cecil and I were seven," Darrell replied frankly. "She left my dad because he couldn't give her all the material things her little heart craved, and when she left, she didn't look back. You'd never know she had two kids."

Serena reached for his hand. "Oh, Darrell. I'm so sorry."

"Don't sweat it. That was a long time ago."

"You," Serena began softly, "you said she died?"

"Yes. Ten years ago. Sickle cell anemia. She knew she was dying, but she never called to make things right."

"God," Serena said, mortified. Then, "Maybe she was too ashamed."

"Like I said, it doesn't matter. If she'd called . . . I would have forgiven her. I wanted to know that she regretted forgetting us, but I guess she didn't. I tried to feel something at the funeral, some sadness, but I didn't feel a thing."

Judging by the grim set of his face and the forlorn look in his eyes, Serena knew that wasn't true. And she could feel that there was a void in his heart.

"That's too bad," Serena said.

"I'm sure the path Cecil chose is a direct result of my mother leaving us. Because we didn't only lose her, we lost our dad. He was crushed and became distant and overly strict, seeking solace for the loss of his wife in as much alcohol he could get into his system. So what does Cecil do now? Scams women, avoids commitment like the plague. That's no coincidence."

"And what about you?" Serena was surprised when she realized she'd actually voiced that question.

"How did my upbringing affect me?"

Serena nodded.

"My mother's abandonment and my father's inability to be a father . . ." Darrell halted, shrugged. "Sure, I wished every day to have a normal family life, but that wasn't the case. So do I believe in that American dream? I've seen firsthand that it's not true."

Serena inhaled a shaky breath, deeply troubled by Darrell's words. "You can't speak for everybody. Like I told you before, my parents were very much in love. They adored each other until the day they died."

"You were one of the lucky ones, Serena. All you have to do is look at the divorce rate today to see that I'm right. Does the perfect woman for me exist out there somewhere? Maybe, but what are the chances I'll ever find her? I was engaged once, but Jessica was only out for my money."

"Darrell, I'm sorry."

"I'm over it," Darrell said, the hint of bitterness in his tone betraying his words. "But it was a lesson to me. Starting with my mother, the only women I've know have been out for what they can get in a relationship."

"Not everyone is like that," Serena said softly.

Darrell shrugged. "Maybe not, but I'd have to be absolutely sure before I ever agree to walk down any aisle again."

A wave of sadness washed over Serena. A thousand

thoughts swirled in her mind, so fast they made her light-headed. She wanted to reply that Darrell would know when the right woman came along, feel it in his heart, but she bit her tongue. She knew he'd have an answer for that.

And maybe he was right. She was a hopeless romantic, still holding out for the kind of love her parents had shared. She hadn't found that yet, but she was still saving herself for that perfect man. That was something even her sister didn't understand, her deep commitment to not simply giving in to lust unless she felt a heart-and-soul connection with a man.

But she hadn't found that man yet, so how could she dispute what Darrell said? Who knew if she ever would?

Still, it pained her in a way she didn't think possible to know that Darrell was so dead-set against the idea of love and commitment. Exactly why, she wasn't sure.

Maybe because he was so passionate, so deeply com-mitted to family in a way he didn't even understand, it would be a waste for him never to experience the joy of marriage and parenthood.

"Cecil's all I have." Darrell spoke out of the blue, star-tling Serena out of her thoughts.

"For what he's done, he's most likely going to do time," Serena began cautiously.

Serena's statement struck a nerve with Darrell. Though he and Cecil were completely different, Darrell had always loved him and always would. But there had been more than one time that he'd wondered what would have hap-pened if Cecil had done some real time in a prison, even as a young adult. Would a taste of what prison was all about have straightened him out then, or simply made him a better criminal?

He suspected the former.

If Cecil had done the crime, then he'd have to do the time. That's just the way it was. Darrell couldn't make this one right for Cecil, no matter how much he wanted to. Besides, it was time Cecil took responsibility for his actions. Darrell only hoped his brother would survive long enough to get to a prison cell.

"Maybe if he had done time years ago, he would have smartened up then."

"For what it's worth," Serena began, "I'll see what I can do about getting the charges dropped regarding my complaint. Provided I get the necklace back."

Darrell's mouth fell open as he stared at Serena. But she didn't meet his eyes. Instead, she pushed her chair back and stood, then reached for her plate.

Instantly, Darrell was on his feet. Serena kept her head lowered as she stepped past him.

Darrell walked behind her as she made her way to the kitchen sink. "Serena." Her name escaped on a raspy breath.

Hearing her name, Serena stopped but didn't turn.

She was an enigma, and Darrell wanted to figure her out. "Why would you do that?"

Slowly, she faced him. "For you."

Darrell couldn't have been more shocked if he'd touched a live electrical wire. "For me?"

"You've been through enough."

She took the remaining steps to the counter and placed her plate there. Darrell followed her.

As if his body held hers captive, Serena froze. He studied her form. Her long, slender neck, her narrow shoulders, her slim waist, her shapely behind.

And then he reached out and touched her, first running a finger along the length of her spine from her neck to the groove above her buttocks. Serena remained very quiet, very still. Darrell ran his hands down both her arms, reveling in the silky softness of her skin.

God, it wasn't enough.

He pulled her against him, and she made a soft mewling sound. He held her soft body against his, pressing his groin against her buttocks. When she didn't protest or move away, but instead leaned her head back against his shoulder, Darrell slipped his arms around her waist and pulled her closer.

"Darrell." His name floated off her lips.

He whirled her around in one quick motion and smothered her lips with his. At first, she seemed surprised and didn't move, but after a moment, her mouth moved beneath his, soft and pliant.

She tasted like heaven—soft and warm and sweet. He urged her closer, pressing her breasts against his chest. Maybe it had been too long, for it felt like the first time he had ever touched a woman.

Serena was dizzy, spinning out of control in a whirlwind of delicious sensations. Why did only Darrell have the power to make her lose all reason with one touch, one kiss? God, she wanted nothing more of life than to spend the rest of it in his arms.

As Darrell urged her closer, she wrapped her arms around his neck and strained her body against his. Lord help her, nothing had ever felt so right.

She could hardly get enough of him.

He pulled away from her to gaze down at her. The scorching look in his eyes brought a hot flush to her cheeks, and a soft moan escaped her lips. He was enticing her into a dizzying world of passion.

"I want to stop playing," Darrell said. He nuzzled his nose against her neck. "You smell so good." He flicked the tip of his tongue across her skin. "Mmm. You taste good. Damn." He gripped her tightly. "God, I want to be inside you."

Serena's breath caught in her throat as her entire body erupted in flames. An alarm went off in her brain, telling her that if she didn't stop this now, there would be no stopping it. Yet she couldn't pull away, not when her body was pressed against his gloriously hard muscles and she felt like a completely new woman in his arms.

This was the woman she'd waited her whole life to be.

"I want you, Serena," he whispered against her ear. "I want you more than I've ever wanted anyone before in my life."

The gentle sensation of his warm breath against Serena's ear sent a searing jolt of excitement right through her. "Oh, Darrell."

"Say you need me," Darrell said. "Say you need me as much as I need you."

"God, I need you," Serena replied.

Darrell ran his hands down her back, smoothing them over her buttocks before slipping them beneath her shirt. His hands were like oxygen to a flame on her skin, making her flesh burn with sexual intensity everywhere they touched.

"The bedroom . . ." Serena managed.

His lips still on hers, Darrell kissed Serena fervently all the way to the bedroom. Man, she was driving him crazy. Everywhere he touched, she responded with a moan, and her soft sounds were like fuel driving him on when a part of his brain told him he should stop. But stopping was out of the question, while she was pressing her soft body to his like she wanted to meld them together.

There were too many clothes between them. Darrell pulled her shorts down and ran his hands over her firm, round behind. A groan erupted in his chest when he discovered she was wearing a thong.

So he was right. Prim and proper on the outside, wild on the inside.

The combination was irresistible.

"Serena," Darrell managed, when he pulled his lips from hers. "If you don't want this, stop me now."

She'd waited twenty-nine years for this, and she'd be a fool to put an end to what felt so right. She wanted Darrell, more than she'd wanted anything else in her life.

So she tipped herself up on her toes and reached for his mouth, throwing her arms around his neck with reckless abandon. When their lips met, she thrust her tongue into his hot, sweet mouth as if she'd invented the art of necking.

When he could no longer stand simply touching her, Darrell slipped his hand beneath the sides of her thong underwear and dragged them over her hips. Serena wiggled her body to help him take them off, then let them fall around her ankles. She stepped back to kick them aside, and Darrell's brain told him that this was another opportunity to stop. But when Serena pulled her shirt off and sat on the edge of the bed, Darrell's brain stopped working.

Lowering himself, he placed one hand on either side of her body, then kissed her softly. Serena stroked his face. Then he slowly urged her backward onto the bed. When she was fully on her back, Darrell straightened himself. His eyes took in the beauty of her naked form. Smooth, chocolatey skin; firm, beautiful breasts; legs that went on for days.

He threw off his T-shirt, then his boxers, and rejoined her on the bed.

Immediately, she placed both hands on his chest, creating circular patterns on his pecks with her short nails. Each stroke made Darrell hotter and harder than he'd imagined possible.

"You're so beautiful," he whispered to her, right before he discovered just how sensitive her earlobe was.

His hands roamed her entire body, stroking, tweaking, exploring, until at last he couldn't take another moment of not being inside her. He spread her legs and settled his body between her thighs.

But he felt her tense, so he asked, "What's wrong?"

"Do you have . . . I'm not on the pill."

"I've got a condom in the other room." He placed a gentle kiss on her forehead. "I'll be right back."

Serena giggled as he got up, and the sound made warmth spread through Darrell's body. For some reason, he was glad to know she didn't keep a supply of condoms on hand.

He returned so quickly, Serena almost didn't know he was gone. Her whole body was alive with wonderful sexual sensations she'd never felt before. And when Darrell eyed her body with a slow, hot gaze, then blew out a small whistle, Serena felt like she was the sexiest woman in the world.

As Darrell covered Serena's body with his, he lowered his head and took her nipple in his mouth. The gentle suckling sent shivers of delight all over her body, it felt so good.

"Oooh," she moaned.

"You like that, do you?" Darrell covered her other nipple with his tongue.

"Oh, my God. Nothing has ever felt so . . . oh!" Serena lifted her head to look at Darrell's mouth over her breast, and a bolt of sensation struck her between the legs. God, the pleasure was like nothing she could ever have imagined.

"Touch me," Darrell whispered, reaching for her hand. He brought it to his erection.

"Oh . . . my!" It was large, hot. She stroked it up and down.

Darrell growled. "Baby, do you know what you're doing to me?"

Darrell devoured her lips, then spread her legs apart. Fleetingly, Serena wondered why she wasn't even a little afraid, why this felt so right.

But she didn't wonder anything else when Darrell entered her with one hard thrust. She felt only the slightest pinch, then a flood of pure pleasure.

Pausing, Darrell looked down at her. She saw the question in his eyes, the surprise at learning she'd been a virgin, and Serena answered the question with an upward thrust of her hips. Once, twice, three times, then Darrell joined her, matching her movements, then taking the lead.

"Oh, Darrell . . . it feels so . . ." Her voice trailed off on a loud moan.

Darrell picked up the pace, deepened his thrusts, reaching a place inside her that was going to send her to white-hot oblivion. With every stroke increasing the friction, she felt herself losing control.

"Wrap your legs around me," Darrell told her.

Serena did. And Darrell's thrusts reached even further inside her, a place that was increasingly getting hotter, and hotter . . .

And then she dug her nails into Darrell's back and cried out when her body exploded with the most glorious of sensations. "Oh, my . . ."

Darrell swallowed her moan with a kiss, and Serena knew she'd found heaven on earth. She'd waited twenty-nine years for this, and good Lord almighty, this had been worth the wait!

As Serena's passionate moans faded, Darrell stopped thrusting. Surely if her release had been this earth-shattering, Darrell's couldn't have gone off without her noticing.

"Hold on," Darrell whispered. "I want you on top of me."

Serena held onto Darrell as he rolled over onto his back. She moaned when his erection went even deeper inside her from this position. Darrell moved his hips upward, and instinctively, Serena met his thrusts.

"God, baby . . ." Darrell threw his head back and grabbed hold of Serena's hips.

Serena's hands covered Darrell's hands. He moved her in a circular motion over him, and the friction started to build again. A long moan escaped her lips, followed by another one, then another, each getting shorter and more intense.

And then she exploded again, her entire body growing weak as her orgasm spiraled throughout her. Darrell quickened his pace, gripped her hips tightly as he thrust hard and deep inside her. Then he moaned long and loud with his own release.

Spent, Serena slumped against him.

"Oh, baby," Darrell said. He kissed the very breath from her.

"That was . . . amazing," Serena finished, not sure how else to describe the life-altering experience they'd shared.

"Yes it was," Darrell said. He wrapped his arms around her and Serena rested her head in the groove between his neck and shoulder. They lay together, neither saying anything more, their ragged sounds of breathing the only thing filling the room.

The moment Darrell knew Serena was sleeping, he let himself have it.

Good Lord almighty, he had just messed up but good!

A *virgin*?

Mentally, he let out a long string of expletives.

Of all the idiotic, monumentally catastrophic things he could have done, this topped the list.

Serena was a virgin. Well, she *had* been . . . until he'd damn well deflowered her.

By the time he'd figured out the score, it had already been too late. And then Serena had started gyrating her hips, telling him in no uncertain terms that she *didn't* want him to stop. She'd felt so good, and so had he, and he'd been powerless to stop something they'd both clearly wanted.

Now, he felt like a jerk.

How had all this started, anyway? Serena had offered to have the charges against Cecil dropped—for him. Hell, most people said a simple thank you when someone did something nice for them. They didn't kiss and grope that person like a horny teenage boy, then take the woman's virginity.

Darrell cringed anew at the realization that Serena had actually given him her virginity.

He'd known from the beginning that getting involved with her was wrong, that there was no future in it. Ultimately, he didn't want to hurt her, and he'd sensed that for her making love would be much more than the physical act. But something about her drew him to her, and he hadn't been able to stop what had been in motion from the first night he'd met her.

But Christ, he had no clue she'd been a virgin! If he'd known that, he sure as hell would have kept his hands off her.

He felt like someone had kicked him in the gut. Talk about complications! Women tended to get all clingy when they gave their virginity to a guy. One look at Serena told him it was already starting. Even in sleep, her mouth formed a faint satisfied smile.

Darrell had been hoping for a no-strings-attached nonmessy romp. Could he have picked a more inappropriate woman?

A virgin? He ground out a frustrated grunt.

His eyes ventured to her face again. He didn't understand. If she'd been a virgin for so many years, why give it up for him?

Slowly, so he wouldn't wake her, Darrell carefully unlinked their fingers, which lay across his chest. Once apart, he edged his body to the side of the bed, then sat up. Surprisingly, he instantly missed the warmth of her body.

Fresh guilt flooded him as he looked over his shoulder at her. She looked so beautiful, so *content*.

How could she be a virgin yet give herself to him with such wanton abandon? What a paradox she was. Serena was all fire and passion beneath that sweet and demure exterior.

*Why me?* The question sounded in his head.

Serena stirred, moaning softly. She reached for him. When she didn't feel his body, her eyes popped open with alarm. But seeing him, she smiled.

"Come back here, you," she said coyly.

*Oh, damn.*

"I was only taking a nap, not down for the count."

Darrell stretched out beside her. "Is that so, Slugger?"

A playful pout danced on Serena's lips. "That wasn't very nice."

Darrell ran a finger along her hips. "Really? Well, how can I make up for that?"

"That's a good start," Serena replied, then rolled onto her back.

Oh, man. Those breasts. That body. Darrell was lost.

What the hell. He'd already taken her virginity.

He couldn't possibly do any more damage at this point.

"Just a second," Serena whispered into the phone. A quick look in Darrell's direction told her he was still sleeping. The poor thing was so exhausted the phone hadn't even awaken him.

Serena's face flamed as she smiled. Darrell certainly had a right to be exhausted after the hours they'd spent in her bed.

Biting her bottom lip to suppress a happy giggle, Serena pressed the hold button on the phone, then got up. She grabbed her robe from the rocking chair and slipped into it. Knotting the tie on her robe, she stole one last glimpse of Darrell before heading out the bedroom door. The sight of his long form stretched out on her bed, naked as the day he was born, did her heart a world of good.

What they'd shared was so incredible, it almost seemed too good to be true. But there was no denying the reality of what had happened, and how Darrell had made her feel.

Part of her brain told her she should feel some regret at losing her virginity to Darrell, but she didn't. Not one little bit. Because Darrell was her Mr. Right. She knew that down in the depths of her very soul.

Serena gently closed the door, then whirled around like a giddy schoolgirl. What an incredible couple of hours. She couldn't wait for more.

Oh, God! Her sister was on hold. An extra pep to her step, Serena practically danced to the living room and picked up the phone there.

"What'd you do, stop to make dinner?" Kiana asked.

"You're so silly," Serena said.

Kiana paused. "And what was with the whispering when you answered the phone?"

"Nothing," Serena practically sang.

"Oh, God."

"Oh, God what?"

"Serena, tell me . . . no," Kiana said after a second. "I must be going crazy to even *consider* that."

"O-kay," Serena replied, chuckling softly.

"Oh, God. You are acting too crazy. Tell me you didn't—"

Kiana stopped short when Serena erupted in a fit of giggles.

"Oh. My. Lord. You *did*."

"Did what?" Serena asked, when she caught her breath.

"You . . ." Kiana's voice was hushed. "You didn't *sleep* with Darrell or anything crazy like that . . . did you?"

"Kiana, why didn't you tell me it was this fabulous?" Serena asked, as though her sister had conspired to keep a secret from her. "I might not have waited this long!"

"Oh, no. Oh, Serena. How could you?"

"I'm sure I don't have to explain the details to you."

"You have gone and lost your mind."

"I don't regret waiting," Serena quickly added. "Like I've always said, I wanted to wait until it was right. And believe me, this was right." Her body throbbed, remembering.

Kiana blew out a long breath. "Serena, what you're feeling now is the euphoric stage. But tell me this, do you even know where this will lead? You barely know the guy."

"I know him." Serena meant every word. In the time they'd been together, Serena knew much more about Darrell than she'd known about any other man she'd ever been involved with.

"Look, I won't give you any lectures. I'm certainly not an authority on love."

Kiana's tone was like a tiny prick in Serena's elated bubble. "Did something happen with Geoff?"

"No." Kiana sighed. "Yes."

"You and Geoff aren't talking?"

"He's mad at me. He thinks I'm using him. I guess there's no other word for it."

"Why?"

"He says I only call when I need something."

"Well . . . that's kinda true."

"What?"

"How often do you keep in touch just to say hi? But when your car got broken into, who did you call—Geoff. When you needed help painting your apartment, who did you call? And you know he's still got a thing for you. So yeah, maybe it's starting to bother him."

"I can't believe you're taking his side."

"I'm not. But you have to admit, it's got to be hard for him."

"He has to get used to the fact that we're friends."

"Because you can't date a cop. Seems to me you knew he was a cop before you started dating, so it's pretty unfair of you to expect him to stop doing that now."

"You don't understand. When he was in that shoot-out . . . he could have been killed. Hell, you're always calling me a worry-wart. How could I deal with wondering every night if he's going to come home?"

"Like you wouldn't worry anyway. It doesn't matter if he's with you or not, because you still care about him. And yeah, I can understand why Geoff is confused. Come on, sis," Serena said. "You can't have it both ways."

"That's not what I'm trying to do."

"Isn't it?" Serena paused. "You don't want to date a cop because it's dangerous, yet you appreciate his job when it's to your benefit."

"Geoff said the same thing."

"Do you love him?"

"Love has nothing to do with compatibility."

"Give me a break. How many couples break up yet remain the best of friends?"

"That's because we're better off as friends."

"Yeah, right. Kiana, there are some things in life you can't control. Who you fall in love with is one of them. What the future holds is another."

"You're in love with Darrell, aren't you?" Kiana asked.

Kiana's question gave Serena pause. "Maybe. Yes, I think I am. God, Kiana. I don't know how it happened. But it did. And it feels right. It really does." A beep sounded on her line. "Call waiting. Hold up a sec," Serena said.

"Actually, I've got to go. I'm behind on my deadline."

"Oh. Okay. Well, take care."

"Uh-huh."

"Later."

Serena pressed a button and clicked over to the other line. "Hello?"

"Who's this?" a woman asked.

Serena immediately went on guard. "Who's *this*?"

"Someone called my place today from this number," came the woman's irritated reply.

"Um . . . oh. Yeah. I called."

"Who are you?"

"My name is Carol. Do you know a guy named Cecil?"

"Yes," the woman replied in a guarded tone.

"Um, I was seeing Cecil, but we've broken up. Anyway, I was going through his little black book and found your name. Sorry, can you please tell me who you are so I won't bother you again? I'm making several c—"

"Tamara. What's this about?"

God, it was Tamara! "Uh . . . I don't know if you're see-ing Cecil now, and I really don't care, but I'm trying to lo-cate him because he has something that belongs to me."

"Yeah, well, join the club."

"What, he screwed you over, too?"

"Yeah, the asshole stole from me. He lied to me and told me he loved me, but that prick wouldn't know love if it hit him over the head."

"Do you know where I can find him now?"

"Wish I did. And good luck tracking him down. He's been AWOL for a while, but I did see him with some nerd at a restaurant a few days ago. She's probably got money, which means Cecil could be anywhere in the world at this point."

"Thanks," Serena said wryly. She swallowed her displeasure. Nerd? Had she really looked like a nerd?

"Oh, and when you find him . . . kick his ass for me, too."

"Yeah, sure," Serena said, then hung up.

Standing, she shook off her disappointment. At least Darrell didn't think she was a nerd.

No, she thought, a smile spreading on her face. Darrell didn't think she was a nerd at all. And that's all that mattered.

# Chapter 21

Kiana was back in the groove of writing her article when the phone rang. Shocked, she gave a start. Then relaxing, she reached for the phone on her desk.

"Hello?"

"Hello. I'm looking for Kiana Childs."

Kiana's stomach instantly dropped. This sounded formal, and considering it was after business hours, formal translated to serious. "This is she."

"Hi. I'm calling from Kendall Medical Center."

Kiana's stomach kept falling, while her heart leaped to her throat. "Oh, God." The words barely made it around her heart. "What is it? What's happened?"

"I don't want to alarm you, Miss Childs, but Geoff Winters was recently admitted."

"Oh, my God."

"He was in a car accident, but he wasn't seriously injured. He asked that we give you a call."

"He did?" Kiana was already on her feet, moving toward her purse.

"Yes. He's here for observation—"

"I'm on my way." Kiana hung up as she grabbed her purse. Then she practically flew out the apartment and to her car.

Darrell couldn't stand another moment of this. Serena was prancing around the apartment like Holly the Happy Housewife. After they'd finally climbed out of bed, she'd made him dinner wearing nothing more than a T-shirt, she'd sat on his lap and served him stir-fry between titillating kisses, then she'd fetched him a beer without a complaint when he'd asked for a cold drink.

It was more than any rational man could stand!

He couldn't do this anymore. He couldn't stay here and play house. The game had been nice, but like every good thing in his life, it would come to an abrupt end.

That much he knew.

And the longer he played the game, the harder it would be to say good-bye when the time came.

"You want to watch a movie or something?" Serena suggested as she gathered his plate and brought it to the sink. "It's kinda late to make any more calls, but we can start fresh in the morning. Besides, a movie will take our minds off—"

"Serena," Darrell said firmly.

Whipping her head up from the sink, Serena met his eyes with a curious look. "Yes?"

Darrell blew out a ragged breath, unsure how to broach the subject. Hell, he might as well just say it. "Look, we need to talk."

"'Talk?'" Serena turned on the faucets and ran water over the plates. "About what?"

Darrell cleared his throat. "Well, we need to talk about . . ."

Serena didn't blink as she waited for him to get his words out.

"About . . ." Darrell swallowed. "Us."

"Us?" Serena turned off the faucets. "What about us?"

*Damn it all to hell. Just say what you need to say and be done already.* "I'm not sure this arrangement is working."

Serena's eyebrows shot up. "*Arrangement?*"

"Us working together. Serena, you have to admit the issue has gotten . . . clouded."

Serena gave him a blank look. God, she wasn't going to make this easy for him.

"We wasted precious hours in bed," he said with difficulty. "Hours I should have been trying to find my brother."

"Wasted?"

"Maybe that was the wrong choice of words."

"What exactly are you saying, Darrell?"

"I'm saying . . . I think we're spending too much time together," Darrell answered. "And getting . . . *involved* . . . well, that was the last thing we should have done. For one thing, we both know it's not going to work, and two, it's a complete distraction from the reason why we're together."

If Darrell had pulled out a gun and shot her, Serena couldn't have been more shocked.

*Not going to work. Last thing we should have done.* Darrell's words reverberated in her brain, bringing with them an overwhelming feeling of despair.

Serena looked away, then back at him. "Clear this up

for me, will you? When is the best time to tell someone you don't think a relationship will work—before or after you get them into bed?"

"That's not fair."

"Isn't it?" Disillusioned, Serena looked at him as if she'd never seen him before. "And we didn't just . . ." Her eyes fluttered shut and she gripped the edge of the counter for strength before her knees gave out on her. "You took my *virginity*."

"God, I know that." Darrell shot to his feet. Frustrated, he ran a hand over his hair. "And I feel awful."

"Awful," Serena repeated in a deadpan voice.

"I don't mean it like that . . ."

She glared at him. "Yes, you did. And I may be a novice at the whole sex thing, but it seems to me you picked the wrong time to decide you didn't like me."

"I didn't say I didn't like you."

"Didn't you?"

"I said a relationship isn't going to work. C'mon. You don't want to get involved with me. I'm related to Cecil, remember? The guy who ripped you off. How many times did you point out that I'm his identical twin?"

"I said it's amazing how completely different you two are."

"Serena, I come from a completely screwed up family. You need someone who's normal, who believes love is more than a fairytale."

Her lips trembled. "How could you sleep with me . . . take my virginity . . . then tell me this?"

"Serena, I'm sorry."

"*Sorry?*"

"Fine. I'm an asshole. I let my libido get the better of me. But now that we're both thinking clearly—"

"I don't remember your judgment being impaired when you told me . . ." Serena's voice trailed off, and she inhaled deeply to quell the disillusionment. "Told me how much you needed me."

Darrell's mouth fell open, but he didn't say a word. What could he say? She was right. Every chance he'd had, he'd been all over her like white on rice. Now, he sounded like a hypocrite.

Or worse, like a guy who'd said the right thing or acted the right way simply to get into her pants.

God, he sounded like *Cecil*.

"Please, tell me you're not . . ." Serena held a hand against her cheek in a worried gesture, the bracelet on her wrist jingling. Her eyes implored him to tell her what she wanted to hear.

When he didn't, her face crumbled. "You *are*. You're serious." She took a step backward, paced a few steps, then took hold of the kitchen counter again as if she'd collapse if she didn't.

Darrell opened his mouth, but not a damn word came out. Words failed him, just as they seemed to elude her.

After a moment, she whirled to face him, disenchantment written on her face in big, bold letters. "What did I do wrong? Am I not attractive enough? Is that it? I know I'm not the most glamorous woman. Am I too nerdy?—"

"No," Darrell quickly said. "God, Serena. Nothing about you is nerdy." He started toward her, the instinct to offer her comfort in his embrace strong. But he recovered and stopped, realizing that would be a bad thing. He couldn't continue touching her while telling her they couldn't have a relationship. "Serena, you are a beautiful woman. You're passionate."

"Then what's wrong with me?"

"Nothing," Darrell replied emphatically.

"Was I bad in bed?" she pressed. "I thought the sex was good, but then, I didn't really know what to do . . ."

God, he literally ached to touch her. But he couldn't. "Serena . . . You were *amazing*." A chuckle of astonishment escaped Darrell's throat as he remembered their time together. She'd given herself to him in a way that was completely open and honest, and she had a natural wild side that drove him crazy. "Honestly, that was the best sex I've ever had."

A spark lit up Serena's eyes. "Really?"

"Yeah," Darrell admitted frankly.

The spark went out. "Then why . . . why walk away from that?"

Darrell didn't know what to say. "I . . . I'm just not cut out for relationships. I know how lame I sound, Serena. God, the last thing I wanted to do is hurt you."

A mirthless chuckle fell from Serena's lips. "Hurt me? It's too late for that." Serena regretted the words as soon as they left her mouth. For pride's sake, she should have given Darrell a blasé attitude about the whole thing, as if what they'd shared hadn't affected her life one way or the other. Because for the life of her, she couldn't fathom how he could stand there and tell her that he'd had the best sex ever with her, yet want to run away.

"I think it's best that I leave," Darrell announced. "Check into a hotel."

"You're going to run away. Just like your brother. Must be something in the Montford genes, hmm?"

Oooh, she got him. She got him good.

And he deserved that, but still her words hurt. Hell, they stung. All his life, he'd prided himself on being different from Cecil, on not making the same kind of choices, and ultimately the same mistakes, that Cecil did. That's what he was trying to do now—do the right thing so he *wouldn't* hurt Serena. But she was right. He was running. Running from something he had no clue how to control. Because the last thing he wanted to do was start to hope, or dream again, only to have the dream blow up in his face.

"You were right," Serena said after a moment, interrupting his thoughts. Her voice now exemplified chilly indifference. "What happened between us . . . it *was* a mistake." She paused. "I see that now. Very clearly."

It was what Darrell himself had said, yet hearing the words from Serena made his stomach twist in knots. "That's what you think?"

Serena steeled her jaw. "Hey, it happened, it shouldn't have, but we're both adults. Neither of us is going to die over this."

Though she jutted out her chin and spoke with confidence, Darrell saw the flash of pain in her eyes. And he felt like shit, because the last thing he wanted to do was hurt her.

"All right," Serena said, her voice traveling on a weary breath. "Now that that's settled, we can get back to the business of finding Cecil."

Darrell stared at her, trying to figure her out. He'd taken her virginity, for Christ's sake, and here she was acting as if she was simply writing off a bad debt. Why the hell would she still want him around?

"But if you don't mind, I'm kinda tired." Serena yawned, as though for effect. "I'm gonna head to bed."

"Serena, I don't like this." He felt like he should say something, *any*thing else. "I feel like a first-rate pig. My timing stinks, I know—"

Serena's eyes narrowed. "Do me a favor, Darrell."

"What?"

"Shut up."

Stunned, Darrell gaped at her.

"I am trying my hardest to forget that the best sexual experience for both of us ever happened. Please don't make this more difficult."

Darrell's jaw was still on the floor when Serena whirled around and headed toward her bedroom.


"Holy shit, Montford, that was smooth!"

Darrell tipped his head back and looked up at the ceiling. As he lowered it, he slapped a palm against his forehead.

He'd handled this thing the wrong way. Yet as he thought back, he wasn't sure how he could have done it differently. When Serena had started on about how bad she must have been in bed, Darrell hadn't wanted her to feel bad, so he'd admitted that sex with her had been the best ever. But given that, the fact that he still wanted to walk away from her made him seem like either a complete jerk or a complete fool.

"Shit," Darrell muttered. Yeah, he'd loved the sex. He could easily imagine himself hanging around with her, having more amazing experiences in bed. But it was the next step he didn't want, because he knew he wouldn't be good at that, and it sure as hell wouldn't be fair to Serena to continue something he knew was doomed from the start.

He had to think of the bigger picture. While his libido had enjoyed every second of their heated moments, he had to remember that crossing the line to sex had been one of the dumber things he could have done. He didn't trust the institution of marriage and he sure as hell didn't want to be a father. Raising Cecil had been job enough.

Darrell strolled into the living room and sat on a sofa, not quite sure why his brain had taken the leap from crossing the line sexually to marriage.

Hell yeah, he did. Serena was marriage material, mother material. Family was important to her, the one thing Darrell couldn't give her.

Lord, he hoped his brother called again.

And soon.

This situation needed to end quickly so that everyone could get back to their lives.

The moment Kiana saw Geoff being wheeled toward his hospital room in a wheelchair, she flew toward him. Ignoring the nurse's startled gasp, she promptly threw her arms around Geoff. "Oh, God, Geoff. Oh, God . . ."

"Ow."

Kiana jumped backward. "Ooh, I'm sorry."

Geoff's face lit up in a smile. "Hey, baby. You came."

"Of course I came. I've been here for a while, but you were having tests . . ." Kiana's bottom lip quivered.

"I'm okay."

"Excuse me, miss. I need to get the patient in the room."

"Oh." Kiana looked at the nurse, whom she'd forgotten was even there. "Of course."

Kiana followed the nurse into the room behind the wheelchair.

Geoff was rising when the nurse said, "Uh, sir. Let me help you to the bed."

"I can manage," Geoff told the nurse. He was now on his feet.

"Hospital policy," the nurse replied matter-of-factly.

Geoff moved to the bed without her help. "I'm not crippled. I'll be just fine."

Kiana hurried to Geoff's side. "I'll help him."

The nurse gave Geoff a reproving look as he sat on the bed and stretched out. "All right. I will see you later. Ring if you need anything."

"Sure thing," Geoff said.

The moment the nurse was gone, Kiana gave Geoff a slow once-over, noting the bandage on his hand and the dressing on his forehead. She gently ran a finger over the dressing. "My God."

"Baby, I'm okay."

"When I got the call . . . Geoff, I was so *scared*."

"I'm fine, sweetheart. Just in a little pain."

Kiana made an effort to stop hyperventilating long enough to ask, "What happened?"

"I was going through the intersection at Miller and one seventeenth. Some guy ran the red light and broadsided me. Luckily, he hit the front end of the car, but I spun around three hundred and sixty degrees before plowing into another car. I don't remember anything after that except my airbag deploying."

"You knocked your head."

"Yeah. I don't remember how that happened. My hand's pretty banged up." Geoff lifted the bandaged hand.

Kiana whimpered as she looked at it. The visible fingers were discolored and swollen.

"But at least I'm still here, baby. That's what matters."

Kiana's eyes flew to his. She was startled to see the hint of a smile on Geoff's face.

"It could have been much worse," Geoff continued. "If the car had hit my door . . . I might not be walking, much less breathing."

Here Geoff was, looking at the bright side even though he was in pain. But he was right. The accident easily could have been tragic. So despite any discomfort, the bottom line was that he was going to be okay.

Kiana threw her arms around Geoff once more and squeezed him, forgetting about his physical discomfort or anything else. She was just so thankful that he was alive!

"Ah . . ." Geoff moaned softly when she held him too tightly.

Releasing him, Kiana said, "Sorry."

"It's okay, baby. I like when you hold me." He paused, then added softly, "I'm glad you came."

Kiana met and held his eyes. "So am I."

"I'm going to be off work for a little while, maybe a few days. Just until my hand feels better, and my neck."

"Your neck?"

Geoff moved it gingerly. "It's a bit sore. Who knows if it will be worse tomorrow? The tests will show if there's any major injury, but I doubt it."

"You'll need a heating pad for your neck. Or is it ice?"

"Ice for the swelling on my hand, that much I know." Geoff looked at his hand, then at her. "I think I'm gonna need a nurse . . . to take care of me. Know any available to do the job?"

"You know I'm gonna take care of you, Geoff."

"You are?"

"Yes. Why, you want someone else to?"

"No," Geoff quickly replied. "I just thought . . . you're always so *busy*."

Kiana placed a palm against his face. "Not for you. Not this time."

"What does that mean?"

Kiana blew out a frazzled breath. "Geoff, I know you're going to say I'm a big idiot—and Serena would no doubt agree—but when I got that call . . . I promised myself that if I got here and you were okay, I wasn't going to take you for granted again."

"Really?" One of Geoff's eyebrows peaked.

"Yes, really. I was always so afraid I'd lose you that I thought I could protect my heart if we didn't continue our relationship. But when I got the call that you were in the hospital, I realized that I'd been lying to myself."

A huge grin formed on Geoff's face.

"My father was a fisherman, and there were risks inherent in his job every day just by his always being out on the boat. But I never heard my mother worry or complain about what he did. She valued the time they had together.

"I think when my parents died in a boating accident, I associated the danger of his job with what had caused his death, even though that wasn't the case. And I kept thinking that if only they hadn't gone out on the water that day, they wouldn't have died. But you know what? In the end, it doesn't matter. You have to live life, enjoy it for as long as you have it. I don't want to live the rest of my life afraid to love because I'm afraid I'll lose you."

"Baby." Geoff placed his uninjured hand on her face. "I want to be straight about what I'm hearing. Are you asking me to give you another chance?"

Kiana's mouth fell open in mild shock, then she smiled at Geoff's signature humor. For months, *he'd* been asking *her* for another chance, yet he'd turned the tables around on her—all, she was sure, to get a smile out of her.

But she said, "Yes. I'm asking for another chance. Think you can give me one?"

"Hmm . . . you know it." Geoff leaned forward and pressed his lips to hers. Then, pulling his head back, he stared into her eyes, his own serious. "I love you, Kiana."

Kiana gave him a playful smile. "I love me, too."

# Chapter 22

When Darrell heard the phone ring hours after he'd retired to bed, he at first thought he was dreaming. But an instant later, he bolted upright.

It was the middle of the night, and the phone was ringing. He threw the covers off and jumped out of bed.

*Cecil!*

Darrell charged into Serena's room without knocking, but paused when he saw her sitting on the edge of the bed, her body hunched forward and her face buried in her hands. Hearing him, she looked up.

That's when Darrell realized something was seriously wrong.

Her eyes were big and round and filled with fear, almost as if she'd seen a ghost. In three quick strides, he crossed the room to her.

"What happened?" he asked urgently.

"Someone just threatened me."

"Who?"

"I don't know. Some man. He said to tell Cecil that his days are numbered and he warned me to stop hanging out with him, or I'd be an unfortunate casualty." Serena's voice trembled as she spoke the last words. "Darrell, someone called here for *Cecil*."

Darrell didn't think of the immediate consequences of her words. Instead, he responded to her fear, sitting on the bed and wrapping her in his arms.

"Why would someone call here for Cecil?"

Her body shook slightly as she spoke, and Darrell whispered, "I won't let anything happen to you, Serena."

"You don't get it. Someone told me to stop hanging out with Cecil. Obviously, they're talking about you. They've *seen* you, and they think you're Cecil." She paused. "God, maybe it was a bluff, but I said . . . I begged them not to hurt him. You. I wasn't thinking. Now, they'll know for sure you're with me. Oh, God."

Still holding her close, Darrell considered her words. "You're right."

"Gosh, maybe my sister was right. Maybe I should have let the police deal with this." She whimpered. "How did this happen?"

Darrell was silent as he thought about her question. "If someone called here, that means they know who you are, or . . . did you block your number when you made the calls?"

"No." Serena looked up at him. "Oh, damn."

"God, I should have thought of that before you made the first call." But he'd been distracted by his attraction to her and hadn't thought about taking any safety precautions.

Serena pulled out of Darrell's arms and rose to her feet. Hugging her torso, she moved to the bedroom window and peered outside. After a moment, she turned and faced him. "You have to get out of here."

He gave her a puzzled look.

"If someone knows where I am and they think you're Cecil . . . God only knows what they'll do. Darrell, it's not safe for you here."

"I'm not going anywhere."

"You were ready to go earlier," Serena pointed out.

"That was then."

"Nothing's changed."

"Of course it has."

"Right. You're not safe here anymore."

Darrell stood. "Do you think I'm going to leave you now, with the very real threat of danger?" When she didn't answer, he continued. "Think about it. Even if I leave, they'll probably think you're still in touch with me. They'll go to you to try and get to me."

Serena moaned her distress. "Oh, Darrell. What should we do?"

"I'm not going to let you out of my sight."

Several seconds of silence passed, then Serena said, "That's not a good idea."

"Why not?"

Serena's eyes narrowed on him in the dimly lit room. "Don't you remember what you said earlier? That we were spending too much time together, that it was clouding the issue?"

"I'll deal with that."

"How?" Serena challenged. "By falling into bed with me again?" At Darrell's stunned expression, Serena added,

"Because say what you want, Darrell Montford, I know you enjoyed being with me, so much so that it scares you."

Serena's words rendered him speechless. How had she so completely figured him out?

"I've seen this struggle before," Serena continued, as if she'd read his thoughts. "With my sister. She's still in love with her ex but is either too blind or too scared to see it."

"Fine," Darrell said, when his mouth was moist enough to speak again. "I'll make a determined effort to keep my hands off you."

Two tension-filled seconds passed before Serena asked, "Why?"

"*Why?*"

Serena folded her arms under her breasts, and the fabric of her T-shirt hugged her as erotically as if she'd been doused with water. "Yes, why?"

"B-because," Darrell stammered, not quite sure what to say in the face of her boldness. "Because I don't want to hurt you."

"I think we're past the hurting stage . . . if you know what I mean."

Good Lord in heaven, who was this woman? Was this how demure librarians talked these days?

She was crazy. If he had a smidgen of doubt about that before, he no longer did. Who else but a crazy woman would talk to him so frankly only hours after he'd taken her virginity, then told her he didn't want a relationship with her?

But God help him, that whole coy-on-the-outside-bold-and-sassy-on-the-inside thing was getting him hot and bothered again. "Why are you doing this to me?"

"If I could stop it," Serena replied, her voice a whisper as she strolled toward him, "I would."

Oh, man. How was Darrell supposed to stay away from her when she came on to him like this? Forgetting everything he'd said about staying away from her, he closed the distance between them in one urgent step, framed her face, and brought his lips down on hers.

Hard.

A soft moan bubbled from Serena's throat instantly, and just like that, he was hard. He pressed his erection against her.

Serena opened her mouth and let him deepen the kiss. He did, his tongue hot and demanding, probing every inch of her mouth. Never had anything felt so thrilling.

Serena suddenly broke the kiss. "I lied," she said breathlessly. "I wouldn't stop this if I could. It feels too delicious."

"Delicious?"

"Mmm hmm . . ." Serena managed before Darrell smothered her mouth with his once more.

God help him, her insanity was rubbing off on him.

Oh, yeah. He was crazy. But this kind of crazy felt too good.


"Maybe we should wait," Jan said, as Rex paced the floor before her. She was suddenly uneasy with what Rex was planning to do. "Cecil promised he'd be in touch in a few days."

"He's been saying that for a few weeks."

"I know." Jan bit her bottom lip as she regarded her husband. Every time she told him they should forget about the jewelry and move on, Rex got pissed. He wanted vengeance, and he wouldn't feel better until he got exactly that.

Rex went on and on about the jewelry and how important it was to him, to them, but in her heart, Jan knew Rex wasn't as upset about the jewelry as he was about what it represented. And that was her fault. She'd had an affair while he was in prison, and boy, had she picked the wrong man. She'd hardly been able to keep her affair a secret when Cecil had stolen the jewelry Rex had given her.

For Rex, getting back the jewelry was like getting back a piece of his pride. And to do that, he'd stop at nothing.

God, Jan just wished he'd forget the whole damn thing!

"We know where he is, so if we're gonna do this, then I say we do it ASAP," Rex declared.

"You think he has the jewelry there?" Jan asked.

"If he doesn't, that's his problem," Rex said.

"I thought the point was to get the jewelry back. Now that we've let his girlfriend know that we know where he is, we should call back and give him the chance to bring the jewels—"

"And give him a chance to call the cops? I don't think so."

"Cecil wouldn't call the cops," Jan countered.

Rex stopped pacing and glowered at her. "You know him pretty well, don't you?"

Jan gritted her teeth. "I'm pointing out the obvious. Why would he call the cops when he's a thief? It doesn't make sense."

Rex didn't respond. Once again, he began wearing a hole in the floor.

Jan bit down hard on her bottom lip. Suddenly, things

had gotten out of hand. She was worried about how far Rex would go. He was a huge man and could seriously hurt Cecil. In fact, huge was an understatement when describing Rex's body. Over the two years he'd spent in prison, his body had grown with extensive working out. Now, he was two hundred and sixty pounds of solid walking muscle.

Unfortunately, Rex had never insured the jewelry he'd given her. In fact, Jan wondered if it wasn't hot when he'd bought it, and therefore he *couldn't* risk insuring it.

The problem was, Jan was glad to have Rex home and didn't want him to go back to jail. But Rex's ego was so big that despite the fact that he was on parole, he wouldn't let *anyone* make a fool of him and get away with it.

She wished she could make him see how crazy it was to pursue this, but when Rex got an idea into his head, no one but Rex could get it out.


Serena's ear-to-ear smile disappeared the moment she rolled over, reached for Darrell, and found the bed empty beside her.

Her eyes flew open. Then her heart sank.

Darrell was gone.

Glancing at the bedside clock, Serena saw it was shortly after six A.M. Miami was still shrouded in darkness, but the sun would soon rise.

But Darrell had already risen, unable to stay in the same bed with her so they could wake up together after the night they'd shared.

Serena rolled onto her side, tucking her hands beneath her cheek. What had gone wrong? While she had felt warm and blessedly content a few hours ago, she now felt cold and horribly confused. She'd sensed Darrell's fear, had told him that, and had assured him that she understood. And Darrell had proceeded to make love to her again. Serena had figured that meant he was ready to deal with his feelings, but clearly she was wrong.

God, she was a novice. She'd foolishly expected that sex would make things better, but now she realized that wasn't the case. Despite how she felt for Darrell, he might never get over his issues.

Yesterday, she didn't allow herself to feel regret, but now it washed over her in waves. She'd waited her whole life to share herself with the perfect person, but she'd blown it.

She'd gone and given her virginity to Mr. Wrong.

When Darrell didn't come out of his room for breakfast, Serena went to him. She softly rapped on his door. Seconds later, he opened it.

"Morning," Serena said cheerfully, though her heart pounded in her chest. Just seeing him again, she found herself growing light-headed. She hoped she wasn't jumping to conclusions about how Darrell felt. Maybe the time away from her had given him time to think, to face his fears.

"Whassup?" he mumbled.

*Whassup?* Last night, he'd been whispering to her how beautiful she was, how good she felt, and today he was greeting her with a *what's up?*

This was bad.

Suddenly, Serena didn't know what to say. Linking her hands together, she wrung them—hard. She'd taken the initiative and seduced Darrell again last night, hoping that would solve everything. She'd held out hope that they could have a romantic breakfast this morning. That's the way the morning after making love for the first time played out in her dreams, with her Mr. Right continuing to sweep her off her feet with a romantic breakfast of strawberries, chocolate, and champagne. But the champagne wouldn't make her light-headed. Mr. Right's affectionate kisses and caresses would.

Instead, she was getting the cold shoulder, served up with a plate of embarrassment.

Serena swallowed her pride, but it didn't make it past the lump in her throat. "Um . . ." *Don't do this,* she told herself. *If he doesn't care, walk away.* But she said, "Last night . . . that was just more sex, wasn't it?"

"If you're asking whether or not . . ." Darrell hesitated, swallowed. "Maybe we should just concentrate on finding my brother. Then all our lives will go back to normal."

*Why are you being so dense?* she wanted to shout. Instead, she said, "I'm going to work." She had been planning to take yet another day off to be with Darrell, to help him search for Cecil—and maybe even have some more wonderful sex. But in light of the brutal reality, she'd now go in.

She could no longer deny the fact that Darrell was Mr. Wrong. And if he was Mr. Wrong, she couldn't share her body with him anymore.

No matter how much she wanted to.

"I'll stay here, then. Wait to see if Cecil calls. If you don't mind, of course."

Serena did a half-turn, fully intending to walk away. But she pivoted back toward Darrell and blurted out, "Yes, I do mind." She looked at him with disbelief. "I gave you my *virginity*, Darrell. And fine, maybe I don't expect a proclamation of love, but I sure as hell don't appreciate the cold shoulder from you."

Darrell didn't know what to say, so he asked, "What do you want from me?"

Serena swallowed, then held her head high. If Darrell didn't care about her, so be it. She wouldn't waste another thought on him. She couldn't change the past, so she'd just have to move on. "I want my necklace back. That was always the plan."

Darrell gave a curt nod, his eyes unreadable. "Good. So we're both on the same page."

Serena forced a smile. "Yeah. I'm gonna go get ready." Not able to stomach being near him another moment, Serena hurried to her bedroom. Inside, she slid down against the closed door. But an instant later, she bolted to her feet. She needed fresh air.

Exiting her bedroom, she hurried to the front door, slipped into her shoes, then headed outside.

The sun was shining in a cloudless blue sky, and the hint of a breeze flirted with her hair. Serena turned toward the lake, then decided that since she always strolled around the lake, she'd take a walk in the other direction instead. There were tennis courts, two pools, and a little park in that direction. Maybe a few minutes alone sitting beneath the scenic palms and cypress trees would help clear her head.

Serena was almost at the end of the walkway from her apartment when she heard squealing tires. Looking up, she saw an SUV speeding toward her. Instinct made her stop and not attempt to cross the parking lot, but as the car got nearer, a chill snaked down her spine. The next instant, she saw something jut out from the passenger window.

She didn't have time to notice anything else, because she was suddenly flattened to the ground. A scream tore from her throat at the same time she heard what sounded like firecrackers.

*Gunshots!* she realized in horror at the same moment she realized it was Darrell's body flattening her to the warm pavement.

"Don't move!" he yelled.

The SUV rounded the parking lot's corner and sped off in the direction from which it had come.

"Son of a bitch!" Darrell stood and scooped Serena into his arms. "You okay?"

"Darrell, what happened?"

"Come on. Let's get back inside."

Darrell slipped his arms around Serena's waist, holding her tight, and Serena clung to him, barely able to think past her fear as he hurried her back to her apartment.

Darrell's heart pumped from adrenaline. The moment he'd seen the Ford Explorer speeding down the parking lot and realized someone was about to shoot, he hadn't been sure he'd make it to Serena in time. Never in his life had he been so scared. If Serena had been shot before his eyes . . .

Even now, he felt a degree of helplessness. And a degree of guilt. He knew he'd sent Serena running. If she'd been hurt, it would have been his fault. If not directly, then indirectly. Cecil was his brother, after all. Because of him, Serena's life was in jeopardy.

Darrell helped Serena to the sofa, but she didn't let him go even as he tried to ease her down. Surprisingly, Darrell felt his heart lift a little. He liked that she trusted him, and that he was able to give her comfort.

Still holding each other, they sat. "We have to get out of here." Slowly, he released her, and she looked up at him. Her eyes were wide with fear, but at least her breathing had calmed. "Grab your purse and let's go."

Serena scrambled to the bedroom, then returned moments later with her purse. Darrell dug the keys to the Viper out of his pocket.

"Can you go to your sister's place?"

"Darrell, I don't want to leave you."

"You'll be better off without me. They obviously mean business, and if you're with me, you're in trouble. Do what we did before. Drive around for a while to make sure no one's following you, then head to your sister's."

"Darrell—"

"No arguments. I'm not going to risk you getting hurt."

Serena whimpered. She didn't want to leave Darrell. She didn't care what the danger was; she'd feel safer with him. Already, he'd saved her from harm.

Darrell flung open the door.

And stopped in his tracks.

"Going somewhere, Cecil?" a man asked, a smug smile on his face as he leveled a gun straight at Darrell's heart.

# Chapter 23

*Serena's blood ran cold as she looked at the mus-*cle man holding the gun and the attractive woman who stood by his side. She shot a quick glance at Darrell, and he met her eyes. Silently, she told him to tell them that he wasn't Cecil.

The man forced his way inside, followed by the woman. Darrell and Serena had no choice but to step backward, but Darrell stepped in front of Serena, shielding her body.

"There's no need for—" Darrell began.

"Shut up and sit down," the man instructed, gesturing Darrell toward the living room.

Realizing he had no other choice but to comply, Darrell led Serena to the living room. He urged Serena down first, then stood before her. But when he saw the lethal look on the man's face, he sat.

Folding her arms over her chest, the woman smugly

strutted toward Darrell. She glanced down at him and sneered, then before Darrell saw it coming, she slapped him across the face.

Serena flinched when Darrell did.

"I've been waiting to do that for a long time, you no good son of a bitch," the woman said.

Serena's eyes flew to Darrell's. She saw pain flicker in his eyes; she felt it in her heart.

Serena's gaze went back to the woman. And suddenly, she recognized her. The woman from the restaurant bathroom that day she'd been at Monty's with Darrell!

"Yeah, it's me," the woman said, smirking as she read Serena's expression.

"He's not Cecil," Serena told her.

"Yeah right, honey. And I'm the Queen of Canada."

"Canada doesn't have a queen," Serena pointed out.

"Shut up," she retorted. Her eyes flitted to Darrell once again. "My point is, I'd know the louse who screwed me over anywhere."

"Darrell." Serena gave him an urgent look, imploring him to tell this psychotic duo the truth. Why, even now, should he protect his brother? This was a matter of life and death!

Darrell replied with a quick shake of the head. A little sob escaped Serena's throat, and what Darrell saw next touched his heart in a way he hadn't imagined possible. Tears filled Serena's eyes. Tears for him.

He looked away because her tears were too much, meeting the stares of first the woman, then the man. "Maybe we can work something out," he said to them.

Serena wiped at a tear that trickled down her cheek.

"Why are you doing this?" But she knew. He was trying to protect Cecil, the way she would try to protect her sister in a similar situation. Right then and there, she knew for certain she was in love with him, and Lord help her if this goon did the unthinkable right in her place.

"You've been promising to work things out for over three weeks now," the man said, stepping forward. He grimaced at Darrell, then looked at his accomplice. "What did you ever see in this pretty boy, Jan?"

"Don't start," Jan said.

"No, I really want to know. I thought you liked your men with a little beef on them—"

"Rex." Jan threw her hands in the air in frustration. "We've already discussed this."

Rex continued. "And he looks like he'd be lousy in bed."

Jan exclaimed, "Rex!" at the same time Serena raised a challenging eyebrow in his direction. She almost blurted out that Darrell was a magnificent lover, but stopped herself.

Besides, Jan's memories were of Cecil.

"Yeah," Rex said, turning his scowl on Darrell. "That doesn't matter. You made a mistake, and I forgive you for that," he added with difficulty. "You, on the other hand." He directed the gun squarely at Darrell's head. "The sooner you're out of the way, the quicker I'll be able to put my wife's *indiscretion* behind me for good."

"So you don't care about the jewelry," Darrell said. "You just want to get rid of me."

Rex's grin was pure evil. "Now you're getting the picture."

"Rex," Jan protested. "You said—"

"Yeah, well, now that I know what he looks like, I'll be haunted by images of you two rolling around together—unless I wipe his ass off the planet."

Slowly, Darrell rose to his feet. He wasn't about to take this threat to his life sitting down. He was a good half-foot taller than Rex, even if Rex was heavier. "If you're so tough, why not put the gun down? Deal with me man to man."

"Rex, we came to get the jewelry."

"Man to man?" Rex asked, ignoring Jan.

"That's right," Darrell said. "Put the gun down."

Rex looked like he was contemplating just that when the front door flew open. All eyes went in that direction.

"Holy mother of Jesus!" Jan cried out.

Rex's gaze darted between Darrell and Cecil, clearly confused. Darrell's eyes filled with relief at the sight of his brother.

"What the fuck?" Rex asked.

While Cecil stepped into the apartment and closed the door, Darrell saw his opportunity and seized it. With Rex's eyes on Cecil, Darrell lunged forward. He hit Rex's thick frame of muscle with an *oomph!* Rex was too big for Darrell to do much damage, but because he caught him off guard, he startled him and Rex stumbled backward. Rex's foot hit the coffee table, and he completely lost his balance. He loosened his hold on the gun as he tried to break his fall.

The gun went flying.

Her heart pounding, Serena jumped to her feet and dove for the gun. Now on her stomach, she scrambled the few inches to grasp the gun in both hands. The semi-automatic secured in her palms, she did a quick roll over onto her back, positioning herself on her butt as she straightened the gun. She'd never held one before, and it was heavy and awkward, but she had to be strong so as not to lose control of things.

She finally analyzed the situation. Cecil had Jan by the arms, and Darrell sat on Rex. Jan whimpered, realizing the tables had been turned. Surprisingly, Rex didn't move.

"Not so tough without your gun, huh?" Darrell asked.

"How can there be two of you?" Jan asked, as if the situation was completely incomprehensible.

"Twins," Rex said, matter-of-factly.

"Very good," Cecil retorted. "Serena, bring me the gun."

Her hands shaking slightly, Serena rose to her feet and did as she'd been told. She handed the gun to Cecil, thankful to be rid of it. If push had come to shove, she would have tried to use it, but who knew if she could have hit a target, even if her life depended on it.

"Go call the police," Cecil told her.

Serena hustled to the living room phone.

"Damn it, Rex," Jan immediately began. "I told you this was a bad idea!"

"If you hadn't fucked around on me—"

"Oh, for chrissakes. I am *not* going to explain myself again."

Rex and Jan continued to bicker while Serena dialed 9-1-1.

Minutes later, the police screeched to a halt in front of Serena's apartment. Serena, who stood alone outside, made her way toward them.

"Thank God!" she said.

Two officers jumped out of the first cruiser, and two jumped out of the second. The closest one to her, the tall male blond, said, "You the one who called?"

"Yes. There's a man and woman in my apartment. They broke in and pulled a gun. The man's really big. Looks like a fridge. And . . ." Just as she was about to mention Cecil, she paused—and thought of Darrell. Suddenly, she decided not to mention Cecil's part in this.

"You know them?"

"No. I can only assume it was an attempted home invasion. My boyfriend managed to get the gun from him. He and his brother, they're twins, are inside with them now."

"All right," the cop said. "Let's go."

Serena hurried with the cops back to her apartment. "Those two," she said, pointing to Jan and Rex. "They're the ones who broke into my apartment!"

"Hey," Rex began in a placating tone. "This is all a misunderstanding."

"You call breaking and entering a misunderstanding?" the cop who approached Rex asked.

"Things got a little out of hand," Rex explained, "but nobody got hurt. There's no need for anyone to get arrested."

"Is that so?" The cop slapped a pair of cuffs on Rex.

"I told you this was a bad idea," Jan snapped as another cop placed her in handcuffs. "God!"

"Fine," Rex said angrily. "Point the finger at me. Are you gonna tell them about your son of a bitch boyfriend?"

"He's *not* my boyfriend!"

"No, you just fu—"

"Okay, okay," one cop said, tightening cuffs on Jan's wrists. "Will you can the lovers' quarrel long enough for me to read you your rights?"

"That punk over there slept with my wife!" Rex exclaimed.

"I can understand you being peeved, but that's not a

crime, sir," the cop informed him, then began reading the Miranda warning.

Both Jan and Rex said that they understood their rights as they'd been read to them—then promptly began bickering again.

"Tell them, Jan," Rex said. "Tell them how you slept with that scrawny piece of shit, and how you let him have all the jewelry I gave you."

"I didn't *let* him have it. He took it! And how many women have you slept with while we've been married? Stop acting holier than thou, Rex. I'm sick of it!"

"God, I'm getting a headache," one of the cops said. "Why don't you two shut up till we get your lawyers?"

"This all started because one of the Bobbsey twins over there stole a fortune of jewelry from me," Jan said.

"Are you making any sense of this?" one of the cops asked another one.

"Naw."

"If you'll listen, I'll explain," Jan said.

The cop holding Rex's arm led him to the door, saying, "How 'bout you both talk at the station? Cause this story sounds like one big mess and we'll need an interpreter to piece it together."

The cop holding Jan chuckled, then started with her out of the apartment.

"You won't get away with this, Cecil," Rex announced.

Serena walked behind the officers to the door. One of the other cops said to her, "You have any idea what those two are talking about?"

"None," Serena lied. As she got to the foyer, she looked at Darrell and Cecil over her shoulder before stepping outside.

Darrell watched her go, knowing she was giving him

and Cecil time alone together, and he appreciated the gesture. He also wondered why she hadn't turned Cecil in.

A smile lifted his lips at the thought that this was finally over, and relieved, Darrell turned to face his brother. Cecil stood a couple feet behind him, a huge grin on his face.

The two brothers flew into each other's arms, embracing tightly. Hands slapped backs and laughter filled the air.

"Cecil."

"Darrell."

They pulled apart and regarded each other, still smiling. Then Darrell punched Cecil in the gut.

Cecil doubled over in pain, and as he raised his head, he stared at Darrell in shock. "What the hell?"

"You almost got me killed, Cecil. You almost got Serena killed."

"Hey, everyone got out of this okay," Cecil retorted.

"*Not* because of you," Darrell pointed out, glaring at his brother. "For God's sake, what were you thinking? Stealing jewelry?"

Regret passed in Cecil's eyes. "I know. It seemed like a good idea at the time. Eddie said it was foolproof."

"A good idea? I can't believe you. Your antics have gone too far this time, Cecil."

"Yeah." Cecil spoke softly. "I know. Eddie screwed me over—"

"Is that all you care about?"

"No, no," Cecil quickly replied. "I'm just saying I know I messed up. Believe me, I know."

"You *always* say you know you messed up. Yet you get yourself into more shit than the last time. I can't . . ." Darrell's voice trailed off as he groaned. "I can't keep bailing you out of trouble. You're thirty-one. Do you know the stress you put Serena through?"

"I'm gonna make it up to her."

"How?"

"Well, I didn't hawk the necklace. I couldn't bring myself to do it, not after everything she'd told me about it."

Darrell gave his brother a stony look. "If you think that's gonna earn you any points in my book—"

"I know."

"Where's the necklace?"

"I've got a van outside. A rental."

Darrell nodded grimly. At least his brother still had it. That was one other plus in this whole messed up situation. "She could have turned your ass in right now. You know that."

"Uh huh."

"I'm not sure you do. That took a lot of restraint on her part, a quality you obviously don't have. If you really want to make this up to her, you have to turn yourself in."

Cecil's eyes bulged.

"There's a warrant out for your arrest. How long do you think it will take for Jan and Rex to calm down enough to explain that you stole from them? Then you'll do what, go on the lam again?" Cecil's expression said he hadn't thought that far ahead. "Cece, it's time you own up to your responsibility. Maybe if you turn yourself in, that'll work in your favor. Gain you a few brownie points."

"C'mon, bro. I've learned my lesson. Believe me. I'm gonna go straight. I mean it this time."

"Bullshit."

"Honestly."

Darrell shook his head with chagrin. He'd heard this song and dance one too many times to get excited now. "I'd like to believe you, Cece. I really would. But let's face it, the next good scam that comes your way, you're gonna jump on it."

"I won't."

"Even if you don't, there's a warrant out for your arrest. That isn't going to go away. Do you honestly want to live the rest of your life looking over your shoulder?"

Cecil frowned, the reality of the situation seeming to dawn on him. "Naw . . ."

"I didn't think so." Darrell paused. "You know how you can prove to me that you're gonna go straight?"

"How?"

"Turn yourself in."

Cecil gritted his teeth. "Man, I don't want to go to jail."

"And I don't want to worry about you while you're on the run for the rest of your life." Darrell paused, met his brother's eyes with a level gaze. "Cecil, I love you. You have to know that. But I can't stick by you if you continue on this criminal path. And I sure as hell don't want to have to travel some place to identify your body because someone you pissed off put a bullet in your head." Darrell's voice wavered. "I don't want to lose you, Cecil. You're the only family I have left."

Maybe it was the hint of vulnerability in Darrell's voice that got through to Cecil, because his brother's eyes filled with tears. "I've made your life a living hell, haven't I?"

"Honestly? Pretty much. But I tell you that because I love you, and because I know you have what it takes to do right."

Cecil's shoulders drooped and he quickly brushed at his eyes. "You're right. I have to do the right thing."

"I'll always stand by you, Cece, but you have to do this on your own."

Cecil nodded.

"The cops said we could head to the station to give our statements, but they're probably still outside."

"I hear you," Cecil said, catching Darrell's meaning. "Thanks, Darrell." He gave him another hug, long and hard. "I appreciate everything. You coming down when you knew I was in trouble. Not giving up on me over the years."

Darrell gave Cecil's back a final pat, then stepped backward. Emotion filled his throat. "They're probably still out there."

Cecil gave his brother a sad smile, then headed out of the apartment. Darrell tipped his head back and looked at the ceiling, then blew out a harried breath. After several seconds, he made his way outside.

While Serena stood beside a cruiser speaking with one of the cops, Cecil made his way to a van. Darrell watched him open the back and remove a small metal box. Serena's eyes went over the cop's shoulder to Cecil as he made his way toward them, and even from where Darrell stood several feet away, he saw happiness shine in Serena's eyes.

And he felt it in his heart.

He was proud of Cecil at that moment, more proud than he'd been of him all his life.

Watching Serena take the metal box with one hand and wipe a tear away with the other, Darrell made his way toward them.

"My name is Cecil Montford," Cecil was saying when Darrell reached them. "There's a warrant out for my arrest . . . and I'm turning myself in."

Serena's eyes flew to Cecil's in surprise, then, as if sensing Darrell, she turned and looked at him. Darrell gave her a soft smile.

When Darrell looked at his brother again, the short female cop was placing cuffs on him. She led him to one of the cruisers.

"Darrell," Cecil said.

It hurt to see his brother being arrested, more than Darrell had thought possible, yet in a way, it was a relief. Cecil was safe. And maybe, by turning himself in, he would end up with a lesser sentence. This should have happened a long time ago, but hopefully it wasn't too late for his brother to genuinely turn his life around.

"Yes?" Darrell softly responded.

"You can keep the car. I won't need it where I'm going."

As she watched Darrell and Cecil communicate, Serena couldn't help feeling a moment of sadness. She hadn't turned Cecil in, giving him some time alone with his brother, and she couldn't have been more surprised when he came out and confessed that he was wanted by police. Even as she'd stared at him in shock, she'd sensed how tough that was for him to do . . . and she couldn't help feeling empathy for him. Perhaps because of everything he'd been through as a child, she didn't see him the same way she had before.

She was simply happy to have the necklace back. She felt a modicum of chagrin at having doubted Darrell. Obviously, Darrell had been right when he'd said that Cecil was probably at a point in his life where he'd want to make amends and start over with a fresh slate.

So she approached Cecil and said, "Thank you. There were a million other things you could have done with this necklace, and for a while I doubted you'd do the right thing, so thank you."

"I'm sorry for everything," Cecil said. "I really did care about you. That wasn't a lie."

His last words left Serena stunned. What exactly did Cecil mean by that? That he'd actually cared about her? And if that's what he meant, was he telling the truth?

But why lie now? Unless he figured that by being nice to her, he could be sure she'd be nice to him in court.

Serena didn't know what to think. All she knew was that Cecil's words made her think of Darrell and what they'd shared. It was Darrell she wanted to hear say that he cared about her.

She stole a glance at him, and her heart started beating doubletime. It wasn't just one thing about him that made her react that way; it was the whole package. He was sensitive, yet strong. Caring and devoted. A wonderful lover.

She wanted more of him, more than he was willing to give.

Yet as Serena remembered how he'd held her after she was shot at, she couldn't stop her heart from thinking he cared about her on a deeper level. Maybe he just didn't want to admit it.

Sensing her, Darrell turned his head slightly and met her eyes. But as if he could read the direction of her thoughts, he quickly looked away.

A lump clogged Serena's throat. God help her, she loved Darrell, but he didn't love her back.

The day had been draining, and by the time both Serena and Darrell gave the police detailed accounts of what had happened at the police station, neither had much to say on the way back to her apartment.

Serena wanted to say so much, but she didn't dare. She knew time was running out. With Cecil arrested and out of immediate danger, there'd be no reason for Darrell to stick around.

The fact that he wasn't saying anything didn't make her feel better. She didn't have any practice in these matters, but she'd already made a fool of herself where Darrell was concerned, and if he wanted something more with her, he'd have to tell her.

And if he didn't . . . well, life went on.

Even if, right now, Serena couldn't imagine how she'd ever live without him.

When had she fallen this hard? That's what she really wanted to know. She'd never doubted that one day she would fall in love, but she couldn't be more stunned at how it had come about. Cecil's brother, of all people? A man who shunned the idea of marriage and family because of his own upbringing. A man who was so clearly wrong for her, given what she wanted from life, yet she'd fallen for him nonetheless.

Butterflies did a nervous dance in Serena's stomach when she and Darrell arrived at her apartment complex. With each minute that passed, she was closer and closer to never seeing him again.

Or to learning that dreams did indeed come true.

They walked quietly to the door, Darrell resting a gentle hand on her lower back. God, just the touch of his hand against her body made her all warm and fuzzy inside. She wanted to feel this way with him forever.

Inside, Darrell said, "So, how you feeling?"

"Relieved."

Darrell nodded, then silence fell between them. "I have to head back. To Orlando. There's so much I put on hold to come down here . . ."

No proclamation of love, but it wasn't like she had expected one. So why was her heart breaking?

"Yes, of course," she managed, forcing a smile. "You have a life to get back to."

"A business to run."

"Naturally."

Pause. "I'm not going to leave right away," Darrell said quickly. "You don't mind if I spend the night, do you?"

"Oh, no."

"Because it's kinda late."

"Mmm hmm. No problem." Serena paused. "I can drive you to the airport if you like."

"Cecil said I could have the Viper, so I'm gonna drive it back. Use the time and clear my head."

*Will you be thinking about me?* Serena wondered. *About us?*

"Hey," Darrell said, his eyes lighting up—and Serena's heart soared with hope. "I almost forgot. I'd love to see the necklace."

Serena's heart fell. But as she went to retrieve the necklace, her mind drifted from Darrell and her feelings for him. Knowing that the necklace was safe with her once again was reason to smile.

She went to the small safe in her bedroom and opened it, then withdrew the old metal box that housed the dazzling piece of jewelry.

Darrell saw both happiness and pride in Serena's eyes as she gently fingered the exquisite necklace. It was nothing short of magnificent, and he was glad that it was back with its rightful owner.

"It's stunning," he said. He reached for it. "May I?"

Serena paused only a moment before passing him the box. Darrell examined it closely. Set in silver, it had diamonds around the entire length of the necklace. The main stone was a ruby, surrounded by tiny diamonds.

"Wow." Darrell let out a low whistle. "I can see why this is so important to you."

"Yes," Serena agreed, taking the box from him. "Every time I look at it, I get goosebumps, knowing so many of my ancestors once held this. It gives me a great sense of belonging." Serena stood. "Let me put this back."

Serena disappeared, and returned minutes later. Once again, she felt tension between her and Darrell. Rubbing a hand on the back of her neck, she asked, "You hungry?"

"Not really. Actually, I'm pretty tired. So I'm gonna head to, uh, bed. To sleep."

Just last night, he'd been making sweet love to her. Now, he could barely say two words to her.

"Good night," Serena said cheerfully.

"Good night."

"He doesn't love me," Serena pined later. She'd filled her sister in on the day's events and the reality that she was in love with Darrell. The reality of the situation was made somewhat more bitter by the fact that Kiana and Geoff were finally working things out. While Serena was elated for them, she wanted some of that happiness for herself.

"Maybe he does," Kiana said. "But it's been nonstop action since he got here. He's been so worried about his brother, he probably hasn't had time to examine his feelings."

"He's leaving tomorrow, Kiana. And I'll never see him again."

"Hey, you don't know that. If he's anywhere near as stubborn as me—" Kiana's voice abruptly stopped and she let out a little shriek. "Geoff, stop *that.*"

"Okay," Serena said. "Sounds like this is getting X-rated."

"No," Kiana managed between giggles.

"Yeah, sure." Not that she could blame them. They'd been apart so long that spending quality time loving each other was exactly what they should be doing. "Anyway, I'm gonna go."

"All right." Kiana didn't protest.

"Call me . . . whenever."

"Oh, sis. You sound so sad. Cheer up, please. I'm sure things will work out once everything's settled down."

"I hope so," Serena said, but in her heart, she didn't believe it.


The next morning, Darrell knocked on Serena's bedroom door, waking her. "Hey, Serena," he said from behind the door. "I'm leaving."

All night, Serena had hoped this moment wouldn't come, that Darrell would return to her bedroom and tell her he couldn't live without her.

She wanted the fantasy, but this was life, and the cold hard reality was difficult to bear.

"Give me a minute," she said, reaching for her glasses beside the bed. She stood and put on a robe, then finger-combed her hair. Out of habit, she gave herself a brief once-over in the mirror, then realized how pointless that was.

No matter how she looked, Darrell just wasn't interested.

She forced a smile as she exited the bedroom. "You hungry?"

"I'll pick something up on the road."

Because he couldn't wait to leave her. Serena nodded. "Okay."

"I do appreciate everything you've done for me."

His words were like a slap in the face. She'd given him her love, yet he didn't appreciate that. Yet she kept her retort in check.

Darrell lifted his suitcase, then moved to the front door. Serena followed him, part of her wondering if she should confess her feelings and assure him she'd never abandon him the way his mother had, or if that would be a waste of time.

But at the door, when Darrell faced her with a smile that said he didn't have a care in the world, Serena made the decision to keep her mouth shut.

Darrell stepped forward and spread his arms wide, as though he intended to hug her. A hug was more than she could manage, considering how strong her feelings were for him. So instead of walking into his embrace, Serena took a step past him and gripped the door handle. She opened the door. "Have a safe trip."

Darrell's lips pulled into a taut line. "Thanks."

Serena held the door open, and Darrell stepped outside

the apartment. And even when she saw his head turn back toward her, she quickly closed the door before she broke down and begged him not to leave her.

And there she stayed, pressing one ear against the door. She listened for sound, but heard none.

Was Darrell standing opposite the door, deciding whether or not he should knock? Or had he already walked away?

*Oh, this is stupid*, Serena told herself. Frustrated, she pressed both hands on the door and heaved herself backward. Darrell hadn't given her one indication that he loved her, so why was she even trying to hang onto the unfounded hope that he'd suddenly realize Cupid was trying to get a good shot at his heart?

All Serena could do now was put their incredible night of lovemaking behind her and move on. Yes, it hurt, and perhaps it always would, but there was nothing she could do about it now. She'd made a colossal error in judgment, and it would haunt her for a long time.

But she would go on. Find someone to love who would love her back.

A sob bubbled up in her throat. God, who was she kidding? She didn't know if she'd ever be the same again. Part of her wanted to open the door and run after Darrell, tell him what was in her heart. But another part didn't want to risk humiliating herself any more than she no doubt already had where he was concerned.

It was better this way, of course.

A quick, emotionless good-bye, and now they could go back to their lives before they'd met.

Darrell had told himself that over and over again as he

drove north along Florida's turnpike, but something still nagged at him. Maybe it was the unreadable look in Serena's eyes as she'd told him to have a safe trip. Until then, he'd been able to read all her emotions easily, and it bothered him that he couldn't.

It bothered him to think she'd stopped caring.

Not that he wanted her to care. In fact, it was better that she not care. He couldn't give her what she wanted or needed. Still, he'd started to get comfortable being around her, had enjoyed seeing her face every morning. It had been nice to know that someone as genuine as Serena actually did care about him, enough to put his concerns for his brother over her desire for justice.

Hell, what was wrong with him? He didn't want her to care, so why even reminisce about things that didn't matter?

Or *did* he want her to care?

He was confused, messed up because of everything that had happened. He hadn't expected to end up in Miami searching for his brother, much less meeting his brother's ex the way he had.

*Why the hell did she sleep with me and not with Cecil?*

Darrell looked out at the scenic view of palm trees and pristine green lawn that lined the highway, trying to make himself think of something else—anything else.

Like Cecil. He was worried about him. The charges of grand theft were serious, and Cecil would no doubt do time. While Darrell had figured this was something his brother needed to smarten up, the thought of Cecil in a prison cell gave him a sick feeling in his gut. Cecil was too clean-cut for prison, and he couldn't help wondering how he'd fare inside. Like the overprotective brother he'd always been, Darrell wished he could make this problem right for Cecil.

*You are not responsible for Cecil.* Darrell heard Serena's voice, soft and supportive, on the wind.

Damn, when would he stop thinking about her?

It was almost hard to believe, but he missed her. Not that he hadn't expected ever to miss her—how could he not miss that sweet smile?—but he didn't expect to miss her already.

Yet he did.

Glancing at the passenger seat, he almost expected to see her sitting there. To know that she wasn't left him with a hole in his gut the size of a basketball.

Darrell gripped the steering wheel and stared ahead at the endless stretch of road. He'd soon get over this feeling and go back to normal.

He had to.

# Chapter 24

*"Who the hell did this?" Darrell bellowed, both* hands planted firmly on his hips. When all the staff in the restaurant's kitchen stared at him in open-mouthed horror, he lifted the plate in question. "This burger needs a pickle on the side."

"Uh," one of his longtime waitresses feebly responded, lifting a jar of pickles, "I was about to cut some up."

"Oh," Darrell replied succinctly, feeling like a fool. "All right, then."

With all his staff watching him, he marched toward the back of the kitchen and his office. Once inside, he closed the door and turned the lock.

Good God in heaven, what was wrong with him? For a full two weeks, he'd been in a funk—raising his voice over things that didn't matter, double and triple-checking orders that were going out. He'd tried burying himself in doing payroll, but he hadn't been able to think. So he'd gone back to wandering around the small hotel, mostly in the dining room, to make sure the guests were satisfied—until one of his bartenders pointed out that he was scaring the guests and suggested that maybe he take a few days off.

Darrell's immediate reaction had been to tell the bartender to mind his own business, but he stopped himself short of saying exactly that when he realized that the very thought was so unlike him.

Besides, Jenny, his assistant manager, had told him that rumors were flying around about him having broken up with someone.

"Broken up with someone?" Darrell had asked, stunned. "I'm not even seeing anyone."

"If you say so," was all Jenny had said in reply.

Women. Darrell didn't even want to know how they started their gossip or how far stories got exaggerated.

After he'd made a nuisance of himself in the kitchen, Darrell had started hanging around the front desk, hoping to make more of an impact there, but after hearing the restless sighs from his staff when he got into everything, he realized he was more of a pain than anything else.

Which made him wonder why, until this week, he hadn't realized that the place could survive without him. He had a great staff—so why didn't he take more time to enjoy himself, enjoy life?

The very thought made him remember Serena. Not that remembering her was hard. Everywhere he turned, he saw her, whether it was at a restaurant table or casually strolling outside.

And every time he thought about her, he wondered how it was possible for someone to get so completely under your skin after knowing them for such a short time.

A thousand times, he'd thought of calling her. A thousand times, he'd actually picked up the phone. But a thousand times, he'd hung up before punching in her home number.

What was he going to say to her? *Hi. Just checking in to make sure you're not an emotional wreck after I took your virginity then practically ran out the door* . . . Anything he could say to her would sound lame.

Still, part of him craved simply hearing her voice.

Yeah, maybe he did need to take a few days off. Because he was infected with the Serena virus, and it was one he couldn't seem to shake.

Darrell tried to pretend that he didn't hear the collective sigh of relief in the kitchen when he told his staff that he'd be heading home early. He only hoped they'd forgive him his foul mood when he returned to his normal self.

He'd pick up a six-pack of beer on the way home, then sit outside and drink a few. When was the last time he'd done that? He smiled. Maybe he'd even buy some bread and walk the lake, in search of ducks.

Damn, Serena was everywhere. It was amazing how much she'd touched his life in the short time he'd known her. But at least she'd touched his life in a positive way, making him realize that it was important to take time to enjoy the small things.

After going to the grocery store, Darrell headed home, all set to have a relaxing evening for a change. But when he pulled into the driveway, he saw Cecil standing on his doorstep.

Darrell threw open the car door and rushed out of the car. Cecil was already walking toward him.

"Hey, Cecil." Darrell laughed, happy. "What are you doing here?"

"I'm out on bail."

"Bail? I figured you weren't getting bail when I didn't hear from you."

"I didn't want to bother you."

"Not bother me?" Darrell asked, mildly surprised.

"You've been bailing me out for years. I feel bad about that, 'cause I know you feel like you're responsible for me—and you're not. So I figured I'd go it on my own this time."

Cecil's words gave Darrell pause. After a moment, he said, "If you're on bail, aren't you supposed to stay within the county where you were arrested?"

Cecil gave a sly smile. "I know, but the police don't have to know I'm not in Dade County right now."

"Cecil . . ."

"Don't worry. I'm heading back tonight."

Darrell shook his head with chagrin. Would his brother ever play by anyone's rules but his own? "So, who bailed you out?"

"Tamara," Cecil responded with a sheepish grin.

"*Tamara?*" Darrell couldn't hide his shock.

"Yeah, she let me sweat it out in the Dade County jail for nearly two weeks, but she finally got me out of there."

"Are you talking about the same Tamara who you ripped off?"

"Uh huh. We're working things out."

Darrell shook his head with disbelief. "God, I don't know how you do it."

"I'm in love with her, bro."

"Come on," Darrell said sarcastically.

"I am. Really. She's beautiful, passionate . . . what's not to like? And she says when I get out of prison, she'll leave her husband. Of course, he may be dead by then."

Darrell rolled his eyes. For Tamara's sake, he hoped Cecil wasn't lying to her—or himself. "How'd you get here? Tamara drive you up?"

"I took the bus."

"From Miami?"

"Yeah. Then I caught a city bus to your house."

"Not stylin' the way you're used to, huh?"

A frown played on Cecil's lips. "Not exactly."

Darrell led the way to the front door. As he opened it, he said, "You have a lawyer, I take it?"

"Yeah. He says I can probably negotiate a lighter sentence if I pay my victims back. But I'll still do some time."

"What are you looking at?"

"Two to three years."

"Man," Darrell said.

"Could be worse," Cecil pointed out. He shrugged. "And you know what, I'm kinda resigned to the fact. Of course, I don't want to go to jail, but this whole experience has smartened me up. I'll do my time, then get on with my life."

"I can't believe you." Darrell sat at the kitchen table, and Cecil sat beside him.

"I had a long talk with Tamara, and . . . what can I say? I can't live like this forever."

Darrell could hardly believe someone had talked some sense into Cecil. Maybe it truly *was* love.

Whatever the cause, it was about time his brother grew up.

"You said you have to pay the victims back if you're going to get a lighter sentence. How are you gonna do that? You already hawked the jewelry, right?"

"Yeah." Cecil made the word three syllables, immediately putting Darrell on guard.

"I sense a but."

"But that's kinda why I'm here. I'm gonna need the car back."

Darrell's eyebrows shot up. "You gave me that car. And I just had it fixed up."

"Sorry." Cecil flashed a boyish grin.

It didn't matter, of course. Darrell would give the car up in a heartbeat if it meant his brother was going to pay back his victims. "No problem."

"I'm also going to have to sell all my homes." He frowned. "Damn, I'm gonna miss that villa in Jamaica."

"How many times did you get there?" Darrell asked, raising a dubious eyebrow.

"Not many, but it was nice knowing I had it for when I wanted to get away."

"Like you had anything to get away from. Welcome to the real world, bro."

"Whatever."

"Did you pay Serena back her ten grand?"

"Yeah. She was the first person I paid back. I figured I owed her the most."

"No doubt."

Cecil gave Darrell a weird look. "You haven't talked to her?"

Darrell opened a can of beer and took a swig. "Me?"

"Yeah, you."

"Why would I?"

"Look, I saw how she looked at you and how you looked at her. We didn't get to talk about it then, but I'm cool with it if you want to see her."

"Who said I want to see her?"

"Why are you raising your voice?"

"I'm not rai—" Realizing that he indeed was raising his voice, Darrell shut up. He took another swig of the cold beer, then placed the can on the table.

"Serena and I, we weren't really an item," Cecil went on. "Oh, I liked her, but she was too sweet. I'm just letting you know it won't bother me."

"It's not an issue."

"All right." Cecil paused. "I never felt good about scamming her."

"Well, I'm glad you've seen the error of your ways. Any other surprises?"

"Man, you sure are in a funk."

"Have a beer." Darrell shoved a cold one into his hand.

"I'm gonna need the car back."

"Uh huh."

"Now."

"Now?"

"I've got to start selling everything. The sooner I do that, the sooner I pay everyone back."

"All right." Just as Darrell had gotten used to the flashy car, he was going to lose it. Oh well. "I've got a few things in there. Let me grab them."

Darrell went back outside. Cecil lagged behind him, drinking his beer.

Darrell was on his knees when he noticed the shimmer

of silver on the floor beside the seat. He thrust his hand down, reaching for the object, and withdrew a small silver bracelet.

Serena's bracelet.

He'd seen it on her wrist. When had it fallen off? When they'd gone to the police station to give their reports after Jan and Rex had shown up?

"Shit," Darrell said, rising.

"What?" Cecil approached him.

"This bracelet. It's Serena's. Damn, I have to return this to her."

"Hey, I'm heading back to Miami tonight. I can do it."

Darrell leveled a skeptical look on his brother. His heart was suddenly beating fast, and he wasn't sure why. "Given everything, you don't expect me to trust you to bring this back to Serena, do you?"

"Oh, come on."

"No, I'm serious. This . . ." Darrell held up the bracelet, filled with star-shaped trinkets, for closer examination. "This could be another family heirloom."

"Gimme a break. If you can't see that bracelet isn't worth more than a few dollars, you're lying to yourself."

Cecil's comment gave Darrell pause. He eyed the bracelet closely. It didn't look like it was worth a small fortune, but how could he be sure? What did he know about jewelry?

"I'm not going to take any chances."

Cecil threw his head back and roared with laughter.

Darrell rolled his eyes. "You laugh now. It might be the last time you get to do so as a free man for a while."

"Hey, that was uncalled for."

"When are you leaving?"

"You're going with me?"

Darrell's stomach tickled with nerves. "Yes, I'm going with you. Like I said, I can't trust you to deliver this to Serena. Bad karma, you know."

"And how are you going to get back to Orlando?"

"I . . ." Darrell hedged. He hadn't thought of that. "I can rent a car. Or catch a flight. They're pretty cheap."

"All because you want to deliver a bracelet to Serena that you could send via courier."

"I'm not going to trust this to a courier. Packages get lost all the time. And if this is worth something . . ."

"It's not," Cecil replied. "Fifteen bucks, max."

Darrell glared at him. "So, you steal a few pieces of jewelry and suddenly you're an expert?"

"Going to Miami just seems a little . . . extreme."

"Whatever." Darrell was annoyed, and he wasn't exactly sure why. "Can I go with you or not?"

"Yeah. I don't mind the company."

"Good. Then let's go."

"Sure thing," Cecil responded, barely suppressing a laugh.

"Darrell." His name escaped on a breathless whisper. "What are you doing here?"

The edges of Darrell's lips lifted in a smile, and his eyes sparkled, as though the sight of her made his day.

"Hey, you. Maybe I can come in?"

Stepping backward, Serena said, "Of course."

Darrell entered the apartment slowly, glancing around with curiosity—almost like someone seeing it for the first time.

Or someone who felt like a stranger here.

Serena's heart filled with disappointment, but she didn't let it get the better of her. At least he was here. Just seeing him did her heart good.

But it also made a lie out of everything she'd told herself over the past two weeks. She had tried to convince herself that she was remembering Darrell, thinking of him constantly, simply because they'd had spectacular sex.

Unforgettable sex.

Which, of course, was why she'd constantly thought of how it felt to be in his arms. Not to mention the tricks your heart played on you when that lover was your first.

But seeing Darrell now, feeling the erratic pitter-patter of her heart, she knew she was in love with him.

"I brought you something."

Serena raised a curious eyebrow.

Darrell dipped his fingers into his shirt pocket. "This. It must have fallen off in the Viper."

Serena looked at the steel bracelet with a blank expression.

"It's a lucky thing I found it." Darrell extended it to her, smiling proudly. "I don't know how much it's worth."

Serena's deadpan eyes went from the bracelet to Darrell. Was he for real? Any fool could tell it was a cheap little bracelet. She'd picked it up for ten bucks in the Grove, simply because she liked the star trinkets.

"You came all the way here to bring me this?" Serena's tone was disbelieving.

"As soon as I found it."

A laugh bubbled in Serena's throat, but she held it down. No matter how much she wanted *not* to hope, she couldn't help herself. Maybe Kiana was right—a little time away, and Darrell realized that he couldn't live without her.

"You didn't have to come all this way. In fact, a phone call would have done."

"Oh." Sounding disappointed, Darrell glanced at the floor.

"Which leads me to wonder what's really going on."

Darrell's eyes flew to hers.

Maybe it was the guarded expression on Darrell's face that made Serena think he was holding his emotions in check, but hope filled her heart, giving her the courage to say, "You come all this way for a ten-dollar bracelet. I'm kinda wondering if the bracelet was an excuse to see me."

God, this woman really was bold. But she asked a good question, one Darrell had been asking himself since he'd left Orlando with Cecil.

In his heart, he'd known the bracelet wasn't worth a fortune, yet he'd taken the trip here anyway. And the smile she'd given him when he'd handed her the bracelet had made the three-and-a-half-hour drive worth it.

He'd missed seeing her smile. And if it meant another three-and-a-half-hour drive, he'd do it again, just to see those beautiful lips curl upward for him.

"How do you feel about living in Orlando?" he blurted out. Serena's eyes bulged with confusion at the question. Hell, she wasn't the only one who was confused. Even now, Darrell's heart and mind seemed to be at odds. The question had come from his heart, while his mind told him he should have kept his mouth shut.

But being near Serena once more, he couldn't imagine leaving her again. It was inexplicable, but he felt infinitely better with her around. And he felt the need to draw her in his arms, to kiss those beautiful lips, make love to her once again. Even more, he wanted to make sure she was safe from all the psychos in the world.

For two weeks, he'd missed her to the point where he'd been going crazy. Why was it that he could only admit that to himself now?

God, he was in love with her.

"Orlando?" Serena asked. "Why would you ask if I want to live in Orlando?"

Darrell shrugged noncommittally. "I hear the antiques business is great up there."

"Really?" Serena asked, her voice full of doubt.

"Yeah. Think about it. There are a lot of tourists who pass through there every day."

"A ton of tourists go through Coconut Grove."

"Not as many as Orlando, I'm sure."

Darrell saw something fizzle in Serena's eyes.

She said, "I'm opening my business in Miami. This is where I live. It's my home."

Darrell opened his mouth to say something, anything, but his tongue was so dry it felt like sandpaper. Why couldn't he simply tell her how he felt? She was frank, bold, said what was on her mind—which was a pretty good way to live your life. Hell, Darrell had come all this way; he had nothing to lose.

Yet he said, "I'd make a lousy father, Serena. I'm not like you. I didn't have a wonderful upbringing. I had a mother who walked out on us, and a father who might as well have. How could I be anything *but* a lousy father?"

For a full ten seconds, Serena could only stare at Darrell. She wasn't crazy. She *hadn't* been imagining his attraction to her. Because here he was, talking about commitment—even if he was afraid to come out and say it.

There was a lot of fear, more fear than she could truly understand. Fear because he'd been hurt in the past by people who were supposed to love him the most. Yet she knew he was reaching out despite that, and the reality touched her heart.

"Of course you'd make a good father. Look at the facts, Darrell. You took care of Cecil all these years. No matter what he did, you were there for him through thick and thin."

"No," Darrell began, shaking his head. "I failed. I didn't raise Cecil into a decent man."

"You weren't supposed to. Your father was supposed to do that."

"I . . ."

"I'll say this one last time, Darrell. You are not responsible for Cecil's actions. My goodness, I doubt your own father felt as much responsibility as you do."

Serena's words struck a chord with Darrell. She had voiced what he'd only been able to think for years. His father had constantly blamed him for Cecil's failures, yet he hadn't taken any responsibility for those failures upon himself. Through those years, Darrell had been seeking his father's approval as much as Cecil had been, and therefore, he'd accepted his father's put-downs and had tried better to make Cecil do the right thing, in hopes that he could gain his father's unconditional love.

Realizing the burden he'd carried but hadn't known until now, Darrell felt a sense of relief. Serena was right. He wasn't to blame for Cecil's failures. Cecil had told him the same thing over and over on the drive to Miami.

It was time he let the guilt go.

"Even with Buford, you were a good father. You made sure he got bread because he was weak and the other ducks were stronger than him. You have a paternal instinct, Darrell, and it's a good one."

Remembering Buford, Darrell smiled.

Tilting her head, Serena gave Darrell an odd look. "Why are you talking about being a good father, anyway? What does that have to do with me?"

Yeah, he must have sounded like an idiot—and incredibly weak. He wanted her; he was in love with her. Why was it so hard to come out and say what was in his heart?

For fear she would reject him, the way he'd been rejected by his mother and his father. But hiding from his feelings would get him nowhere. And given how miserable he'd been the past couple weeks without her, he had to take a chance—even if she *did* reject him.

It could be no other way.

"Darrell?"

"Because Orlando wouldn't be the same without you." Serena opened her mouth to say something, but Darrell continued before she could. "And because . . . I'm in love with you."

Serena didn't react. Didn't smile, didn't frown, didn't flinch. And Darrell's heart plummeted. He'd taken a chance, had jumped off the deep end only to find there was no water in the pool.

Then Serena screamed, startling Darrell. For a second, he didn't know what was going on. Coming from Serena, he wasn't quite sure if this reaction was good or bad.

But then Serena jumped toward him, throwing her arms around him, and leaving Darrell with no choice but to gather her up in his arms. Her screams of delight turned into laughter.

Yeah, she was crazy, Darrell realized, his heart filling with warmth. Who but a crazy woman would want to be with the brother of the guy who'd ripped her off?

But her laughter was contagious, and Darrell found himself laughing with her.

"Oh, Darrell," Serena said when she caught her breath. "I love you, too."

Darrell pulled his head back to stare at her. "So you'll move to Orlando? Be with me?" Darrell paused, then continued. "Marry me?"

"Oh, Darrell." Serena's eyes misted. "Oh, yes. Yes!"

She squeezed the hell out of his neck as she started that laugh/squeal thing again, but Darrell didn't mind. He didn't mind one bit.

She may be crazy, but this was one crazy woman he wanted to hold onto—forever.

Coming Soon . . .

**TELL ME SOMETHING GOOD**

by Lynn Emery

May 2002 from HarperTorch

Enjoy the following sneak peek!

*Lyrissa's voice died away when she looked into a* pair of eyes the color of dark amber with a hint of green. Shapely, masculine eyebrows lifted above them. The man stood at least six feet three inches tall. His skin was the color of vanilla caramel candy. His face was framed by dark, thick bronze curls cut into a short, neat style that suited him. The custom-fit navy linen and silk jacket did not disguise broad shoulders. Lyrissa imagined an equally broad chest covered in downy curls that matched the hair on his head. For a moment she forgot to be embarrassed as she pictured this man naked to the waist. Before she could undress him further he spoke again, breaking the spell.

"You get paid to eavesdrop?" His full mouth lifted at one corner as his dark eyebrows arched even higher.

"Yes. I mean, of course not!" Lyrissa blinked her way back to reality. His smart-ass tone pinched a nerve. "May I help you?" she said in her best chilly tone.

"Nice collection," he said mildly, untouched by the frost in her voice. He waved a large hand back toward the main gallery. "Mr. Taylor deserves his reputation, Ms. . . . ?"

"Lyrissa Rideau. I assist Mr. Taylor in acquisitions and appraisals." She extended her hand.

"Hello," he said, and took it.

Lyrissa felt a shock of warmth like a soft electrical charge at the sensation of his large hand closing around hers. His palm was dry and smooth, like soft chamois. He smiled and revealed even white teeth. Her breath went shallow for a split second at the sight. The man went from being merely tall and good-looking to drop dead gorgeous in the blink of an eye. He let go too soon.

"I'll just look around a bit more."

"Yes." Her answer was more a sigh than a word. She watched his broad back retreat.

Mr. Taylor opened his office door. "I'll just check on that, Mrs. St. Denis." The short wiry man literally bowed his way out into the hallway. He bumped into Lyrissa. "Where's the café au lait?"

"Um, just on my way," she said, craning her neck to keep the stunning vision in sight.

"Excuse me," Mr. Taylor said sharply. "This is Georgina St. Denis, okay? You don't keep this woman waiting for *anything.*"

Lyrissa inhaled, then let out a deep breath. "Right, right. It'll just take me a few minutes to get it."

She flashed an encouraging smile at her jittery boss, then scurried out the side entrance. Thankfully, the coffee shop wasn't very crowded. Frank, one of the owners, helped her. He filled a small black insulated pot with coffee. Next, he added hot frothy cream that formed white foam on top. Lyrissa was back at the gallery within ten minutes, as she'd promised Mr. Taylor. She went to the kitchen and put the pot, white china cups, and a matching sugar bowl on a red lacquered Chinese serving tray. With skills gained from working her way through high school and college as a waitress, she balanced the load expertly on one hand.

The handsome gentleman appeared from nowhere again. "Need help?" he said in that sonorous voice that could melt the clothes right off the coldest woman.

"I've got it, thanks." Then Lyrissa stumbled, causing the cups to rattle ominously.

"Here, let me." He opened the door to Mr. Taylor's office. Lyrissa rushed to block his view into the room. She imagined Mr. Taylor's eyes bulging with alarm. Mrs. St. Denis was known for her obsession with privacy.

"Thanks, but I'm fine. This is a private meeting and— Damn!" she muttered when the carafe of coffee wobbled.

He steadied it with one quick motion. "There you go."

Mrs. St. Denis sat in one of six forest green leather chairs arranged around a highly-polished oval table. "What in the world is going on? Well, it took you long enough to get here!"

I'm sorry, Mrs. St. Denis. But—" Lyrissa began, then realized the royal disapproval was directed at the man beside her.

"It's not easy finding a parking space around here, Grandmother. Let me help you." He took the tray from Lyrissa and set it on a long rosewood table against the wall.

Her mouth open in surprise, Lyrissa barely registered his action. She held her arm up as though the tray was still there. "Grandmother?" she repeated.

He flashed another dazzling smile at her. "Noel St. Denis at your service. I'll pour."

Mrs. St. Denis pursed her lips as she accepted a cup from him. "We don't have much time, Noel Phillip. We have a meeting at the office in another hour."

"We've got plenty of time; Henderson canceled. Ms. Rideau." He handed Lyrissa a cup.

"Thank you," she managed to mumble before she sank onto a chair across from Mrs. St. Denis. Noel sat in the chair next to his grandmother and sipped from his own cup.

Mr. Taylor returned. "Ah, here we are." He looked at the newcomer.

"My grandson, Noel. He's CEO of Tremé Corporation."